The impulse overtook him suddenly. She had her back to him, nestling into him and breathing quick and hard as he smoothed hot hands over her flesh: tracing the curves of arm, waist, thigh, and up to pert breasts. Bolder now, he began to undo the buttons on her blouse and slid one hand inside.

The delicious contact of the cool flesh was like a spark igniting the furnace within him. It came upon him as it had never done before: the sudden sense of power invading him and empowering him to do anything.

He flung her forward, took hold of her blouse and skirt and just ripped them off – tore at the fabric until it gave way. Then the bra, the flimsy lace panties. The seamed stockings and high-heeled shoes he spared: he loved to have a woman in black stockings and suspenders . . .

Kiss of Death

VALENTINA CILESCU

NEON

A NEON PAPERBACK

This paperback edition published in 2005 by Neon
The Orion Publishing Group Ltd.
Wellington House, 125 Strand
London WC2R 0BB

A CIP catalogue record for this book is available
from the British Library.

Printed and bound in Great Britain by
Mackays of Chatham.

ISBN 1-905619-09-X

Kiss of Death

1: Winterbourne

It was happening at last.

The Master was awakening: his immortal soul was rising through seas of consciousness, thoughts unfreezing, clarifying, memories melting the icy prison of enforced forgetfulness.

His spirit hovered, like a formless black shadow of unspeakable evil, above his motionless body, trapped and impotent within the unforgiving crystal; looked down upon the heavy lid of the sarcophagus and was filled with rage, grief and the longing for sweet revenge.

But his powers were still at a low ebb. There was a dim flickering where before there had raged a sulphurous furnace of chaotic energies, the servants of his perverse and terrifying desires.

He was going to need time, imagination, cunning. But he was patient. He could wait. The world would know his power once again, and this time there would be no mistake.

There had been long years of imprisonment, betrayal, defeat. But he was back now. The arrogant fools had thought they could kill him: that in trying to kill his body they could annihilate his spirit. Soon they would know that there are some things in this world that are beyond understanding: some things that never, ever die.

He wondered what had provided the stimulus to his reawakening, what had struck the spark of consciousness into his frozen heart. In his weakened state, he was still blind. He could not even see his own face, fixed in an expression of unbearable agony beneath the heavy stone coffin-lid. He did not even know where he was. His memories were muddled, clouded by pain and long slumber. A dark cellar, somewhere beneath a great stately home. That was all he could recall. A silent and deserted place, walled up and forgotten for – how many years? He could not tell.

But he could feel. And already he sensed the power-source, as yet just a trickle of feeble electricity, but soon, soon he knew, to burst forth into a great surge of life-giving energy.

The sexual energy on which he fed. The power-surge generated out of the chaos of frenzied coupling. Someone, somewhere very close at hand, was preparing an orgy and, although they did not realise it, the Master was to be their honoured guest.

The girl wore nothing but a thin white shift made of the thinnest, most diaphanous cotton lawn. Her body was pale, firm, perfect: the body of a young and beautiful girl. She could not have been more than eighteen years old at most.

'Beautiful,' breathed Delgado, reaching out a bronzed hand and running an incautious finger down the girl's cool, white arm. She shivered slightly, as though she were cold, but she did not flinch. The girl seemed unusually docile, and her eyes stared almost sightlessly before her. 'You have drugged her?'

'Of course,' replied Madame LeCoeur. 'A little injection to calm her down, a shot of something to make her more . . . receptive. Our lovely little child will enjoy her initiation, never fear. It was so good of Herr Königsberg to volunteer his daughter's . . . services . . . for our opening night. Such beauty should not be wasted. Among us, she will learn to be a skilled whore. One day, she will thank her father for what he has done to her tonight . . .'

Delgado surveyed the girl and took in her charms. Tall, slim-waisted and full-hipped, her body was enough to delight any man. The bright blonde triangle of her pubis showed clearly through her thin dress and proved that she was a natural blonde. Her pert breasts were cherry-tipped and hard, bearing witness to the efficacy of Madame LeCoeur's aphrodisiacs. Her eyes were a brilliant blue: clear and deep as an August sky. He was pleased with her. He turned to Madame LeCoeur:

'You are quite certain that she is a virgin?'

'You would like to see, perhaps?'

Delgado nodded. He was not easily moved by feminine beauty. A lifetime spent masterminding white slavery and the brothels of Marrakesh had left his palate jaded, and it took something exceptional to whet his appetite these days. He noted with approval and some surprise that he was salivating, and his hardened penis was bulging appreciatively inside his Savile Row trousers.

'Lie down on the bed, child.'

Slowly, mechanically, like a sleepwalker, the girl obeyed. Her pale golden hair flowed over the pillow as she lay down on the blue silk bedspread.

'Pull up your shift.'

She did so, wriggling to free the flimsy material from underneath her ivory-pale buttocks. Madame

LeCoeur stepped forward and took hold of the girl's knees, pulling them apart to expose the treasures within. The girl offered no resistance: in fact, Delgado thought he heard her breathing quicken.

The girl's cunt was appetising and rosy-pink as Madame LeCoeur parted her nether lips and revealed the gleaming pearl of her clitoris. Delgado felt a surge of unstoppable desire, and it was all that he could do to prevent himself taking the child there and then on the bed – but of course he couldn't. He couldn't rob Winterbourne Hall of this costly virginity – and on its opening night at that. There would be some very important and exclusive guests at the Hall tonight: guests who would pay dearly for the pleasure of deflowering and debasing such a delectable virgin. Each *maison de passage* must offer its own specialities, and this fresh young girl was Winterbourne's very own *spécialité de la maison*.

'You wish to check her for yourself?'

Delgado did not need asking twice. He burrowed an exploratory finger into the young girl's tight cunt, finding to his surprise that it was both hot and wet. She did not even wince as his finger came up against the leathery hymen. The child was excited, her young woman's body crying out for the first thrust of a hard, insistent prick.

Instinctively, without thinking what he was doing, Delgado began to move his finger in and out of the girl's fast-moistening cunt. Her lips parted and she began to moan quietly.

'Be careful, Delgado,' warned Madame LeCoeur.

'Don't worry, I won't damage the merchandise,' he replied with grim humour. 'Just a little induction course for our new trainee . . .'

4

The girl was writhing about now, and her cunt was glistening with moisture. Smiling at the power he was exerting over her, Delgado climbed on to the bed and knelt between her thighs. Still frigging her, he stretched out his other hand and thrust it up underneath the shift until he made contact with her hard-tipped breast. She groaned with pleasure as he pinched a nipple between his knowing fingers.

Delgado could resist her no longer. Even if he could not fuck her, he knew he must come inside her. Those pretty lips: sweet and gentle and innocent, and ripe for defilement . . .

He unbuttoned his flies and exposed his prick. It was fine and hard, throbbing with unrestrained delight. He turned around on the bed so that he was lying over her, his head between her thighs and his prick poised over her mouth. Greedily, just as he had hoped, she took it between her lips, and in turn he began to lick her clitoris.

Madame LeCoeur's aphrodisiac had worked its spell on the girl. Totally inexperienced and yet so, so knowing, she gave him such pleasure that he felt his head swim, his senses reel. And he could feel her own pleasure mounting as her clitoris swelled and throbbed beneath his tongue. Then she moved her hands up towards his balls and began to caress them gently, firmly, almost lovingly.

It was the strangest sensation: at that moment, Delgado felt as though he were no longer in control of his own body, as though some other, much more powerful presence had entered him and was sharing and magnifying his sensations, spurring him on, making him lick the girl faster, more and more obscenely.

He was floating, spinning, reeling, falling: a wheel within a wheel, a cloud within a cloud. There was a voice within him – he could not make out the words, but it was calling to him, urging him on, amplifying his desire, taking hold of his very soul. For a second, he thought he glimpsed a face: a strange, dark face containing all the evil of the world and yet so handsome, so seductive, so irresistible that he felt drawn into the flame-red, furnace-hot eyes. And then the fleeting vision was gone, and only the sensations remained: the aching desire in his loins, the velvet caress of the girl's moist tongue, the feel of her fingers on his balls, the scent of her untried womanhood in his nostrils. He felt as though he were losing his mind.

It was all too much for him. He exploded into her mouth and she swallowed his semen like a practised whore, eagerly, as though she relished the newness of its taste in her virgin mouth. Seconds later, Delgado felt the girl's own orgasm tearing through her, setting up great waves of pleasure that racked her whole body and left her exhausted and panting on the bed beneath him.

'She is ready,' decreed Delgado, buttoning his flies. 'Have her prepared for tonight.'

Far below, in the forgotten and bricked-up cellars of Winterbourne Hall, the Master's spirit feasted on this gift of raw sexual energy, and slowly began to understand. Tonight he would grow in strength, and one day, very soon, he would be free.

At last, his deliverance was at hand.

Winterbourne Hall was playing host to guests for the first time in almost half a century. And they were very important guests. Guests who relished Winterbourne's isolation, deep in the English countryside, because it gave them the secrecy they demanded. Guests who could not afford to be seen frequenting this type of establishment.

In the dark days of World War II, Winterbourne Hall had been commandeered by the authorities and used for billeting officers and training agents for SOE. When the time came for it to be returned to civilian control, there was no-one left to hand it back to. The last Earl had died, his son had been killed at Dunkirk, and the family fortunes had taken a tumble. In any case, there were some funny stories about odd goings-on at the Hall in the latter days of the war, and the place had earned itself a dark and mysterious reputation.

No-one wanted to know about Winterbourne Hall. Better to retreat to a nice compact villa in the South of France, and leave Winterbourne to rot, conveniently forgotten by the world.

No-one seemed interested in buying a huge ancestral pile requiring millions of pounds of investment. A few property developers considered acquiring it for the land, but nothing came of it. Like Sleeping Beauty's castle, Winterbourne Hall stood lonely and forgotten, hemmed in by the encroaching greenery of neglected hedgerows and untended gardens, for over forty years.

Until Delgado found it and realised its true potential.

He had been holidaying in England one hot August, and stumbled quite by chance upon the old house. Still gracious after all those years, it nestled in forlorn gentility among ancient woodland

and was virtually inacessible. Even the locals had almost forgotten its existence. It was perfect for a high-class house of entertainment for a really exclusive clientele. Delgado began discreet negotiations ('We're turning it into an institute for sociological research'), and within a few weeks his organisation had gained possession of yet another house.

Months of renovation work and millions of pounds of money from shadowy international sources had completed the transformation of Winterbourne Hall, from decaying ruin to palace of pleasure.

There were dozens of bedrooms, each one decorated according to a theme: Ancient Rome, Dynastic Egypt, the French Revolution, Nursery Rhymes, and even Outer Space. There was something for even the most discerning of tastes. And the Great Hall had been completely refurbished to accommodate wonderful all-night 'parties' which everyone knew would really be orgies on the grand Classical scale.

Choosing the girls had been the most difficult and the most skilful task, and this had been the joint responsibility of Delgado and his assistant, Madame LeCoeur, who had come to him from another of the organisation's houses, in a select district of Paris. Madame LeCoeur was herself an accomplished whore: a voluptuous woman of forty-five who had lost none of her allure and whose great delight it was to cater for the most perverted of tastes. She could awaken the most jaded of palates and titillate men who had been impotent for years. Delgado himself could vouch for her talents. 'A fellatrice of distinction,' was how he described her after a night spent sampling her unique charms. He trusted her judgement implicitly in matters sexual.

The girls they had picked were all remarkable whores: dedicated and ready for anything. Best of all, they loved their work. Each was a beauty, and each a specialist in her own way. There was rosy-cheeked Madelon, the French whore, who looked more like an angel but had all the works of Satan in her luscious arse. Rosie, the Philippino who had spent ten years in the girlie-bars of Manila and could enslave a man with one sinuous movement of her tawny thigh. Consuela, the devout Spaniard whose novel way of taking confessions had intoxicated penitents from Cadiz to Cairo and beyond. Birgitte, the towering Danish farmgirl with bright blonde plaits and breasts as massive and as comforting as feather pillows.

In all, there were forty girls, all at the peak of their perfection and as gifted as fine musicians, skilled in playing perfect concertos on the bodies of tired and jaded clients. Perfect, as indeed they must be to cater for their exclusive clientele. And drawn from dozens of different countries.

It really was a United Nations of sex, mused Delgado, lighting an expensive Cuban cigar and admiring himself in the full-length mirror in his bedroom. He looked good. Tall, swarthy-skinned, hair still dark and slicked back; only the walking-stick he carried a reminder of the backstreet brawl in Algiers, twenty years ago, which had left him with a knife-wound a hair's breadth from his heart, and a badly broken leg. Now only the slight limp remained to take his mind back to those days of poverty and dangerous living in the North African slave towns.

He glanced at his watch. Almost eight o'clock. The guests would be arriving shortly. He took up

9

his silver-handled cane and went downstairs to the Great Hall.

He had been saving himself for this moment for a very, very long time.

The Hall looked magnificent, softly yet clearly lit by dozens of massive candelabra and huge wrought-iron chandeliers blazing with hundreds of candles. For a moment, Delgado looked into the flickering shadows and thought he glimpsed the silent revels of gathering ghosts: the forgotten souls of earlier inhabitants, awakened from their slumbers and brought here by the memory of what it was to be young, alive; to fuck.

The decorations followed a Classical Roman theme, with a wonderful erotic mosaic floor which had been especially commissioned. Many of the paintings around the walls were copies of obscene murals found at Pompeii: pictures of naked men and women coupling with frenzied passion, enjoying every obscenity. In the very centre of the hall was a sunken bath, big enough for twenty or thirty revellers and filled with a constant supply of rose-scented warm water. Low benches were arranged around the pool, and in the darker recesses of the hall were soft couches and cushions.

All of Winterbourne's exquisite whores were gathered in the Hall: reclining on cushions, talking and drinking wine, or swimming naked in the scented bath. The costume was Roman too: semi-diaphanous togas and no underwear. Some of the girls had been cast in the role of slaves: wearing nothing but jewelled belts and tiny decorative aprons, these girls had been chosen for the exceptional beauty of their breasts, which stood out proud and stiff-nippled in the evening air. Stiff, not with cold but with excitement, mused Delgado with satisfaction, feeling his own prick begin to twitch with delicious anticipation.

The guests were arriving: distinguished, greying men with unspeakable lusts in their tired eyes. As each one arrived, he was introduced to Delgado, and taken away to be robed by Madame LeCoeur. The introductions sounded like the guest list for a Royal garden party or a charity gala night . . . Sir Roger Linford (the Queen's press secretary), Harold Winterson, Edmund O'Rourke and Sir Jeremy Hunter (cabinet ministers), and David Roehampton, the TV journalist . . . Men in whose hands lay the future of the country; men who could not afford the merest breath of a scandal; exactly the sort of men for whom Winterbourne had been created.

'Let the revels begin!' Delgado nodded to Madame LeCoeur, and the procession of guests filed into the Great Hall, almost unrecognisable in their togas and sandals.

He clapped his hands, and at once there were two whores beside each man, taking them by the arms and leading them to the benches beside the scented bath. They sat down on the stone benches, and the 'slave-girls' brought in silver trays laden with food and wine.

They ate greedily, fed and waited on by their whores, and watching two naked girls frolicking in the pool. They were twins: exotic coffee-coloured girls with a hint of the Dark Continent; long glossy-black hair streaming out behind them in the water

11

as they swam, weaving about their shoulders and breasts like some strange chimerical seawrack.

At first, their play seemed innocent enough. The girls were excellent swimmers, and moved sinuously like tawny eels through the pink-tinged water. This was deeply erotic in itself. As they glided through the water, it ran like a loving caress across their gleaming buttocks, moulding the ever-moving, ever-glistening curves and awakening long-suppressed desires in the watchers. And the watchers themselves were being caressed, gently, subtly, knowingly: doubly caressed, a beautiful semi-naked girl on either side, twin goddesses of love for every man.

And then the water-games became more adventurous. The girls swam towards each other and began to lavish caresses upon each other. One picked up a cake of soap from the side of the bath and began to rub it lasciviously over her sister's skin: so bronzed, so perfect, that she might have been one of the statues standing in the candlelit shadows of the Great Hall. The tormentor laughed merrily as she ran the soap vigorously over her sister's nipples, delighting in the way they leapt to attention, darker brown mounds at the ends of her firm young breasts.

Nor was the first sister indifferent to the charms of the situation. Her own breasts were hardening, trembling deliciously as she worked away vigorously at her twin's body, the mirror-image of her own vibrant sexuality. Her twin moaned and moved her legs apart, bracing herself on the tiled floor of the bath as her sister slid the soap downwards and inexorably towards her juicy cunt. A well-soaped finger slid inside, and the girl began to writhe

12

about, groaning and flinging her head from side to side.

On the benches, the men wanted to lift up the hems of their togas and masturbate. Some longed to dive into the scented water and take the girls there and then. But their knowing, skilful companions shook their heads and smiled, and whispered secret words into their ears: 'This is just a beginning, an apéritif'; 'Save yourself for later'; 'The best is yet to come . . .' And they soothed and aroused them with knowing kisses, caresses so skilful that they awakened and prolonged desire, eternally retarding the moment of orgasm until desire became so acute that it was almost pain, and arousal became sheer torment . . .

The girls were now climbing the steps that led up out of the pool. Dripping wet, glistening and with rivulets of water coursing down their impassive faces, their breasts, their bellies, their thighs, their brown bodies seemed even more as though they were cast in bronze: ancient statues discovered by exultant archaeologists and drawn up from the far fathoms where they had lain lost and forgotten for centuries, their perfection unimpaired by time.

'On the floor, Calypso,' commanded the first twin.

'I obey, Sappho.'

And Calypso lay down upon the mosaic, her bronzed flesh framed by the lewd brightness of prancing satyrs and wanton naked nymphs. And Sappho began, with the utmost lasciviousness, to lap up the droplets of rose-tinted water from her sister's taut-muscled body. She began by licking the water from Calypso's closed eyelids, where little rose-scented pools had gathered like tears of ecstasy.

The girl trembled, not with cold but with desire: trembled as bronze vibrates when it is struck into sudden and unexpected harmonies.

Sappho's tongue ventured downwards, lapping greedily at her twin sister's long, slender throat and plunging ever-downwards to the foothills of her glorious tawny breasts. Her own breasts were hardened with desire and she was breathing heavily as her lips fastened on Calypso's nipples: first the right, then the left, until each was taut and hard with pleasure and the girl began to thrust her pelvis slowly and seductively upwards, as though seeking an invisible lover who would thrust his massive penis into her cunt and end the delicious misery of her frustration.

But the lover had no need of any penis. Her tongue – long and muscular and lively – was all she needed to satisfy her sister's cravings. Slowly and tantalisingly, she moved inexorably downwards over Calypso's flat belly, lingering a little while to send her tongue wriggling playfully into her navel and delighting in the little spasms of pleasure which contorted the young woman's body.

Calypso was moaning loudly now, and her cries contrasted markedly with the tense silence among the watchers: men of power rendered powerless by the sight of these two lovers who had no need of them. So powerless that they could not even reach for their straining pricks and masturbate themselves to release, for their hands were restrained by their strong-willed companions, and in their heart of hearts they knew that they must hold back their desires for there was better – much, much better – to come . . .

Sappho had rested her slender hands upon her twin sister's strong-muscled thighs and was now insinuating sly fingers into the hot, moist place where those thighs met, tormenting and persuading the girl to give in to lust: to open her legs and display her treasures. It was a pretty game, for it was obvious for all to see that Calypso's saintly self-restraint was entirely for the benefit of the important guests watching her twist and turn and cry out in her fury of lust.

The *coup de grâce* came after an eternity of playful licking and half-hearted resistance. Sappho began to lick her sister's pubic hair, wriggling into the jet-black frizzy mass and twisting the curly strands around her tongue, tugging lasciviously at that most sensitive part of Calypso's body. With a cry – half despair, half pain – the poor victim surrendered herself body and soul, and flung her thighs so wide apart that none of the watchers could have been in any doubt about her excitement. Her cunt glistened, pink and wet. And that wetness owed little to the rose-scented waters of the bath. Her own juices were flowing freely, welling up out of her secret spring like healing waters, redolent with mystery and power.

Sappho began to play with these rosy treasures, running her index finger luxuriously down the sopping crack, scooping up the juices and using them to lubricate her sister's mound of desire. Calypso gasped as her sister's finger reached, and applied skilful pressure to her yearning clitoris.

'No, please, no . . . !' she cried.

But Sappho was pitiless. With a wicked smile she began to rub harder at her sister's clitty with her left hand, whilst plunging her right index finger into Calypso's tight but amply lubricated hole. The girl's eyes flew open in ecstasy, and she thrust her pelvis forward to take in her sister's finger up to the knuckle.

Struggling to sit up, Calypso grabbed hold of her sister's shoulders and pulled her head down, down, down until it was between her thighs. Sappho made great play of struggling, resisting, but the outcome was a foregone conclusion: Calypso would have her own victory. The punters mustn't be disappointed, as Delgado mused to himself, gently and surreptitiously stroking his penis as he looked on from the shadows.

He was far too preoccupied to notice another, less formless shadow that seemed to grow darker and more substantial as each second passed, as the excitement mounted and the sexual energies in the room grew ever stronger.

Sappho's face was now pressed hard against her sister's cunt, her lascivious serpent of a tongue darting in and out of the fragrant depths and her finger still rubbing ever harder on Calypso's erect clitoris.

Calypso came to her climax, crying out and writhing on the mosaic floor; and Sappho fell upon her, panting. They lay there for a long time, long coffee-coloured limbs entwined like tired young animals curled up together for warmth.

The room grew darker as the concealed electric lights were dimmed. Now the only light came from the hundreds of flickering, dancing candles warming the gloom and bringing the lewd figures in the wall-paintings strangely to life.

A blood-red velvet curtain at the back of the hall

twitched and swished back, revealing a dreamlike procession. Two tall negresses in long white robes led the way, their ebony skin gleaming eerie and blue-black in the light from the flaming torches they carried. They wore long white robes which clung to the swell of breast and hip and revealed a sinuous ripple of muscular strength.

Behind them came four young blond men, naked save for tiny loincloths which bulged with the promise of their manhood. They carried an ornate curtained litter with gauzy curtains, behind which could be glimpsed the vague form of a woman. At the rear of the procession came Madame LeCoeur, plump and appetising in her guise of Roman procuress.

The whores were chivvying their guests to their feet, and leading them over to join the procession. They seemed slightly dazed, slightly drunk, though they had consumed little. They were not to know that the sweet wine they had drunk had been laced with a little concoction of Madame LeCoeur's own devising, guaranteed to sweep away all inhibitions and convey whoever drank it into a realm where dream met reality and fused seamlessly with it.

The guests would enjoy the spectacle, rise to new heights of ecstasy, experienced undreamed-of orgasms tonight. And their pleasant memories would be bound to ensure their swift return. No man who had once stepped into the world of Winterbourne Hall would ever quite escape its special charm, its seductive lure.

The curious procession wound its way slowly around the Great Hall six times, accompanied by sensual music whose beat grew gradually more insistent and its rhythms more and more lewd.

The guests processed behind the litter, flanked by their whores who continued to caress and excite them, always withdrawing their subtle fingers before their victims could reach orgasm. The atmosphere was heavy with sex and anticipation.

At last the tall negresses led the way to a softly carpeted corner of the Hall, strewn with rugs, floor-cushions and rich wall-hangings. In the middle was a low bed with a soft mattress. At a sign from Madame LeCoeur, the blond youths set down the litter and stepped away into the shadows, almost regretfully, as though they were loth to miss what was going to happen next.

This was what the men had been waiting for: the highlight of their evening's entertainment; the special, piquant pleasure which they could buy nowhere else. A young girl's flesh, unsullied and fresh as a dew-kissed fruit still clinging to the bough, just begging to be plucked and defiled. Men licked their lips, forgot the seductive delights of their companionable whores, and all their eyes turned to feast on these new wonders, these delights chosen especially to revive their flagging tastes, their much-abused libido. For these men had the power and the money to afford any perversion, any baseness, any indecency they craved . . . and they craved this young flesh which they had not yet even seen, craved it because they delighted in the perversion of innocence, the sight of fear darkening cloudless eyes, the power of doing wrong.

Delgado stepped forward out of the shadows and addressed the throng. In his immaculate black tuxedo, leaning on his silver-topped cane, he looked strangely out of place in this satyric *mise-en-scène*.

18

Out of place but superior, he knew that. He was the ringmaster, and these guests, however rich, however powerful, were merely the beasts in his circus. He enjoyed that kind of power. A sardonic smile played about his lips as he began to speak:

'Gentlemen, you are gathered here tonight to witness and take part in an erotic pageant – the greatest the world has to offer. Already you have witnessed a little spectacle, which I believe we all found enjoyable.'

There were nods of agreement.

'Well, gentlemen, now we come to the highlight of the evening: an auction which I know will interest and excite your passions. Within this litter sits a girl of rare beauty, innocence, docility. Innocence most especially. I personally have verified her virginity, and I can tell you she has been with no man in her young life. A mere child, a slip of a girl, inexperienced, filled with fear.'

One of the watchers had found his voice:

'How do we know she's a virgin?'

More nods. Drugged or not, these men had lost none of their business instincts.

'Yeah, let us check out the merchandise before we part with our money.' It was Gavin de Lacy, the well-known City broker with an equally well-known penchant for young men and women – sometimes both at once.

'All in good time,' replied Delgado. 'You shall have ample opportunity to . . . examine . . . the girl before you place your bids.'

This seemed to placate the guests, so Delgado continued:

'Gentlemen, whichever of you is the highest bidder

shall have the great joy of taking this girl here, on this bed, in front of us all. He shall have the singular pleasure of being the very first to thrust his manhood into her cunt, to tear into her and destroy her innocence. And he shall have his will with her until he is sated. After which,' he added, with a conspiratorial glance around the room, 'anyone else who desires her may have her. And of course any others of our magnificent whores who take your fancy. And the orgy shall continue until dawn.'

He signed to Madame LeCoeur, and she drew aside the curtain. Inside, Joanna Königsberg sat unmoving, pale, trembling slightly. She seemed not to know quite where she was or indeed who she was. Aided by Madame LeCoeur, she climbed out of the litter and stood obediently in front of her would-be purchasers.

She was dressed in full Roman costume, with her breathtaking blonde hair piled up in an ornate style, perfect ringlets framing her ivory cheeks. Her firm breasts thrust against the diaphanous material of her robe and the nipples were hard as iron.

'Delicious.'

'Good enough to eat.'

'Like a little white dove just before the eagle swoops down and devours it . . .'

Appreciative murmurs came from all sides. Like the slave master at a slave auction, the French madame led the girl around the circle of men, letting them see, touch, handle. Joanna submitted silently to every indignity, standing docile as the gazelle waiting for the lion to strike.

Lewd hands clawed at her dress, tugging it from her shoulders. The fabric gave way and the bodice dropped down, leaving her naked to the waist. Fingers plucked at her perfect pink nipples and for the first time it was obvious that Joanna was feeling not only fear but the beginnings of pleasure through her drug-induced trance. Her breathing became halting and her eyes half closed. More hands, and the rest of the dress fell to the ground.

She was entirely naked underneath. The broad perfect sweep of her hips and the blonde curly triangle of her pubis were breathtaking. A bold hand ran down her taut belly and toyed with the blonde curls. Instinctively the girl began to open her legs almost imperceptibly, until at last her feet were several inches apart and the man's finger was teasing the gateway to her maidenhead.

'Lie down on the bed,' Madame LeCoeur commanded her, leading her across and sitting her down on the satin sheets. She took the pins from the girl's hair and it tumbled in a blonde wave over her ivory shoulders.

The girl obeyed and stretched out full-length on the bed.

'Spread your legs.'

She did so, and Madame LeCoeur beckoned Gavin de Lacy.

'Feel for yourself that she is a virgin.'

He needed no second bidding. Roughly, quite without gentleness, he thrust two fingers into the girl's damp crack. Joanna gave a little cry, perhaps of pain, perhaps of anticipation, and she began to tremble. De Lacy gave a self-satisfied grunt and withdrew his fingers reluctantly. His rock-hard penis was clearly visible, beating an insistent tattoo beneath the fabric of his toga.

21

He looked around the gathering and nodded.

'She's a virgin all right. And tight as a sparrow's arse,' he laughed. And his laughter was as cold and unfeeling as the night wind shrieking cruelly through the woods enshrouding the Hall.

The girl lay, oblivious and unmoving, on the bed: legs splayed wide and her virgin wetness glistening in the candleglow. She seemed younger than her eighteen years: a protected, sheltered child with a body as precious and fragile as Dresden porcelain. Her extreme youth and innocence had delighted Delgado the very first moment that he set eyes upon her: not because those qualities appealed especially to his own tastes, but because he knew that they would appeal to those of his guests. Herr Königsberg had provided a precious commodity in offering his daughter as a sacrifice to the prosperity of Winterbourne Hall: her virginity would fetch an excellent price.

'Then may I start the bidding?' Delgado continued. 'What am I bid for this luscious fruit, this fresh rosebud? Who will start me off at two thousand?'

'Two,' came the prompt reply.

'Two thousand five hundred.'

'Three thousand.'

The bids came thick and fast. These were men for whom money was no object, and who would stop at nothing in their quest for new frissons of pleasure. Delgado knew that the atmosphere of the auction itself was exciting them: men who thrived on competition and got a hard-on whenever they ruined a decent man or starved out a widow and her family.

'Eight thousand.'

'Eight thousand five hundred.'

There were only two bidders left now: de Lacy and a fat old man called Harry Blomfeld – ironically, a business associate of Joanna's father. Delgado knew he had lusted after the girl for years, had even offered her father cash to fuck her. Obviously not enough cash. But Blomfeld was a wealthy man – far wealthier than de Lacy – and it looked as if he was finally willing to pay whatever it took to get his kicks. The outcome was a foregone conclusion.

'Ten thousand.'

De Lacy shook his head, regretfully.

'I guess I'll just have to have her later,' he concluded.

'Can I have her somewhere private? I've paid good money for the slut: I'd like to enjoy her a little, play with her maybe . . .'

Delgado shook his head. He knew that Blomfeld was a noted pervert with a reputed taste for sadism. He might not stop at 'playing' with his prey. They didn't want any scandals at Winterbourne, not on the first night. 'The rule is that you must take her here, in front of all the guests. Of course, if you're unwilling, I'm sure Mr de Lacy . . .'

But the victor was already taking off his toga, to reveal a flabby, sixty-year-old body and a surprisingly lively-looking prick: long and hard and glistening at its tip with the long anticipation of this moment.

Blomfeld stared glassy-eyed at the girl and licked his lips. He really was a repellent man. He reminded Delgado of some disgusting flesh-eating reptile: a Komodo dragon, perhaps, or a carrion-feeding dinosaur. He leant over the girl and began kneading her breasts, tweaking the nipples so roughly that

Delgado could not believe she was not feeling pain. And yet the girl was smiling strangely in her drug-induced trance, and began to writhe about under her tormentor's touch.

Somewhere close at hand, a dark shadow was drawing ever nearer, now with a purposeful intent.

As his hand slid gradually downwards, Blomfeld felt the strangest sensation taking him over. It was as though he was no longer within himself, or that he was sharing his inner identity with another, and much stronger, personality.

The sense of power took his breath away. Always a little, insignificant man, he had compensated with ever-greater cruelties and perversions of the weak and defenceless. But never, never in all his life had he felt such power. It soaked into him like a dark mist, filling every crevice of his being with an unspeakable evil. He welcomed it in, like oxygen to a suffocating man. It was everything he had ever wanted to be: evil, dark, strong, cruel, merciless.

The Master's spirit entered Blomfeld's body and laughed to see his soul so feeble. He brushed it aside like a tiny fly, and rejoiced in this temporary gift of sight and sensation. Blomfeld's body was flabby, old, inadequate and decaying: ordinarily it would have disgusted him. He would have scorned it. But in his weakness and need the Master seized it gratefully, drank at the fountain of life and rejoiced at what he saw before him.

The girl was beautiful, perfect, innocent, untouched. Her frail purity excited him so much that he could control himself no longer. He used the body he had 'borrowed' to slake his terrible, terrible thirst.

The other guests looked on in surprise as they saw

the sudden transformation in Blomfeld, the glint of pure evil in his eyes, the ferocity of his assault upon the girl. He wrenched her legs wide apart, and – without the least preliminaries – thrust his thick, hard penis into her tiny virgin cunt. She cried out, but there was an inexplicable ecstasy in her cry of pain. He thrust into her a second time, and broke through her hymen, sending a deluge of bright red blood coursing down her thighs.

With a cry of triumph and monstrous delight, the Master wielded Blomfeld's body once again and the old man found himself biting into the girl's neck, drawing forth another trickle of blood. He lapped at it greedily, continuing to paw at the girl's defiled body and thrust frantically in and out of her.

His cry of ecstasy was also the Master's cry of victory. As his semen mingled with the girl's blood, a massive orgasm tore through Blomfeld and through the girl, and the power of that orgasm flowed abundantly into the Master's enfeebled soul, bringing for just a moment the revelation of what his powers had once been, and what they would soon be once again.

When at last the waves of pleasure and life-giving energy ebbed away, and the Master's soul lost possession of the body it had taken over, it remained stronger – almost imperceptibly stronger – than it had been before. Now he knew that Winterbourne Hall would be the scene of his resurrection. No-one who stepped within its walls would be safe from his ever-growing power.

'What's wrong with them?' demanded Madame LeCoeur, panic-stricken.

Blomfeld and the girl lay in a tangled heap on the bed, a slow trickle of blood still flowing from neck and cunt. Delgado hauled Blomfeld's inert body off the girl and saw that they were both smiling. It was a strange, chilling smile – self-contained and surprisingly macabre. They were unconscious but breathing normally. To all intents and purposes, sound asleep.

'Take them upstairs and put them in the Rose Room,' ordered Delgado. 'They'll soon come round. Now: let the revels begin!'

Winterbourne Hall lay still and silent as dawn's grey light touched the tops of the trees. In the Great Hall, bodies lay entwined and sleeping in the aftermath of a night of sexual excess.

In the Rose Room, Joanna slept on, the effects of the drugs still strong in her body and consciousness of her defilement mercifully yet hours away. And when she awoke, there would be an inexplicable tiredness: a weariness of the soul which could not be attributed to physical causes. A long-lasting weariness which no doctor would be able to fathom . . .

And when Blomfeld awoke, it was with the sense of having been changed, possessed, altered so radically that he would never be the same. It was as though there was another, darker presence with him, a presence which would never leave him.

He had the strangest sensation that he would never be alone again. And a sudden dark shadow of fear clutched at his coward's heart.

2: Cheviot

Sir Anthony Cheviot could not believe his good fortune. An invitation to Winterbourne and a lunch-date with a beautiful young debutante, all in the same week.

It was many years since Lady Cheviot had given him any sex. A lot longer than that since she had given him any good sex. A succession of anonymous call-girls had seemed the safest solution in his delicate position. One had to be so careful. Kiss-and-tell memoirs in the *News of the World* didn't do you any good at all when you were supposed to be a right-wing, God-fearing MP with a strong line on sex, violence and immorality.

And then he heard rumours about Winterbourne. A discreet haven for distinguished men with needs to satisfy and reputations to protect. Perfect. But how to go about getting an invitation? Luckily enough, in one of his visits to a 'private party' in Sussex, he had met a man called Delgado. Delgado had understood perfectly. It was almost as if Delgado could read his mind.

Within a fortnight, he had found himself at the gates to Winterbourne Hall, as excited as a schoolboy out on a first illicit assignation.

It was hard to choose a girl. There were so many

to choose from. He liked Madelon, the plump-buttocked French whore – but buggery wasn't his style. He wanted a girl with lips like a vacuum cleaner, who would suck him dry and then coax him into hardness again and let him screw her till she begged for mercy. On the advice of Delgado, he chose Lim Pei, a breath of the mysterious Orient with fire in her jewel-dark eyes. Lim Pei, otherwise known as Nemesis.

He had paid his money and the girl was his. She led him up the carved sixteenth-century staircase, and down a long carpeted corridor. He marvelled at the names on the doors as he passed: 'Dark Angel', 'Winged Hope', 'Juno', 'Eden', 'Paradise Found', 'Serpent of Nile'.

At last they stopped outside her room. There it was – the plaque on the door read: 'Nemesis'. For a moment, he felt just a twinge of unease. The word was not a particularly erotic one. It wasn't even one he was comfortable with. Let's face it, he'd done enough iffy things in his life to wonder if one day he might really get his just deserts . . . But no. It was just a word. Just the sort of thing an advertising agency might come up with to add a little frisson to their latest marketing campaign.

'Try Nemesis today: and really get what's coming to you . . .'

He laughed, licked his lips and followed the girl into the room. It was very dark, and he blinked as his eyes accustomed themselves to the dim candle-glow. Half-blinded, he felt Lim Pei's tiny, butterfly hands fluttering over his body, awakening his desires, teasing him and – when he reached out to catch her and pull her to him – flying away just out of reach.

He could hear her breathing, soft and urgent. And something else. He could have sworn there were other shapes, moving, gliding in the shadows.

But no. He was mistaken. He'd paid for one girl, and one girl was what he'd got. He was going to enjoy her. He wondered if Delgado had recommended her for a reason. It seemed unlikely. For if the mysterious dark-haired brothel-keeper had done his research properly he would have known that Sir Anthony liked to be dominated. He liked to be overwhelmed. He liked to be submerged and punished and left begging for mercy. Begging for more.

No, Delgado had got it wrong. This so-called Nemesis was so frail she couldn't harm a fly. Couldn't defend herself against a midget, let alone his not-insubstantial bulk.

'Come here, my lovely,' he breathed, still straining his eyes to make out shapes in the half-darkness.

She came towards him and smiled. His cock reared in his pants, thrusting its head painfully against the inside of his zip. He readjusted himself and felt the dampness already soaking through his trousers. She was luscious.

Her lips glistened in the flickering candle-light, and she ran her tongue over them hungrily. She had taken off her long robe and was wearing nothing but a sort of jewelled bikini: all blues and brilliant greens and gold, with suggestive tassels where he knew her nipples were hiding.

He wanted to bite those nipples. Sink his teeth into them until she cried out in pain.

Heart thumping, he reached out and took hold of her right shoulder-strap. She made no attempt to move away, and with a gasp of triumph Cheviot

29

tore at it roughly. It gave way and the cup fell away, exposing her right breast. He fell upon her, licking and biting. He was surprised to feel her stand her ground. She winced slightly as the tips of his teeth dug into her flesh, but still she withstood his assault. He felt slightly disappointed: he hadn't planned on spending the night with a submissive little geisha. He might even ask Delgado for his money back.

But then he felt her hands searching for him, finding the bulge in his trousers and rubbing at it with obvious pleasure and considerable skill. He could not suppress a low moan of satisfaction as her fingers ran lightly over his testicles and fastened on his shaft, gripping it purposefully. Then she unzipped him, and that was heaven. The unbelievable coolness of those tiny fingers on his immense hardness, holding him just hard enough to drive him wild, just lightly enough to stop him coming all over her hand.

He thrust his penis against her, ground it against her belly suggestively. Maddened with lust, he tore at the other bra strap and in seconds she was naked to the waist: two perfect globes, soon glistening with his saliva; firm-fleshed and erect.

The panties. He must get her panties off her. Got to get into her juicy cunt. Got to fuck her, fuck her, fuck her. His brain was reeling. Had that Frenchwoman slipped something into his drink? He felt so randy he knew he couldn't control himself much longer. He lunged for her panties but, to his amazement, the girl drew away from him with a wicked smile.

'What . . . ?'

Something was moving towards him out of the shadows. Not something. Some things. There *were* shapes in the margins of the room, and now they were moving in on him. He began to sweat, panic, turn around and look for the door. No good. They were all around him. There must have been . . . eight of them at least.

Closer and closer . . . and hands reached out from behind him and began to run all over his body. Hands, hands – how many hands? Four? Six? More? It felt as though he was floating in an ocean of hands, fluttering fingers taking the place of the treacherous currents. He tried to turn around, but the shadowy figures were in front of him, too.

Now he could see them. Women. Tall women clad in black leather. Black leather and studs. Leather-girls with cruel whips. They were all smiling; smiles without warmth; smiles full of malice and desire. They were going to punish him. He didn't know whether to cry out with fear or desire.

Strong hands. Hands that picked him up and carried him, struggling, towards the futon bed at the far end of the room, haloed in candles. There was a heady scent of incense that made his head spin even more. His prick felt as though it were on fire.

Hands. Hands that tore at his clothing and wrenched it from his body. The Jermyn Street handmade shirt and the Savile Row suit, torn from him without a thought of how much they had cost. Hands that squeezed his hardness lasciviously through his under-pants, then tugged roughly at them. He was naked and struggling.

He found his voice: 'Let me go!'

But only mocking laughter greeted him. Strong hands held on to his wrists. And all the time he was gazing up at Lim Pei, who had straddled his face and was masturbating herself obscenely and unashamedly only inches above him. He longed for her tight cunt on his prick, but all he could feel were hands, hands gripping his ankles, forcing his thighs apart, splaying his helpless body across the bed, kneading his flesh so eagerly, so violently that he winced with pain.

He gazed up at Lim Pei, marvelling at the olive skin of her inner thighs, the hot and steaming furrow that ran between them, the halo of dark bristles guarding the entrance to her love-palace. The desire to fuck her overwhelmed him, and still the cruel hands refused to wank him off, refused to release him from this torment. His poor tormented prick twitched and ached to burst inside some hot, wet slit, or to explode on to the surface of some knowing tongue.

Lim Pei knew how to make a man suffer. First, she ran the edge of her hand though her hot crack. It sank into the flesh like a hot knife into butter, and when she took away her hand it was wet and fragrant. She wiped it on Cheviot's face, and he groaned at the sweet muskiness of her powerful smell.

Then she moved both hands down her pubis and began to toy with her belly, her genitals, teasing not only Cheviot but herself, running fingertips gently and deliciously over the hypersensitive flesh of her inner thighs. The flickering candlelight gave a dream-like quality to the sight of this lovely woman playing with herself, pleasuring herself and her audience in the semi-darkness of a bordello where nothing was forbidden, everything permissible and indeed encouraged.

Her playful hands moved upwards towards her

cunt, and Sir Anthony heard her give a little sigh of pleasure as their very fingertips reached her pubic bristles and began to twist them around, tugging at them, clearly enjoying this sensation of mingled pleasure and pain. Then, delicately, as though parting the petals of a fragile lotus-blossom, Lim Pei pulled apart her cunt lips and displayed the glories within to her transfixed victim.

Glistening, running with rivulets of shining love-juice, Lim Pei's dark-fringed cunt swayed inches above Cheviot's face and mesmerised him, like the golden pendulum of some diabolical hypnotist. Swaying, glistening, fragrant and heady like summer wine and bee-harvested lavender honey. Instinctively he stuck out his tongue, and with a laugh of glee Lim Pei lowered herself on to his face. He felt his tongue go straight to its target, and as he licked at the girl he could taste her juicy abundance as it flowed freely down his face.

Groaning, she came and the fragrant corolla of her cunt opened and closed on his enchanted tongue. His brain reeled, he felt himself floating, submerged in the blue-green light of submarine grottoes, drowning, drowning.

When she climbed off him, he was only dimly aware of what was happening to him. Until the hands began to torment him again, tormenting him in earnest, pinching and stroking, kneading and scratching with their long, merciless fingernails. The pain was excruciating: a nail raked up his inner thigh and he could feel a warm trickle – of blood? or was it sweat? – coursing down the flesh.

He gazed up at the women: tall leather-girls in spiked boots. Masked and identical, like the multiple

33

images cast in some horrific kaleidoscope. Strong bodies moulded in black leather catsuits, slashed open at the crotch and with holes through which their identical breasts protruded. Breasts whose brown, stiffened nipples were cruelly pierced and ornamented with silver chains, forming a weird, fantastic bridge between right breast and left. Breasts that glistened palely in the half-light.

They raised their whips and – before he could cry out in fear – began to lash him, at first gently but then with greater insistence, infinite and Mephistophelian skill. The thongs were of the softest, most flexible leather, and the torture was exquisite; exactly calculated to arouse a stinging pain which turned swiftly to an agonisingly, deliciously pernicious warmth in his loins. Their whips studiously avoided his penis and testicles, yet with every measured stroke he held his breath in terror, expecting to feel the bite of the lash on those tender parts.

His prick was bursting with desire. His balls were tense and hot and hard. He writhed and moaned, and tried desperately to wrest his arms free from his torturers' grasp, but the strong, leather-gloved hands held him fast and in his heart of hearts he didn't want them to let go. Not ever.

Suddenly the strong hands lifted him up, wriggling and elated, turning him over in mid-air; and he found himself face-down on the futon, breathless, helpless, desperate. And the lashes came stinging down on his backside, making him arch his back, thrust out his buttocks in pain and insatiable desire.

It was then that he felt it: the cold presence between his buttocks: at first gentle, caressing, pleading; then gradually more insistent, more persuasive.

'No!' he cried, and tried to wriggle free; but it was no use. His cries were muffled by the mattress and his flabby body was held fast. He was the helpless victim, and there was not a thing he could do about it. There was something wonderfully erotic about such helplessness.

The dildo insinuated its way further and further into his backside. Without lubrication it was painful, but he welcomed it in, feeling his prick harden still further as the smooth hardness forced a path into the very heart of him. Further in, further still: his mouth was contorted in agony. And then a last cry of pain as, with a final violent shove, the dildo was pushed right into him and disappeared inside. He felt as though he would most certainly explode. And all this time, the lashes were still stinging down on his striated backside.

Once again picked up, thrown harshly on to his back. He blinked in the sudden candlelight. The masked faces around him looked sinister, blurred, confused. It was as though he was being raped by a many-headed, many-armed monster with a black shiny skin and sharp, raking claws. The dildo inside his arse pained him and aroused him, like a red-hot poker joined to the root of his penis.

Suddenly, Lim Pei reappeared, completely naked now. Two of the leather-girls began to massage her body with sweet oils, and the scent of bergamot and sex made Cheviot groan as beads of love-juice appeared at the tip of his sex-hungry penis. The leather-girls held him down, legs spread and penis jerkingly erect.

Slowly and seductively, Lim Pei – Nemesis truly named – came forward and knelt between his thighs.

She stretched out her delicate, perfumed hands and began to work sweet oil into his groin, then over his balls, and along his shaft. He knew that in a few moments he would come . . .

But she stopped. And with one swift movement climbed on to his penis, sliding her well-lubricated cunt like a silk glove over his yearning hardness.

'Nemesis . . . !' he groaned, as she laid her body down on his, and he felt her warm breath on his cheek.

He waited for her to move, but she lay still on top of him, her warm, moist cunt throbbing gently on his hardened shaft. Waited, but she did not move a muscle. Why did she not move? He tried to thrust in and out of her, but the leather-girls had him fast and he could not move his pelvis. With a strangled sob of realisation, he saw that it was all part of the torture, all part of his Nemesis. How long would they leave him like this, unsatisfied and frantic with lust? How long would they keep him in this terrible limbo?

And then the strangest thing happened.

It was only a feeling at first. Like a scarcely heard whispering in his head. A curious shadow cast over his face, clouding his brain, suspending the moment in time and space. And then it grew to a great, formless blackness that chilled and then inflamed him, swamped him and augmented him.

It felt as if the Devil himself was taking his hand and leading him through fire, burning away all that was light and good and weak and helpless. And the seed of dark strength grew until it filled the universe, and in terror he realised that he was gazing deep into two fiery eyes, brimful of evil joy. He no longer knew where his own spirit ended and that of this

conquering evil began. He had become someone –
something – he no longer recognised.

The strength surged through him like fire through
a tinder-dry forest, and with a cry of triumph Cheviot
wrenched himself free of the leather-girls holding
him down. They struggled to hold him but he brushed
them aside like small children, and – as though
they understood that what they were dealing with
was something far more sinister than a fat, elderly
Cabinet minister – they backed away and made no
further attempt to restrain him.

Lim Pei tried to resist him, but it was futile. Within
a second, he had flung the tiny woman face-down
on the mattress and was wrenching her arse-cheeks
apart. He was into her arse like an express train and,
with the glorious sensation of the dildo still buried
in his own backside, he was able to feel it all: to
be the buggerer and his victim, the ravisher and the
ravished. And still the fiery eyes burned deep within
him and it was as though everything he felt, he felt
through another, stronger body, saw through those
other eyes.

The girl squealed in pain: Nemesis meeting her
own fatal destiny, paying for all her excesses, all the
men she had ever tormented.

And he looked down at her and in that moment he
was the stallion, serving the mare with a huge erect
penis that bruised and tore and violated. And with a
huge cry of elation and lust, he lunged for the nape of
the girl's neck and buried his teeth in her sweet flesh.

They came together, in an explosion so vast that
they both sank into unconsciousness and did not
wake for many hours, overcome by a weakness that
was as much of the spirit as of the body.

* * *

Cheviot fondled the debutante's arse and she gave a little low growl of pleasure. The drink had weakened her resolve, just as he had planned. There was no way he was going to let her get away from him. He needed sex, and he was going to get it.

Ever since he had met Nemesis, his sexual appetites had increased alarmingly. Masturbation – for years his number-one hobby – no longer satisfied him for long. He needed firm young flesh. He needed a place to bury his yearning prick and shoot up his load of thick, frothing sperm. He hadn't had needs like this since he was a young man. His hungry penis was a daily torment to him. And he was loving every minute of it. Funny, really, but he felt like a new man.

He had met the girl at the launch party for a glitzy new showbiz autobiography. He had weighed her up at first sight: aristocratic, a little straightlaced, but with a basic sensuality which he was sure that a combination of drink and flattery could easily bring to the surface. Besides, he prided himself that few girls could resist the attentions of such a rich and powerful man as Sir Anthony Cheviot. She'd drop her knickers for him before the night was out, and he licked his lips in glorious anticipation.

Back at his place, she'd seemed quite tipsy and he'd worried initially that he'd overdone the drink. But no. A few discreet gropes, an 'accidental' hand on her breast, and she'd started to get friendly. From then on, it was easy.

She was giggling now, and still drinking heavily. He didn't want to overdo it so he gently took the glass from her hand. She protested, but he silenced her with a kiss on the mouth: tentative at first, and then passionate as she began to respond and breathe heavily as he pressed himself against her. The urgency of his desire had been a constant surprise to him in recent weeks. Already he was rampant and wet for the girl, and all he wanted was to bury himself inside her.

Steady now. Mustn't frighten the little slut. Got to keep her sweet. Make her feel good. *Then* get inside those pretty little panties of hers.

And so he caressed her hair, her shoulders, whispered sweet nothings in her ear and waited for his moment.

They were standing behind the sofa when the sudden impulse overtook him. She was standing with her back towards him, nestling back into him and breathing quick and hard as he smoothed his hot hands over her flesh: tracing the curves of arm, waist, thigh, and back up to her pert breasts. Bolder now, he began to undo the buttons on her blouse. She seemed to be enjoying it so he slid one hand inside her bra.

The delicious contact of the cool, sweat-moistened flesh was like a spark igniting the furnace within him. It came upon him as it had done at Winterbourne: the darkness; the sudden sense of power invading him and empowering him to do anything; filling him with the awesome, infinitely destructive powers of chaos.

And he flung her forward over the back of the sofa, knocking the breath out of her. As she lay there, arms dangling over the back, he took hold of her blouse and skirt and just ripped them off – tore at the fabric until it gave way. Then the bra, the flimsy

39

lace panties. The seamed stockings and high-heeled shoes he spared: he loved to fuck a woman in black stockings and suspenders.

And, without further ado, he pulled out his well-hardened prick and shoved it deep into her: deep into the tight, slippery little cunt she was shamelessly offering to him, arse thrust backwards, eager to swallow him up.

And he fucked her like that, hands clenched tight on her naked breasts, tightly enough to bruise and hurt her yet she did not cry out.

She did not cry out until, with an unearthly scream, Cheviot felt the spunk rising in his balls and lunged hungrily for her pretty white throat.

The Chief Whip paced up and down in his Westminster office. The police inspector waited patiently for his response. At last he broke the silence.

'You're sure he did this to the girl?'

'You've seen the photographs.'

'It'll have to be hushed up, of course. You do realise that? Cheviot is a very important man at Westminster. A senior Cabinet minister, maybe even a candidate for the number-one job. We have our own methods of disciplining our black sheep – you have my word that he'll be dealt with severely. Do I have your undertaking that you'll keep this thing out of the Sunday papers?'

The police inspector thought hard for a moment. He was a realist.

'I'll do my best, sir,' he sighed.

3: Andreas Hunt

Andreas Hunt didn't make a habit of picking up girls in bars, but he was beginning to wonder if he ought to make an exception in this case. This one was something special.

He took a long pull at his pint, settled back into his chair and began to watch her. She was stunning: dressed in a skin-tight Lycra off-the-shoulder sheath-dress that clung to her like a lover's embrace, moulding the curves of breast, hip and thigh so intimately that Hunt felt he already knew her body almost as well as she knew it herself. She had really made him sit up and take notice when she strode into the bar, alone and proud, tall and scarlet-lipped, her black hair falling in silky waves over her bare shoulders.

But it was her backside which really turned him on, made his cock twitch in his trousers – so suddenly and so uncomfortably that he had to surreptitiously wriggle his hand down into his underpants and arrange it flat against his belly. It was hot; hot and throbbing. It wanted to be inside that girl. Never mind standards of public decency: Hunt felt a terrible urge to throw the girl over a table, pull up her dress, rip off her panties (was she wearing any? He couldn't see any tell-tale line . . .)

and take her like a rutting beast in a primeval forest.

He put his hand to his brow and wiped away beads of sweat. Funny. He didn't normally get to feel like this after only two pints and not even a grope. Maybe the beer was off. His prick felt hot and urgent inside his underpants. Over by the bar, the girl shifted position on the bar-stool and her gorgeous buttocks moved so temptingly that Hunt felt a tremendous desire to wank himself off.

Luckily it was dark in the cellar-bar, and Hunt was sitting alone in an alcove, pretty much hidden from casual glances. The table in front of him ought to safeguard him from prying eyes. Surreptitiously, and pulling the sides of his raincoat over his lap for extra protection, he unzipped his flies, slid in his right hand and pulled out his penis. It felt smooth, hard, magnificent in his sweating palm, and he began to caress it straight away, with long, loving, rhythmic strokes.

The girl was still sitting with her back to him, drinking alone and exchanging few words with the men who tried to chat her up. So sexy, and yet so uninterested? Not a high-class hooker, then? Or maybe just a very choosy one . . . Hunt began to fantasise about her taking her clients back home, ushering them coolly into some million-pound penthouse flat.

Taking *him* back to her penthouse flat. Pouring him a drink. Bending over to pour the drink, knowing the action would thrust back her beautiful bum-cheeks and push them against the taut red stretchy fabric. Knowing the sight would so inflame Hunt that he would be red-faced and panting by the time she handed him the whisky and soda; smiling maliciously when he took a mouthful of the drink and found he could not swallow for the lump in his throat . . .

And then she would make her excuses and go off into the marble-lined bathroom to get ready for him. And he would be left in an agony of indecision: what should he do whilst she was gone? Ought he to get undressed? Get into the king-size bed? Or maybe give in to the irresistible urge to rub his aching cock? No, no. Save it all for her. Give her all his spunk. Let her feel it flooding out of her tight little cunny-hole.

Hunt was pumping his shaft rhythmically and hard now, so excited that he knew he could not stop. Still gazing lust-crazed at the girl, he fantasised about screwing her, letting himself go and letting her work her wiles on him. All the tricks of the trade. Teach a dog new tricks. He was fucking her doggy-fashion and she was howling with pleasure like a bitch on heat. And he was biting into the back of her neck as the dog bites the bitch, the stallion bites the mare as he mounts her. He was clutching her luscious arse-cheeks, grabbing great handfuls of her flesh and squeezing, squeezing as he rammed into her cunt.

He was dizzy, dizzy with excitement and through half-closed eyes he only dimly saw the girl as she slid off the bar-stool and turned to look at him. All he wanted to do was come. All he could think about was the incandescent heat of his throbbing penis. All he desired . . .

'Hello there.'

He surfaced from the trance, panting and dazed, and the climax that had been so near receded, leaving him frustrated and ashamed. The girl was standing over him, smiling to herself and looking him straight in the eye. Surely she couldn't see what he was getting up to underneath the table? Surely . . . ?

'No need to hide it, darling,' she breathed. And to Hunt's amazement she sat down on the padded bench beside him and slipped her hand under the tablecloth. It met his own, still firmly clamped to his hardened shaft. He stared back at her in absolute horror, mingled with the most exquisite pangs of desire. She was truly breathtaking. Sloe-black eyes and glistening, scarlet lips moistened constantly as the tip of her tongue passed across them, lascivious and irresistible. 'I could show you a good time.'

She tossed her hair back over her shoulders, and Hunt noticed the crystal-studded choker she was wearing. All those facets of multicoloured light had a mesmerising quality. He felt himself drifting, losing his willpower.

Hunt tried to pull himself together.

'I don't pay for it,' he protested. 'Never have. But thanks for the offer.'

'No, no. You've got it all wrong,' she breathed. Her voice was as smooth as melted chocolate, dark and aristocratic and sophisticated. 'I like you. I *want* you. This one's on me, darling.' And she prised his fingers from his shaft and began to masturbate it herself, slowly and skilfully so that she took him once again to the very brink of oblivion.

'One hour, my place,' she said. And she slipped a small card into Hunt's jacket pocket. Then she was on her feet again and away, stepping confidently between the tables, attracting all eyes, and finally eclipsed by the crowds of businessmen and their secretaries standing by the door.

44

She was gone.

Hunt let out a great sigh – half of relief, half disappointment. He swiftly put away his penis and did up his flies. The woman had unnerved him, and he didn't like that. A hardened investigative journalist, working on one of the major tabloids, and still a girl with a juicy arse could reduce him to jelly. He ran a hand nervously through his shock of dark hair.

He was a handsome man: over six feet tall, muscular, with delicate hands and compelling blue eyes. Had he wanted, he could have had his pick of women. Lord knows, he interviewed enough of them every day: society whores, page-three girls, actresses, housewives – every story brought its share of shapely women and a fair number of them were ready, wet and willing.

But Hunt was a bit of a loner. And he was choosy. Exceptionally so. Ordinary women bored him. He'd rather have a good wank than boring sex. When he did take a girl to bed, it was usually a one-night stand. A good fuck and so long, no hard feelings. He was independent. He didn't want to get involved – at least, not yet. He liked to think he had a cool head, didn't get carried away.

So why had this one girl had such a powerful effect on him? How come he couldn't get her out of his mind? It was some sort of trap, of course. All his journalistic instincts told him not to take the bait. She'd probably got her pimp back at her place, waiting to beat him up and pinch his wallet.

He took the card out of his pocket and gazed at it for a long time. It wasn't quite what he expected. He had thought it would be one of those gaudy

cards you find in London telephone boxes – garish
advertisements for 'executive massage' or 'spanking
by angry miss'. But it wasn't like that at all. It was
an ordinary white business card, quite tastefully produced. It read: 'Anastasia Dubois: society events and
exclusive catering service', and gave a very upmarket
address in an exclusive mews development, about
half a mile away.

Not a whore then? Hunt was puzzled. But why the
hell should some high-class bimbo like this one set
her sights on someone like him? Granted, he wasn't
bad looking; but he was one heck of an acquired
taste, and the nearest he'd ever got to Ascot was
the time he'd done that feature on bent jockeys.

She must be some kind of weirdo. But she was
dynamite, and the fuse was still burning. No, he
wouldn't go. It was either a trap, or she was some
kind of pervert.

He mustn't go. But he knew he would anyway.

Anastasia Dubois lived in one of those exclusive
Kensington apartment blocks that *real* people never
live in. Hunt was used to visiting people – indeed
harassing them – everywhere from back-to-backs to
Buckingham Palace; but he still felt vaguely uneasy
as he spoke into the entryphone:

'It's me . . . Andreas Hunt . . . from the wine bar.'

He half expected an awkward silence. Maybe
she'd been drunk. Maybe she'd only done it for a
bet. Maybe she'd changed her mind. He turned to
go, but a smooth voice purred out of the crackling
entryphone:

'Mr Hunt, I'm so glad you could come. Come right
up. Fifth floor, flat number nine.'

As he stepped into the lift and the doors closed behind him, Hunt became aware once again of the erection throbbing insistently in his trousers. An hour since he'd seen her and still he was hard. He gave himself a little rub, enjoying the well-lubricated sensation of the glistening tip against the inside of his underpants.

The lift stopped on the fifth floor and the doors glided open. The corridor was luxuriously carpeted and the whole place made Hunt feel thoroughly cheap and nasty. It was like walking out on to the set of a lavish American mini-series dressed in an old anorak and Wellington boots.

Flat nine was at the far end of the corridor. He rang the bell and waited for the longest few moments of his life. At last there was the sound of a bolt being drawn back, a safety chain being unhooked, and the door swung open.

'Come in, darling. Everything's ready for you.'

She was even more arousing than she had seemed in the half-light of the cellar bar. Her skin was so pale it seemed almost translucent, the blue of her veins clearly visible through the ivory surface. Her great dark eyes burned with an inner light which both excited and disturbed Hunt. Something deep inside him was still preparing him to run away, still convinced that this was some crazy woman.

But he stepped inside, and allowed her to take his raincoat and sports jacket. The interior of the apartment was just as luxurious as the corridor outside had suggested: Chinese silk carpets and oriental porcelain, Liberty-print sofas, embroidered wall-hangings – all the marks of tasteful affluence.

'Would you like a drink, Mr Hunt?'

47

'I'll have a whisky and soda, please. Look, call me Andreas, will you? Under the circumstances I don't really think we need stand on ceremony, do you?'

She handed him the drink: 'Andreas.' She mouthed the word as though it contained some seed of irresistible, forbidden eroticism; as though his name were some mystic talisman of sex. 'Andreas the Hunter.' Her smile broadened. 'And now you have hunted me down.'

'I'd hardly say that, Anastasia,' replied the journalist, thoroughly perturbed but not caring for anything as long as he could glut himself on that glorious sweep of backside, those 'come-here-and-fuck-me' eyes. 'Some might say you were the hunter – hunting down poor defenceless men like me! And what do you want with me anyway?' he added, though he had a fair idea by now.

'Shame on you, Andreas,' she grinned. 'You know very well what I want. I want you. I want your cock inside me. I want you to squirt your semen up into me until it overflows out of my cunt.'

Such direct words from such a sweet mouth, spoken in such cultured tones, really threw Hunt off balance.

'Are you a . . . ?' Words failed him.

'No, I am not a whore. Not a prostitute. Not a streetwalker. Do I look like a streetwalker, Mr Andreas Hunt?'

'Right now, you look like the most beautiful, the most desirable thing in the world,' he replied. The tension in his groin had reached such heights that it was almost painful. He could feel dampness spreading out from the yearning tip of his too-long-deprived tool. 'I'm sorry: no, you don't look like a whore.

But what are you? Why have you asked me here?
Why me?'

'I told you. I want you. I desire you. You have
a magnificent body. Very strong, very supple. A
powerful sexual drive. I want you to make love with
me many times tonight, Andreas Hunt.'

Hunt looked into the woman's eyes and saw
that they gleamed with an almost fanatical zeal.
Still she was licking her lips in suppressed hunger.
This woman needed sex like other people need
food or oxygen. And then she stretched out one
scarlet-tipped finger and brushed against his groin.
It was the gentlest, the faintest, the merest of touches
but it inflamed Hunt's already-smouldering passions
and at that moment he knew he would sell his soul
to get inside that glorious body.

Anastasia took him by the hand and led him
towards the bedroom door. It was every man's
dream come true. So why did he feel as though
she was going to eat him alive?

Anastasia pulled Hunt towards her and sank softly
on to the big bed. She bent his head down to her face
and he thought she was going to kiss him, instead she
parted her glistening scarlet lips and murmured:

'Fuck me.'

The words sent Hunt's cock wild with anticipation,
and he began to fumble for the zip on the back of
the girl's dress. Coolly, almost casually, she reached
behind her and and pulled down the zip; then slid
the dress down over her perfect body.

Underneath, she was stark naked. No bra, no
panties. Not even stockings. She kicked off her
shoes and lay naked before him, save for the ornate

crystal-studded collar she wore. He reached out to unfasten it, but she turned angry eyes on him and pushed away his hand:

'No!'

'OK, OK,' he breathed. And he kissed her passionately as she undressed him, feverishly, ravenously, desperate to seek out his throbbing hardness and pull it into the warm, wet heart of her. At last he was naked and she was sucking him into ever-greater hardness, her muscular tongue winding around the tip of his penis like a wicked serpent in Eden. And he was indeed in paradise.

'Take me.' It was a command, and he obeyed, thrusting into her eagerly and almost as hungrily as she swallowed him up.

He took her many times that night. At last they fell into a troubled slumber, and it wasn't until the first glimmers of sunlight came creeping through the curtains that Hunt really had time to take a close look at his companion. She was lying on her side, with her back to him, and her hair swept forward, baring her neck.

The clasp on the crystal collar had come unfastened, and the collar had slipped down, revealing her white neck beneath. A white neck spoiled only by a single blemish. Hunt had never seen a human bite before, but he knew that was what it was. The scars left by human teeth biting into the back of her neck.

'I'm sorry.'

Anastasia looked at him as though he had tried to rape her.

'I told you not to take off the collar.'

'I didn't. I've told you. I woke up and the clasp had come undone. So tell me, how did it happen? Who did that to you?'

'Who? How do you know it's not an animal bite?'

'It's not. Those are the marks of human teeth. If you don't want to tell me, it's OK. God, but there are some pretty weird people in this world, though . . .'

The girl looked at him for a moment as if trying to weigh him up, decide if he was trustworthy.

'I ought not to tell you. There's been . . . pressure . . . on me not to tell anyone.'

Hunt pricked up his ears. He was glad he hadn't told her he was a tabloid journalist. He began to wonder if there might be a story in this somewhere.

'He picked me up at a party and got me drunk. I'd never have done it with him otherwise – he's old and fat and disgusting. He took me back to his place and then he fucked me . . . I was half-unconscious by the time . . . and then he just went mad and started biting my neck. It was terrible – he was like an animal, a wild beast.'

'But who was it?'

She hesitated, then gave in.

'Sir Anthony Cheviot. The dirty bastard.'

Hunt's mind was reeling. 'Cheviot? Are you serious? You mean the Cabinet minister?' His journalistic instincts were sounding red alert. This could be the big one. This could get him the news editor's job.

The girl was talking again, but he was hardly listening.

'And do you know what the weirdest thing of all

51

is?' she went on. 'You'd think a thing like that would put you off sex for good, wouldn't you?'

Hunt nodded.

'Well, the funny thing is that ever since it happened I can't get enough of it. It's terrifying. I'm turning into a raving nympho. I mean, d'you think I make a habit of picking up men in seedy wine bars? These last few weeks, it's been so bad I'll do it with anyone, anywhere, anytime.

'Come here and do it to me again.'

It was a request no gentleman could refuse.

4: Mara

Mara Fleming lived life as she wanted to live it, not as anyone else wanted her to. That, basically, was the cause of all her problems. Psychic, pagan and traveller, and beautiful to boot: that was a heady combination. And one which most men thought they really ought to resist. Few managed it. And after knowing Mara Fleming, however briefly, no-one was ever quite the same again.

Glastonbury had been good for Mara this year. She had given a lot of Tarot readings, done a lot of healings, colour therapy, and she had met up with plenty of like-minded people: musicians, Druids, Greens, travellers like herself. People for whom sex was an expression of life and a celebration of the eternal cycles of birth, death and rebirth.

Sex meant a lot to Mara Fleming. Through it, she had found that she could get into closer contact with her psychic powers, commune with the soul within herself and raise and expand her consciousness. Sex for Mara meant spiritual growth, and spiritual growth was her only real ambition.

It was a fine summer morning, and the early sunlight was already caressing the sleeping travellers with warm fingers. Mara threw off the blanket she had wrapped around her to keep her from the night chill, and stretched out her lithe, naked body to the sun's eager caress. She felt restored, renewed, chosen.

Mara delighted in her body: in its youthful vigour, its sleek, strong perfection, the naturalness of its urges. She was proud of its demands, its wilfulness. She knew it more intimately than any lover, and because of that she knew exactly how to make love to herself and bring herself to ecstasy every time. If there was no man to share her bed, or take her roughly on the warm-veined earth, no matter. She did not need a man to give her pleasure. Pleasure radiated from her fingertips, like the healing fire that had restored so many of the sick and despairing to health and life.

With a little murmur of delicious enjoyment, Mara began her complex ritual of self-love. Taking a little bottle of lavender oil from the embroidered bag she always carried, she unscrewed the top and let a few of the cool, viscous drops fall on to her breasts, her belly, her thighs. Then she set to work on her taut young flesh; set to work to bring herself the ultimate in pleasure.

First of all, she ran her index finger lightly over her flesh, gathering up the drops of fragrant oil and drawing curious little patterns on her sun-bronzed skin. A pentacle, moons and stars and other, less familiar, shapes. The sun had already warmed the oil, and Mara felt as though she were lying on some faraway desert sand, whilst a mysterious dark man in voluminous robes bent over her and prepared her for the rites of love.

Slowly, luxuriously, she laid the palm of her hand flat upon her belly and began to move it upwards, enjoying the warm sensation and the lingering, envigorating fragrance of lavender floating up off her flawless skin. Her hand travelled still higher, and reached the blessed place where belly becomes breast: a hot, humid crease. She slipped her hand under her right breast. It was firm, yet overflowing and ample. She had beautiful, full breasts that stood out in womanly contrast to her otherwise gamine body, wiry and sleek and spare. The exuberance of her big breasts was a joyous assertion of her womanliness, her vitality, an affirmation of her belief in the universal earth-mother, the giver of life.

Mara's breasts were truly breathtaking: each one too big to fit into any man's hand. Her rounded globes were lightly bronzed, for in the summertime Mara lived as much of her life as possible in a glorious, natural state of nakedness, living whenever she could in remote places, so that she and her companions could walk naked without fear of being discovered.

She cradled a breast in either hand, loving the sensation of fullness, revelling in the amplitude of the flesh which escaped from her fingers, and refused to be confined within their limited compass. They were hot, moist and fragrant with lavender oil, and the nipples were rapidly hardening into long, brown hazelnuts begging to be cracked between eager teeth. She pinched them hard, and felt a tremendous shiver of pleasure pass through her, momentarily tightening the muscles of her vagina and triggering the flow of love-juices which would soon turn her cunt into a raging torrent.

Now she was massaging the oil into her breasts with a loving, circular motion that made he breathe hard with deep satisfaction. The veins were standing out, bluish and obscene, and the nipples were straining under this terrible provocation, crying out for someone – anyone – to come and suck at them, bite them, pinch them, give them some release from this ordeal of sexual torment.

She smiled to herself. The sun climbed higher in the perfect blue of an August sky, and rays of caressing sunlight filtered through her half-closed eyelids. She was bathed in sunlight, caressed, adored by the loving rays. They recognised her as their own, their lover, their mistress; and washed her lovely body in torrents of mellow sunshine. The warmth penetrated her limbs, her breasts; soaked into her skin with the sweet-smelling oil; insinuated itself into every fold and crease, every nook and niche of her smooth-skinned loveliness.

Her breasts were hard and hypersensitive now. Each time a practised finger slid over a well-oiled nipple, it felt as though there was an electric current linking breasts and loins; and she could feel the juices in her cunt flowing free, cascading in ever-more-dangerous rapids until her pubic hair was dew-sparkled and her thighs running with the dampness of mounting desire. And she sighed deeply: sighed with the enormous pleasure of it all, physical and spiritual fulfilment combining in these solitary rites of love.

She slid her right hand down her flank, delighting in the smooth, silky sensation of the oil on her warm skin. Her fingers met her pubis and began to tease and torment the luxuriant dark hairs they found there. Warm sunlight caressed her loins and she could resist no longer: her thighs began to move apart, revealing the moist and wonderful world of her cunt, far more fragrant and more sensual than the essential oils she was working into her skin.

With the fingers of her left hand, she gently parted her cunt lips, gasping with pleasure as the sun's warmth soaked into these most sensitive, secret parts of her. All at once she was united with all the power of the sun, suffused with its life-giving energies, vibrant with golden light and strength. Her right index finger began its delicate journey down her gleaming wet furrow, and she shivered with pleasure as it glanced across her clitoris, hard and throbbing.

She began to rub at the little pink pearl, and immediately felt herself floating on a great tide of pleasure. It was a feeling she had had many times before: a sensation of being out of her body, a soul floating free and joyful in a world of pleasurable sensations, a world full of whispering voices where she met and communed with her deepest, uttermost self – her immortal soul.

Her cunt was dripping juice now. Almost mechanically, instinctively, Mara reached out with her right hand and picked up the dildo which she always carried with her. Carved from green obsidian, it was a massive and breathtaking representation of the erect male organ: cool, hard and worn smooth with use. It had belonged to many generations of psychic women in her family, and had gained a truly ritual significance. The orgasms she experienced with it inside her had a spiritual, all-consuming quality which she could not explain.

Restraining her eagerness, she forced herself to take it inside her cunt slowly, luxuriating in the delicious sensations as it slid further and further in, millimetre by millimetre. Its coolness contrasted exquisitely with her sun-warmed, lust-hot cunt, and it slipped in and out of her luscious wetness with consummate ease.

She could feel the thick stone phallus stretching the walls of her cunt, and groaned with delight as it encountered the neck of her womb, filling her up, possessing her yet freeing her soul to fly with the spirits of fire and air.

Eagerly now, and urgently, she used the fingers of her left hand to massage her burning clitoris whilst with her right hand she masturbated her cunt with the inanimate phallus which seemed paradoxically to radiate a cold life of its own.

As she climbed towards orgasm, she felt – just for a split second – as though she were being watched by some invisible, faraway presence. Far away, and yet so powerful that its unspeakable, seductive evil could reach into her soul and almost, but not quite, possess it. She felt as if she should have been afraid, and yet the presence seemed to wish her no harm. It was willing her to orgasm, lending her fingers strength and skill. There really was magic in her touch that day.

And as she reached the summit of orgasm, it was as though another massive, cold penis was joined to the obsidian prick within her tight-stretched cunt, doubling the intensity of her pleasure as she cried out in her delirium.

As she came to her senses, and lay panting on the warm earth, wondering at the strange hallucination she had just experienced, Mara reached down to take out the stone dildo.

It was impossible, but it had happened. The stone shaft was cracked from tip to balls, and as she held it in her hand the phallus split into two halves, its magical power destroyed by some other, infinitely greater, force.

'Morning, Mara.' A tanned face peered down at her and a roughened hand slid down her backside. A hardness, too. He was awake and ready for anything.

Mara had grown fond of Gareth. He had a rough Welsh charm and had been a traveller all his life. They had met up two years previously, at the Midsummer Festival at Stonehenge, and had thrown in their lot together. There was nothing jealous or possessive about the relationship. Mara shared her favours not only with Gareth, but with his two mates, Jason and Clem, who travelled in the van with them. They were young and vigorous and exuberant, and Mara enjoyed sex with them. And anyhow, they were all New Age People: being there for each other was what it was all about. Having sex was good for the bonding, the closeness, the spiritual growth.

'Want me?' Gareth took hold of Mara's hand and drew it back to rest on the hardened shaft of his penis. He was proud of his penis. He had every right to be. It was thick, long, beautifully shaped, and years on the road had taught him how to satisfy a woman with it.

'Want you.' Mara snuggled backwards under the blanket, so that her backside nestled against Gareth's hollowed stomach. His erect shaft twitched as it pressed against her curving buttocks. She took hold of it firmly and began to masturbate it slowly and lovingly.

'Don't tease!' groaned Gareth, in an agony of pleasure.

'I want to make sure you *really* want me.' She gripped Gareth's prick a little harder and made the strokes longer, more deliberate.

'Much more of that and I'll cream myself!'

'You're so impatient!' But she gave in, pulling apart her own buttocks to let him inside her nicely moistened cunt.

'No, not your cunt. I want to fuck you in your arse,' breathed Gareth into her ear. 'You will let me, won't you?' She needed no second bidding. Mara gave a little shiver of pleasure as he slid a finger into her cunt and used some of the abundant juices to grease her tight little arsehole, weakening its feeble resistance by sliding that same fingertip in and out of the sphincter a few times to drive her mad with desire.

'Now?'

'Now! Go on! Stick it in me! Bugger me, Gareth; bugger me now!'

He placed the head of his impressive tool into the amber furrow between her tanned buttocks and rammed it in hard. It slid in first time, right up to the hilt, and they groaned together with the pleasure of it. Gareth slipped his hand round underneath her and searched out the rosebud of her clitoris. She gasped at the heavenly sensation as he rubbed at her, and slid her own hand backwards to cradle Gareth's balls, which were already tensed and hardening.

Gareth rode her hard, pulling her towards him so that his prick stabbed into her right up to the balls;

and she cried out with mingled pain and pleasure as her clitoris swelled beneath his insistent fingers.

'I'm coming, I'm coming!' she gasped.

'Wait for me!'

And they came together: Gareth's burning spunk searing her violated arsehole and frothing out on to her buttocks and thighs.

They lay there together for a long time, hearts racing and heads spinning. Then, half-asleep and still dazed with pleasure, Mara felt Gareth moving away and one . . . no, two . . . people sliding under the blanket with her.

Jason and Clem were twenty-four-years-old twins and, like all good twins, they liked to do everything together. They settled down under the blanket, on either side of Mara, and rolled her on to her back. Then they began a strangely symmetrical exploration which left her wondering if she was hallucinating. An identical blond youth on either side; identical smooth hands gliding over her flesh; identical sensations on both sides of her body.

Jason was on her right, Clem on her left. As the older twin, Jason always took the lead – but his brother was never far behind. As Jason's eager fingers slid to her right breast, Clem's promptly followed suit, and Mara sighed deliciously as she surrendered to the hypnotic, circular motion of playful fingers dancing in ever-decreasing circles around her rapidly stiffening nipples.

Now they were bending their heads to suck at her breasts like babies, hungry for the comfort of her firm young flesh. Electric charges of pleasure went rippling through her at each rhythmic movement of lips, tongues and teeth upon hardening, rubbery

61

flesh. She lay helpless, unable to move even if she had wanted to. Her golden breasts held her in thrall, as securely as if they had been iron chains. She was locked in a world of pleasure from which there could be no untimely escape, only patience and eventual release.

Mara stretched out her hands and began to stroke the firm, athletic bodies lying on their sides beside her. Their identical beauty added to her delirium: which was Jason, which was Clem, and where and who was she? She was floating in a dreamworld of desire, and the two strong bodies beside her felt like the solid walls of some pleasure-barque, drifting on an ocean of passion and carrying her away, effortlessly, towards the shores of ecstasy.

Muscular arms and strong shoulders; broad chests dusted with a light down of blond hair; flat, hard bellies and thighs as solid as marble columns, but so warm, so pulsating with life . . . And what were these two other columns, hard and hot and throbbing to their own crazy rhythm? She let her fingers glide over them, so lightly that they were scarcely touching the smooth, dry flesh, and yet she could still feel the incredible heat radiating from those beautiful twin pricks and burning deep into the palms of her eager hands.

The boys were sucking harder at her breasts now, nibbling lightly and teasingly at her engorged flesh, so skilfully that she felt as if she might even come – like this, surrounded by golden flesh and with her two grown-up babies at her breasts.

With a sigh of contentment, Mara began to stroke their balls, lovingly and simultaneously. The identical twin sacs were pursed and puckered, pubic hairs erect on gooseflesh that quivered and oozed beneath her fingers, almost as though it could hardly bear the exquisite agony of her caress and was seeking to escape before the pleasure and pain became too great for it.

The victory was hers. After only a few moments of gentle caresses, the boys' balls began to harden under her touch, marshalling their spunk ready for the heart-stopping moment when they would send it surging up twin shafts and into some warm nook of her love-hungry body.

As she began to pump their hardened shafts, she felt their hands move downwards from her breasts and glide down towards her enticing groin. Instinctively, she drew up her knees and opened wide her thighs, yearning for the sweet sensation of a finger on her clitty. But which finger? Whose finger would it be? The hands moved ever nearer and began to torment her raven curls, already bedewed with her love-juices, welling up from the fountainhead of her ready sex. But neither made any attempt to enter her, though her thighs strained apart and her cunt-lips gaped, begging to swallow up some long, hot token of thrusting manhood.

The pricks in her hand had grown even stiffer in homage to her reverent caress, and she used the drops of clear liquid glistening at their tip to lubricate each shaft and work it more easily up and down. She could hear Clem and Jason breathing hard, urgently; knew that they were holding back so as to prolong the enjoyment; knew, too, that with a deft flick of the wrist she could bring them both to orgasm on her golden belly. But that wasn't what she wanted. She wanted this red meat inside her, screwing her, fucking her, stuffing her fit to burst.

'Fuck me . . .' she breathed, desperately, longingly.

'Patience, patience,' whispered Jason.

'All in good time,' added Clem.

And they began to stroke her thighs, slowly and tantalisingly, just skirting the outer lips of her juicy cunt, and from time to time brushing against the thick black curls that fringed it. Each fleeting contact was like an electric shock, swelling her clitoris still further so that it felt as if it might burst if anyone so much as breathed on it. With their free hands, the lads began once more to torment her nipples, tweaking and rolling them between finger and thumb so that she cried out an writhed in an agony of pleasure. She pumped away frantically at the twin shafts, and she knew that they, too, must soon take her or explode.

At last they moved theirs fingers inwards, to the heart of her sex, playing and carefully circling her clitoris so as not to bring her off too soon. Mara sighed and tried to engulf their fingers in her hot wet cunt.

They had other plans for her.

Pulling their hardness out of her grasp, Jason and Clem lifted her astounded body in strong arms and flipped her over on to her front, half-kneeling so that her backside jutted up obscenely into the air. Clem propped two pillows behind his back and settled himself down underneath and in front of her, so that he was able to pull her head down towards his groin and force his hard prick inside her willing mouth. She began to suck at it greedily, running the tip of her tongue around the purple head and savouring the saltiness of the lubricating fluid.

Jason, meanwhile, was now kneeling behind her, pulling apart her thighs so that she was kneeling doggy-fashion on the bed, and admiring the beautiful and obscene view she was presenting to him. A still-wet trail of semen was trickling out of her pretty little arsehole, and her buttocks were spattered with the pearly droplets. Jason ran his finger through the stickiness and began to spread it over her arse-cheeks, rubbing it in like an expensive body-cream, massaging and kneading with strong fingers.

Then he moved back to her little brown arsehole. Pulling apart her buttocks, he ran his fingertip over the sopping-wet amber rose, drawing sighs of pleasure from Mara as he tickled the sensitive perineum. Then he began a more intimate game, wetting his index finger well and then gliding it into her arse – first only a little way in, then right inside, up to the knuckle.

Inside her arse, it was like a tropical rainforest: hot and steamy and wet. Well-greased with semen, the elastic walls yielded willingly to his insistent caress. In and out, in and out, he buggered her with his skilful finger, and all the while she kept on sucking at his twin brother's cock, arousing and delaying him with her clever lips and tongue.

He let his finger roam in a circular motion, stretching the walls of the girl's arse and enjoying her shivers and sighs at each new, forbidden sensation.

But his own prick was leaping impatiently, rearing its head and ready for the fray. It longed to be inside her. With his free hand, Jason reached round underneath Mara and felt for her clitoris, foraging through her thick undergrowth, parting the lips of her cunt and feeling inside. There it was: her hard button, harder and bigger than he had ever felt it before, and throbbing with the intensity of her insatiable desire. With a grunt of extreme pleasure, Jason thrust his hardness into her yearning vagina, feeling its walls contract around him and imprison him in a web of irresistible sensations. Slowly, and still stimulating her clitoris and arse, he began to fuck her.

There was a vision inside her head. At first, just lights in a dark sky, dancing shapes in a formless void. Faraway voices that whispered to her and urged her on, unseen hands that caressed her everywhere, every way, bringing her to the brink of orgasm and refusing to let her step out into the sunlight of ecstasy.

And then she saw him. A dark man in a dark cloak, his head turned away from her. She shivered as she saw him unbutton his trousers and take out a long, gleaming-white prick so terrifying that she felt it must be the talisman of some ancient evil. And he began to masturbate – to masturbate over the face of the dead woman who lay at his feet, arms crossed across her breast and a withered lily in her waxen fingers.

And as he came, and his semen fell in huge, white droplets upon the dead woman's face, Mara saw her breast rise and fall in a first breath of renewed life. Then the eyes fluttered open, and the woman turned her sightless gaze on Mara.

She found herself looking into her own, long-dead eyes.

Her orgasm was as unexpected as it was cataclysmic, shaking her with sobs of agonising pleasure as she felt her mouth and cunt fill up with a great flood-tide of semen.

They lay together, semi-conscious, for a long time, hardly breathing, hardly moving. And the picture in her head stayed for a long, long time: the picture of a dead girl brought obscenely to life. A dead girl who was Mara Fleming.

The following morning saw Mara on the road by six a.m. Gareth, Jason and Clem were still sleeping, oblivious that she had gone. They wouldn't have understood.

And then again, what was there to understand? A vision, a feeling – for that was all it was – a feeling of being pursued relentlessly by something evil and growing stronger by the minute.

She knew she had to get away. Try to escape, before it was too late. Where to? What did it matter? She had a terrible sense of foreboding. A sense that, wherever she should go, the presence would not be far behind.

The Master was elated. Trapped and yet every second more powerful, more able to transcend the confines of his prison. His spirit had reached out blindly into the blackness of the night, the wild vastness of the storm, and had, by some incredible stroke of luck, encountered another spirit almost as remarkable as his own.

The spirit of a woman. He had not had the strength he needed to see her face, but he had seen into her mind, her soul. A woman with the power. A woman who might have the key not only to his freedom, but to that of the one he had thought lost eternally.

He must find her. He must know her. He must possess her.

5: Flight

Andreas Hunt locked his car door and turned to face the sea. It glared back at him, grey-green, foam-flecked and irritable. A sudden gust of wind slapped him across the face and caught him off balance. He held on tight to his trilby and pulled the collar of his raincoat up around his chin. He liked his trilby and his raincoat. They made him feel like a proper investigative journalist – not a hack struggling for that first big break which would take him into the big league.

Maybe Whitby would give it to him.

It was a draughty place, even in the late summer sunshine. He stood shivering on the cliffs and looked down on the sort of seaside town ignored like the plague by fax salesmen and multi-national burger chains. At least it had that in its favour.

Life here was out of step with the modern world, and proud of it. Below him, a drab and rusty dredger was chugging out of the estuary with yet another load of silt. To the right of him, and a little way down the hill, a pair of enormous bleached jawbones were arranged as a sort of triumphal arch, suggesting that Whitby folk had little time for saving the whale. Gangs of frozen pensioners in Pacamacs were scuttling over the swing bridge

69

like worried ants. Makes you wonder what Dracula ever saw in the place, mused Hunt. I mean, that guy had style.

Over on the other bank of the Esk, a heart-attack-inducing flight of stairs wound a tortuous path up the side of the cliff towards a black and glowering ruin. It might be a castle. No, a church maybe. No, too big. Oh, who cares anyway? thought Hunt, and picked up his suitcase. A stiff drink, that's what he needed. And a thermal vest.

The hotel wasn't a disappointment. Then again, he hadn't expected much. It had an organic look to it somehow, like something regurgitated by a seasick cormorant; and it clung to the cliffs with all the horror-stricken tenacity of a stranded Boy Scout, watching the tide come in. But at least the hotel bar was open. He ordered two double whiskies and flopped down into a squeaky leather armchair in the corner by the window.

'Staying long, sir?' The barman set his drinks down on the sticky tabletop and gave the ash tray a cursory wipe with a damp rag.

'Couple of days, maybe more. Depends how things go.'

'Business trip, is it, then?'

The barman wasn't as daft as his pebble glasses might suggest. And these local characters were always good for a bit of gossip. Hunt decided to pump him for information.

'Sort of. I'm a journalist. I'm doing an article on provincial MPs and their constituencies, and I was rather hoping I could get an interview with Sir Anthony Cheviot.'

'Aye, well, you've come at the right time. Hardly

ever here, he is. Spends all his time down in London
with his la-di-dah Tory mates. Lucky if we see him
twice a year, not that I'm complaining. If it wasn't
for all the rich farmers round here, he'd never
have got in last time. Anyhow, you're in luck. Just
so happens he's opening some Tory party fete on
Sunday. Can't think why you'd want to bother with
him, though.'

'So he's not a popular MP? Not what you'd call a
man of the people?'

The barman laughed and pushed his glasses back
up his nose.

'The only people he cares about are the ones who
can get him a peerage. And his poor wife – don't
know how she puts up with him.'

Hunt pricked up his ears.

'Not all sweetness and light at home, then?'

The barman looked suddenly evasive.

'Well, I don't know as how I'd want to talk about
that sort of thing. I mean, you're a journalist and
I've heard all about slander, you know. Mebbe I've
already said too much. A man's private life's his own,
as I reckon.'

'Look, off the record. Just out of interest. It won't
go any further, I promise,' Hunt assured him, fingers
crossed behind his back to free himself from the
promise, just in case.

'Off the record? No names?'

'I always protect my sources.'

'OK. Well, it's common knowledge anyway.
Cheviot's a pervert. Everyone round here knows
that, but they keep it hushed up, you know. Likes
being tied up and whipped, that sort of thing. Kinky
bondage stuff. He's got a mistress up here, so they

say, but I don't know if it's true. Someone he's
known for years. She's discreet, so it suits him to
keep her on.'

'You've no idea who this woman is, then?'

'No, but . . .'

'Go on. It's OK.'

'Look, I haven't said this, but I've heard a few
rumours about her. He's been seen visiting Ship
Street, down by the docks, late at night. A red-haired
woman.'

'Oh, come on. This is a small town by anyone's
standards. And you're telling me you don't know this
woman's name?'

'I'm sorry, sir. I've said too much already. Now
then, can I get you something to eat with that
whisky?'

Hunt ordered a ploughman's lunch and sat back
in his chair, gazing out of the window at the
surly sea below. It wasn't much to go on, but
he wasn't going to let this one slip away from
him.

He could feel it in his bones. This was going to
be the big one: the one he'd been waiting for all
his life.

Somewhere outside, a seabird called mournfully
across the bleached blue sky. It sounded for all the
world like the last, despairing cry of a soul cast
forever into the wastes of Hell.

Mara Fleming had never seen herself as a seaside
sideshow. But now here she was, giving psychic
readings in a seafront booth usually rented out to
'Gypsy Rosa: Romany Princess', and feeling like a
complete fraud.

A fraud, not because she was telling lies to the gullible, but precisely because she wasn't. These day-trippers expected ten pounds' worth of home-spun advice from a woman who was no more a Romany Princess than Kylie Minogue; an amateur psychologist whose readings depended less on her psychic powers than on her well-honed ability to listen to her customers' problems and give them the answers they wanted to hear.

And what was Mara giving them? Something they couldn't cope with. True powers; true readings; true visions. She couldn't lie. The power within her wouldn't lie. The Tarot told the truth, however much she wanted to distort it and make it less painful. When she looked into the crystal, she saw the bad as well as the good, and honesty did not sit well with tact.

Maybe she wasn't cut out for this game. But since she'd left Gareth and the twins, she'd begun to find her own way, seek her own path. And here, with hundreds of miles between her and the bad experiences of a few weeks ago, she was beginning to feel free of the awful pursuing terror that had dogged her footsteps and peopled her dreams with nameless chimeras.

Here, she was at last beginning to feel safe.

The customer paid and left, and Mara sat back in her chair and surveyed the scene. On the beach, children were playing French cricket and throwing handfuls of wet sand at each other. Chilly parents cowered behind windbreaks and dreamed of the Costa Brava. Mara smiled to herself and looked up. A tall, dark man in a brown trilby and a trenchcoat was wandering along the promenade,

Valentina Cilescu

eating an ice-cream cornet. He looked totally out
of place and uncomfortable in this end-of-the-road
seaside town, and Mara watched him with interest.

He was good-looking in an unusual kind of way:
tall, slim, with deep-set blue eyes and black hair.
His face was striking and unforgettable: high cheek-
bones, a strong jawline and a long, aquiline nose
gave him the profile of an argumentative eagle.
Mara felt strangely drawn to him, and in a sudden
flash of insight felt she could see into his soul, read
his thoughts, understand his motivations. A sudden
flash of insight, and it was gone, and she was left
wondering how and why this man could get so far
inside her head.

And he hadn't even noticed her yet.

He kept on walking towards her, still gazing out
to sea, not really looking where he was going. Then
he bumped into a woman walking in the opposite
direction, and in the confusion he turned his head
towards Mara and their eyes met.

In that moment she wanted him and knew he
wanted her. She could feel the electricity of the
kisses they had never enjoyed, and probably never
would; was shocked to find that she could feel his
hand on her breasts, his hard penis in her crack, his
kiss on her throat.

It was the most erotic, the most uncommon
sensation: and yet it did not feel dangerous or
threatening. It was as though their bodies had been
made for each other, their sex-organs custom-built to
fit together seamlessly: engines of irresistible, match-
less pleasure. So aroused was she in that split second
of desire that she could almost believe she could
bring herself to a climax, simply by concentrating

on the sensations which she could feel, so very real, so overwhelmingly strong.

He looked away; and the spell was broken. Mara sank back into her chair, breathing heavily, and ran the back of her hand over her forehead. It was damp and clammy with sweat. The man was looking at her again now, though less intensely, and had begun to walk towards her again. Had he felt anything of what she had felt?

Hunt approached the garishly painted booth and read the name over the door: 'Gypsy Rosa: Romany Princess'. Funny, the girl inside didn't look like a gypsy; nor did she have that tired, shabby look of your average seaside fortune-teller. She was fresh, vibrant, absolutely stunning.

The girl was quite tall, very slender, very dark. Her eyes were huge and a striking shade of violet. Hunt had never seen eyes like that before. The girl wore no make-up: she didn't need any. Those enormous violet eyes dominated and lit up her face like precious stones set in ivory. Her hair was long and thick, hanging down her back in a glossy plait tied with a green velvet bow. She was dressed like a hippy: fringed skirt, sandals, peasant blouse swelling with the promise of two perfect breasts which seemed surprisingly large and mobile for such a slender girl.

No doubt about it. She was a bit of all right. Wouldn't kick her out of bed. Maybe he'd chat her up. He flashed her his most dazzling smile.

'Morning.'

'Hello.' She seemed a little nervous, almost afraid of him. Maybe he was coming on too strong? 'Would you like a reading?'

'Well, I don't know. I'm not really into all this

75

. . . stuff.' It was an understatement. Hunt had written countless stories debunking this kind of mumbo-jumbo. On the other hand, she was a real looker, and those breasts . . . 'What do you do and how much does it cost?' Oh damn, he thought. It sounds like I'm trying to pick up a prostitute.

She didn't seem to have noticed the clumsiness. 'I do Tarot readings, palm readings, phrenology, crystal gazing . . .'

'How much for a Tarot reading?'

'Ten pounds.'

He gave a sharp intake of breath. 'Bit pricey isn't it?'

'You won't find cheaper anywhere. Not from a genuine seer.'

'A what?'

'A seer. One who has the gift of sight.'

Hunt thought about taking the piss, then decided against it. If he was going to pull, ten pounds and a bit of mumbo-jumbo was a small price to pay for Heaven on earth and a good squeeze of those knockers.

'OK, then.' He handed over his money and stepped into the booth. Mara indicated a rickety camping chair and he sat down, conscious of the lack of space which forced him to crumple up his long legs and made him feel like an adult on an infants' school chair. He took off his hat and balanced it sheepishly on his knee.

She looked at him long and hard, and it made him feel uncomfortable. For a second he almost believed she really could see into him. If so, she could be in no doubt that he fancied her like crazy. He was grateful for the trilby, hiding his burgeoning erection as he gazed back at her, dry-mouthed and sweaty-palmed.

Mara picked up the pack and began to deal out the cards, face-down, on the green baize surface of the table in front of her. She wondered if he could see her hand trembling as she fought to control it. Now that he was there, in front of her, the feeling was overwhelming. She was almost drowning in the weight of the thoughts she could feel spilling out of him, lapping around her and washing over her like wild ocean waves. She fought the feeling, but it pressed on, insistently, and in that split second she closed her eyes and gave way to the weight of his will, the force of his fantasy . . .

It was a dark room, but warm – almost oppressively so. She was standing there, in the pitch blackness, unable to see anything, but knowing that somewhere close in the darkness a presence was watching, waiting. She felt fear and yet arousal. It was coming to get her, coming to take her and possess her. Her cunt felt damp and her nipples hardened as she waited for it to come and find her. She realised that she was naked, and she tried to cover herself with her hands.

But suddenly there were other hands: curious, insistent hands intent on exploring her every delight, her sinuous expectant flesh. And instead of trying to escape, she opened herself to the hands, strained to offer herself to their obscene caresses, their frank indecency.

Lips now, brushing the tips of her breasts. A moist and lascivious tongue running over her flesh and adding its own contribution to her willing wetness. Teeth nibbling gently at her buttocks, the tops of her thighs, tinging pleasure with the piquancy of pain.

The unseen figure surprised her from behind. Strong hands threw her forward, so that she found herself bent almost double over the back of a chair, rump thrust out and breasts dangling down. Fingers explored her most intimate places, not ungently but sparing her no embarrassment, no modesty. Her buttocks were prised apart firmly and a practised fingertip ran straight home to the target: diving into her slippery cunt as lithe as an eel, wriggling deliciously now in and now out of her, making her gasp with pleasure.

Now the finger was exploring farther afield, using the abundance of juices to lubricate the whole of her intimate crack, from pubis to arse; and the wetness was dripping out of her, glistening on her slender tanned thighs. As he pressed close to her, she could feel the rhythmic beat of his erect penis as it slapped against her backside, eager for the fray. She was eager for it, too, and tried to reach behind her and pull him into her. But he resisted, deflecting her fingers and making her hold on to the chair-back to support her lust-weakened body.

Her unseen lover, shadowy and silent, hot-bodied and sweet-breathed, was becoming bolder still. His fingers moved away from her cunt and slipped slowly, deliciously backwards until they were circling her tight brown arsehole.

'Yes, yes . . .' she moaned, straining to thrust herself still further backwards and meet his incautious caress.

But the fingers teased her still, refusing her the offices she so craved, refusing to batter open the gates and enter the temple of delectable, unholy rites. They circled the amber rose and it strove to open, to flower in response to this careful gardener's secret skill. But the coquettish fingertips slid away again, diving once more into the hot sweet depths of Mara's cunt, making her cry out with the pain of frustration and desire.

At last the fingers returned, suddenly and bolder than before. Mara's arsehole was so eager for the caress that there was no need to force it. The fingertip rested for only a moment on the sensitive membrane before it was swallowed up, engulfed in that most secret of nooks.

Mara groaned and began to writhe about as the finger slid gradually further into her, wriggling about so as to titillate the fragile walls of her rectum, stretching the narrow tunnel, dilating it; then pressing up against the wall of her vagina. She longed to feel fullness in all her orifices, to be stuffed full to bursting, to be nothing but an engine of pleasure, filled with desire and fulfilment.

He had steadfastly ignored her clitoris, and it was throbbing painfully, resentfully. Mara tried to touch it herself but he prevented her. All at once, she felt his hot prick nuzzling into the brown furrow between her buttocks, and in a single, fluid movement, still keeping his finger in her arsehole, he filled up her juicy, yearning cunt with another, longer, much thicker finger of flesh which forced the path and made her groan with the exquisite pain of it.

The cock was unexpected, miraculous, magical. It was much broader, much thicker, much more massive than anything she had ever had inside her before: It felt as if she were being screwed by several big cocks at once. It felt as if half a dozen men – no, more – had come together to desire her and possess her; and, being unable to decide which should have her first, had come to an entirely civilised arrangement:

they would all have her at the same time. Her cunt was stretched beyond the limits of endurance by this massive, multiple cock; and the feeling that she would at any moment burst open, be rent in two, only added to the ecstasy of this unbelievable fuck.

Now he was removing his finger from her arsehole. She moaned in protest but her dissatisfaction soon turned to pleasure as his hand moved forward to cup her left breast in his hand, skilfully pinching her nipple between finger and thumb. It felt like an electric shock, running right down her body from nipple to cunt; and Mara could feel the juices overflowing her tight-stretched vagina, lubricating her unseen lover's thick shaft and dripping down in glistening beads on to his thick pubic hair. His hot, sweaty balls were bouncing off her arse-cheeks, taut and full of spunk. All for her.

And then he took pity on her and slid his right hand round underneath her, foraging in the dark curly triangle of her pubic bush until he found the secret door and passed through it, into the humid, fragrant world of her crack. She howled with pleasure as his well-lubricated finger slid further down until at last it made contact with the hard, erect bud of her throbbing clitoris.

A few more thrusts; a few more strokes of his fingertip upon her clitoris, and she would come . . .

A sudden voice brought Mara back to her senses. 'Are you all right?'

She shook her head to clear it: she was still dazed, still clouded by the vision of oncoming ecstasy which had so cruelly deluded her. Looking up, she saw Hunt gazing at her and something in his eyes frightened and excited her. It was the reflection of her own lust, the realisation that they had shared that vision – that he had been her unseen lover and she his willing plaything.

And the feeling of incredible sexual arousal was still with her, trembling her hand and her voice as she set out the cards. Could he feel it too? He was clutching his hat so hard that his knuckles were white, and staring at her with an intensity which she found hard to bear.

She turned up the first card.

'The Hanged Man.'

Hunt winced.

'It's OK. It doesn't mean what it looks like. The Hanged Man just means there are going to be changes in your life.'

'What kind of changes?'

'It's difficult to say. Something that alters the quality of your life. Are you . . . searching for something in your life at the moment?'

'Could be.'

The feeling was still there, intense, insistent. She closed her eyes but that only made it worse. Then, she was there in that room again, being screwed in the dark by a shadowy man – the man who was sitting in front of her, seemingly innocent but she knew he could feel it too. Her clitoris was throbbing in time to her racing pulse, the tom-tom beat of an insolent desire that made her head spin, made her nipples hard and tensed the fragile flesh on her ample breasts. She could actually feel his fingers pinching her nipples, feel his massive, hardened shaft and the way the walls of her vagina were sucking away at it eagerly, insatiably.

The excitement was mounting in her; racing,

climbing, striving ever higher – and in spite of herself she began to breathe heavily, haltingly, and her left hand moved involuntarily under the table to touch her clitoris, ease her aching need.

She dealt the next card.

What she did not know was that Hunt was also living the fantasy, enslaved and enchanted by the dark vision in which he toiled silently inside the glorious wet cunt of this dark girl he had never met, never even touched. His penis felt massive, granite-hard, smooth as silk. And more than that. It felt like someone else's penis. Though he was feeling the pleasure, he had the curious sensation that he was feeling it through someone else, or that someone – or something – else's consciousness was feeling the sensations through him.

As though something else was using his body for its own pleasure.

But he was locked away in a world of unbelievable sensual pleasure: a world in which only he and the girl existed, united by this strange consciousness which was playing with them as though they were pawns in a bizarre chess game.

He could feel a lake of sperm, heavy and turbulent, collecting in his tensed and aching balls. And, very slowly and surreptitiously, and all the time still looking deep into the girl's deep blue eyes, he reached for the zip of his trousers and pulled it down.

The contact of hand on shaft sent electric shivers through his body, and – although he had meant only to touch himself passively and go no further – he could not resist the overwhelming urge to pump his shaft. His hand was shielded from view by the table, and his hardened prick hidden by the trilby on his lap, but nevertheless he felt delicious pangs of danger as he began, very slowly and carefully, to masturbate himself.

He knew he could not hold out for long. His prick was already oozing lubricating fluid and slid easily and delightfully between his practised fingers. Indeed, he had never before derived such pleasure from the simple act of masturbation. Was it the fact that the situation was spiced up with danger? Was it the knowledge that the girl was returning his gaze and was also beginning to breathe more quickly, tellingly? Or was it the fact that it felt for all the world as if another, silken-soft hand was manipulating his willing tool?

Mara's trembling hand turned over the card and, mechanically, they both glanced down at it. It transfixed them and they could not tear their eyes away from it.

'The Broken Tower,' she gasped. And could say no more.

The card depicted a tall, slender tower: no longer broken but phallic and thrusting, strong and suggestive. And, as they looked, the strangest thing happened. The tower changed shape and form – at first subtly, then blatantly – until at last it had become a penis: a long, thick, hard penis thrusting up out of a dark pubic thicket. A penis throbbing with its own life. A penis jerking up and down as though thrusting into an unseen cunt.

And as they watched, it seemed that this magical penis was thrusting into their own hearts and minds, forcing its obscene majesty into them, uniting them in defiance of their will, shooting its torrent of unearthly semen into them and fertilising them with an evil seed – a seed of fear and forbidden pleasure. And somewhere above them, below them, deep within the darkest parts of them, a cold black voice was laughing, laughing; and fiery red eyes were burning into their souls, remorseless and uncompromising.

And they came together, not daring to cry out but gazing fixedly into each other's eyes, completely unable to look away – locked into an embrace so powerful, so indissoluble that it needed no touch, no kiss. They came together in floods of cunt-juice and semen; trembling silently as they sighed out the last waves of their passion, and slumped, free at last, in their chairs.

When he came to his senses and looked up, Hunt realised that she was gone. He stood up unsteadily and gazed after her, but she was too far away by now. He just caught a momentary glimpse of her glossy black hair and she was gone: engulfed in the crowds of holidaymakers.

All that was left to remind him of their bizarre coupling was the damp, dark stain spreading over the front of his trousers. That, and the tarot cards strewn in terrified chaos across the table in front of him. One caught his eye: The High Priestess. He wondered vaguely if it meant anything, pocketed it and prepared to leave.

He wondered if he would ever see her again. For some unaccountable reason, he was convinced that he would.

6: Lost and Found

Hunt had almost given up hope of seeing the girl again. He'd made enquiries but no-one seemed to know where she was staying. She ought to have faded to a vague memory by now: some wild phantasm dreamed up by the sick mind of a man who hadn't had a woman for too long. But he just couldn't get her out of his thoughts.

He had managed to find out one thing about her. The woman who normally rented the fortune teller's booth had told him the girl's name was Mara: Mara Fleming. At least his phantasm had a name. Somehow that was comforting – having established that she was real, and had a name just like everyone else, made him feel that he might yet track her down.

And anyhow, he had other fish to fry. Sir Anthony Cheviot, to be precise. His journalistic nose told him that if anyone deserved to fry, he did.

His main lead was the red-haired woman Cheviot was rumoured to visit on his infrequent visits to the town. Further discreet enquiries had produced a few more helpful details. A local tradesman had told him – in an indiscreet moment induced by half a bottle of Glenfiddich – that the woman was called Viviane, that she had once been one of the highest-paid tarts

in London, and that Cheviot had set her up in her
own house here in Whitby. In return, she satisfied
his whims whenever he was in town. It was a funny
old world. The word was that Viviane lived near the
harbour, in one of the 'yards' that subdivided the old
town into a maze of discreet alleyways, perfect for
smugglers and clandestine assignations.

Maybe if he kept a close watch on the area he'd
find her. Maybe he'd be luckier still and catch
Cheviot going into the house. He loaded up the
Leica just in case, and pocketed the telefoto lens.
Never knew when you might get the chance of a few
candid close-up shots.

The first three evenings produced nothing. A
couple of brushes with local drunken yobbos and
a pointed enquiry from a beat constable convinced
him he needed to be a little less obvious. He lurked
in doorways, waiting, watching, yawning, chewing
gum, getting thoroughly pissed off – even playing
with himself through his raincoat pockets when the
boredom got too much.

And then, on the fourth evening – just as he was
giving up and going back to the hotel – he saw her.

He was half-watching, half-dozing in the doorway
of a grotty baker's shop on the corner of Ship Street
and Miller's Yard, when an anonymous black car
slid past, weaving its way with difficulty through the
narrow streets. It had darkened windows and there
was something sinister, something clandestine about
it. What's more, it looked very out of place in this
quaint but rather run-down part of town.

The car was moving very slowly, so Hunt crept
carefully out of his doorway and followed it at a
safe distance. It turned into a side-street and drew

to a halt outside the peeling dark green door of what seemed to be an uninhabited cottage. Hardly the place you'd expect a high-class mistress to be living. But discreet, certainly.

The car door swung open and out stepped a tall, statuesque red-haired woman in a black coat with a massive fur collar. She could have been thirty, forty – she was agelessly attractive, fine-boned as a thoroughbred racehorse, yet muscular beneath her expensive clothes. The car sped away into the night, its driver a shadow behind tinted windows.

The woman was left standing on the pavement, alone, somehow out of place in this world of everyday things and commonplaces. Holding his breath for fear of being spotted, Hunt stepped just a little way out of the shadows and lifted the camera. One shot was all he'd have time for. One shot and then he'd be running away into the night, as fast as his legs would carry him. Maybe he shouldn't bother. Maybe he should be patient, wait until he could get a picture of them together. Yes, that was it. Be patient.

Sweating with the tension, Hunt lowered the camera and made to step back into his hiding place. But at that very moment, the red-haired woman turned to unlock her front door and found herself staring straight into his eyes.

Hunt was transfixed. For an instant, his instincts deserted him. He knew he ought to run away but his feet were rooted to the spot. His mouth was dry. His palms sweated. She looked into his eyes and all the strength drained out of him. It was as though she was sucking out his very soul, and to his amazement he felt his legs giving way, buckling under him, and he felt himself slide slowly and untidily down the wall.

It was almost like fainting and yet he was conscious throughout.

Viviane's spiky red heels clicked across the cobbled street and Hunt struggled to tear his lifeless head away from her stony gaze. Without success. He could feel nothing save the burning sensation from those glittering dark eyes – jet-black and fathomless in the cold moonlight. And he offered no resistance as she bent down, took hold of his limp arm and drew him to his feet, supporting him with her own strong arms as she half-walked, half-dragged him, unprotesting, across the narrow street, unlocked the door and led him inside.

Mara was finding it difficult to sleep. Every time she managed to doze off, she was troubled by the same disturbing dream.

She stood by the window and gazed out on to the moon-reflected sea, trying to clear her head of the vision which haunted her and would not go away.

Somewhere, very far away – perhaps far away in time as well as space, she could not tell – a young woman was in the grip of a terrible fear – knowing that her sweet-fleshed young body was about to be violated by sinister, sallow-skinned men with shaven heads. The men had cast aside their robes and the girl was screaming in terror as they held her down on a cold stone slab and ripped off her white gown.

Some were young men, rampant and hard-muscled. Others were old, bent, with flaccid erections, dribbling and salivating with disgusting desire. But all wore the same expression of cold-eyed vengeance. This was no ordinary rape of a young girl. This was a sacred rite. A punishment.

Mara held her head in her hands, as though by some effort of will she might be able to reach inside her mind and tear out the nightmare, the unwanted guest; claw it out of her ailing, aching brain and fling it over the sleeping rooftops, into the depths of the cold, glittering sea far below. For she knew this was no ordinary dream. It was a vision of something real: something faraway in space and time, yet something which would in time come to pass, or which had already been played out in some part of history, some far-off land . . .

But why was she being tortured with this vision? Mara was a true seer. Others might mock, but the Tarot spoke truths for her. When she gazed into a crystal ball, she had no need to invent what she saw. She saw the future, and had often wished that she did not. Her gift was also a curse. And now she had been forced to suffer this vision of terror and pain. Why her? What possible relevance could it have for her? And what was the girl's fate? Up to now, all she had seen was the girl's terror of anticipation. Maybe she would be spared the rest.

She sighed and got back into bed, drawing the light bedcovers up under her chin. A pleasant, late-summer breeze was drifting in through the open window and played gently across her naked skin. Mara always slept naked, even in the winter. She loved the world of sensations, and her extraordinary abilities made her hyper-sensitive to every stimulus. Sex, for her, was as natural and as indispensable as breathing.

She missed them now, her three erstwhile companions. She missed the hardness of their pricks in her hands, running over her flesh, burrowing into her every nook and hollow. She missed it all so desperately.

Her nipples were hardening, and her fears melted away as she began to caress the perfect fullness of her golden breasts; letting her fingers glide expertly over the firmness, the divine heaviness, and lingering on her nipples just long enough to tantalise, and very nearly enough to bring her to sudden orgasm.

She gave a little shiver of delight and stretched out in the bed, thoroughly enjoying the cool, insistent caress of the silk sheet against her flawless skin. It felt as though some feather-light, ethereal being had lain down on top of her, making love to her as only spirits can, caressing almost without touching, bringing her exquisite lovemaking in a whisper of smooth black silk.

Her desire grew, and she felt herself growing hot and wet between her legs. Her breath was coming in little urgent gasps, and she slid her right hand down her belly and began to toy with the jet-black pubic bush that crowned her tawny thighs. It was dew-spangled and she rubbed her fingers in it, then brought them up to her face to savour the strong taste and heady fragrance of her womanhood. Then she began to caress herself, working her fingertips slowly and luxuriously between her protuberant cunt-lips and scooping up the abundant, frothing cunt-juices which she then used to lubricate her throbbing clitoris.

With her left hand, she pinched her right nipple between finger and thumb, groaning with pleasure at the electric shocks of pleasure which shot right down to her cunt, and sent floods of love-juice coursing down the walls of her vagina, flooding out on to her thighs. With her right index finger, she skilfully manipulated her clitoris, stroking, circling, massaging, rubbing harder and faster now, faster and more boldly, triumphantly, as at last she felt her pleasure approaching and cried out with the sheer joy of it. Her thighs spread wide to accept the tribute from an imaginary penis, her back arched and she threw her head back in ecstasy, catching stars and sliding down waterfalls.

In the afterglow, she snuggled down under the sheet and, through half-closed eyelids, watched the constellations move in stately procession across the night sky, towards dawn.

And as she lay there, she drifted down, down once more into sleep. Sleep filled with disturbing images . . .

The young woman was screaming still, her face turned away from her tormentors. Mara saw them more clearly now. It took four of the men to chain her to the stone slab: heavy irons at wrist and ankle held her fast to unyielding iron rings at each corner, splaying apart arms and legs in a parody of a lover's open-armed embrace. One man, taller than the others, stepped forward and, with a razor-sharp dagger that seemed hewn from pure flawless crystal, slit the girl's diaphanous robe from ankle to throat. He tore away the flimsy fabric and bared her slender nakedness.

The young woman became suddenly silent, surprising her captors. Her skin glowed amber in the unearthly light from the flaming torches hanging on the walls. There seemed a nobility in her, despite her humiliation and powerless though she was to resist the vile caresses of her torturers. She refused to turn her head; refused to look at them; as though to acknowledge their existence was also to acknowledge her subjection. She lay still and almost lifeless, showing her defiance in the only way she could: by detaching herself completely from her own violation.

The tall man flung himself upon her without the slightest pretext of gentleness, ramming into the girl as though she were some piece of meat, some common whore. Mara knew that this woman was no whore. This woman was something special.

He rode her like a stallion covering a mare: with no more consideration for the woman than an animal has for the female he couples with and then deserts. She lay unmoving as he shot his load of sperm into her unwilling cunt and climbed off, panting slightly but emotionless.

Others followed. Many others. Mara wanted to cry out, to struggle for the girl, to help her escape from her torment. It angered and pained her to see her so passive, so silent – thighs wrenched apart and robbed of every last vestige of her modesty. But, like the girl, Mara was utterly powerless.

It was over. The last of the men climbed off the inert body of the girl and they began to chant in some strange gutteral language which Mara did not recognise. It sounded like a religious chant. The girl lay motionless on the stone slab, head still turned towards the protecting shadows, and a flood of semen trickling out of her on to the cold surface beneath her.

The vision faded, and for a moment Mara almost relaxed, believing it had left her and would not return. But the picture came back into focus. She saw the same dark, torchlit chamber, the same stone slab.

And on it, a body. A body, swathed, tightly bound in bandages. A dead body, yes, that was what it was. A corpse prepared for burial, intricately bound and ready for the afterworld.

An Egyptian mummy . . . ?

The same dozen men were there, still chanting. But now they were dressed in long, white robes with exquisite serpent-crested head-dresses. They looked somehow familiar, and yet Mara could not quite recall . . .

They were bending over the table, putting the finishing touches to their handiwork. Four of them appeared, bearing an ornate wooden coffin, in the Egyptian style, which they placed upright against the wall so that Mara found herself looking right inside it. Then the men lifted up the corpse from the slab and carried it over to the coffin, placing it reverently inside, so that it appeared to stand motionless with its hands crossed in prayer across its breast. It was the body of a young girl, the face bandaged and unrecognisable.

Then they fetched the painted lid of the coffin and fitted it on to the base, nailing it shut then gliding away into the shadows, chanting their long and baleful litany. Only the coffin remained: propped up against the wall in the half-light.

Mara awoke screaming hysterically. Outside, it was a beautiful late summer's day and the seagulls were wheeling overhead. Everything seemed perfect. She leant out of the window and breathed in the crisp morning air, dizzy and sick with the shock of the vision.

And she understood for the first time that the horror would never leave her. For she knew, with a terrifying, sickening certainty, that the girl in the coffin had been the girl she had seen violated on the stone slab. And that when she had been put into the coffin she was still alive, silently screaming and powerless to escape her terrible fate.

And she had seen the face painted on the wooden coffin.

And that face was her own.

Far away, beneath the secret halls of Winterbourne, where naked men and women slept in shameless disarray after wild, untrammelled pleasure, the Master sent out his ever-growing spirit into the world and revelled in his newly-restored gift of sight. He could see across the miles, into hearts and minds, into the souls of men and women.

And as he roamed the astral plane, looking down upon mortals and searching for what he knew he must inevitably find, he once again encountered the timid, yet wondrous soul of Mara Fleming and knew that in her, he had found the missing key to his eternal freedom and the eternal damnation of mankind.

When Hunt came round, he felt dizzy and disorientated. He blinked his eyes and tried to shake his head but, although there was nothing there to impede movement, it felt as though was held fast in some contraption of iron and steel. He tried to cry out, but the breath hung, frozen, in his throat as surely as if he had been gagged. He could hardly breathe, and realised with a start that he was lying on his stomach on some sort of bed or couch, untied and yet fixed to the spot as securely as if he had been tied there with straps and manacles. He was stark naked.

Memories rushed through his head in mad procession: waiting in the darkness; the car; the woman; her hypnotic gaze; being dragged through the open doorway . . .

So where was he now? Was this all the woman's doing? And if so, what was the secret of her strange power over him? How could she imprison him here like this, without chains or physical force? He struggled desperately to free himself, but the force that held him spreadeagled on the bed was far, far stronger. He gave up and lay there, panting with frustration.

A silken voice behind him cut through his thoughts:

'Who are you? You must speak the truth. In the name of the one true Master, I command you.'

The pressure on his mouth and throat lessened, and he was able to gasp his reply:

'My name is Hunt.'

'And what do you seek?'

Hunt had every intention of lying, but somehow he could not. That same force that had given him back the freedom to speak was also denying him the freedom to lie. In horror, he found himself blurting out the truth:

'I'm a newspaper reporter. I'm investigating Sir Anthony Cheviot. I wanted to speak to you because I have been led to believe that you are his mistress.'

The woman laughed. It was a soft sound, but not a pleasant one. There was a mocking quality to her voice, laced with a hint of sinister power.

'And what have you discovered about Sir Anthony?'

'Nothing. No-one will tell me anything.'

'What of me, then? What have you learned about me?'

'That you are called Viviane. And that you are very beautiful.'

Hunt could not believe he was hearing himself say the words. And yet they were true. Lord knows, they were true. The force acting upon him refused to allow him to speak anything but the truth. And it was an incontrovertible truth. Viviane certainly was a beautiful woman, and Hunt was a connoisseur of beauty . . .

'Do you desire me?'

'I desire you.'

'Do you wish to have sexual congress with me?'

'I do.'

'I warn you, Hunt. In approaching me, you thrust your hand, unprotected, into a white-hot flame. It is a flame which few can resist. It may well be that you will be destroyed, or transformed, or consumed by this flame. Only the very strong can take the flame into their hearts and feed upon it. Now answer me this question, and mark me well: your answer must be true. Are you willing to risk your soul for sexual union with me, to perform the sacred rite and enter the flame within me?'

Despite himself, despite his natural caution, Hunt found himself unable to hesitate or resist. It was as though a voice spoke for him, from the very centre of his soul:

'I am willing.'

He was afraid, blindly afraid as a child is afraid of the dark. He could not even see the woman. What if she was not alone? What if all this mystical nonsense was just so much hocus-pocus as a prelude to doing him some very serious wrong?

But the power she had over him was so strong

that only the shadow of the fear touched his waking mind. The fear lay buried within him. Maybe she had drugged him. He felt almost as though he were floating above his own body, not a part of it any more, only experiencing events through it and not truly identifying with it. Or maybe it was hypnosis. Yes, that must be it. It was the power of hypnotic suggestion holding him in invisible chains that bound not only his body, but also his helpless mind, devoid of the will to resist.

It was then that he became aware of the music. He didn't so much hear it as feel it, pulsing into his bloodstream along his arteries and veins, washing over him like a sea-borne mantra and soaking through his skin. The music, like the woman's voice, was silky smooth and hypnotic. But it did not make him want to sleep. Quite the reverse. It lulled and soothed his mind, but it played upon the nerve-endings in his body like a cool sea-breeze, or crystal-clear mountain spring-water, over naked skin. It danced over his body and filled it with desire.

He could feel his penis beginning to stiffen, and his balls grew deliciously heavy beneath his helpless body. He wanted to cradle them in his hand – gently, lovingly, teasingly – as he always did when he was aroused and preparing to masturbate. He wanted to touch his shaft, feel it grow smooth as silk, turgid and rampant between his fingers. He wanted to measure its width in his proud hand, then measure its length in the woman's moist and tender quim . . .

A futile longing, an unattainable vision of ecstasy. For he was lying helpless, face-down on a bed, and the woman he desired was behind him, tormenting him with her voice, the voice of sex, the voice of pitiless domination and desire. There was not a thing he could do. Only instinct convinced him that this was the same woman he had seen outside in the narrow cobbled street, the woman who had gazed into his eyes and robbed him of his will. He was utterly powerless now. He could not hurl himself upon her, take her with his potent manhood, dominate and possess her. Why, he could not even touch his own aching tool, buried beneath him and begging to be touched, caressed, released.

The swish of the cane as it cut through the air came only a fraction of a second before he felt its pitiless bite on his buttocks. He cried out and tried to wriggle away, but the invisible force held him motionless upon the bed, compelling him to offer himself up to the cruel snake-bite of the slender bamboo cane.

At first, the pain was all he could see or hear or feel. The pain was his world: he became the pain, lived inside it, heard his screams echo within it, beat invisible fists against its inner walls and begged for escape.

But when the beating had gone on for so long that he no longer quite understood where or who he was, the feelings began to change. A treacherous warmth began to spread through him, numbing away the hurt and filling the void with a deepening sense of wellbeing, excitement, desire. Hunt could barely believe it: everything he had heard was true. Pain really could be the path to an exquisite pleasure, and he was treading that path now, feeling the softness of its grass and wild flowers beneath his bare and willing feet.

And he heard his voice, moaning soft and low:
'Take me, take me, please take me . . .'

The beating had stopped now, and he lay quivering with lingering hurt and growing desire, still helpless, unable to move or to see his tormentor.

The warm, liquid sensation on his skin was unexpected but infinitely pleasurable. A heady fragrance he could not quite recognise spread through the air, and the warm liquid oozed across his wounded flesh like the healing touch of the summer sun. It was a sacred scent: a scent redolent of temples and secret rites, a scent that reminded him of incense and temple bells and dark-haired priestesses of some ancient cult. His senses wafted him away to a new world where pain was replaced by pleasure, and when strong but gentle hands began to work the oil into his skin he could not help moaning with enjoyment, helpless though he was.

They were knowing fingers, skilled in the arts of provoking pleasure . . . and pain. From time to time, the long nails bit into his skin as the woman worked the oil in deeply, making him wince as the sharpness scored the raw flesh and the weals she had raised on his back and buttocks. But he could not move to escape her ungentle touch. She had become his nemesis, his dark fate. And he must endure.

And just as the sting of the soreness was becoming unbearable again, she would ease up and begin once again to massage gently, hardly more than stroking his fragile flesh with the flats of her palms, letting them skim his skin on a wafer-thin film of fragrant oil.

He realised that her fingers were moving down the muscular curve of his torso, stroking his flanks and teasing the sensitive flesh where back becomes belly. He longed for her to ease her hands round underneath him and make contact with the wild electric eel thrashing about furiously in its dark prison against his belly.

But she was merciless. Moving away from his waist, she began to slide her hands downwards over his hips and thighs, massaging the firm flesh and teasing the dark hairs foresting his olive skin. He shuddered with pleasure as she let her fingers glide between his thighs, and he was surprised to feel his legs move apart, though he had no power over them. It was exactly as if she had command of his every muscle, like a puppet-master manipulating the strings of a marionette.

Her fingers were teasing the hypersensitive skin of his inner thighs, and Hunt was in seventh heaven. It was the most delicious agony imaginable. He wanted her to move her fingers further up and in, to take hold of his balls – and yet he also wanted this marvellous suspense to continue: the wonderful moment of anticipation which you want to go on for ever. For the anticipation of extreme pleasure is almost better than the fulfilment of that pleasure itself.

He was so aroused, he almost felt he could ejaculate without so much as the merest touch on his erect shaft. He needed only to imagine her fingers on his hardened prick and it twitched convulsively beneath him, craving warm, wet places in which to hide its purple, glistening head.

And then it happened. She slid her fingers further inside his thighs and made contact with his balls. Immediately they tensed, and Hunt was convinced that they would contract and spew out their heavy load of pent-up spunk. But, to his amazement, although he seemed to rise towards new plateaux of exquisite enjoyment, he did not ejaculate. And with a start, he realised that this woman really was in complete control of him. She was able even to command his orgasm: to summon it forth or restrain its impetuosity simply by the force of her Titanic will.

The knowledge of this ought to have disturbed him, he knew that; but the woman Viviane had befuddled his brain and robbed him of the critical judgement Hunt so prided himself on. She had captured him whole and was playing with him as a big cat plays with its prey, just before it settles down to devour it . . . But Hunt was swimming sightlessly in an ocean of indescribable pleasure, in which only his prick existed, and in which the intensity of his desire, his need to reach orgasm, forced him to relax and surrender himself to the faceless one who could bring him joy or agony with just one touch of her slender fingers.

All at once, he felt the strangest thing happening to him. It was impossible, of course, but it was happening anyway. His body was rising slightly off the bed. Levitation? But surely that was impossible! People don't just rise into the air and float there. That was hocus-pocus, and Hunt didn't believe in that sort of thing . . . but it was happening, whether he chose to believe it or not.

Floating helpless and immobile in mid-air, Hunt looked down and saw the bed about a foot or so beneath him. He had no sense of danger, or fear of falling. The warm, knowing hands were still stroking his inner thighs, teasing the taut sac encasing his balls, but they were not supporting his body. They were resting gently on his flesh, and he could feel the incredible heat soaking into him and filling him with unbearable desire.

It was a wonderful feeling of being detached from space and time, reborn into a world of pure sensation. Although he could not move of his own free will, his body felt free and disconnected from the base earth of daily life.

Viviane now lay down upon the bed, her feet at his head and her face underneath his groin. He could not see her face. She had slender, graceful legs surmounted by a bright chestnut pubic bush which testified that she was a natural redhead. He yearned for her to touch him.

And now he felt her lips upon him, soothing and tormenting him into granite hardness. Surely he must come to orgasm . . . He was riding on a tide of uncontrollable passion, felt like a surfer about to ride the crest of that one last, mountainous wave, tumbling down into the foaming water, laughing and crying and breathless. But no. She kept him there, a microsecond away from the great pinnacle of pleasure; refusing to push him off the diving-board into the welcoming, sun-kissed ocean.

Her tongue worked its way around the base of his glans: probing, exploring, insisting. It wriggled its shameless tip into the moist eye at the very tip of his penis, licking up the tears which had gathered there and making him shudder with the velvet intimacy of it all.

Half-swooning with pleasure, he felt his eyes closing, and the room began to spin, faster and faster, making his head swim and robbing him of the little rational thought he had left.

When he opened his eyes again, he realised that he was lying on the bed, now on his back but just as helpless as before. He looked up and saw Viviane towering above him, clad only in a miniscule outfit of black zippered leather, thigh-high shiny boots and a studded collar. She looked sinister, threatening, capable of exerting great violence, and yet he was not afraid. He looked at her and all he felt was desire.

The red-haired Valkyrie stood silent and imposing beside him, running her scarlet-nailed fingers down his expectant body. Hunt could see she was enjoying the power, knowing she was inflicting discomfort but that her victim could do nothing to stop her. He tried to speak but the words froze in his throat, intercepted by that soul-deep, steely gaze from those cold blue eyes.

She climbed on to him, leather-booted thighs encasing the sudden vulnerability of his body. And she drove down upon his penis with such a force that he wanted to cry out with pain and pleasure. He was utterly helpless. After two or three powerful strokes, she stopped moving and Hunt thought he would die of unsatisfied lust. She seemed to have entered a trance, and was chanting softly to herself as she sat there with his erect penis deep within her womanhood.

Time passed. Time as Hunt had never before experienced it. It was as though each individual second was chiselled out of crystal and had many coloured facets which glittered elusively in the candle-glow. Each second was an eternity, a test, something to be endured. For – although this too seemed impossible – with each second that passed as they lay coupled on the bed, his desire and pleasure grew. He knew now that he was not moving towards an ordinary orgasm. The orgasm – when she chose to let him achieve it – would be something beyond the experience of ordinary mortals, something of another, more mystical world of which he had always been profoundly sceptical.

He lay there, utterly helpless, and enjoyed the sensations which surrounded and engulfed him. The velvet rings of her cunt enclosed his manhood like a close-fitting glove, opening and closing slightly like the mysterious mouth of some rare sea-urchin. He gazed up into her eyes and saw . . .

Eyes like flaming coals, eating into his soul. A cruel twist of the mouth, contorted into a parody of a smile. Teeth as sharp as needles. And, as he realised that his orgasm was almost upon him, he also realised that this terrifying vision was more than a vision. It was a woman, a terrible, evil, predatory woman, and she was lunging at him, lunging for his throat with those wickedly sharp teeth . . .

And the force of his terror, or maybe some super-human effort of will, at last broke through the spell and unlocked his gaze from hers. He did not know how he had succeeded in doing it, but all at once the realisation hit him: he was free, and he was in mortal danger.

The power of sound and movement flooded back into him and he howled with terror:

'No, no, keep away!'

But she was fast and she was relentless. He caught hold of her wrist as it came down to hold him fast, and gripped it for dear life. She spat and writhed in his grasp, no longer the sensual seductress but the destroyer-goddess, come to kill him and eat up his soul.

Dim recollections of his army training lent him speed and he rolled swiftly sideways, pulling her on to the floor with him. They clawed at each other's faces and bodies, raising red welts and in some places breaking the skin. As the blood began to trickle down his face, he heard a weird, unearthly moaning and realised that it was coming from Viviane. Her face was contorted with an expression which fascinated and disgusted him. An expression of lust, desire, greed, hunger.

She was hungry for his blood.

For a moment he lost control and could only lie and stare up at her, mesmerised, as she opened wide her scarlet lips to reveal wickedly sharp, pointed canine teeth. She was smiling – a horrible, carnivorous smile. The smile not of a soft and sensual woman, but of a ghoul from the chill, dark, outer wastes of Hell.

She lunged at him, but he parried, suddenly realising what she was doing, what she wanted. She was going for his throat . . .

What was she? Some kind of vampire?

He would have laughed out loud if he had not feared for his life, his sanity. His strength returned to him and he cursed himself for a weakling and a coward. With a roar of anger and triumph, he took hold of her mane of red hair and pulled her head back, until it was a safe distance away from his bare throat. He held her fast and marvelled at her animal viciousness, her wild snarling and spitting as she writhed and scratched in frustrated fury. It was then that he tore off her jewelled necklet and saw the marks.

The two tiny scars, like the faded traces of teeth-marks, on her throat.

Horror lent him a final surge of strength, and Hunt flung her away from him, hoping only for a second or two's respite to allow him to make a run for the door. But as she stumbled backwards she clutched at an iron poker propped up by the mantelpiece, and began to swing it wildly at him. He ducked and backed away, but still she came, cold-eyed and relentless. The realisation left him numb, too shocked for fear.

She was going to kill him. Unless he killed her first.

Hunt was no killer, and he knew it. And certainly no killer of women. He knew that if it came to it, he couldn't do it. For an instant, he imagined his strong hands around that milk-white throat and a flash of insight let him experience what it would feel like to squeeze the life out of that comely body. And then the thought struck him: was she really alive? Was she a living woman?

He was going mad. She must have drugged him. He was losing his mind. She lunged for him with the poker but he dodged her and she fell forward, stumbling and – it seemed almost in slow motion – struck her head against the mantelpiece.

It was a very slight blow. Scarcely enough to stun. But she fell to the ground as though struck by lightning. For an instant, Hunt could have sworn he heard the sound of faraway laughter, echoing somewhere deep inside his brain.

Maybe she was pretending. But no. He touched

her. She was cold – unearthly, deathly cold, and so still . . . so very still. He felt for a pulse. Nothing. Not dead, surely? Not dead . . .

And as he watched, something impossible happened. He blinked, wondering if his eyes were failing him, if the shock had blurred his vision. But there was nothing wrong with his sight. He gaped, incredulous, as Viviane's white skin became luminous, waxy, translucent. It was like looking into a milky, swirling mist. He reached out to touch her again – and touched empty air. He tried again, but his hand passed straight through her.

Viviane was melting away, fading like a cloud of smoke on the night air, dispersing as though she had never existed.

Hunt covered his eyes in disbelief, shook his head. Maybe it was all a dream. Maybe when next he opened his eyes, he would find himself back in his hotel bed, or the red-haired woman would be laughing at him and congratulating herself on the excellent joke she had played on him.

He opened his eyes. She had gone. And nothing remained to remind him of her, save a tiny, sparkling crystal, glittering defiantly up at him from the faded blue carpet.

He ran and ran and ran, away into the night. He did not look behind him.

7: Victims

Hunt was beginning to wish he had never heard of Sir Anthony Cheviot, and Whitby was starting to give him the creeps.

The episode with Viviane chilled him to the marrow every time he thought about it. He'd tried to convince himself that the whole thing had just been an unpleasant dream, to put it all down to a couple of bad pints and an iffy pork pie, but how do you explain waking up in your hotel room at four a.m. wearing nothing but your raincoat and Doc Martens? He couldn't remember a thing about how he'd got back to the hotel. What if somebody had spotted him? And there was the camera, too. His editor wasn't going to like it when he told him he'd lost the Leica *and* the telefoto lens. Of course, he could always go back to Miller's Yard and ask Viviane for it . . . And then again, maybe not.

He shivered, and splashed his haggard face with cold water. Come on, Hunt, he told himself. Make the most of yourself, you lazy git. At least try to look the part. We've got important fish to fry today.

Today was the day of the annual charity fete – quite a glitzy event by local standards, and Cheviot was sure to be present as he had been asked to open the proceedings and give a little speech. Hunt

109

intended to take the opportunity to ask him one or two pertinent questions. Maybe Cheviot thought he could play silly games. Maybe he'd thought his little secrets were safe for good. If so, he'd underestimated Hunt's sheer bloody-minded determination. Like the Mounties, Andreas Hunt always got his man.

Mara felt tired and confused. Her psychic energies seemed to be draining out of her, directed against her will towards something – or someone – her whole being told her to resist, wanted to resist: but could not. She tried to keep busy – after all, she had to earn her living – but in the middle of a reading she would be overwhelmed by a type of psychic 'interference': an astral 'static', blocking the pure waves of thought and the pure visions of truth, and filling her mind with insistent and obscene messages, only half-heard, only half-perceived. She couldn't get those words out of her mind:

'Whore, bitch, bitch on heat . . .'

'Sex-hungry little slut, filthy temple whore . . .'

'Open your thighs, bitch: you know you want it . . .'

'Go on, finger your clitty . . . Feel the heat . . . Aren't you just longing to have my meat inside you . . . ?'

She shook her head, held it in her hands, trying to reach into her deepest self and tear out the invading thoughts, cast them away from her and be free. But the soft, venomous, insidious voice hissed on inside her head:

'Pretty little bitch, smooth-buttocked, firm-thighed whore: I'm going to have you . . .'

'Soon, soon . . . Look, you're all wet between your thighs, you dirty little slut . . .'

'You *know* you want it . . .'

And it was true. She was ashamed to feel the spreading moisture, the damp crotch of her knickers sticking to her most intimate places, the subtle titillation of the crumpled fabric rubbing against her hardening clitty. She knew the words were a lure, a deception of some kind. She knew in her heart that they emanated from some source of evil: that same source, she sensed, that had pursued her across England and which remained with her, tormenting her, refusing to let her go, to let her live her life in peace.

She was in an almost constant state of sexual arousal, tortured day and night by erotic impulses she could not control. Every man she saw, she now saw as a potential sexual partner. She wanted to stroke their pricks through the fabric of their trousers, grab hold of them and feel them hardening, lengthening in her hand. She longed to unzip their flies and take out their love-shafts, teasing and masturbating them to within a hair's-breadth of orgasm, then holding back and watching their tormented faces, mouthing 'Please, please . . .' She craved that power; craved the delicious despotism of the hot, wet crotch over the starving prick.

Night after night, she had gone early to bed and lain down on her bed, naked, in front of the long mirror on the front of her wardrobe. Head and shoulders propped up on pillows and cushions, she drew up her knees and parted her legs wide, so that the image of her dark glossy muff stood out vividly against the light gold colour of her tanned skin.

And night after night, she had abandoned herself to the voice that whispered to her of pleasure, pleasure, pleasure . . .

Lovingly, she ran her right index finger down the length of her snatch, at first so lightly that she merely brushed the dark fleece with her fingertip, and then more insistently, more wickedly, diving down into the plump flesh as though her finger was a knife, sinking into a soft and deliciously juicy fruit.

Carefully but greedily, she parted the flesh and exposed the glistening treasures within: moist pinkness, as sweet as honeydew, and in the very heart of the oyster, the pearl – a little sphere that seemed to grow and pulsate and radiate its own life.

This pearl had become the centre of Mara's universe. How often, on these long summer nights, she had stroked it, teased it to the far-off accompaniment of a voice she could not quite hear, raucous breathing filling her head . . . She could almost feel unseen fingers plucking at her flesh, hot breath caressing her breasts.

And each time she came to orgasm, the same fiery eyes seemed to burn into her, and she imagined she could hear that evil, wonderful, obscene, seductive voice breathing its message of terror and shame . . .

And anticipation.

'Little slut, little princess, little temple whore: I shall have you. Soon now. Very soon. And you'll never be alone again . . .'

Mara looked up from her reverie and was surprised to discover that she had been daydreaming: it was noon and the sun was high in a perfect, eggshell-blue sky. It all looked so innocent and so impossibly pure: so English! The whole of the scene belonged to a world in which unseen evil spirits were wholly out of place. And yet, all this was happening to her.

She allowed herself a little ironic half-smile. This was a strange sort of a place: why, she'd be believing in Dracula next.

There had to be some escape from this persecution. Maybe it was all in her mind. Maybe she was going mad. She needed time to think, fresh air to clear her head, some sacred place to purify her and drive out the thoughts that were destroying her peace.

She picked up a light summer jacket and slung it around her bare shoulders. As an afterthought, she put on the Egyptian amulet Gareth had given her: 'It will protect you,' he had said. 'And somehow it looks just right on you.'

It felt right, too. She had always had a special affinity with ancient Egypt and Egyptian magic. The minute the cool stone amulet had touched her skin, she had felt calmed, whole, peaceful. And right now, she could use all the peace she could get.

Hunt hated garden parties, fetes, summer 'fayres' and all the other Merrie England nonsense so beloved of English villages and provincial towns. Morris Men, maypoles and guess-the-weight-of-the-cake competitions reminded him painfully of his days as a cub reporter on the Macclesfield Bugle, and he'd sworn he'd given them up.

And here he was, queueing up with the rest of the rabble to pay his 50p and see the big cheese himself

– The Right Honourable Sir Anthony Cheviot MP –
cut the ribbon and get his gleaming bridgework on
page three of the local paper.

Hunt was feeling unusually jittery. He felt guilty
about not reporting the incident with Viviane to the
police – but then again, what would they have made
of it? 'You see, officer, she bumped her head and
when I touched her to see if she was OK, my hand
went straight through her. Oh yes, and then she
dematerialised completely.' They'd put him in the
funny farm for sure.

The odd thing was, there was nothing in the papers
about it, nothing on the news about a young woman
disappearing. Nothing at all to disturb the seamless
fabric of an English afternoon.

The more he looked into this case, the more he
was convinced that something very weird indeed was
going on.

He had a cursory wander round the stalls, exchanged
small-talk with a few local dignatories and drank a
couple of pints of Sam Smith's in the beer tent, but he
didn't manage to glean any useful information about
Cheviot. Blimey, he thought, these Yorkshiremen
are tighter than a crab's arse.

Sir Anthony and Lady Cheviot arrived – the
regulation ten minutes late – and ribbons were
cut and pleasantries exchanged with the Mayor and
Mayoress. No chance to get anywhere near – this guy
was as slippery as an eel. For the next half-hour, Hunt
kept one step behind him, following him round the
stalls and waiting for his moment. It didn't come until
Cheviot's glossy black car arrived to take him back
down to London. Cheviot paused for a moment to
shake hands with his constituency agent, and Hunt

saw his moment. There were few people around – now was the time to strike.

He pushed through the small huddle of onlookers, briefly flashing his Press card for the benefit of Cheviot's burly PA-cum-minder, who instinctively tried to bar the way.

'Sir Anthony – can we have a word?'

'About what, precisely? This really is an unpardonable intrusion.'

The man's voice had a mesmerising quality, and Hunt found it intensely difficult to tear his gaze away from Cheviot's piercing grey eyes. It became almost impossible to articulate the questions he wanted to ask. It took a supreme effort of will to get the words out:

'About . . . your involvement with a certain young lady in London. And another here in Whitby. About certain . . . incidents . . . which you might not wish to discuss here, in front of all these good people.'

'No comment,' snapped Cheviot.

'Of course,' sighed Hunt, irritated but hardly surprised. He tried again, a little more insistently: 'What does the name Anastasia Dubois mean to you, Sir Anthony?'

Cheviot was not even slightly fazed. Hunt realised that he was sneering at him.

'I haven't the slightest idea what you're talking about, Mr . . . ?'

'Hunt, Andreas Hunt. *Morning Chronicle*. Can I just ask you . . .'

'Listen, Mr Hunt.' The eyes were steely now, and narrowed. And as they gazed deep into Hunt's blue eyes, they seemed to rob him of the power of speech, to paralyse him and leave him open-mouthed and idiotic in the MP's wake. 'If you wish to arrange an interview with me, you'll have to contact my Press Secretary at the House of Commons. And now, perhaps you'll do a great service to the good people of this fine town and go back to London, where slime like you belong.'

A brief stare at Hunt – as cold and as bleak as a January night on the North York Moors – and Cheviot turned on his heel and climbed into the black limousine. Hunt was pretty sure it was the same one he'd seen three nights ago, in Miller's Yard.

Hunt stood and watched the retreating limo, and desperately wanted to kick himself. What had gone wrong? What had robbed him of his native cunning, his famous journalistic expertise? He was baffled. It felt just as if some unseen force had drained all the energy out of him. He was still weak, still shivering.

Let's face it, he'd blown it, and in a big way. What the Hell happened to the big showdown he'd planned? Now he'd have to start all over again, keep on trying. And maybe blow it all over again.

He was thinking of leaving, when he caught sight of the fortune-teller's tent at the far side of the field. Maybe, just maybe, it would contain that same, unforgettable girl. Maybe it would have been worth his while coming to this horrible garden fete, after all.

The fortune-teller's tent seemed to have few customers. It looked deserted, but as Hunt approached the door, a soft and somehow familiar voice drifted out:

'Come inside. I won't eat you.'

It was a pleasant, silky voice and Hunt reckoned

that, even if it didn't belong to the girl he was looking for, its owner would probably be worth meeting: so he ducked inside.

It was one of those old hexagonal bell-tents that Boy Scouts used to go camping in, in the days of wide-brimmed hats and knee-length shorts. Inside, it was hung with eastern draperies and there was an old Afghan carpet on the ground. The place smelt strongly of joss-sticks, and a faint smoky haze hung on the air, dimly lit by the filtering daylight and a few flickering candles, tastefully arranged.

The fortune-teller – 'Madame Zara' of course (couldn't they think of any other names?) – was heavily veiled and swathed in luxurious Eastern fabrics: brocades, silks, satins, all in sensuous shades of burgundy and purple. Her face was hidden behind layers of silver-spangled tulle, save for her handsome, night-dark eyes, which peered at him intelligently and (he guessed) with some amusement as he sat down hesitantly on the rickety folding chair.

He wondered if she could read the disappointment on his face. Dark eyes: not, then, the girl who had taken him to Heaven and back, just those few days ago, and then disappeared like an opium dream from an addict's trance. And, like the addict, Hunt was disturbed to realise that he still craved his fix. The craving simply wouldn't go away.

Still, now he was here he might as well have his money's worth.

'Tarot, palm or crystal ball, darling?'

The voice was as smooth as double cream, poured temptingly over a cold silver teaspoon.

'Not Tarot.' The memory was too strong, the fear lingering at the back of his brain. So many strange things had happened over the last few days, and he couldn't risk setting off some psychological trigger, buried deep in his troubled brain. Somewhere, in the darkest recesses of his cynical journalistic mind, hidden in a place so dimly lit he could barely perceive it, lurked the deep, ancestral fear that stalks all men in their worst nightmares.

The fear of going mad.

'Then let me read your future in the crystal. You have an interesting face. I feel sure I shall see a fascinating life in the crystal.'

'How much?'

'Only one pound fifty. And it's all for charity, of course.'

'Of course.' He handed over a heap of small change, and felt a whole lot better. The thought that he was paying some woman (who was probably the grocer's wife and hadn't the faintest idea about fortune telling) to read his fortune in a lump of glass, seemed so prosaic that a slight smile twitched at the corners of his rather saturnine mouth. He wondered what she'd manage to come up with, and prepared himself to be thoroughly entertained.

She slipped the midnight-blue velvet cover from the crystal, and passed her ringed hands over the smooth surface. Funny, but Hunt could have sworn it began to glow slightly in the semi-darkness. Amazing what you could do with a bit of subdued lighting and auto-suggestion.

'Before we begin, show me your palm. It will help me to pick up on the correct vibrations, tune into the images of your future which lie imprisoned within the glass.'

He obeyed, enjoying himself now. She wasn't half

bad for an amateur, a real little actress. She took hold of his hand and turned it palm upwards, lightly caressing his fingers and making him shiver slightly with pleasure. She had the touch of an experienced whore: she'd definitely missed her vocation.

'You are an ambitious man. Impatient sometimes, a perfectionist. Is that true?'

'Yes, it's true . . . but can't you be a little more specific?' Hunt was willing to stake a tenner that she couldn't.

'You are a seeker after truth. And a man of great passion, inexhaustible sexual energies. A man whose passions sometimes lead him into danger. You enjoy danger, perhaps too much. As to the specific, I must look deeper, into the heart of the crystal.'

'So – will I lead a long and happy life, then?'

She paused, in a way which unsettled him. Why didn't she just give him the usual crap about 'you will meet a blonde-haired girl and have three children?'

'You have an unusual life-line. Unlike any I have seen before. I can't quite make it out. But an interesting life, I do not doubt. Now, let me look into the crystal. Come, look into it with me, share the visions.'

Now this *was* unusual. A fortune-teller inviting her client to look into the crystal. What was she going to do – hypnotise him? But he decided to go along with it, just for the kicks.

Unconvinced he peered into the glass ball as the woman passed her hands over the surface again and again, all the time muttering a low-voiced incantation which he could not quite make out. He began to feel a little light-headed, but still saw nothing. Why didn't she just get on with it and tell him any old bullshit?

'See: there – can you make it out?'

He blinked and rubbed his eyes, but there was no doubt about it: something seemed to be stirring deep within the crystal. At first, it seemed that a cold blue fire was burning there, a seed of fire and ice combined, beautiful and ever-changing, but so very far away. It seemed to draw him into the crystal, calling to him silently, and he knew that he must follow.

The blue fire gave way to a swirling red mist, through which Hunt could at first distinguish nothing. But as he watched, it began to clear and he realised that shadowy figures were moving beyond the mist. As the mist thinned and parted, leaving a vignette of clarity within a swirling red frame, he realised with fascinated horror that he was looking at the image of himself and one other.

The two figures were naked and sweating, their golden skins perfectly matching as they writhed and intertwined in a silent dance of lust. Although the male figure was facing away from him, Hunt would have known instinctively that it was himself, even if he had not recognised the familiar birthmark in the small of his back. He was looking down on his own self, and his own self was busily screwing a beautiful girl with firm tits, glossy dark hair and satin-smooth thighs dripping moisture. He could feel every stroke of his hard penis inside her, and he realised that his own penis had hardened in sympathy.

But who was the girl? He could not make out her face, hidden by her long black hair and by his shoulders as he pumped away at her. Oh, the ecstasy as he felt the thrusts of this other man who was himself, felt the slick, warm wetness of the girl's tight vaginal walls, subtle and firm as a hand closing around his hardened tool.

And then the man moved slightly to one side, and the girl's face was revealed. Her eyes were closed as she climbed towards ecstasy, but he knew her instantly. It was the girl from the fortune-telling booth on the promenade, the girl he had been seeking for the last week. But what was the significance of this 'vision'? Could it be just some fevered daydream, born out of the wishful thinking lodged deep in his own brain? And if it was more than that, what could it possibly mean?

He glanced up at the veiled face of Madame Zara.

'What does it mean?'

'Don't look away. You must keep looking . . .'

He returned to the strange vision in the glass, strangely detached and yet inextricably a part of what he saw. As though in a dream, he felt his other self climbing towards orgasm, and he could feel the girl's joy and excitement too, felt the blood pumping round both their bodies, felt the juices rising within them, ready to rush out and unite them. The girl's fingernails, long and red, were digging painfully into his back . . . no into the back of the *other* Andreas Hunt . . . but he didn't care, he just wanted to come. He wanted to feel that hot white jet, abandon himself to the thrust and pump and spurt of that engorged prick which was, and was not, his own.

But, just as the crisis seemed within reach . . . no going back now . . . he saw the girl's face again, and it was changing, changing subtly from approaching ecstasy to something very different.

Approaching terror.

As he watched in horrified fascination, the girl's face contorted into a parody of its former serene beauty, each muscle clenching in terrified apprehension. She was staring wildly in front of her, at something so horrible that her mouth opened in a soundless scream.

And the man who was also Andreas Hunt felt and saw her terror and twisted his head round to look behind him. But the face which turned towards Hunt was not his own: it was a terrible, strange, unearthly face – handsome and yet unspeakably evil. And the eyes, those terrible eyes . . . two burning red coals set in a waxen skin, hot coals that burned into him. And that smile, the cruel smile that twisted the corners of that implacable mouth. And the mocking laughter . . .

Hunt tore away his gaze and staggered to his feet, upsetting the table and sending the crystal rolling across the carpeted ground. He felt dizzy, disorientated and very confused. Anger surged through him and he wanted to lash out, hurt someone, show that he was not a victim, not just the plaything of a force he could neither see nor understand. He knew it was irrational – how could he blame his weird hallucinations on some tin-pot astrologer? – but somehow he sensed that this woman was at the heart of all his troubles.

He lunged at Madame Zara, but she stepped back neatly, parrying his wild lunge and moving out of his reach. But Hunt kept on coming, furious, resentful, sure that this woman was playing games with him. Maybe she was in the pay of Cheviot? Maybe he'd been drugged somehow . . . he had to know. And she was going to tell him.

She was as far away as she could get now, and trapped – her back against the far canvas wall of the tent and nowhere else to run. And yet the woman's eyes seemed calm, almost mockingly so. Hunt picked up the table and threw it out of the way, then approached the woman, irritated that she seemed not at all worried by him, not at all cowed before his anger.

Now he was gazing into her eyes, those cold, dark eyes with their irresistibly mesmeric quality. But this time he was strong enough to withstand them. He reached out and took hold of the veils covering her face. She made no attempt to stop him as he tore away the layers of flimsy fabric.

She stood revealed before him, and the blood froze to ice in his veins.

'Viviane . . . but how . . . ?'

But the red-haired woman – this woman who could not be Viviane and yet she surely was – simply threw back her head and laughed, and her sharp little teeth glinted like diamonds in the lamplight.

8: The Abbey

It was five a.m., and Mara walked slowly down the deserted side-street, relishing the peace and freshness of the early morning. Seagulls wheeled overhead in the perfect blue of a late summer sky, and the disturbing thoughts which had plagued her in the hours of darkness seemed to have no place in a world of sunshine and sparkling sea.

She paused to glance into a jeweller's shop window, admiring the display of Victorian jet, then catching sight of herself in the glass, smiling as she surprised herself with her own beauty. She was an exceptionally good-looking woman, and the troubles of the last few weeks had done nothing to spoil that sensuous, full-lipped face. Her tanned skin glowed with health, and her low-cut T-shirt did ample justice to the two juicy amber fruits nestling within, their twin stalks pressing eagerly against the taut white fabric. An amulet swung temptingly between her breasts on its long silver chain. Her tiny waist flared out into smoothly curving hips and a pert backside, deliciously delineated by her skin-tight jeans.

Mara realised with a sudden start that she hadn't had a man in weeks, not since that last time with Gareth and the twins. Her only companion had been her own subtle fingers, and she began to realise that it was no wonder she'd been having these weird sexual dreams and fantasies. Maybe she'd over-reacted. Maybe they really were only fantasies, the inventions of her own sex-starved mind, and not the premonitions or visions she had believed they were.

And yet they were so real. She could not clear her head of that vision of the past, the young girl who had faced such brutal violation and a horrible, slow death. The young girl who had worn Mara's own face.

And the thing which worried her most of all was the fact that, mixed up with the horror and the disgust, the fear and the bewilderment, there was a grain of pleasure, the merest touch of sexual excitement. There was a tiny part of Mara which wanted to be that girl, to feel the bite of the lash upon her delicate skin, to feel the brutal hands and the urgent pricks entering her and toiling away inside her belly. Even now, as she tried to dismiss the image from her mind, Mara could feel a spreading warmth in her loins and her finger strayed momentarily to the swelling bud of her clitoris.

Pulling herself together, she took a last glance in the shop window and straightened her hair. Her nipples were standing proud and erect, and her heart was beating faster than usual. She took a deep breath, and headed on towards the Abbey stairs.

The stairs – a good two hundred of them – wound steeply up the cliffs towards the ruined Abbey of St Hilda. At this time of the morning, it stood alone and sentinel-like against the sky, dark and lonely and yet friendly. An ancient and holy place, its holiness probably pre-dating the Christianity which had made it a place of pilgrimage and sanctuary.

'If I can't find peace there, I'll never find peace anywhere,' Mara told herself, and began to climb the steps.

Delgado rubbed his hands together with satisfaction. Business was good. Even better than he could have expected. From that very first moment when he had caught sight of Winterbourne Hall, deserted and tumbledown and forgotten, he had known that it would be perfect for his purposes, and he had been right. His international masters were pleased with him. They trusted his judgement now, and he knew that any suggestions he made would be accepted without question.

Winterbourne was fast becoming the playground of the rich, the famous and the influential. A whorehouse for politicians and princes. A sweet-trolley for palates spoiled by too much of the rich and the exotic. A man could find anything he wanted at Winterbourne. If he couldn't, it simply didn't exist.

He ran his hand down the silky flank of Kushka, the pretty little Indian whore he had chosen for the night, and she purred with genuine satisfaction. All the whores at Winterbourne loved their work. They sucked cock with an almost religious fervour, begged their clients to bugger them, to bite their nipples till they bled, to fuck them to the point of unconsciousness. They played their allotted roles with every bit as much conviction as Oscar-winning actresses – no, more: for they weren't acting. That was the great thing about Winterbourne girls. Their clients might be perverts – but so were they.

He signed to Kushka and she picked up the leather

127

thong and knelt with her thighs on either side of his head.

'Now,' he commanded.

And she began to lash the swarthy skin of his naked backside with a genuine enthusiasm that gave Delgado such a huge hard-on that he almost came there and then.

Delgado sighed with pleasure. Life was good. Business was even better. Why, if things went on like this, they might have to think about expanding.

The Master's restless spirit filled its prison like a poisonous gas, swelling and pressing against the walls, desperately seeking some means of escape, some way to sever the link with its helpless, useless body. And yet his hope of life lay within that body: the hope of a resurrection that would release him from the tenacious embrace of the crystal.

It was no ordinary crystal. Magic had created it. Magic protected and empowered it, endowing it with strength and resilience that no man-made implement could gouge or shatter. Only magic, its creator, could be its destroyer, and the Master's powers, though returning to him slowly, could never be sufficient on their own to release him.

He needed help. He needed the woman, the psychic, the white witch. And he craved her sweet and juicy flesh, longed for the feel of his own flesh against hers, the glory of his own senses, of being master of his own body once again. He needed her help. And that made him angry. He wanted to play with her and lure her and use her and break her. Take what he needed and destroy the rest. Squeeze out her sap and then crush her pretty petals.

The Master needed no-one. She would pay dearly for her fleeting power over him.

He concentrated his spiritual energies and willed himself away from this place. He was going on a journey, a journey of the spirit. A journey of exploration into the mind and body of the woman called Mara Fleming.

Mara drew her jacket closer round her shoulders and stepped out across the grass towards the Abbey ruins. They looked perfectly at home here, in this wild and forlorn place, this place hanging between sea and earth and sky, not quite part of any element. It was as though the earth were striving to extend its yearning arms towards Heaven, only to be held back by the cold embrace of mortality and the trivial mind of man.

The clifftop hung suspended between sea and sky, between life and death, between yesterday and today and tomorrow: and its timelessness struck Mara immediately, made her feel at her ease. This was a special place, a spiritual place. She could feel a tangible psychic presence here, and it wasn't difficult to see what had drawn St Hilda here to build her abbey, more than a thousand years ago.

She crossed the grass, strangely lush even though the greenery everywhere else had been baked dry and brown by the late summer sun. Hillocks and gentle swellings betrayed the sleeping monuments beneath a soft green canopy: the works of man, gently obliterated by the forces of nature.

Most of the Abbey church was in ruins now, but the outline of the nave was clearly delineated by fragments of crumbling stone wall and austere tiled floor. And the towering east end of the church remained, defiant against wind and rain and time, the early sunlight pouring through the skeleton of the great east window, casting ghostly pools of forlorn light on the wreck of what was once an altar.

Mara tried to imagine what it must have been like to have been one of the nuns here, all those centuries ago when it seemed that civilisation was under siege and only the religious remained to bear the flickering lamp of knowledge and enlightenment. A time of shadows and fear, of magic and devils when all pleasure was forbidden and the only escape was through those forbidden pleasures . . .

Mara laid her hand upon the dark, smooth stones, not yet warmed by the morning sun. Their coldness soaked into her bones, but it was not coldness which drew her attention. It was the sounds of the stones as they spoke to her, whispering fountains of words and thoughts and pictures overflowing in her head. This was an ancient place, a place that had seen much of both good and evil.

Suddenly, she felt nauseous, dizzy, colder than the fresh morning air around her. She shook her head to clear it and looked around her. Everything seemed slightly out of focus. A wave of vertigo hit her again, harder this time, and she put out both hands to steady herself against the wall of the nave.

At once, the vertigo took hold of her and she felt as though an icy electricity was flooding into her through her hands, paralysing her and taking away her breath. It froze her blood in her veins, and she became an ice-crystal in a hailstorm, blown hither and thither and falling, falling, to land she knew not where.

Dizzy and sick, and unable to open her eyes, she clung to the wall because it was the only thing within reach, the only anchor in the hurricane – even though she knew in her heart that to do so was a mistake. The stones themselves were the source of this new terror, and in touching them she had plugged into a rich vein of psychic experience. And yet she had never experienced anything quite like this before, nothing as strong as this. She was afraid, more afraid than she had ever been in her entire life. It was as if her psychic powers were taking over her life, and she was merely their unwitting, unwilling pawn.

The dizziness began to subside, and Mara's breath came back, at first in painful gulps and then more easily. Slowly and tremulously, she opened her eyes and could not believe what she saw.

It had grown suddenly dark, save for the glimmerings from many candles. Mara blinked and looked around her. She was still standing in the Abbey, but not in its ruined state. Nor was it restored to its Gothic grandeur of stained glass and towering stone. The building in which Mara stood was unrecognisable as the Abbey, and yet instinctively Mara knew that was what it was. She was standing in the Abbey church as it had been a thousand years before: a simple building of wood and stone, with a beaten earth floor and a small wooden altar at one end. The candles were held by a procession of a dozen nuns, dressed in rough habits and processing silently into the church.

With a sudden sickening lurch, Mara realised that she was not merely watching the nuns process past: she was one of them. She looked down and saw that she, too, was dressed in a rough brown woollen shift, a white wimple and knotted sash, a heavy wooden cross around her slender neck. She was a part of this silent procession. Was it a dream? Or could she somehow have been transported back in time to the earliest history of the Abbey? She closed her eyes, pinched herself, tried everything to bring herself out of the trance, but it was no trance. A drop of burning wax on the back of her hand shocked her into the reality of her situation: this was no dream.

The nuns were standing together now, singing. Mara was singing with them, instinctively knowing the words, the music, and not knowing how or why. The women's faces gleamed ghostly and unreal in the half-light, shadows flickering and leaping in their eyes.

They were young women for the most part, doe-eyed and comely-faced. But there was sadness in their eyes, and fear too. Mara looked at them questioningly and immediately understood: they were praying for safety, for protection, for deliverance from the terror from across the wild sea.

It happened so quickly, with such brutality that Mara had no time to collect her thoughts or register what was happening to her. The shouts, the flames, the battle-axes slicing through the sturdy timbers of the church door. The sisters flinging themselves to the ground, hiding their terrified faces in their skirts. The Northmen were coming!

Mara whirled around, confused and terrified. She realised that she was shivering uncontrollably in her rough habit, her bare feet cold and vulnerable in their sandals. And she shivered with fear, for already she could see what was about to happen . . .

The Northmen had broken down the door of the

church, and were thundering towards the huddled women with cries of triumph, their eyes wild and arms eagerly stretching out for their prey. They were laughing, laughing, as they tore the clothes from the women and feasted upon their untouched flesh, glorifying in the defilement, the ravishment of perfect innocence.

A tall, blond warrior with a straggling gingerish beard had taken out his hard prick and was even now between the trembling thighs of a doe-eyed novice who could not have been more than seventeen. As he toiled away inside her, she cried out lustily – whether in pain or pleasure, Mara could not tell.

Everywhere the same scene was being played out: women dragged to their knees, stripped bare so that their poor pale bodies trembled in the cold night air, nipples erect with cold and fear. Women flung to the ground, legs prised apart, men lying upon them, the thin high cries that could be distress or pleasure . . .

And in the middle of it stood Mara, frightened and confused and yet detached, waiting for the moment when she too would succumb to the deadly embrace of her tormentors.

A wild impulse took over her, and she tried to run away, to head for the door which led – if not to safety – at least to the chance of escape. She made it to within a few feet of the door, but a strong, calloused hand fastened on her arm and drew her inexorably back. She fell to her knees, sobbing now, afraid to look back at the other sisters – her sisters – for fear of what their fate might be.

'Look at me.'

She could not. She stared in terror at the ground,

hands clenching and unclenching and sweat trickling down into the small of her back.

'I command you to look at me.'

The voice was authoritative and harsh. She dared not disobey, and lifted her eyes to peer into the man's face. He was tall and muscular, about thirty-five or forty – a real giant of a man, a bear, with a mane of golden-brown hair and blond-fleeced arms and chest. And only one eye – the other a closed socket, slashed across by a massive scar running down his face from hairline to jaw. He was leering at her, spittle drooling out of the corner of his mouth, and as she watched he tugged down the front of his goatskin breeches and pulled out his cock.

It was a beautiful cock for such a devil of a man: smooth and long and sleek, hard as iron and thick as a woman's wrist. Even in her fear Mara was dazzled by its beauty. His fine, hairy balls hung rounded and tempting as fruit on a tree.

'Take it in your mouth.'

Mara was quick to obey, kneeling up and slipping the glistening head into her mouth. He thrust suddenly, forcing the shaft down her throat, and she gagged, afraid that she might suffocate on such bounty. It tasted strong, and she sucked at it with growing pleasure, enjoying the sensation of burgeoning hardness. She longed to stroke those tense balls, run her fingers over his pubic curls, burrow into the hot cleft between his strong thighs, but her hands were tied behind her back and he held her fast. All she could do was suck, suck.

She ran her tongue around his glans, probing under the foreskin and teasing the little dew-spangled eye that threatened to open and pour forth its tears in abundance.

And with a roar of pleasure, he exploded in her mouth: a salty tide of frothing spunk that bubbled and fizzed as it shot down her throat; and she swallowed it with relish.

He pulled back, and she raised her eyes to see how well she had done, to receive his praise. And saw, instead, his mighty arms raised above his head, and the broadsword poised to strike her down.

And after that, all was blackness.

Not dead? Not murdered by a mad-eyed Viking with a greedy prick and a pitiless sword-arm? Mara blinked her eyes and opened them, half-expecting to find herself back on the grass, clinging to the stones of the ruined Abbey wall, half-fearing that she would look up to see the sword still poised to strike the life from her.

But no. She was still in the Abbey, but the Abbey was greatly changed once again. This was neither a ruin, nor the humble wooden church, put to fire and the sword by pitiless pagans. This was the Abbey in its medieval glory, a vibrant pageant of colour and incense.

She rubbed her eyes and took stock of where she was. She was kneeling alone, near to the altar. Looking down, she saw that she was still dressed in a nun's habit, but of a finer, smoother fabric that said much about the Abbey's new-found wealth. She looked up and saw the great east window restored to its full glory: a riot of exquisite stained glass. The morning sunlight was flooding through the glass, casting pools of green and blue and red on the cool tiled floor. The faint scent of incense hung on the air.

'I am a penitent,' Mara told herself. 'I am here to do penance for my offences against decency and morality.'

But what crime had she committed? What had she done to offend against the honour of her religious house? She continued to kneel there in silence, afraid to get up and leave, and somehow sure that very shortly something would happen to show her what to do.

The door at the west end of the church swung open, creaking slightly on its heavy iron hinges. The sound echoed through the church, joining the staccato tap-tap of sandalled feet on the tiled floor.

The footsteps came nearer, but Mara dared not look behind her. She wondered who this could be. Was it some other nun, come to give her a message perhaps, or to tell her that her penance was at an end? She hardly dared hope, and the breath caught in her throat as the footsteps came to a halt, just feet behind her.

She could hear breathing, rather quicker and noisier than normal, as though the person were out of breath. Or excited by something.

The voice was as cold as ice, cutting through the chill air like a blade through hard-packed snow. Cold, yet something in its timbre spoke to Mara of a dark and forbidden sensuality, of some horrible perversion marrying pleasure and pain.

'Do you know why you are here?'

Mara was astonished to hear herself reply, in a hushed voice that trembled with terror:

'I have sinned.'

'And what sin have you committed?'

'I . . . I dare not tell.' She craned her head sideways in an attempt to see her persecutor, but he admonished her:

'Look before you and do not attempt to look at me. Now speak, I command you.'

'I . . . I have committed the sin of self-pleasure.'

'Describe to me what you did.'

'In my cell, last night . . . I . . . touched myself to give myself pleasure.'

The voice had become quieter now, but far more menacing:

'I told you to describe what you did. *Exactly* what you did. Now relate all the events to me, in detail, or it will be the worse for you, child.'

The tide of words poured out of her, seemingly without any intervention on her part:

'It was late at night, after Compline, and I was very tired, but I could not sleep. I was troubled by . . . unclean thoughts. Thoughts of the handsome young merchant who stayed overnight in the Abbey guest house a few nights ago.' She hesitated, afraid to go on.

'Proceed.'

'I lay down on my bed and tried to sleep, but whenever I closed my eyes I saw this same young man. I was troubled with what I had seen that night when I had taken up the hot water for his bath. He was . . . unclothed . . . and I had never before seen such beauty, such perfection of form.

'At first, he did not realise that I was standing there, in the doorway, and I was able to admire the roundness of his buttocks, his firm young thighs, his muscular back and shoulders; the downy golden hairs

137

on the back of his slender neck. I felt such strange stirrings in my belly, at the tips of my breasts.

'Then he turned round and saw me. I was afraid that he would be angry with me for looking at him, but he smiled and beckoned me towards him.

'He was so beautiful, so manly. I had never seen a naked man before. The fragrance of sweat upon him made me feel strangely intoxicated, put a new kind of hunger into my belly. And his manhood was so perfect and so responsive. He bid me take it into my hand and stroke it, like a wounded bird cradled in my palm. And lo! The wounded bird began to revive, and then to grow!

'I could hardly believe what I was seeing, feeling. I felt an unbearable desire to take it into my mouth and taste it. The young man saw my desire and bade me kneel before him and reverently take the tribute between my lips and suck at it like a babe at a breast. Oh, how exquisite the flavour, the texture. Little salty tears wept from it on to my tongue. With what wonderment I touched the velvet bag that carried his twin treasures. And at last, a great torrent poured forth into my mouth, almost choking me as I struggled to swallow it.

'I was in utter confusion – convinced that I had done wrong and yet aflame with a desire I had never experienced before. The tips of my breasts had grown hard and were pressing insistently against the rough material of my shift, and my loins felt as though they were on fire – begging some touch or caress which my own inexpert fingers were too innocent to provide.

'With another sweet smile, the youth hoisted the hem of my robe and – despite my blushes and protestations – silenced me with a kiss in my most intimate place. He then began to caress me there, probing my maiden intimacy with incautious and insistent fingers. I bit my hand to stifle my cries of pleasure as his caresses grew bolder still, and I felt a rush of warm liquid trickling down my thighs as he massaged a curious little button which seemed to have sprung up from nowhere.

'I felt sure that something wonderful was about to happen to me – a great tide of pleasure was building up within me – when there was a noise on the stairs and I heard the Almoner's voice calling to me. I pulled abruptly away from the young man, though every fibre of my being cried out for me to stay and discover the secrets of womanhood which he wished to reveal to me. And I ran away from him, back down the stairs to the refectory, where the Almoner was waiting to scold me for my tardiness, the taste of the young merchant's seed reminding me of the secret pleasures I had been forced to abandon: a second novitiate which, perhaps, I was never to undergo.

'I lay there on my bed last night, and I simply could not forget the young man and his wonderful caresses, his beautiful, perfect body with its smooth skin; and the marvellous flower-stalk, blossoming miraculously out of a thicket of curly brown hair.

'My excitement began to return: that same excitement which he had evoked in me, only two nights before. I unfastened the tapes which held my shift modestly together at the neck, and my fingers strayed, unbidden, to my hardening nipples. I touched them tremblingly, cautiously, half-afraid of what would happen to me, what it would feel like. For never before had I ever stroked myself in such a lewd and shameless way. Why, I half believed I would be struck down where I lay for such wanton behaviour.

'The touch of my unpractised fingers on my hardened buds electrified me, awoke in me the sudden understanding of what I had been denied in entering the Abbey. For I was dedicated as an oblate to this house when I was no more than a tiny child, and it is many years since I have seen the world beyond its walls. And I know that I am a well-formed young woman, with a young woman's desires, though they have long been buried deep within me. The searing pleasure of caressing my own nipples maddened me, banished all self-restraint, corrupted me utterly and damned me to self-pleasure.

'I abandoned myself to my own inexpert caresses, learning little by little how to procure the most intense sensations. My nipples were as hard as little stones now, and I began to imagine the mouth of that young, smiling merchant, sucking and nibbling away at my breasts. I was breathing heavily and I could feel wetness from between my thighs, beginning to soak into my shift.

'Trembling and full of guilt, I reached down and pulled my shift up above my waist, so that my loins and thighs were bare to the cold night air. I did not feel or even notice the chill of the night, so transported with guilty delight was I. I scarcely knew what I should do, for all I had to guide me was the memory of that young man's fingers – probing me, exploring me, working away at me and sapping my will.

'I ran my fingers through my curls and parted my nether lips. Inside, all was fragrant moisture and warmth. I searched with my fingertips until at last

I found the impudent button, pulsating like the very heart of me beneath my touch. I sighed and began to rub it – at first gently, and then, as I grew bolder, with a ferocious intensity. And all the time I imagined that the young man himself was stroking me, bringing me to undreamed-of pleasures.

'And I climbed once more towards that elusive summit of joy, desperately stretching out for the pleasure which I had never before tasted. But, just as I began to understand that I was standing on the threshold beyond which there was no going back, the door of my cell opened and there stood our Mother Abbess. Her wrath was terrible. She ordered me to be bathed in freezing water, and then locked me overnight in the punishment cell. And now she has ordained that I must come here, to the chapel, to do due penance.'

The silence seemed unending, unbearable, but she dared not break it with a question or a plea for mercy. Then the voice spoke again, velvet-smooth yet merciless:

'And penance you must do, my child. Prepare yourself to receive your punishment.'

But nothing had prepared her for what happened next. For the hand which reached out and held her by the shoulder, whilst the cold steel blade ran like lightning from nape to hem of her habit, slashing the fabric and leaving her bare-backed and trembling.

Hot, strong hands pulled roughly at the cut edges of the fabric, tugging them apart, baring more and more of her flesh. Terrified though she was, Mara found it strangely pleasurable. Startled and afraid, she cried out:

'Please, no! Please stop . . .'

141

But her entire being screamed silently for the punishment to go on, and on, and never end. Already she was naked, yet she wished with all her heart that she could peel off even more and deeper layers of herself, so that she could be more naked still. Her rebel body would not accept that punishment must not bring pleasure, and she realised that her insolent nipples were even now stiffening – and not merely with the cold.

The girl whom Mara had become knelt timorously yet with a growing excitement at the foot of the altar steps – terrified lest she was committing some terrible profanity, yet all the time telling herself: 'How can this be wrong? I cannot see this man's face, but he must surely be the Father Confessor . . .'

'Prepare to feel the weight of your sins, child,' hissed the voice she was beginning to desire as much as she dreaded it.

The first stroke caught her unawares and sent her reeling forwards against the chill stone of the altar steps, breathless and tearful with the shock and the pain. The flesh of her back and buttocks seemed to sting and burn in a thousand different places, and she guessed that this unseen tormentor was punishing her waywardness with strokes of the discipline: that wicked cat-o'-nine-tails, whose pitiless thongs were each tipped with a tiny ball of lead shot. A device made to deliver the maximum suffering with the minimum of effort. But this particular exponent seemed determined to give it his all.

She clambered back on to her knees but the lash fell again, and Mara cried out with the sudden agony of it: it felt as though a thousand red-hot needles were sinking into her flesh at precisely the same moment.

142

A third stroke threw her forward again, and this time she did not have the strength to haul herself up on to her knees. She lay sprawled on the steps, flesh mortified both by the lash at her back and by the cold, sharp edges of the stone steps, biting into the soft and delicate flesh of her belly and breasts.

The unseen hand continued to flog her for a long time, raining stroke upon stroke on her poor back, and Mara sobbed uncontrollably on to the unresponsive stones, her fists clenching and un-clenching with each agonising stroke.

Then her tormentor began to direct his efforts more specifically, concentrating on her luscious ripe backside. The first strokes raised red weals on the soft flesh, and a rain of blows followed, breaking the skin and causing a hot trickle of blood to run into the furrow between her buttocks, and down the inside of her thighs.

Strange to tell, the excruciating pain began to be transformed into a very different feeling. A curious warmth began to mingle with the searing agony of each stroke of the discipline: a warmth which began in her backside, but which rapidly spread to other parts of her nubile young body. This girl was a virgin, but a virgin ripe for defilement: trapped within her body, Mara sensed the girl's amazed excitement as, little by little, the pain of the punishment began to transmute into the pleasure of anticipation.

The warmth was in the girl's belly now, moving deliciously downwards into her cunt; and the girl was twisting and turning under the lash, writhing like a lascivious serpent in the dust of its own baseness. Another warm fluid was trickling down her thighs now: a clear, fragrant fluid from the depths of her womanhood, honey from the honeypot, milk for the cat to lap up as it explored her with its many sharp-barbed tongues.

'Repent!' cried her torturer. 'Repent your wickedness and surrender yourself utterly to the punishment!'

'I repent, I repent!' sobbed this girl whom Mara had become, desperately seeking both to escape the wicked pain of the lash and to offer herself up to it more completely. She realised with a horrified start that she was actually thrusting her backside out towards the lash, as though begging for more of its unremitting punishment, welcoming each and every stroke as it bit into her flesh. She was groaning and sighing now, and her breathing was harsh and quickening.

Suddenly, the pain stopped. He had finished beating her. Perhaps he was exhausted . . . or maybe he had other plans for her, other punishments to inflict upon her? Mara's mind was full of a heady mixture of terror and excitement, now re-experiencing – through the body of this wayward novice – the unbearable suspense of the virgin longing for the first intimate touch, the first excursion into her womanhood.

'Now, now is the time of your atonement,' hissed the tormentor's voice, very close to her ear. Mara could feel his hot breath on the back of her neck, and realised that he was very close behind her indeed – so close that he was virtually on top of her.

He began to caress her buttocks with the flat of his hand. The ungentle pressure of his hot palm on her lacerated flesh made her wince with pain, but the heat radiating into her added to the warmth already in her belly, and she twisted and turned even more under the sway of an emotion she did not yet recognise as lust.

His hand worked its way into the crease between her buttocks, and almost instinctively Mara began to part her thighs to allow the intruder to pass. It slipped between her bum-cheeks, lingering for a while on the puckered rosebud of her arsehole. She groaned as he worked the tip of one finger inside her forbidden palace, brutally destroying all her resistance. So this was atonement: the complete surrender of even her most secret places to an unseen stranger; the utter humiliation of her pride through the power of lust . . .

Now his fingers were between her thighs, and she was straining to thrust them wider apart, to urge him further in. He massaged her inner thighs, mingling the blood from her wounded backside with the sticky love-juice from her throbbing, yearning cunt, and she began to murmur 'Please, please, please . . .' without really knowing what it was she was begging him to do to her.

Then, still behind her, he grabbed hold of her thighs and knelt down between them. The girl in whose body she was trapped was afraid and confused, but Mara knew what was going to happen next, and wanted it. She heard a rustling as the confessor pulled up his robes, and pulled out his prick; then felt its tip as it nudged eagerly at the girl's virgin cunt.

He pushed a little. His erect penis was massive, and the girl's cunt was tiny and the way barred. He pushed harder, and she cried out with pain and distress. A third thrust, and he was inside her at last. Mara felt the stabbing pain as he tore through the girl's thick hymen and a torrent of virgin blood cascaded down her thighs. She was sobbing now, but her sobs were mingled with the urgent breathing and moaning of a girl who is being initiated into the rites of love.

He fucked her roughly but expertly, and before long the girl realised that she was once more climbing the hill that leads to exquisite pleasure. This time, this time she must not be thwarted.

As though reading her thoughts, her tormentor reached around underneath her and began to pinch her nipples hard. The pain was sufficient to bring the girl to the threshold and beyond, and with a great sob of ecstasy she reached her very first orgasm.

A second later, he gave a final thrust and felt his twitching prick discharge its load of sticky semen into the cunt he had just violated. He withdrew immediately, and stood up. At that moment, the girl whom Mara had become took her courage into her hands and turned to see his face.

It was the face of evil: elegant, smiling evil in a monk's cowl. The face was half shadowed by the full hood, but Mara knew she would never forget those eyes, for as long as she lived. Eyes like burning, fiery coals that reminded her irresistibly of the fires of Hell.

When she came to her senses, she was still clutching the walls of the old Abbey church, but she realised with horror that she was totally naked, and in some pain. Her clothes lay tattered on the grass beside her. They looked as though they had been torn off – maybe even cut off with a knife.

Luckily, it was still very early and there was no-one in sight.

There was blood on her back and buttocks, and she winced as she sank to the grass and tried to cover her nakedness, shivering both with the early-morning chill and with the shock of her experience. And what had truly been the nature of that experience? Not a dream, not an hallucination, surely – for she bore the physical marks of her ordeal. Self-inflicted injuries? Surely not. In her heart she knew that it had been no dream, that it had been the most powerful psychic experience she had ever had. A psychic experience which she doubted had been triggered solely by the memories contained in the ancient stones she had touched. A dark suspicion chilled her heart and made her fearful. Fearful of whatever – or whoever – had had sufficient power to manipulate her mind and misuse her body, so adeptly, so cruelly.

If she had ever believed that she had escaped the dark shadow which had been pursuing her for so many weeks, if she had ever managed to convince herself that she had reached a safe haven where evil could not touch her, all her feelings of security now deserted her, and a slow tear trickled down Mara's cheek.

From his hiding-place a few yards away, amid the ruins, Andreas Hunt surveyed the scene and didn't know what to think, what to believe. Was he supposed to believe his eyes? But they were telling him lies, surely. For had he not seen a girl apparently stripped, beaten and fucked by some invisible force? Had he not heard her cries, seen first the weals and then the blood appear on her smooth, tanned back and softly curving backside?

And the slow, mocking trail of semen, trickling coldly and defiantly down Mara's bruised and defeated thighs.

He knew he ought to go to her, to help her, but there was a feeling of something so unspeakably evil in the air about him that Hunt found himself trembling and rooted to the spot. A choking, stifling presence that felt as though it were sucking all the oxygen out of the air. Hunt tried to step forward and go to the girl, but something prevented him: it was like a hand clenched tightly about his throat, squeezing out his breath and making him gasp for air. An icy hand, the hand of death . . .

He turned and ran away, not daring to look behind him.

9: Discovery

It was Saturday morning, and the public library was thronged with borrowers and guilty fine-payers. Posters on the noticeboard advertised Children's Book Week, the local Bee-Keepers's Association, a Harvest Supper and – last but not least – a Psychic Fair. Hunt shivered and turned away. He'd had enough of the paranormal to last him a lifetime – no, several reincarnations.

And the girl . . . he couldn't get her out of his mind. Every time he stopped to think, the image of her tortured face floated into his mind's eye with a painful insistence. He didn't want to think about her. He tried his damnedest not to. But still he found himself alternately fascinated and repelled by the uncannily clear recollection of what he had seen amid the Abbey ruins.

He recalled the smooth curves of her back and buttocks, caressed by the gleaming black tresses which fell in long, sensuous waves across her luscious flesh. He remembered the tremendous excitement he had felt as, disbelieving yet bewitched, he had watched some ferocious unseen force apparently tear the clothes from the girl's body, exposing it in all its juicy perfection. The sight of her full, firm breasts, pendulous as bunches of ripe grapes as she knelt and

149

supported herself on her hands. How he had wanted
to reach out and caress them, massage them with
sweet oils until she moaned with ecstasy, and then
– only then – lie beneath her and take those hard,
tempting nipples into his mouth and suck on them as
he weighed the glorious fullness of her breasts in his
greedy hands.

And then, inexplicably, she had begun to twist and
turn as though under some invisible torturer's lash.
Why, he had even seen the marks the cruel thongs
made as they seared her delicate skin. But how could
it be? He could only watch and wonder.

He had winced with her as the lash broke the skin
and the blood began to trickle down her back and
thighs. And yet his prick had stood erect in homage
to the supreme eroticism of the scene, almost bursting with excitement as Hunt realised that whoever –
or whatever – it was that was torturing the girl was
also preparing to fuck her. He watched as she parted
her thighs and then thrust backwards, as though to
receive the big hard prick he himself longed to bury
deep inside her.

When, at last, she had reached her climax and
fell back on to the damp dewy grass, Hunt had felt
aroused, yet terrified. His emotions were in tumult.
He had wanted to rush forward and ask her if she was
all right, look after her, hold her tight. And he had
also wanted to rush forward, throw her down on to
the earth and thrust himself into her up to the hilt,
oblivious to her pain and protestations.

And, in the event, he had been unable to do either
because of the bizarre atmosphere of foreboding
which had overtaken him. The sensation of an icy
hand about his throat was still vivid in his mind. He

could still conjure up the awfulness, the choking and gagging, the breathlessness, the terrible premonition of evil.

He had run away, and he wasn't proud of it. The guilt stung his conscience, and the feeling of failure hurt his pride. Andreas Hunt didn't run away from confrontations. In fact he regularly sought them out. Yet Andreas Hunt, ace investigative reporter, had run away three times in less than a week, and there was a danger that it might get to be a habit.

What's more, he still hadn't had a decent lead on Cheviot, and his editor was pulling him back to London tomorrow. It was hardly surprising he wasn't too chuffed: a week at the seaside on expenses, and all Hunt had come up with so far was a collection of garbled nonsense that would have him on the psychotherapist's couch if he wasn't careful about shooting his mouth off.

So he'd decided to come to the library to do a final bit of research on Sir Anthony. Maybe if he could find out something about the companies Cheviot was a director of, he might be able to dig up some dirt from a different angle. He wasn't giving up that easily. He asked the reference librarian to direct him to the stacks where the business directories were kept.

And then he caught sight of the girl.

Mara went back to the flat, made herself some strong black coffee and ran herself a hot bath to soak away some of the pain. The sight of the blood swirling away like fantastical feathers made her feel dizzy and nauseous. Her head was spinning with confusion and – with a suddenness that surprised her – she burst into uncontrollable sobs. How did she know that someone, something, somewhere, was profoundly gratified by her tears, drank them in like the sweetest nectar, and smiled with evil satisfaction?

She soothed her wounds with cold cream, collapsed into bed and slept through most of the next day, exhausted by her ordeal at the Abbey, and desperate to escape the hideous memory of it. But even in her dreams she found herself forced to relive the events in all their terrible clarity, feeling every stroke of the lash upon her martyred flesh, every painful thrust of the pitiless prick in the virgin cunt which belonged to that frail, yet luscious, body which was and yet was not hers. She tossed and turned under the satin sheet, and awoke in the morning sore and bathed in sweat.

But the strangest moment of all came when she caught sight of her nakedness in the mirror on her dressing-table. Where, the previous night, there had been massive bruises, red welts and weeping flesh, all was now silken-smooth and flawless. She turned her back to the mirror and looked over her shoulder at her reflection. Nothing. Not a mark. Nothing at all to show what she had suffered. Had it then been some bizarre hallucination? She knew that it had not.

For the bath towels still bore the clear traces of blood from her wounds: wounds which somehow – impossibly – had disappeared overnight, leaving no sign that they had ever been there.

Mara sighed and sank on to the sofa, clutching a cushion to her as though it might contain answers to the insoluble questions which thundered through her brain. There were no logical answers, that was clear. The wounds had been there and the evidence that

they had existed was still all around her: the stained
towels, the cotton wool and the antiseptic. And she
could still remember the pain, as vividly as if the cruel
thongs were still stinging her fragile flesh. But now
all that existed was a vague stiffness in her limbs –
something that could have been explained away by
a restless night's sleep.

Only Mara knew that the truth was far stranger, far
more macabre. Someone or something had gained
access to her mind, and was manipulating her psychic
powers for its own ends. Ends which she could not
even begin to guess at. Not for the life of her. And
she realised, with a shiver of fear, that her life might
indeed be at stake.

She had to do something. Otherwise, she was
going to go mad. Mara slipped on her coat and
headed off towards the Abbey. Better to go back
there now than to live in fear of the place for the
rest of her days. If this thing was out to get her, she
was going to need all her strength to fight it.

It was an unusually warm day, and the wind had
died down to a light breeze. The Abbey looked
picturesque and innocent in the midday sun: golden
light caressing the stones which had shown themselves so powerful and so treacherous only the day
before. Tourists were milling around the ruins: happy
smiling people with cameras and noisy children
running about in the sunshine. Mara felt like a
sleepwalker in a nightmare landscape, completely
alienated from the comfortable normality around
her, dry-mouthed and afraid.

She found the place: an innocent section of the
ruined wall of the Abbey church, almost apologetic
and irrelevant, carved with the graffiti of decades

of ignorant tourists. Surely there could be nothing sinister here?

Mara stretched out a fingertip and, trembling and holding her breath, touched the weathered stone. It felt comfortably warm under the noonday sun, but nothing more. Relieved, she smoothed her palm over the stone and concentrated hard on the faint vibrations she could feel rising up from the heart of the stones.

All stones felt alive to Mara, for all stones are ancient, and all have a story to tell. Over the years, Mara had discovered that she could 'read' many stones, tuning in to their vibrations and briefly glimpsing the most important events in their history as pictures in her mind's eye. But nothing to compare with the experience she had undergone the previous day.

At first, little came out of the stone, save a confused murmuring of voices, then Mara glimpsed one brief image in her mind – the picture of nuns in procession, peacefully and reverentially chanting their plainsong . . . and then nothing more. The stones were silent again, and would not give up their secrets. But the stones could not lie. If this was all that she was getting from them, then this was all that was stored within them. Which meant that the incredible visions she had seen had come, not from the stones, but from some external force which wished her to believe that they came from the stones.

She opened her eyes and stepped back from the stones. Children were still laughing and running about. Japanese tourists posed for photographs and a fat middle-aged American couple were oohing and aahing over the incredibleness of it all.

And then she caught sight of it. It hadn't been there before, she was sure of it. She had already searched the grass at that point. Just a tiny glint among the long grass gave it away: the glint of something sharp and bright. She bent down and parted the grass to reveal it. It was a small silver dagger with a blade of pure crystal, wickedly sharp and glinting with defiant flashes of light in the sunshine. So beautiful, so perfect, so bright: and yet there was something malevolent about the dagger that made Mara want to drop it and leave it where it lay.

She could not. She turned it over and over in her hands and felt a power within it, a pulsating life-force at once compelling and terrifying. An indefinable eroticism that made her mouth go dry and her heart beat faster, to the rhythm of her ever-eager cunt.

But something else also made her heart race. There was dried blood on the tip of the dagger, and Mara knew with unswerving certainty where that blood had come from. It was her own, shed as the hungry blade had slashed the clothes from her back and its wicked tip had grazed her fragile flesh.

The crystal-bladed dagger lay on the desk in front of her: a beautiful object, clearly very old and very valuable. Its silver hilt was carved with strange symbols which Mara did not recognise, but which she sensed instinctively had some magical significance. Certainly they were very ancient in origin – perhaps Sumerian, Phoenician or Egyptian. Oh yes, it was a real find. Any collector would be delighted to have it, especially a collector specialising in the occult. So why did it give her the creeps? Why did she sense that it was inherently evil? And why did she not have the will to get rid of it?

Maybe if she could find out something about the history of the Abbey, she would be able to get closer to finding out who – or what – was persecuting her, and why. Why it had such a keen interest in manipulating her through her sexuality. And maybe she would find out something which would bring her nearer to an understanding of the inscription on the crystal dagger, and to the identity of the person who had hidden it in the grass at the Abbey.

The public library had an extensive local history collection, and the librarian proved helpful:

'Which period are you particularly interested in?'

'I'm not quite sure . . . the thirteenth or fourteenth century, I should think. Do you have anything on that period?'

'As a matter of fact, we have some rather interesting original documents dating from that period. They're all in Latin, of course, but our Mr Fletcher is something of a dab hand at medieval Latin, and so we've had most of them translated into English.'

'Could I see them, do you think?'

'Well, yes. But I do feel I must warn you that some of the writings are . . . well . . . a little earthy. We keep them under lock and key, as we feel that in the wrong hands . . . But of course, yours is a specifically academic interest, isn't it, Ms . . . ?'

'Fleming, Dr Mara Fleming', she lied. 'I can assure you they'll be read with purely academic interest.' She felt quite amused that anything from the Middle Ages could be considered indecent today, and wondered what on earth all the fuss was about.

Apparently satisfied, the librarian led Mara into a

room at the back of the reference library, where the local collections were kept. It was a gem of a room: straight out of the 1930s. Dusty, with high ceilings and a yellowish light from a greasy 60-watt bulb with no shade, lots of mahogany panelling and row upon row of tall bookcases.

The librarian unlocked a glass-fronted cabinet and took out a sheaf of typewritten pages:

'I'll leave you to it,' she said. 'Let me know when you've finished and I'll lock them away again.'

The door closed and Mara settled down to read through the papers. Most of them were the tedious transcriptions of account-books or the annual agricultural records of the manors held by the Abbey. Surely these weren't the 'earthy' documents the librarian had been so worried about!

Mara turned to the next sheet and knew immediately that she had happened upon something much, much more interesting. A diary. Fragments of a diary which – according to the spidery notes scrawled at the bottom of the first page – had been written by a young novice, Sister Honoria. It had been found and partially burned by the Abbess at some time during the thirteenth century. The first few fragments spoke of the daily round of Abbey life. But then Mara came upon a more substantial piece of text:

'I know not whether I am blessed or cursed, for last night I was initiated into a new world of which formerly I knew nothing. I had been instructed by Mother Prioress to take hot water to the guest house for the young merchant who is lodged therein. Alas for my immortal soul, for I lingered too long on the stairs and saw far more . . .'

Here the passage ended, with a note to the effect

that the rest of that entry had been destroyed by fire. But Mara's breath quickened as she recognised the tale told by the girl whose body she had dwelt within the previous day.

'More, there must be more . . . ,' whispered Mara, quickly turning the page.

'And he chastised me for my terrible sin, flayed my cowering nakedness until I bled and cried out for mercy. And yet mercy he showed me not, for assuredly I deserved none. And I now know that the pain and humiliation which fell to me were indeed my just punishment, for even the searing pain of the discipline awoke the basest lusts in me. Lusts which even now rage within me and – in spite of prayer and fasting – refuse to be stilled.

'I could not see the face of he who punished me, only feel the bite of the discipline as it cut into my flesh. And oh, the shameful warmth of the lust which crept into my loins. But he who flayed me saw this in me and sought a just punishment; and, seizing my mortified flesh, he thrust his carnal lance deep into my shameful womanhood, causing me not only the horrible pain of retribution, but the glorious ecstasy of redemption through atonement.

'And when the punishment was done, and he stayed his hand against me, I turned to thank him for his godly offices and saw that my chastiser was the dark stranger who came here lately from a religious house in the East: the one they call the Master . . .'

Mara's mouth was dry with excitement, the hairs erect on the back of her neck. She sensed that this dark stranger, this 'Master', might be the key to her own persecution. She skipped the next few pages, which dealt only with trivialities, and then read on:

'Tonight the Master commanded me to meet him in the Abbey church, where he stripped me and bade me lie upon the icy floor. He chastised me with his fleshly lance, running me through time and time again until I begged for mercy and cried out as he brought me to a vision of ecstasy. His eyes have the power to burn the soul: I cannot look into them without fear and amazement, for it seems to me that those eyes contain all the secrets of life and death. He spoke strange words over me: words that I could not understand; and I felt myself floating . . . I seemed to be looking down upon my body and I believed that I understood all things. And he embraced me and it was as though not only his manhood but also his spirit entered me, and I felt pain and ecstasy and I became his utterly.

'The Master showed me a strange dagger, with a silver hilt and a blade of a beautiful carved crystal. He told me that, if I will offer myself up to its power, it will grant me immortality. But I am afraid and also I am uneasy that this cannot surely be the work of God. And if the Master, my confessor, does not derive his power from God, then from whence does it come? Weariness overcomes me and I can write no more. God grant me the strength to resist all evil, God protect me from the darkness, God forgive me my transgressions, God grant I lose not my immortal soul . . .'

The diary came to an end at this point. For a long time, Mara sat and gazed at it, wondering, guessing, frustrated by the inability to know what became of the girl. Were her fears justified? Did she escape the corrupt influence of this man she called The Master? Or did she meet an untimely death at his hands?

Or, thought Mara to herself, hardly daring to consider the possibility: did she surrender herself to the dark power of the crystal dagger, and find that immortality which her Svengali had promised her?

Of course, that was impossible. Then again, it was impossible that Mara should, that very day, have discovered a dagger. A silver dagger with a crystal blade. Either someone was playing a very elaborate practical joke on her, or something very strange was going on. In her heart of hearts, she knew it was no joke.

At that moment, the door opened and in walked a tall man in a raincoat and trilby. Even if she hadn't recognised his face, she would have known him instantly by the jaunty angle of his hat, his slightly dishevelled yet quietly stylish appearance. It was the man from the fortune-telling booth: the man with whom she had shared that frightening, yet exhilarating, sexual experience. She knew he had felt it too.

Did she want to meet him again? She had been dreaming of it for the last week, and yet she wanted to run away and hide, afraid of what might happen, the potential dangers of such dramatic chemistry, such a psychic bond. And there was also the worry which followed her everywhere, which occupied her mind at every moment: was this a spontaneous chemistry, or was it simply yet another manifestation of the force which was toying with her, enjoying making her its prey?

In any event, she had little choice in the matter. A few moments in which to observe him, unseen, from behind a bookcase, and then he walked around the corner of the shelves and saw her.

He stopped in his tracks, mouth slightly open, all the breath knocked out of his body. So you feel it too, thought Mara, her knuckles white with tension as she clutched the pencil she had been using to make notes.

There was a long and uncomfortable silence, and then he stepped forward and took off his hat:

'Hello again,' he said, with a strained smile. His voice sounded trembly and hoarse, despite the bravado. 'My name's Andreas Hunt and you're not moving an inch until you tell me what yours is. I've spent an entire sodding week trying to track you down.'

'Mara . . . Mara Fleming.' She couldn't find any other words. Only the terror held her fast – the terror that it was beginning again.

Hunt took off his coat, tossed his hat on to the desk, pulled up a chair opposite Mara's and sat down.

'Doing some research?'

'Just a little work on the Abbey,' Mara replied, perfectly truthfully but economically. She liked him, but couldn't yet be sure that she could trust him. 'I have a special interest in it from a . . . psychic . . . point of view.'

'You're a psychic then? And I thought you were just a fake gypsy fortune-teller.'

'Please, Mr Hunt, don't make fun of things you don't understand.' Mara was angry, and stood up to leave.

'No, don't go. Look, I'm sorry – my big mouth again and all that. Tell me about it. I'm all ears.

In fact . . . well, to be honest, I've had some pretty wacko experiences myself these last few days. You wouldn't believe the half of it. I can hardly believe it myself.'

His hand was on her shoulder, pressing her back down into her seat; but she prised his fingers away and turned on him:

'I suppose you think "psychic" and "wacko" mean the same thing – well, do you? Look here, Mr . . . Hunt, or whatever your name is, it's bad enough having the gift without having it ridiculed by know-it-alls like you.'

'I'm sorry. It's my job to be sceptical.'

'What do you mean?'

'I'm a journalist. You know – one of those no-good scumbags who can't even write. We journos suffer from clichés too.'

She smiled a tired smile. 'I'm sorry.' She looked up into his face and liked what she saw. Nor had she been unmoved by what she had seen of Hunt as her gaze travelled downwards: nice broad shoulders, slim waist and hips, promising bulge at the crotch – a bulge that seemed to be growing larger, if she wasn't much mistaken . . . Maybe it was happening again, but there wasn't anything paranormal about it: he had a nice body, almost certainly a good-sized prick; she had softly curving hips and breathtaking tits. Hardly surprising they had the hots for each other.

He reached across the table and touched her shoulder again. This time she didn't flinch or draw away. In fact, she smiled and took hold of his hand, kissing it lightly and placing it carefully on her left breast. He needed no prompting, and began to stroke the firm flesh, unrestrained beneath her tight T-shirt.

It felt good, very good. The rosebud of her nipple was firming, hardening, growing, blossoming, and he could feel a delicious warmth spreading through his groin as his prick swelled to the electric charge of sexual energy sparking its way through his fingertips to her welcoming flesh.

He looked into her violet eyes and saw that the pupils were hugely dilated, betraying her mounting desire. She was smiling: the secretive half-smile of a martyred saint approaching the moment of ecstasy – loving every moment of his carefully measured caresses. Not too fast, nor too slow. Not too violent, but not too gentle either, or she would not derive the full benefit from his touch. Hunt was no libertine, but the extremes of desire gave his fingers the gift of second sight, made him an expert in the art of stirring the deep, dark waters of Mara's sexuality, troubling them into vast breakers of turbulent passion. Her lips parted, and she began to pant, very quietly, very discreetly . . . they mustn't make a sound, for at any moment the elderly spinster librarian might overhear and open the door, putting an end to this long-cherished fantasy.

Gently, Mara removed Hunt's hands from her breasts. Seeing his look of worried surprise, she silenced his fears with a smile and whispered words of promise and comfort:

'Relax . . .'

'What . . . ?'

'Relax . . . just sit back and let me . . .'

Hunt obeyed, nonplussed but at the peak of excitement. Mara slid down in her seat, and for a moment he wondered if she was going to slide under the table – but no. She slumped in her chair and all of a sudden Hunt felt a subtle presence, a gentle but insistent touch on the lower part of his leg. Footsie. The girl was playing footsie with him.

He reached down and stroked her ankle, pulling off her shoe and caressing the naked flesh beneath. Strange how erotic it could be to touch a naked foot, to draw a fingernail gently across the sole and feel the toes flex and squirm delightedly at the touch. Strange how good it felt to feel the blood pulsing beneath the cool flesh, and to feel the lithe and sensual strength of muscle and sinew.

He let go of Mara's foot, and let it roam wherever it would. It explored his calves, climbed playfully up towards his knees and insinuated itself between. Almost instinctively he clenched them together, afraid in a childish, subconscious way of what might happen next, but the continued caressing broke down his resistance and, little by little, he let himself relax and his knees began to part.

Once it had breached the defences, there was no stopping Mara's adventurous little foot. It nuzzled between Hunt's knees and began to forge a path further into the warm furrow between his thighs. Hunt gave a low growl of pleasure and opened wide to let her in. Mara slid still lower in her seat, and thrust her foot further, deeper, into uncharted territory.

He gasped as her toes burrowed into his crotch, teasing the crease between thigh and pelvis, between thigh and testicles. His balls tensed anxiously as she skirted their extreme sensitivity with cautious caresses; but he sighed with relief and gratitude as he realised that she was not going to hurt him, but bring him to the very brink of ecstasy.

Her toes seemed every bit as sensitive as fingers: better, even. They were like the butterfly-soft fingers of a child, yet with the strength and confidence of tempered steel. They danced in a circular motion about his loins, teasing him and calling him to play their own delectable game of catch-as-catch-can. Oh, how he longed to catch them and force them to linger endlessly on the burgeoning flower-stalk of his penis, straining to meet them and yield up its essence as joyfully as the blossom yields its pollen to the questing bee.

He could hear her breathing quickening as she began to rub harder at his hardness, every bit as excited by what she was doing as he was himself.

'Harder . . . please, harder. A little higher . . .,' he heard himself beg, and was stunned to realise the extent of the control she had over him. For a brief instant he was paralysed with terror: what was this leading to? What if they were discovered? Maybe they should stop this, right here and now, before they went too far . . .

But could he have stopped himself, even if he'd wanted to?

Mara was enjoying herself immensely, but was tiring of playing with her prey across the frustrating partition of trousers and underpants. There must surely be some way to make the contact more intimate . . . With the subtlest of movements, her toes climbed a couple of inches up his flies, tracing the line of the zipper, and found the little tag protruding at the top.

With the utmost concentration, she pressed on it with her toe and succeeded in pushing it down about an inch. Another try, and it yielded another half-inch. A third go, and the fly was open wide enough for her to wriggle first her big toe, and then all the rest of her toes, inside.

The first barrier was down. Now only the underpants were between her and her conquest, her goal. He was wearing silk boxer shorts, and she amused herself toying with his wonderful rigidity through the slinky fabric, enjoying the sensation of thin silk sliding over hard, swollen flesh. The silk grew damper and damper as his love-juices began to gather at the tip of his prick and soaked into the flimsy fabric.

The vent in his boxer shorts was already gaping with the pressure exerted on it by Hunt's massively erect penis, and it was easy for Mara to slide her toes inside and liberate her prey from its lair. Oh, how beautiful it was in its smoothness, its perfection; how exciting it was to feel its heat, its vibrancy against her own flesh. How could she ever have known how sensitive toes could be?

Hunt gave a groan of pleasure as his penis sprang forward out of his trousers and was caught and devoured by Mara's eager foot. It seemed to be everywhere at once: under his balls, stroking the underside of his shaft, tickling his glans . . . it felt like heaven.

But he knew that this was only the threshold of heaven, not heaven itself. There was more, much more, to come – and he wanted it. He simply had to have it.

He caught hold of Mara's foot and, despite her wrigglings and protestations, held it fast. Slowly and inexorably, he began to pull it forward, forcing her to slide further and further down in her chair.

'What are you doing?' breathed Mara. 'I'm going to fall on the floor!'

'Aren't you just!'

And he pulled a little harder, and sure enough Mara did slide on to the floor, in a giggling heap of silent laughter and raging lust. Pulling his trousers down around his knees, Hunt slid down under the table with her, and silenced her helpless giggles with a kiss. One hand held her down, whilst the other began to explore underneath her skirt, wriggling an exploratory finger inside her knickers, round the side of the gusset. She was wet, soaking wet, and he could feel her cunt pulsating slightly, as though it could already anticipate the orgasm he was about to bestow upon it.

Sliding his finger out of the sopping hole, he moved it up a little and sought out the throbbing pearl of Mara's clitoris. He had never felt such a huge clitoris: it really was like a little penis, fully three-quarters of an inch long, and throbbing with a life all of its own. He pinched it lightly and Mara gave a little cry, half-pain, half-ecstasy.

No time for preliminaries, not now. He had to have her, and he knew she felt the same way. She was writhing about underneath him, and the hard tips of her pillow-soft breasts were grinding irresistibly into his chest. But how could they – here, now, when they might be discovered at any moment? Oh God, what were they going to do? If his prick didn't find a soft, wet place to bury its head, it was going to explode . . .

'I want you, I want you . . .,' she moaned. 'Take me, please take me now . . .'

'But . . . here? How dare we . . . ?'

Her only reply was to reach out and grab hold of his penis, tormenting it with her soft, strong hands so skilfully that he knew he could take no more. With a stifled sob of irresistible desire, he pulled aside the gusset of her knickers – no time to take them off, too far gone, got to have her right now – and thrust his member deep into her.

And that really did feel like heaven. Only better. His hardness slid into her like polished steel into a velvet scabbard, and he felt her grow wetter still as her womanhood welcomed him in, yearning and exultant.

The fear of discovery stifled their cries of passion, but the hoarse cadence of their breathing rose to a crescendo as their loins beat time and they swam together in the warm sea of pleasure, borne up together on the wild, surf-crested wave of a perfect orgasm.

Afterwards, they lay together for a few moments, breathing slowly quietening. Then they hurriedly rearranged their clothes and sat back on their chairs to get their breath back.

Not a moment too soon. For at that instant, the door opened, and in walked the librarian – fortunately, an unobservant woman.

'Sorry to disturb you,' she said. 'I just wanted to see if you'd finished.'

'Thank you,' replied Hunt, with his most ingratiating smile. 'I think I can safely say we've just brought our research to a very satisfactory conclusion. We'll be out in a minute.'

When the door had closed behind her, they collapsed into another fit of giggles, letting out all the relief they felt, not only at their narrow escape, but at the release of tension after so many days spent worrying about what was happening to them.

It was only after she had gone that they noticed the book lying on the floor under the table. It definitely hadn't been there before.

'Perhaps she dropped it,' suggested Hunt, unconvincingly.

'Don't be a prat,' Mara chided him. 'You know she didn't.'

She picked it up. It was a very old book, bound in vellum, with a Latin title on the spine.

'Chronicles of . . . the Master,' she translated, in a shaky voice, trying not to betray her sudden fear.

Hunt took it from her trembling hand and opened it. Whatever he was expecting to happen, it wasn't what actually did happen next. The book was no more than a sham, an empty shell – the centre portion hollowed out to form a little storage space. As he opened the book, something fell out and rolled across the table.

It was a ring. A broad silver band set with a single crystal, and bearing a strange inscription.

Mara picked it up, and the colour drained from her face.

'What's the matter?' asked Hunt.

But Mara said nothing. Already Hunt had her marked down as some kind of New Age nutcase. How could she tell him what had been happening to her? How could she explain to him that the inscription on the ring was identical to the one on the crystal dagger she had found at the Abbey?

It was a full moon, and the sky was so clear that each star glittered like a cut gem in the blackness.

Below, bathed in the cool white light, Andreas Hunt and Mara Fleming lay naked and entwined on the still-warm sand.

'I want you,' said Hunt, stroking her flank and making her shiver with delight.

'I want you too.'

'I have to go back to London tomorrow morning. Say you'll come with me.'

Mara was silent.

'You know you want to.'

Which was true. Never before had she experienced orgasms of such intensity. Already she was addicted to this tall, dark man with the quiet voice and the eager prick. But the shadows of persecution were still around her – a little further away, but who could say when her tormentor would strike again? And she recalled the time at the fortune-telling booth, when they had shared their lust and their fear.

Who could tell if the evil force which pursued her might not also strike at Andreas Hunt? Who could tell if it might not even strike at her through him?

She looked across at him and saw that he had drifted off into a peaceful slumber. Carefully, silently, she disentangled herself from his arms and got to her feet. Gathering together her clothes, and not daring to risk a backward glance, she tiptoed softly away across the sand.

10: Serpent of Nile

The gym was crowded, and it was some time before Mozzini noticed Delgado standing in the doorway. He left the lad beating hell out of the punchbag and strolled over, towel slung across his shoulders. He was a big man with a lived-in face that had seen plenty of action inside and outside the ring, and he towered over Delgado. But Delgado was welcome here, for well-built lads were often in demand at Winterbourne, and more than one aspiring boxer had acquired the money to turn professional through 'services rendered'. No questions were ever asked.

'Evening, Signor Delgado.' He smiled affably and extended a bear's paw of a hand. 'And what can we do for you tonight?'

'I'm looking for a young man.'

'Understood.'

'Ah, but this time I'm looking for someone a little . . . special. Mid-twenties, I'd say. A nicely built young black fellow. Broad shoulders, slim hips, tall . . .'

'. . . And a nice big dick, eh, Signor Delgado?'

'You read my thoughts every time, Guiseppe. Have you anyone in mind?'

'Si, si, Signor Delgado. Come with me and I'll show you round.'

171

Business was good, and the gym was packed with the beautiful, muscular, sweating bodies of young men training, sparring, honing their bodies to the peak of perfection. Delgado was spoilt for choice. Why, he even began to wish he were gay . . .

'Ibrahim, take a break and come here a moment, would you?'

A tall, glistening, black figure vaulted effortlessly out of the practice ring, and stood questioningly in front of Delgado.

'Signor Delgado, this is Ibrahim. He's very keen to make it in boxing. Came here last year as a refugee from Ethiopia. Filled out nicely since then, he has.'

Perfect, said a voice inside Delgado's head. No friends, no ties, no-one will miss him.

And he was undoubtedly beautiful, too. Fully six feet six, glistening black skin and broad shoulders; rippling muscles and bulging thighs. Delgado had already made up his mind. He would be perfect, just perfect.

And no-one would ever miss him.

Mozzini turned to Ibrahim and introduced him: 'This is Signor Delgado, Ibrahim. He's been very good to us here at the gym. Signor Delgado has a proposition for you.'

The Master was growing impatient. The girl was ideal and yet proving difficult to lure. His powers were not yet sufficient to sustain his control of her mind, and without her he knew he could not hope for release from his torment.

But he was at last beginning to gain ascendancy in the mind of the procurer, Delgado: a man whose licentious nature and spiritual corruption made him particularly vulnerable to the Master's growing power. That power, although still limited, could take his spirit briefly into the world outside in its search for allies, and already Delgado's mind had opened to him as a flower opens to the sunshine. It was a promising beginning, for the man's mind was not entirely petty: he had a certain cunning, a sadistic finesse, and he would prove a useful tool to the Master in his search not only for regeneration, but for the memories of his past.

For parts of the life which had been his were still unclear to him in his weakness, his mind still clouded and his recollections incomplete. Only slowly, by degrees, was the Master beginning to piece together the whole of the long, dark story of his life. A life which had been interrupted for a few short decades, but which soon – very soon – would begin again and never cease.

No, not life, but death in life: the bittersweet gift of living death, which – once he had regained his lost powers – the Master would broadcast like a deadly germ until at last he had infected the whole of mankind.

Delgado was delighted with life. For some reason, he felt more alive than he had ever done before. He awoke each morning with a sparkle in his eye and a renewed sense of purpose. In fact, ever since Winterbourne had opened, he had felt as though a guiding hand was steering him towards ever-greater success. What's more, his sex-life was better than ever, too, though he had begun to develop the bizarre conviction that he was sharing his sexual experiences with someone else . . . as though that unseen someone were looking over his shoulder all the time, sharing his sensations, feeling them through his body.

But whatever doubts or unease filtered through into his brain, Delgado had no difficulty in chasing them away with the warm glow of success. Ever since he had managed to persuade not one, but two members of the Royal Family to become regular patrons of Winterbourne, Delgado was convinced that the venture could not fail.

Such certainty of success demanded a celebration – something really glitzy and lavish. That was a great idea of his, to hold an Egyptian orgy. These days, Delgado was full of great ideas. He wondered idly where they were all coming from.

The guest-list was even more impressive than usual. The regulars of course – Blomfeld, de Lacy, Cheviot, Spender, van Linden and the rest . . . but what a star-studded cast-list Winterbourne had assembled tonight. Prince James and Edmund, Duke of Mexborough, several multi-millionaire businessmen, numerous MPs and wealthy lawyers, a couple of Arab oil magnates and Andrew Diamond, clean-cut, firm-jawed host of the *At Home Tonight* programme. Delgado smirked to himself at the entertaining thought that thousands of bored housewives wet their knickers every day over Mr Diamond. He wondered if they'd be so hot for him if they knew how much he liked having beautiful young men shove their fists up his arse.

The scene had been set most impressively in the Great Hall at Winterbourne. Piers Seaton, celebrated West End theatre designer and undisputed queen of the cross-dressers, had done the job for a very modest fee, in return for an invitation to the fun and the promise of an introduction to Andrew Diamond.

The Roman trappings had long been cleared away, with the dried blood and the semen and the cunt-juice that had stained them and told the story of a wild night and a rueful morning after; and the hall had been completely redecorated in the style of an Egyptian dynastic palace.

Pretty boys dressed as eunuchs (but in fact gloriously well-endowed and carefully selected to appeal to Andrew Diamond) guarded the doors and stood at the head and foot of gorgeously painted couches, strewn with embroidered cushions. Their perfect young bodies had been oiled from top to toe with the sweetest and most expensive of Eastern aromatic oils and spices, and their nipples had been pierced to carry golden rings and jewelled chains which hung across their gleaming chests. Bidden to serve without question or complaint, these Eastern delights were forbidden to speak.

The central pool had been filled to the brim with a fragrant blend of rosewater and genuine asses' milk (not an easy commodity to come by and not cheap either, but then Delgado wasn't footing the bill). Six of Winterbourne's most exotic whores were reclining by the edge, clad only in gauzy diaphanous shifts, and wearing the heavy wigs, gold jewellery and kohl eye-paint which added a touch of authenticity to the scene. Delgado firmly believed in attention to even the tiniest of details.

Tables laden with exquisite fruits and sweetmeats stood beside each couch, and naked maidens were charged with the task of filling each goblet with wine as soon as it was empty.

For those who had had too much wine – and those whose sexual abilities did not quite match up to their aspirations – Madame LeCoeur had prepared genuine Egyptian aphrodisiacs, concocted from ancient recipes discovered in the Valley of the Tombs of Kings. The fact that most of these contained substances highly illegal in the West was of no great concern either to her or to Delgado, since the Drug Squad were hardly likely to prosecute their own Commissioner (a regular since that first heady night at Winterbourne) and, even if they did, he'd be sure to be baled out by one of the three (or was it four?) High Court judges who relied on Winterbourne for regular recreation.

In the centre of the pool a dais had been built, with a narrow footbridge joining it to the side of the pool. On the dais were two wooden thrones, gilded and decorated with painted hieroglyphs. This was to be the setting for the evening's great set-piece: Ibrahim's moment of glory. The sort of success he'd never see in a boxing-ring, mused Delgado, strangely elated and spurred on by the voice inside his head which now so often guided him and told him what to do.

Delgado surveyed the scene and was well satisfied with the preparations. The dark shadows at the corners of the room were filled with darker shadows still: the shadows of fantastical creatures: human from the neck down, but bearing the heads of animals and mythical beasts upon their shoulders. The gods of Egypt were here in force: Thoth, Bes, Anubis, Hathor, Set, Osiris and Amun-Ra, waiting in the wings to take their cue. Delgado had to concede that Seaton's papier-mâché animal heads were extremely effective.

The lights dimmed, and the great velvet curtain was drawn across to reveal a figure from a mystic's dream. The goddess Isis, earth mother in diaphanous white shift, stood for an instant on the threshold, and then began to walk slowly and solemnly into the great hall, flanked by naked youths bearing baskets of rose petals, which they cast on the polished floor before her feet.

Delgado had dressed his guests as Egyptian noblemen, and had instructed them to join in the ceremonial. As Isis approached, they too began to prepare her way with flowers and incense – cleverly laced with an aphrodisiac perfume devised by Madame LeCoeur. Excitement was beginning to mount.

So skilfully prepared had she been that none of those watching recognised the Mother Goddess as none other than Joanna Königsberg, so very recently a timorous virgin, sold by her father to feed the base appetites of world-weary connoisseurs and perverts like Harry Blomfeld. Delgado had been astounded at her transformation over the past few weeks.

From fearful victim to sex-hungry vamp, Joanna had come a long, long way. To Delgado's amazement and delight, she seemed to have a natural, even instinctive understanding of the ways of lust. She had a wonderful aptitude and appetite for sex and – far from wanting to run away from Winterbourne – she had begged to be allowed to stay and become one of Delgado's costly whores.

Not that she had needed to beg. The girl was dynamite. Customers had begun to ask for her by name. She was the natural choice to be the star of this evening's entertainment.

With her bright blonde hair hidden under a dark wig and heavy make up adorning her ice-maiden face, Joanna made a perfect Isis. Her pale skin contrasted dramatically with the dark wig, and under the subtle torchlight she seemed to have a ghostly, ethereal pallor. Her pink nipples had already puckered with excitement, and were clearly visible through the flimsy fabric of her robe. A heavy gold pectoral hung about her neck and between her breasts, and a fine golden powder sparkled on her cheeks, eyelids and limbs.

The air was heavy with sex and Madame LeCoeur's aphrodisiacs were doing their work well. Gavin de Lacy was stroking his testicles and longing to wank off, only barely managing to save himself because he knew that more and better was to come. Harry Blomfeld had already ejaculated once, into the hand of one of the naked slave-girls, and was working up a second, equally impressive erection: Madame LeCoeur certainly knew her job. Meanwhile, Andrew Diamond was eyeing the naked youths and licking his lips, snake-like and greedy.

Isis stepped on to the bridge and began to cross the scented water towards the central dais. She reached the larger of the two thrones, and sat down, allowing her slit robe to fall in graceful folds on either side of her knees, revealing an eternity of pale, gold-shimmering thigh and the teasing shadow of a golden pubic bush. She raised her hands and clapped them three times.

Delgado stepped forward, resplendent in the costume of a wealthy Greek merchant, and spoke:

'Let the King approach his consort.'

Trumpets and cymbals sounded, and the curtain swished back once again, this time revealing Delgado's chosen King – the exquisite Ibrahim. He betrayed not a trace of self-consciousness, for Madame LeCoeur's expertise had been put to good use. Besides, what healthy young man would refuse the offer of being paid to screw a sex-goddess like Joanna Königsberg? Ibrahim strode into the great hall with all the confidence of a true aristocrat, and stood before the assembled throng in all his glory: the King who must be wedded to the Earth Goddess in order to bring fertility to the land of Nile.

Ibrahim was naked, save for a cloak of golden cloth, embroidered with hieroglyphs and symbols of fertility. His dark, oiled flesh was fragrant with sweet oils and his muscles rippled as he walked. With each step he took, his thigh pushed forward and the cloak parted, revealing the glories within. Fully ten inches of dark, glistening manhood sprang out from a mass of black curls, and two plump and tempting bags of love-juice swung heavily between those vice-like thighs.

This young stallion brought gasps of astonishment, desire and envy from Winterbourne's clientele and whores alike. What better symbol of fertility than this superbly endowed young animal?

And the Master, too, was present and looked on in approval. Delgado had done well. If all went according to plan, tonight would bring a feast of sexual energy which would allow his powers to grow tenfold in the space of but a moment.

Ibrahim crossed the bridge and stepped on to the dais, kneeling before the Mother Goddess and planting the tenderest and most reverent of kisses on her feet, her ankles, her calves, her thighs . . . and at last burying his face deep in the fragrant golden bush in which nestled her regal cunnyhole.

The face of the goddess was radiant, transfigured with joyful lust; and she cradled her crown prince's noble head in her hands, stroking his neck, his forehead, raking her long painted nails lightly across his ebony shoulders.

And when he raised his head she smiled her approbation and beckoned to her High Priest: one of the 'eunuchs', shaven-headed and wearing only a belted loin cloth with a staff of office thrust into the belt. He crossed the bridge towards her, bearing a cushion covered with a black velvet cloth, spangled with magical symbols in gold and silver thread.

Isis removed the cloth to reveal two crowns: circlets of gold surmounted by golden serpents with ruby eyes and darting tongues. Nodding to the priest, she bowed her head and allowed him to place one of the two crowns on her head. Then she herself picked up the second crown and placed it on Ibrahim's dark curls, touching him lightly with the priest's staff on either shoulder.

'Stand, my King. Stand before me, that I may pay you your due homage,' she commanded him.

And Ibrahim stood before her, his breathtaking manhood springing forth satyr-like from the folds of his satin cape.

'Remove your robe,' she commanded him. And he obeyed with an alacrity which betrayed his eagerness to satisfy his own desires, as well as hers. She gave the satin cape to the High Priest, who crossed back over the bridge and joined the assembled throng.

The priests and priestesses (pretty young whores with shaven heads and skilled in the most lewd and enchanting versions of snake-dancing) set up a slow, hypnotic chant to the beat of a sacred temple drum:

'Isis, Isis, meet our need;
Suck the King and spill his seed.'

Gradually the guests began to join in with the chant as Isis inclined her head and pulled Ibrahim's immense erect prick into the satin cave of her hungry mouth. He gave an involuntary cry as he felt her lips close over him and her tongue darting its tip lewdly around his glans.

Lord knows, he was a good-looking lad and he'd had his share of sexual adventures since his arrival in England, but this girl was the best little cock-sucker he'd ever had, no doubt about it. And yet she looked so young! Where had she learned the tricks of this delectable trade? Not in a convent school, that was for sure. She had a mouth like a vacuum cleaner: he could feel her drawing his prick out, sucking it so hard that he could feel it growing even longer than its incredible ten inches. And those fingers! She had the devil in them, she must have. With her right hand, she was cradling and gently squeezing his balls, evidently savouring their heaviness and the promise of not one, but several great floods of spunk this auspicious night. They were growing, maturing fruits, ripening in her hand as though it were the baking African sun. He groaned and moved his feet apart to give her more room to play with him, and the onlookers gasped at the size and beauty of his twin fruits.

181

With her other hand, she was reaching around behind him, stroking and kneading his taut buttocks, revelling in the way they clenched and unclenched to the rhythm of her caresses.

And to think he was getting paid for this!

He could hear her breathing accelerating, becoming hoarse and laboured. She was getting excited, just from sucking his cock. He reached down and felt her titties and realised with a joyous start that she was indeed excited: her nipples were iron hard. He pinched them, cautiously at first, and was rewarded by a muffled groan of pleasure. He pinched harder, and felt her tremble, not the regal goddess but the mortal woman, subdued and subjugated by her own pleasure, by the power of his fingers. And that was in itself supremely erotic. He just knew he wasn't going to be able to hold out much longer . . . but then again, who cared? He was young and at his physical peak: there was plenty of spunk in his bollocks; plenty for everyone . . .

And then she retaliated with her own touch of power. Moving her left hand down a little, she began to insinuate her fingers into the crack between his buttocks. He almost blushed with embarrassment. No woman had ever done that to him before. It felt good, and he felt confused: was it OK for a straight guy to like having his backside played with? Oh, but it felt good!

Her caresses grew more incautious still, as she began to search for the secret pouting mouth of his arse. She found it and he gave a start of shameful pleasure as she began to titillate and torment it with her oh-so-expert fingers. In the frenzy of his excitement, he tweaked her nipples harder than ever, and she took this for a sign that he wanted her to be bolder still. Without the slightest compunction, she licked her index finger and wriggled it inside his virgin arse.

This was just too much for the newly crowned King, and his heavy balls prepared themselves to shoot their load of spunk.

'I'm going to come!' he gasped, powerless to stop himself.

And, just as his cock began to twitch and pour forth its abundant tribute, Isis pulled away from him and threw herself back on to her throne, pulling apart the two sides of her flimsy bodice and exposing her pert little breasts:

'Pour forth your seed upon me, my lord!'

And he obeyed, as readily as could be. Huge, pearly drops of semen fell on to the girl's face, her shoulders, her breasts, lodged in her navel and on the heavy pectoral she wore round her neck; and settled on her closed eyelids like a sacred kiss.

When he came to his senses, Ibrahim realised that – incredibly – he was ready to begin all over again. Whatever it was that that Frenchwoman had given him, it had certainly had an impressive effect on his libido. Normally it would have taken even him ten minutes or so to raise another good, strong, erection; but the drug he had taken, and the aromatic ointment he had had rubbed into his penis and testicles, had restored complete potency to him within less than a minute. He looked down at the girl and he wanted her, wanted her now. But carefully, he'd got to play by the rules Delgado had taught him, however stupid they might seem.

'Lie down, my King. Lie down upon the dais.' It

was not so much a command as an urgent entreaty. He looked into the young woman's face and saw the desperation of her lust, the longing for his body that was every bit as strong as his for hers.

The priests and priestesses set up a new chant:

'Fertile Isis, meet our need;
Ride the King, bring forth his seed.'

And they began once more to cast rose petals on to the platform, rose petals and little silver coins, their offerings for fertility and abundance. Soon, the glossy black body of Ibrahim, King for one night, was almost obscured by rose petals. Only his magnificent phallus rose forth out of the pink and white scented carpet, rearing its head as proudly and nobly as any pharaoh's. A black serpent, uncoiling and preparing to strike, about to spit forth its deadly venom.

Isis, already naked to the waist, began to remove the rest of her flimsy garments: the golden belt in the form of a serpent with its tail in its mouth, the ceremonial staff and flail and, finally, the remains of the thin, gauzy white robe which concealed so little and revealed so much.

Delgado gazed at her and desired her all over again. He recalled that first evening with her, when he had given her the trial of his tongue, and had felt her soft virgin lips sucking at his ripe manhood. And now she stood before him, unattainable once again, a golden icon at a carnival of lust, the glamorous pawn in a chess-game of desire. And he knew only too well that it was this very unattainability which made her so desirable, not only to Delgado but to the punters who had shelled out thousands for the chance to take part in this beautifully choreographed farce. Exquisite and exotic it might be, he mused, but it was none the less still just a story of cunt and cock. And his own cock was already dancing wildly to the tune.

Isis bent to pick up the flail, and was careful to part her legs just far enough to give the onlookers behind her a really tantalising view of her bum-crack and the golden tuft of her generous pubic bush. Those in front were treated to the spectacle of her firm young breasts, hanging down in front of her as she bent down, their tips as hard as iron but as pink and appetising as sugar-candy.

She picked up the flail – the implement used by the Egyptians to winnow their grain, and the symbol of the fertility of the Nile lands. She stroked it and ran the long tails across her pale, gold-dusted flesh, working the flail downwards until it passed across her cunt. Then she turned it round so that the long handle pointed upwards, and began to work it up inside her cunt, using the fingers of her left hand to hold her cunt lips apart whilst with the right she manipulated the handle of the flail into her secret crack.

The handle of the flail was thick – as thick as a woman's wrist – and it did not enter her easily. But her crack was well-lubricated with love-juices, with the offerings of Ibrahim's reverential tongue, and with the sweet oils which Madame LeCoeur had used to douche her cunt as a preparation for the rigours of a long night of unremitting copulation. With a sigh of immense satisfaction, she succeeded in pushing the handle into her cunt and groaned as she rammed it home as far as it would go.

The onlookers grew ever madder with desire for

this untouchable, inaccessible, miraculously lewd goddess of sex as she tormented them with her shameless rite of self-love. Ibrahim, her King for a night, lay panting at her feet, prick twitching desperately as he gazed up at her, masturbating with evident enjoyment and scorning those lust-crazed eyes, those yearning hands.

The handle of the flail moved in and out of her juicy cunt, glistening with drops of love-juice and the thongs of soft leather forming a trembling curtain between her smooth, pale thighs. With her left hand, she felt for her clitoris and began to rub it, at first gently and then harder and faster, bringing gasps of pleasure from between her full, painted lips.

Isis neared orgasm but did not give in to the overwhelming impulse to bring herself off. Oh no, this orgasm must be savoured, enjoyed and indulged to the full with her King's beautiful prick inside her. She longed to feel the spasms of his twitching prick as it disgorged its torrent of spunk into her young, yearning cunt as the Nile breaks its banks and floods the fertile land.

She now turned her attentions to the young King, Ibrahim, who still lay panting and inconsolable on the painted dais. Raising the flail in her right arm, she brought it down upon his torso, scattering the rose petals strewn across his body. A rain of blows followed, the soft leather thongs causing more pleasure than pain, and raising the rose petals in clouds like a pink-and-white snowstorm. Ibrahim twisted and turned under the flail, writhing in ecstasy as Isis brought the flail down skilfully upon his genitals. The delicate lashes irritated and excited the already-bursting flesh, and he wondered desperately if he could possibly hold out much longer. Her touch was so exquisite, her cruelty so welcome. He was her King, her consort, her devoted slave.

Isis saw that she had brought her King to the very brink of orgasm, and knew that it was time for them to be joined.

The hypnotic chanting began again:

'Mother Isis, meet our need;
Ride the King, bring forth his seed.'

The flail had now served its purpose, and Isis flung it into the crowd of onlookers, who scrabbled desperately on the rush-strewn ground for a touch or sight or scent of the sacred toy. Gavin de Lacy emerged, breathless, from the throng, bearing the trophy aloft in triumph. Lust-crazed, he grabbed the nearest slave-girl and threw her face-down on to the floor, tearing off the thin skirt which was her only covering, and wrenching her legs apart. With a savage cry of victory, he parted his own robes to reveal a vigorous and straining prick, which he rammed into the girl's slippery cunt, swiftly following with the thrust of the flail-handle up her unsuspecting arse. She howled with pain and pleasure, but all eyes were still fixed on the dais, where Isis and her king were about to consummate their union.

The mother-goddess knelt astride her consort and gently brushed away the remaining rose petals from his taut black belly. Then, in one swift movement, she slid smoothly on to his upstanding prick, and they roared in unison as they felt the glorious union of their divine loins.

'Let the festival begin!' cried Delgado as, slowly

and reverentially, the goddess Isis began to ride her sacrificial King . . .

It was like an explosion of lust, an unbridled celebration of life and lust in which no sexual act was too perverse, nothing forbidden; in which every smiling mouth was a safe haven for a hard prick or a dripping cunt; every tongue ready to entwine itself around heavy balls or to feast upon clitoris or tight bum-hole.

And the old gods and goddesses came forward out of the shadows, forward to join the celebrations.

'Do what thou wilt' shall be the whole of the law,' breathed Delgado, the unfamiliar words coming suddenly and inexplicably into his mind, as though bidden by the dark shadow that had come to dwell within him. And a cold hand laid itself upon his shoulder and the voice within him whispered to him again:

'Do what thou wilt . . .'

And he obeyed, driven with a surge of lust that surprised even him, the old libertine who had seen everything, done everything, had every woman – and man – he had ever desired. He forgot the infirmity of his twisted leg, and threw away his silver-topped cane. Grabbing a slave-girl around the waist, he began to tear away her clothes.

Under the cool shadows of fans held by four beautiful boys knelt Andrew Diamond, crouching on all fours and howling with bestial pleasure as he was buggered by Anubis the jackal god, their brutal rutting matching the wild rhythms of the temple drums.

Beside a fountain, filled with blood-red wine, three temple prostitutes with naked painted bodies were licking an aphrodisiac paste of honey and eastern spices from the penises of three well-known City stockbrokers.

And Harry Blomfeld was enthusiastically whipping a naked girl as she licked out the juicy cunt of a pretty Nubian slave.

Everywhere was a mass of heaving bodies, sticky with sweat, sweet oils, spices and semen. The flames of lust burned higher, higher still, and the lord of chaos looked on and was well pleased.

And all the while, the mother goddess was slowly fucking her King, riding his hot hard prick and rising towards the summit of their shared orgasm.

The Master gathered all his strength and once again entered the body of Delgado: it was a poor, flawed body, unworthy of such a great spirit, yet it welcomed him in as a kindred soul welcomes its long-awaited lord and master.

Delgado had done well. He was an excellent subject, an excellent servant. Inspired by the Master's soul-deep whispered commands, he had instructed the designer to produce exactly what the Master had wanted.

He exulted in this fleeting gift of sight, sound and sense. Impatient to feel warm flesh once again, he forgot the imperfections of Delgado's body and glorified in the taste and smell of the slave-girl. She was fragrant, young, juicy, appetising; and he fucked her with a joyous rage that shook Delgado's body and drew heartrending cries from the girl, bent-double with his prick threatening to split her poor little cunt in two.

But all the time his attentions were taken up by the

mother goddess on the dais, the false Isis sweating and straining as she rode her sacrificial beast to his innocent, unsuspecting doom. The sight of her awoke memories in him, memories that came flooding back after so many years of darkness and oblivion.

Memories of a chamber very much like this. A temple in ancient Egypt, long ago . . .

The torches flickered, casting fantastical shadows on the walls of the inner sanctum. On the altar, the massive block of crystal gleamed and sparkled, a thousand bright blades of light flashing from its many facets.

The young priestess knelt before the altar, her head bowed in reverence or terror, he could not tell. No matter, very soon she would have no more reason for either. For she was his chosen one, the one who was to become his Queen. The only one worthy to stand beside him throughout all eternity.

The choice had been easy. Alone among the priestesses of Isis, Sedet had shone out to him like the pure fire in the very heart of the crystal, the great magical crystal which had already bestowed immortality upon him, and which he was about to use to make her immortal, also. Already he had rendered her soul immortal: now all he had to do was to speak the incantation which would preserve her body from all age and decay.

Soon she would be godlike, as he was.

He recalled that first sighting of her: full-breasted and softly curving, eyes modestly cast down as she walked in procession with her sister priestesses towards the temple of Isis, there to be welcomed by the High Priest, the Master himself.

He saw her, and desired her immediately, irresistibly. He had long sought a woman worthy of him in mind, body and soul, and as soon as he saw her he knew he had at last found her.

'I want you, little temple slut.' He sent the thought rushing through the ether and into her mind, and to his immense joy she looked up at him, suddenly, frightened like a cornered deer, yet fascinated, excited, alive. She had heard that thought, and immediately he heard her own silent reply:

'What is it that you want of me, O Master? I am but a simple priestess . . .'

'I want all of you. I want your body and soul. I want to stick my prick into your tight little cunt and make you scream with pleasure. I want to fuck your arse and your mouth and your big firm tits. I want to fuck you until you beg for mercy, and cry for more. And more still: I want to take you and make you my immortal Queen, little temple whore.'

'I do not understand.'

'You understand me well enough. And the rest, you shall understand later. You will have many centuries in which to learn to understand.'

'How is it that you can speak to me through my mind, without a sound, with only thoughts?'

'How is it that you can understand me when I speak to you in thoughts? Do not question, child. Come to me in the inner sanctum of the temple tonight, at moonrise. I shall be waiting for you.'

And he had waited for her, and had feared that she might not come. He, the Master, who had solved the great mysteries, who had conquered life and death and become greater than either or both: he had been afraid because he knew that she was the one, and

191

without her his triumph would be incomplete. He waited in the darkness for a long time, with the crystal-bladed dagger and the ring of power, and began to wonder if his wait would be in vain . . .

But she came to him, trembling for cold and fear, and she fell upon her knees and begged him to have mercy. He showed her none, forcing her to strip naked in the darkness and cold of the temple, and making her kneel before him and suck his cock. Oh, it had felt so good, that timid little tongue on his world-weary prick – fresh and young and vibrant, and so worthy of immortality. And as she squeezed his balls and brought him to orgasm, he had thrown back his head and laughed for the sheer joy of knowing that he would be able to feel like this forever, because he had joined the ranks of the immortals and would never grow old.

Ruthlessly, he had silenced her terrified protests and forced her to lie down on the altar of Isis, pulling apart her slender, silken thighs and placing his fingers on her clitoris. She had gasped as he began to caress her, awakening desires which she had never dreamed she had. Her cunt became a brooklet, a stream, a mighty river as he pressed upon her hard little button and brought her to a raging, soul-rending orgasm.

Afterwards, he had held her down on the cold stone altar and forced her to listen to him:

'Child, you are beautiful.'

'You are very gracious, O Master.'

'Do you not fear growing old and ugly?'

'Of course . . . but is that not the lot of every man and woman?'

'It need not be, child. It is not my lot.'

'How can that be?'

'See, child. Mark well what you see and know that it is true.' And the Master took up the crystal dagger with the silver hilt. It flashed fire as he held it aloft for a moment before plunging it deep into his heart. Sedet screamed and tried to turn her head away, but he held her fast, forcing her to look at him.

Smiling, he pulled the dagger from his chest, and there was blood on the crystal blade. But within seconds the wound had disappeared, had healed as though it had never been there at all.

Sedet gasped, and stretched out her hand in disbelief, to touch the place where the mortal would had been.

'You see, my child. Death is but an illusion which man can conquer. I alone have conquered it. None else has the secret of immortality. But I have chosen you to share my glory with me. Tonight, child, you shall become immortal.'

He raised her up and made her stand before him. She looked up into his eyes, still questioning but full of eagerness now.

'Child, I have chosen you and you shall be my worthy consort, my immortal Queen,' explained the Master. 'You shall have powers beyond your wildest dreams: you shall have immense sexual power to enslave all men and feed upon their energies as you copulate with them; these energies will make you stronger, and feed your powers. Once you have gained physical immortality, you shall have the power to travel through time and space, to change your form, to grant life and death, to impart immortality to others.

'Child, with me you shall share power and dominion over all the earth. Nations shall bow down before

Valentina Cilescu

us. The unworthy shall be enslaved to feed our
needs and desires. And our empire of immortals
shall endure for all time. Now, come: and I shall
grant your flesh immortality.'

He bade her kneel before the altar, her small white
hands laid upon the surface of the crystal, and began
the incantation.

As he spoke the words of power, Sedet began to
feel a change coming over her, a weakness as though
all her mortal self were being absorbed by the great
block of crystal. It felt no longer cold under her
hands, but warm and throbbing with a mysterious
life that emanated from the heart of fire burning
deep within it.

As he ended the spell, he touched the crystal with
the tip of the ceremonial dagger, and Sedet felt a
tremendous surge of power rushing back into her
body, washing away the woman she had been. But
it was a surge not of clear bright light, but of dark
energy, dark power that made her scream out with
the terror and the realisation. At that second, she
saw in her mind's eye a vision of her former self:
warm-blooded, vibrant, fresh and young; and of
herself as she would henceforth be: a creature of
crystal, as hard-hearted as the stone itself, as dark as
a crystal when no light shines upon it, enduring not
as a living, breathing thing but as a creature hovering
for eternity between the worlds of the living and the
dead, driven to feed on the energies and blood of
mortals in order to continue its cursed existence.

'No!' she cried, as the dark force surged through
her veins, and the coldness clutched at her heart.

But it was too late. The transformation could not
be stopped now – and already Sedet felt her mind

clouding, adapting, becoming eager now for the life of evil she must henceforth lead.

The Master spoke again, in a voice full of excitement and desire:

'Come, child, and be joined with me as my immortal Queen.'

He picked her up, frail and unresisting in his arms, and laid her once again upon the altar of great Isis. And he lay on top of her, sliding his hard penis inside her so that she shuddered with pleasure, and riding her hard like a thoroughbred filly. Gradually she began to move, to meet his thrusts with the upward tilt of her pelvis, to thrust back and grind her pubis against his, accepting his immortal manhood with eagerness.

Her cunt began to pulsate about his stiff prick, like a tight and greedy mouth, hot and wet and urging him on to ever-greater ecstasy. And as they fucked, their minds were also joined, filled with the vision of the greatness they would share when their empire of lust had spread across the whole wide world. The aphrodisiac of power, glimpsed and savoured, brought them rapidly to the brink of ecstasy and eternity . . .

At the moment of orgasm, the Master threw himself forward, and she thought for a moment that he would kiss her. But instead he lunged for her throat, sinking wickedly sharp teeth into her golden flesh. She cried out in mingled pain and ecstasy as her cunt-juices flowed and the blood spurted out and began to trickle down her neck.

And she knew in that moment that she had received not only the touch of immortality, but the kiss of death.

'Now, child, your spirit is immortal,' whispered the Master. 'My kiss on your throat has released your mortality with your blood, and your soul cannot be destroyed. Arise, my Queen, my empress, my consort: for soon, very soon, we shall inherit our realm.'

As the Master used Delgado's body and that of the slave-girl, he gazed again upon the false Isis and recalled, with a pang of guilt and rage, the events which had followed the triumphal crowning of his immortal Queen.

Secrecy had been vital in those early days. Move with stealth, build up power in secret before the Way could spread like a deadly virus throughout the world, infecting and transforming all in its path. A little death, such a little death, and their victims would be freed for ever from the fear of old age and mortality. Their total servitude to the Master seemed a tiny price to pay for the gift of eternal existence.

In the long run, they would see his point of view. They would be grateful to him.

At first, they contented themselves with experiments to test the limits of their powers. They discovered, to their great joy, that they could cloud the minds of men and women, provoke an insatiable sexual need, unbridled lust from which they, in turn, could feed. For they needed and craved these powerful sexual energies in order to grow in power. How they had laughed as they drove their victims to wild frenzies of copulation. How they sighed with pleasure as they felt their strength grow, and joined their own immortal loins in the great rites of power.

And then, growing bolder, they had begun to initiate others into the Way: bewitching them, copulating with them, biting their throats and releasing their mortality so that they might have the honour of serving the Master and his Queen throughout eternity. Only a very few victims, for fear of discovery. For the process did not always go quite according to plan. Sometimes the preparation was incorrect, or the outpouring of blood too great . . . Sometimes, the victim died.

Inevitably, they began to arouse suspicions, hostility, fear. And Sedet was too bold, too indiscreet. He felt the agony clutch at his heart – the heart he had believed invulnerable to the mortal emotions of love and grief and guilt – as he remembered his Queen's terrible fate.

It happened one starry night, as Sedet was initiating a victim – a priest of Amun-Ra whose mind she had clouded and whose body she had bewitched. He would be a useful slave for the Master's cause. She had lured him, unbeknown to the Master, to the inner sanctum of the Temple of Isis, and was fucking him on the stone floor, naked save for the powerful crystal which she wore perpetually on a golden chain around her neck.

As the rite neared its consummation, the Master awoke from a restless slumber and saw in his mind's eye what was happening. It was a trap. He saw the approaching doom and – knowing he could not reach the temple in time to save her – tried to telepath a warning message to his Queen. But her mind was too full of the exultation of victorious lust to hear his urgent commands until it was too late.

The priest-magicians broke in and surrounded her.

Laughing, mocking them, she had believed she was invulnerable; that no mortal could harm her. But they had been watching her, had discovered a little of the secrets of her immortality. And, knowing that it was impossible to kill her, they had learned the way to trap her and disable her magical powers through their own magical means. More than that, they craved the secrets of eternal life.

They could not kill Sedet, but they could hurt her. Protected by their own magic from her telepathic powers, they tortured her for many hours. But she would not reveal the truth which they craved, the betrayal which might have saved her.

Loyal to the end, she denied absolutely that the Master had anything to do with the 'conspiracy'. He was a High Priest and no more. She alone had discovered the secret of immortality. She protected him and he, poor coward, had not dared to intervene, forcing himself to believe in his desperation that he would be able to rescue her later, when their enemies had forgotten about her.

And so Sedet went to her doom alone: brutally violated by a dozen lecherous priests; humiliated and scorned; taken alive and bound in the linen bands of a corpse, then placed in a sarcophagus and bound to her captivity by magic. Alone. Still living, but helpless.

This much he had learned, but no more. Too late, the Master realised that his enemies were stronger than he had thought. The priest-magicians had not only hidden his Queen from him in some faraway place: they had also hidden her from him by sorcery, casting a dark curtain about her through which the Master could not see, could not reach her . . .

Except that, from time to time, he heard her faraway voice crying to him across the darkness, alone, helpless, not knowing where she was.

No words; no sign of where he might find her. For all he could hear was the screaming.

As soon as he learned this, the Master had fled Egypt, lest he suffer the same fate. But he had not given up. Throughout the centuries and millenia to come, he would search the world and never give up until he found the one he had chosen to be his Queen. She alone had refused to betray him. None other would ever stand beside him at the head of his evil empire.

And now he, himself, was trapped. Soon, soon, he must break out of his crystal prison and wreak his revenge upon a world which had thought it could destroy him.

Bitter and crazed with lust, the Master urged Delgado's body towards its orgasm, and – as he felt the spunk rising up his shaft – sank his teeth into the back of the slave-girl's neck. Her back arched and she groaned beneath the yoke as she yielded to the dark force of lust and passed through the threshold of fear into the world of the undead.

Still panting, the Master looked up. The surge of sexual energy from the orgy had strengthened his powers, but this brief time of freedom was ending; already he could feel the link with Delgado's body dissolving, the body in the crystal calling him back to endure more darkness, more blindness, more helplessness. When, when would it end? A fury of envy swept over him, and he craved his revenge.

The girl lay insensible beneath him. He climbed

off her and forgot about her immediately – a broken toy, holding no further interest for him. The orgy was still raging about him, twos and threes of naked bodies, copulating frenetically, fanatically, like creatures from some medieval bestiary. No-one noticed him as he staggered weakly towards the dais and raised his hand towards the false Isis, commanding her attention.

Isis turned and looked into his eyes, still astride the writhing form of Ibrahim. She understood what the Master wanted, and raised herself off Ibrahim's massive prick, in spite of his groans of protest. Kneeling between his muscular thighs, she began to caress the mighty prick, and he relaxed and sighed with pleasure as she used her velvety tongue to toy with the well-lubricated glans.

Within a few moments he came, spurting his abundant seed all over belly and loins, and roaring with the immense pleasure granted him by his magnificent body.

Smiling grimly, the Master raised his hand again and gazed deep into the eyes of his false Isis. She returned his smile and, obedient to the last, sank her teeth into Ibrahim's thigh, biting through the artery and laughing like a madwoman as the scarlet blood fountained out of the wound and cascaded over her white flesh like a second skin.

Droplets of blood sprayed on to naked faces and bodies, and somewhere in the throng of copulating bodies a woman screamed, and the whole tableau froze to sudden silent stillness.

'Oh my God,' gasped Delgado, suddenly coming back to his own self as the Master's mocking presence left him. 'What are we going to do now?' And then he remembered, with a sigh of relief, that a careful instinct had made him choose Ibrahim precisely because he was expendable. A lucky decision.

Poor Ibrahim, the sacrificial victim, scarcely had time to realise what was happening to him, as he drifted away within moments into unconsciousness, oblivion, utter darkness.

Madame LeCoeur looked puzzled as she knocked on the door of Delgado's office.

'Can I have a word?'

'What's up?'

'I can't understand it. That body we put in the storeroom . . .'

'What about it?'

'Well, you'll never believe this, but . . . it's disappeared.'

11: Rasputin

One of the most popular diversions at Winterbourne was the Imperial Russian room, which catered above all for the tastes of some of the house's discerning female clientele. Delgado was delighted with the success of his attempts to bring ladies of taste and discernment to Winterbourne.

All in all, the experiment had been a great success. Already he had attracted the butter-wouldn't-melt children's TV presenter Maggie Tinsworth (sophisticated dyke and leather fetishist – whatever would the parents say?); a couple of bored duchesses with gay husbands; Arianna Hadjopoulos, the classical percussionist with a shoe fetish; and a bevy of well-connected women who wanted their connections lubricated in style.

Tonight, the Russian room was to be dedicated to the pleasure of a real-life princess, no less. Princess Marie-Louise of Lichtenstein claimed descent back to the Romanovs, and was quite obsessed with the belief that she was the reincarnation of the ill-fated Czarina Alexandra. Added to which she had a strong masochistic streak – all of which made for great visual entertainment; so good that Delgado had arranged for a select clientele of discerning voyeurs to pay a little extra for their tickets and watch the whole spectacle from the next room, through the two-way mirror he had so thoughtfully provided for just such an eventuality.

He made sure that his six 'special guests' were safely installed in the adjoining room before he made the final preparations for the evening's Russian frolics. Couldn't risk his princess getting wind of the fact that she was being made a spectacle of . . .

The Russian room was decorated to represent the Czarina's bedroom in one of the imperial winter palaces: opulent brocades and ornate hand-woven carpets, silks and tapestries. The central feature was a huge four-poster bed with a rich red and gold canopy and the imperial crest carved at the head of the bed. Beside it stood a carved wooden prie-dieu, worn smooth from the pressure of penitential knees, and with attachments for straps and belts so that the penitent could be secured to the prie-dieu and not escape the full wrath of the chastiser. The room was filled with religious relics and the scent of incense hung heavy on the still, silent air. Dimmed oil-lamps lit the gloom with a flickering, ghostly light. A fire burned low in the hearth. There was an atmosphere of tension, of expectancy.

The door opened and the Princess Marie-Louise entered, eyes bright with anticipation but lowered modestly to maintain the charade. She was richly dressed as the Czarina, and looked every inch the part: tight-waisted in a boned corset which pushed up her breasts and displayed their bounty at the low-cut neckline of her watered silk gown. The watchers in the next room had noted the fine white swell of her breasts and were already unzipping their trousers and teasing their pricks into enthusiastic rigidity.

Marie-Louise – or should it be Alexandra? – sat down at the dressing-table and called for her maid. A pretty girl in a maid's uniform entered, and began to take down and brush her hair. It was long, dark and glossy, and hung in opulent waves to her slender waist.

At that moment, the door burst open and a dark, powerfully built figure thundered into the room. He was tall, unkempt, with a wild look in his eye: a very fair representation of Rasputin, in fact.

Marie-Louise looked up with fear in her eyes . . . fear, and another emotion, a troubled, turbulent lust that mingled the desire for pleasure with the desire for pain.

'I am most displeased with you, Empress,' thundered the wild-eyed monk, not at all cowed by the grandeur of the scene or the regal presence before him. 'You have been neglecting your spiritual purity. If you do not purge yourself of sin, how can you expect your son to become well again? Will you not listen to my teachings?'

Marie-Louise fell to her knees, hands clasped in a gesture of exaggerated humility:

'Forgive me, Father – it is so hard for me . . . tell me what I must do to make amends . . .'

In response, the wild-eyed monk grabbed her by the arm, squeezing the fragile flesh until she cried out and leaving red marks that would soon turn into garish bruises. He dragged her across the room towards the prie-dieu, forcing her to kneel upon it and attaching her wrists to the top with leather thongs. She was panting hoarsely, not entirely with fear . . .

'Mortification of the flesh!' cried Rasputin. 'That

is the only way to achieve purity of the soul.' And he grabbed at the costly fabric of her dress and ripped it from her delicate back. Then he took a knife from his belt and slit the stay-laces that held her sweet flesh imprisoned in her corsets. The watchers gasped with pleasure and began to wank their turgid pricks enthusiastically.

A shadow within a shadow, darkness within darkness, lurked in the corner of the room. The Master was again playing the spectre at the feast, looking on with approval and preparing to join in the game. Slowly, imperceptibly, he drew nearer and entered the body of the false Rasputin, urging on his host to ever-greater obscenities, worthy of the man he represented. He tore away the dress and the corset, to reveal pure silk knee-length bloomers, open at the crotch, and a curious, rough garment – a sort of bodice which covered the Czarina's torso from shoulder to waist.

With a grunt of satisfaction, Rasputin slit away the hair shirt to reveal the poor mortified flesh beneath, sliding his rough, dirty hands around to the front of her body to give himself the extreme satisfaction of causing her pain: rubbing his calloused skin mercilessly across her tortured flesh, and enjoying the sound of her pitiful little cries of distress. The distress which, he knew only too well, brought her sexual desire to fever-pitch.

'Harlot!' he cried. 'You mortify your flesh and still my touch provokes lewd thoughts in you.'

'What is my punishment, Father? I will accept anything you impose upon me, truly I will.'

'Since you crave pain, then pain you shall have!' he replied, and he ran the point of his knife down the line of her spine, very lightly but just hard enough to bring beads of bright blood leaping to the surface of her skin. 'But first, harlot, you shall serve my pleasure and in so doing, commit a mortal sin. For, as I have taught you, it is only through sin that we can feel remorse and so attain redemption.'

He untied the girdle about his waist, and slipped off his filthy robes above his head. Underneath, he was dirty and smelt disgusting. His massive cock reeked and he was crawling with lice. Smiling grimly, he walked around to the front of the prie-dieu and lifted up the Czarina's head, enjoying the look of terror and disgust in her eyes.

With two of his fat, grubby fingers, he forced her lips apart and – without further ado – rammed home his cock, well-nigh suffocating her as it slid down her throat. He ignored her stifled cries, and provoked a little more of the pain which so gratified them both, by leaning down and pinching her nipples very hard, between finger and thumb. Then he took his cord belt and wound it in a figure-of-eight pattern around her breasts, pulling it so tight that they stood out from her chest like twin turrets, and she gasped with pain as the rough hempen cord cut into her already-bruised and blistered flesh.

When he had amused himself with her to his – and the Master's – satisfaction, he emptied himself into her mouth and forced her to swallow his jism, though it almost choked her and her stomach heaved with nausea. Then he walked behind her again and took the long, leather whip from the wall. Raising it above her shuddering back, he cried out:

'Prepare to accept your penance, harlot!'

The Master was enjoying the vigour of the man's

huge, bear-like body but despised his poor intellect. The fellow had clearly been chosen for his physical attributes, not the quality of his mind – which made of him a sadly flawed representation of the real Rasputin, for that man had been far more than he had seemed – a fact which nobody knew better than the Master . . .

Over the centuries, the Master had moved like a black shadow across the face of the earth, never staying too long in one place, changing his identity frequently: his constant obsession the search for his chosen queen, the priestess Sedet. Although from time to time he heard her cries of distress across the miles, across the centuries, he was no nearer to finding her than he had been when he started.

Early in 1907, he swept like a whirlwind into the Court of Czar Nicholas of all the Russias, bewitched the Czarina with the power of his black soul, and became the most powerful man in all Imperial Russia. Yes, the filthy, lice-ridden vagabond became more powerful than the Czar himself, who did not even realise that his own Czarina was being screwed nightly by her beloved Father Rasputin.

Little did the Czarina realise that her son's haemophilia derived neither from God nor nature, but from the Master's own dark intent. His power to work 'miracles' over the child had blinded the foolish woman to the truth: that he had made the child ill in the first place. And the energies he was able to suck out of the child through the bloodletting were making him stronger and stronger.

He had bewitched women in every village in Eastern Europe, and many had become first his mistresses and then his victims. They, in turn, had initiated their husbands and lovers. Soon, very soon, the ranks of the evil undead would become a mighty host, invincible and eternal. And when at last the Czarina fell victim to his evil kiss of death, he had truly believed that the hour of his dominion was at hand: the hour when he would call upon his mighty host to follow him to glory.

It happened one wintry evening when a blizzard was raging outside the winter palace, and the Master was at last alone with the Czarina, in her apartments.

'Tell me, great teacher, how can I redeem my poor, unclean soul and attain the bliss of eternal life?'

'Only through sin, remorse and penitence, as I have told you, Czarina Alexandra.'

'But I do not understand. I am not clever. Your teachings are too complex for me. Will you not show me the true path, Father Rasputin?'

And she had gazed into his eyes as though to tell him: I know exactly what you wish to teach me, and I wish to be your willing pupil. I wish you to take me and mould me and punish me and fuck me . . .

'If you will put yourself in my hands, Czarina . . . ?'

'I swear it.'

'Then you must obey my every command.'

He had begun her torment with a savage glee. It felt good to topple icons, to ridicule these empires of poor mortals who called themselves kings and princes.

He looked out into the freezing night, and laughed to himself for the sheer joy of it. And then he stripped off her shawl and commanded her:

'I wish you to walk, barefoot and naked, across the rose garden to the private chapel.'

She gazed at him with terror in her eyes:

'But Father Rasputin, the earth freezes, there is a blizzard, I will die. And if someone should see me . . .'

He silenced her with a look from his fiery eyes. Hypnotised by their blazing depths, Czarina Alexandra believed that she was gazing upon the purifying fire of holiness, and not the beckoning fires of Hell . . .

She stripped off before him, and he felt his prick leap to instant attention at the mature beauty of her body – her underused body, he thought to himself. Here is a woman who has lived too gently, too tentatively; who has seen far too little of life. I shall take it upon me to complete her education.

'Now go!' he commanded, opening wide the French doors of the drawing room and pointing towards the private chapel, some fifty yards away in the pitch darkness and driving snow. The wind's icy blast sent the curtains billowing inwards, and stinging clouds of snowflakes attacked the Czarina's poor naked body. She fell to her knees, weeping, and implored her tormentor:

'No, please, anything but that . . .'

'You swore a sacred oath. Now go, I command you.'

And, sobbing her heart out, she stepped tentatively into the snow, which was crisp and powdery beneath her naked feet. It was over a foot deep, and she cried out with agony as the cold attacked her legs and the wind-borne snowflakes whipped her martyred flesh. The Master walked before her, bearing a lantern to light her way; relishing her every sob and laughing inwardly each time she stumbled and fell in the snow.

When at last she stumbled into the chapel, she was blue with cold and shivering uncontrollably. She fell at his feet and implored him to help her.

'Have no fear: I shall warm your flesh, my Czarina,' he replied. And he began to whip her with such ferocity that the blood did indeed begin to return to her poor frozen flesh, drawing patterns of scarlet and livid blue-white on her noble skin.

Wrenching her legs apart, he began to whip her inner thighs and pubis, being careful to strike her just hard enough to cause an agreeable mingling of pleasure and pain.

'Mortification of the flesh!' he roared. 'Surrender yourself utterly to the shame, to the humiliation. Surrender all self-pride and rise towards redemption.'

And then he lay upon her and thrust his beautiful, proud prick into her aristocratic cunt. It slid in like a knife into butter, for the Czarina's crack was well-oiled. He had calculated well: the slut enjoyed a little rough handling.

She fucked clumsily at first, as though she had no idea what to do; and the Master guessed that she was more accustomed to lying passively on her back than to giving a man a good time. So he rolled over on to his back, taking her with him, and forced her to take the active role.

'Ride me, harlot,' he commanded. 'Ride me as though I were a fine stallion from the Czar's Imperial stables.' And he grabbed hold of her waist and pushed her up and down on his prick, showing her how it was done. He took hold of her right hand and made her squeeze his balls, and run her finger forwards through the hot, hairy crack between bollocks and arse. She learned quickly, and her explorations began to give him pleasure.

Certainly she was a fine woman: mature in the sense of ripe, juicy – and almost virginal in her inexperience and docility. Revelling not only in the pleasure she was giving him, but in the ecstasy of total control, he reached upwards and searched out her clitty. She gasped as his fingers found her love-button, and from the look of amazed delight on her face he guessed that she had no knowledge of her own body. No-one had ever taught her the little games that bring ecstasy.

He stroked her skilfully, and ensured that, as he shot his own load into her cunt, she climbed up to the sunny summit of her own orgasm, drenching his prick with clear love-juice at the very moment that it inundated her cunt with spunk.

She slumped forward on to his chest, weeping with ecstasy; and he took advantage of the opportunity to nuzzle into the crook of her neck.

She scarcely noticed his sharp teeth sinking into her flesh.

For ten years, Grigori Rasputin held sway. The Czarina Alexandra proved an insatiable lover, an invaluable ally, and her son a useful source of blood and energies upon which the Master could feed. Gradually, discreetly, the circle of the undead began to widen. And he had all the time in the world . . .

But the Great War came, and with it a decline in fortunes. People grew suspicious of the filthy, wild-eyed priest who had so much control over their Czarina, and who was more famous for his lechery than his piety.

The end of Grigori Rasputin came one night in 1916, when he unwisely accepted an invitation to a drinking party with some junior army officers. They got him drunk; spiked his drink with deadly poisons – which of course had no effect; stabbed him; shot him and finally drowned him. For some reason, he simply would not die . . .

And when they were satisfied that he was dead, they cut off his magnificent cock and put it in an ornate box. A gift for the Czar, they laughed, as they threw his mutilated body into the river.

The Master smiled to himself as he recalled the truth of that dark night. For what history did not recall was that, the next morning, not only Rasputin's body but his severed cock had disappeared.

And it and its owner were reunited and merrily on the road to Sicily, there to assume a new identity and join the disciples of an interesting young man known as Aleister Crowley . . .

The false Czarina writhed about under the lash and cried out for mercy, though her cunt was dripping with juice and she was wriggling her thighs ever wider apart, and thrusting out her buttocks to welcome the bite of the whip.

The Master, suddenly weary of this game, of this trivial masochist and her unintelligent torturer, was overcome with a wave of uncontrollable rage, which communicated itself to the false Rasputin. With a roar of demonic pleasure, he dropped the whip and placed his hands about Marie-Louise's throat, despising her because she, like himself, was stupid and unworthy to join the ranks of the undead.

He squeezed tighter and tighter, and her eyes began to bulge out of her head. When at last the onlookers managed to prise his fingers away from her throat, she fell to the ground half-unconscious and raving, but smiling the secret smile of the masochist for whom the only real pleasure is the apprehension of the approach of death.

With a final roar of rage and hatred, the Master picked up one of the Louis XIV chairs and flung it through the two-way mirror, showering the voyeurs with broken glass and interrupting the progress of more than one orgasm.

When at last the Master left the body of the false Rasputin, he was angry and dissatisfied, and bent on revenge. If the girl Mara Fleming did not come to him soon, of her own free will, then he must ensure that she would come by other, more devious means.

Trapped once again in the bricked-up cellar, chained to the useless body which refused to let his spirit go free, the Master raged in his frustration and plotted a way to recover both his greatness and his Queen.

12: Berchtesgaden

She was a big girl: Nordic-looking, tall, with an impressive bust. She was also clad in skin-tight black leather and wore swastikas on what passed for a uniform. It was hardly standard issue. Two circular zips on the front of the clinging bodice indicated the quick and easy way to the alluring playground of her mountainous breasts, whilst another zip ran between her legs, from navel to coccyx, signposting the entrance to her pleasure-palace.

Not that these facilities were available just for the taking. Ilse was an extremely assertive young woman, who believed in strict corrective measures for those of her clients who offended her. And they all invariably did. At this very moment, she was grinding her spiky-heeled boot into the naked upturned backside of a well-known member of the General Synod. He was clearly appreciating her firm stand on matters ecclesiastical.

'Englischer Schweinhund!' growled Ilse with predictable Teutonic wrath.

'Yes, yes, punish me! I've been so wicked . . .' whined her wriggling prey, thrusting his pimply white arse Heavenwards for the satisfaction of the pain she would graciously inflict upon him.

She did not disappoint him: tossing back her

ash-blonde mane, Ilse flipped the trembling cleric over on to his back as easily as if he were a pancake, and began to walk over the prostrate body of her willing victim, making sure that her not-inconsiderable weight lingered longest on his softest and most sensitive parts. And oh! How he groaned and screamed with the exquisite pain of feeling his flabby testicles being ground beneath the eager heels of this latter-day Valkyrie.

In fact, it hurt so much that he came, shuddering, all over the spotless polished surface of her spike-heeled jackboots.

With a mighty roar of rage, the leather-clad torturess took the bullwhip from her belt and swung it down upon her victim's defenceless belly. The first blow was so excruciating that he felt his prick beginning to stiffen again already . . .

The atmosphere was heavy, and the air stifling. It smelt of piss and shit and blood and fear. The room was gloomily lit by a single 40-watt bulb, fly-specked and dusty, which hung from a bare flex in the centre of the ceiling. Nazi flags flanked the heavy dungeon door with its tiny grille and iron-studded surface. Beside the banners stood men in SS uniform, armed and jackbooted and ready for anything. The room was bare of all humanity and comfort: in the centre stood a rickety wooden table and two chairs, whilst one wall was lined with an array of fearsome-looking instruments of torture: whips, thumbscrews, mana-cles . . . And underneath stood a narrow wooden bed with attachments for hands and feet. It was no use asking to be excused: no-one left this room before Ilse had finished with them.

The Reichskammer was one of the most popular

rooms at Winterbourne, combining the very worst in aesthetic taste with the very best in sado-masochism. The Third Reich held a perverse fascination for some of Delgado's most influential clients – particularly churchmen, MPs and ex-public schoolboys, he mused idly as he stood guard in the corner, immaculately dressed in the full uniform of an SS corporal, circa 1943. He liked to get these little details right: it gave him such job satisfaction to know that his customers were happy.

The Reichskammer was decked out as an interrogation room, in which 'victims' could be stripped, abused, tortured . . . or whatever turned them on. One of Delgado's most regular clients, a merchant banker called Piers Wellesley, was obsessed with the life and perversions of Adolf Hitler; and every time he visited Winterbourne, he insisted that one of Delgado's German whores dress up as Eva Braun, serve him herb tea from a silver tray, and then jab his balls with a darning needle.

Each to his own, thought Delgado – musing pleasurably on the last time that adorable half-caste Perdita had lashed his backside. He could understand the need for the unusual, the corrupt, the unacceptable.

Indeed, ever since Winterbourne had opened and he had felt the protecting presence in his head, the dark but avuncular hand on his shoulder, his own tastes for the unusual had been sharpened. These days, his appetite for sex of all kinds seemed inexhaustible – even after a night-long marathon of screwing and fellating, even after orgies that lasted days and left him feeling more drained than he could have believed possible, Delgado's prick would leap

defiantly to attention and fill his restless sleep with
images of luscious bodies, glistening orifices, and
fountaining spunk . . .

The Master's spirit slipped silently into Delgado's
body and remained quietly within him, simply watching, waiting, remembering. He looked contemptuously upon the charade and recalled a time, not so
very long ago, when he had been a part of the world
so crudely parodied within this room: those glorious
days when he had last walked the earth; when he
had believed that, at long last, he was coming into
his kingdom.

Ilse's willing victim groaned with pleasure as she
strapped him down to the rack and began to turn the
handle, stretching muscles and joints and tendons to
screaming-point. Then she placed her hand upon her
pubis and began to unzip her pleasure-palace . . .

Early-morning light warmed the stones of the ancient
stronghold, and flooded the wooded valley below
with a golden wash of sunshine. Eager fingers of sunlight played in the girl's soft brown hair and sparkled
in her eyes as she ran and turned exuberant cart-
wheels on the terrace of the mountain-top retreat.
Her body was lithe and slender, with fine muscle-tone
and the golden, glowing skin of a healthy young
peasant girl.

She gave a final backflip and landed adroitly on
both feet, panting and laughing. Looking towards
her lover, she called out:

'*Liebchen*, will breakfast be ready soon? I'm so
hungry, I could eat an ox!'

The Führer was displeased. The war in the East
was going badly. His indigestion was troubling him.

And Eva Braun was a stupid young woman who was beginning to get on his nerves. Only those inexhaustible golden thighs had thus far saved her from the firing-squad.

The only bright light on the horizon was that Goebbels had come up with something – a surprise, he had said. Something that would help his Führer to smite his enemies into the ground and allow the German jackboot to stamp upon the faces of the whole world. But this had better be good: he was tired of phoneys, and he was not a patient man.

'*Komm herein*,' he commanded Eva, who scampered to his side. 'You will suck me off before breakfast.'

Hitler felt an instant affinity with this new man, this strange, dark-haired man with eyes that burned with all the ferocity of the nether fires of Hell. This man who wore strangely outdated clothes and affected a long black velvet cape. And what's more, he knew what attracted him to this bizarre itinerant sorcerer. He could see at a glance that the man was unspeakably evil.

And that filled him with the indispensable glow of reassurance.

'You are an experienced sorcerer?'

'I refined my art in the Sicilian temple of the great Aleister Crowley,' replied the Master with an imperceptible smile – omitting to mention that he had in fact taught Crowley all he knew. And that he personally had initiated many of Crowley's more delectable female followers into the ranks of the undead.

'You have the gift of sight?'

'I have the power to see the future and the past, and to see across great distances and into the minds of your friends and enemies.'

'Then I command you to look into my mind and tell me what you see there.'

The Master laid his hands upon the Führer's forehead and thought deeply for a moment.

'I would rather not speak before these other people, lest I cause you embarrassment, mein Führer.'

Intrigued, Hitler dismissed his henchmen to the corridor outside his study, and when the door had been closed and bolted behind them, he turned his attentions once again to the Master, waiting patiently with hands folded and eyes downcast.

'Now tell me: what thoughts did you read in my mind?'

'I read this: that you crave power and wish me to give you the information that will win this war for you . . .'

'Any fool could tell me that. And the rest . . . ?'

'I read also that you have a great and growing sexual desire: that you are thinking of Eva Braun and her taut buttocks, which you find so so delightful to spill your seed upon . . .'

The Führer's face was crimson with fury:

'How dare you! How dare you imply such things. I could have you led outside and shot!'

'For telling the truth, mein Führer? So you do not wish for a true seer, but only one who tells you what you wish to hear?'

'Continue,' replied the Führer, icily.

'And I read this: that you also desire my body. That you would very much like me to remove my clothes, suck your penis until you achieve erection, then bend over your desk and invite you to commit an act of sodomy with me.'

Silence.

'I am right, am I not?' And the Master threw off his cloak and began to unbutton his trousers. His penis was long, stiff and inviting, and the Führer felt a sudden surge of desire. This strange, dark man had been right: he did desire him, did want to feel those sensual lips closing around his jaded member, weary of Eva's willing but inexpert touch.

Still in silence, he allowed the Master to unfasten his uniform belt, then his jacket and trousers, growing impatient and hastening the process by wrenching off his tie and throwing it on to the floor.

Now naked, the Reichsführer shuddered with exquisite pleasure as the Master knelt before him and applied the gentlest degree of pressure to his balls, making them tense and heavy in his hand. Instantly, with an unprecedented eagerness, the Führer's prick leapt to attention, ready for anything. Seeing this, the Master bowed his head, opened the warm, moist cavern of his mouth and took in the willing member.

He did not suck at the Führer's prick for very long, for his expert touch divined the closeness of his orgasm. He took him to the edge, to the very brink, feeling the Führer's hands stroking his head and the back of his neck almost tenderly, as though in gratitude for this great gift of pleasure.

The Master now pulled away from the straining prick, and stood up. The Führer looked at him aghast, uncomprehending, until the Master turned his back and bent forward over the broad mahogany desk, pulling apart his buttocks so as to make it plain what he intended.

Well-greased with saliva, the Führer's prick slipped easily into the Master's arse, and he rammed it home with a jubilant cry.

'Quiet, mein Führer – you don't want them to overhear,' hissed the Master, reminding Hitler that guards stood only a few yards away from them, waiting in the corridor on the other side of the study door.

But to keep silence was sheer agony, when all he longed to do was shout and scream and sink his teeth into the Master's smooth, tanned back; when all he dreamed of was to come in a great crescendo of screaming and spunk.

He was not long in coming: nine or ten thrusts, and he felt his balls tense for that delicious moment of expectation before they sent the semen rushing up his over-excited shaft. And, with a muffled cry of ecstasy, he came into the tight, welcoming arse of this uncommon man who had read his desires and would soon be reading his victories in the stars.

The trouble with being Hitler's black magician, recalled the Master, was that he would not listen to the predictions he was given, true though they undoubtedly were. He would listen only to what he wanted to hear, which was rarely what he was told. Consequently, the other genuine psychics recruited by Goebbels eventually gave in and joined the charlatans in providing him with the sort of crap he was paying them to produce.

He began to lose more and more battles, more and more support. The Master realised that he had hitched his wagon to a falling star. This small, inadequate, angry man was in no way worthy to join the ranks of the undead, or to assist him in his own quest for world domination. He made his decision: when the time came, he would allow Adolf Hitler to sink without trace.

The one link which bound him still to Berchtesgaden was the woman they called Hedwige Lutjens – though she was known to the faithful as the Mother of the World. She worked as an astrologer and witch for Hitler, drawing up predictive charts and casting spells to punish, restore or bind. She was particularly in demand for her aphrodisiacs, which had restored potency to the flagging Führer on more than one occasion.

Hedwige had a talent which made her indispensable to the Master: her ability to roam the astral plane in search of lost spirits. She also knew the secret of raising those spirits and conversing with them. Could this, at last, be the one who would help him to locate his lost Queen, the companion of his future triumph?

It was not long before she became the Master's confidante, then his lover – though she refused to let him initiate her into the realm of the undead, for fear that this would cause her to lose some of her special powers.

One day, Hedwige came to the Master with great news:

'I believe I have spoken to her on the astral plane.'

'And where is she, where is my Queen Sedet?'

'She could not tell me. She is blinded and bound by sorcery, and can reveal nothing except that the place where she is imprisoned is dark and cold, and she is afraid.'

The Master clenched his teeth and punched the wall in frustration:

'Can we do nothing to find her?'

'There may be a way, I am not sure. A spirit-raising ceremony. It may be that I can break through the barrier of sorcery by my own magical means. But I will need your co-operation and assistance. Meet me tonight in the caverns beneath Berchtesgaden, and I swear I shall do all that is in my power.'

Hedwige held her magical ceremonies in the deserted salt-mines which formed a network of eerie caverns beneath Berchtesgaden. By order of the Führer, only she, her close confidants and the Führer himself were permitted to enter this magical place.

The Master followed Hedwige down hot, narrow corridors of crumbling brownish stone, sparkling dully with rock-salt – a magical place indeed, the purifying properties of the salt offering protection to the magician from the spirits he might raise in perilous ceremonies. The flaming torches they bore cast grotesque shadows on the walls: the shadows of elementals and horned devils. This was a place in which the Master felt thoroughly at home.

They reached a massive natural cavern with a lofty ceiling and a floor of beaten earth. It contained four concave mirrors and an altar with a white marble top, encircled by a chain of magnetised iron. The sign of the pentagram was engraved and gilded on the white marble surface, and embroidered on a new white lambskin stretched beneath the altar. In the middle of the marble altar stood two chafing-dishes, in which burned alder, laurel, cedar and sandal woods.

'Undress. You must be sky-clad,' whispered Hedwige; and she stepped out of the long white shift she had flung over her soft, naked flesh. Taking up a ceremonial sword, she placed its tip upon the Master's excited penis. 'Feel the power enter you,' she said: and it was true – he could feel an energy rushing through him, making him desperate to fuck her. He reached out and touched her breasts, stroking, questing.

'No, you must not have me. You must save your powers,' decreed Hedwige. And she picked up an earthenware pot of salt and handed it to the Master. 'You must describe the pentacle. None other may do it, or it will not have the power to protect you.'

Carefully measuring as he went, the Master sprinkled salt in the form of a pentacle, roughly nine feet across.

Hedwige clapped her hands, and a figure glided towards them out of the shadows.

'Come,' commanded Hedwige. 'And offer yourself to the Master, for his delight.'

The Master gasped as – momentarily – he looked into the face of the girl and believed that she was his Queen, come to him again from beyond the curtain of night which had been thrown up around her. But his heart sank once again as he realised that she bore merely a passing likeness – the same dark hair, almond eyes, full lips. She was naked, and her snow-white body seemed as pure and as vulnerable as a child's.

She approached the Master, knelt at his feet and kissed the tip of his penis, reverently and with great ceremonial. Then she waited for further commands.

Hedwige took up a silver goblet, filled to the brim with a crimson liquid, and handed it to the Master. His nostrils filled with the intoxicating scent, the scent of death and life and energy and eternal youth. It was warm, salty, coppery-smelling. It was fresh blood.

'Draw the sign of the pentagram and the sign of Sedet, priestess of Isis, upon the body of the girl,' instructed Hedwige. And, revelling in the wonderful richness of the warm liquid, the Master resisted the urge to drink it down and instead dipped in his finger, and used it to inscribe the magical symbols upon the girl's pure white flesh. The blood trickled down her flesh irresistibly, so irresistibly that he desperately wanted to stick out his tongue and lap it all up.

'What now?' he demanded.

'Now you must fuck her. You must place your essence inside her body, if she is to be the vessel through which we make contact with your queen. But remember: you must stay within the pentacle at all times, or I cannot answer for your safety. We are dealing with some of the most dangerous forces in the universe – the forces which gave you immortality, and which can – just as easily – deal out death and destruction.'

Hedwige laid the girl down inside the pentacle, and opened her thighs. The Master knelt between them and tried to insert his penis into her vagina. He was surprised to meet resistance, and looked up at Hedwige questioningly:

'A virgin?'

'Only a virgin will suffice, Master. And this girl has

KISS OF DEATH

saved herself solely to be of service to your cause.
She will be your devoted slave.'

With a second, harder thrust, he succeeded in
penetrating her, and almost came on the spot as
she screamed her pain and he looked down and
saw rivulets of scarlet virgin blood coursing down
her martyred thighs. But he held back and tried
to pace himself, so that he could enjoy her to the
full. She felt wonderful, as tight round his prick as
a clenched hand, yet velvety and smooth.

All too soon, he shot his load into her and was
gratified by the look of surprise on the girl's face
as she experienced her first orgasm with a man's
cock inside her. He longed to bite her lily-white
throat, but knew he must not, for fear of ruining
the magic ritual.

'Lift her up and place her upon the altar,' decreed
Hedwige. And together, they carried the girl across
and laid her upon the gilded white marble top, legs
wide apart to reveal the violated treasures within.
Droplets of mingled blood and semen trickled out
of her crack, falling like a slow, red rain to sully the
white lambskin beneath.

Hedwige extinguished all but one of the candles,
and began the incantation. With each word, the
darkness seemed to grow vaster, more impenetrable.
Straining his eyes in the gloom, the Master realised
that he could make out a vague shape, a denser
black in the darkness, hovering over the prostrate
body of the violated girl. He watched in breathless
excitement, as it grew closer and seemed to disappear
into the body of the girl, who began to writhe about
and moan as if in pain, or struggling with some
unseen enemy.

227

As they watched, a shape began to emerge from the girl's body. Only this time it was not a formless darkness. It was the misty shape of a young woman, white-faced and hollow-eyed. She was wrapped in a long white cloth, like a shroud. Her mouth was open in a soundless scream, and she seemed to be holding out her arms and imploring them to help her. There were two tiny red puncture marks on her neck . . .

'Sedet!' cried out the Master, stretching out his hands towards her.

'Keep within the pentacle!' Hedwige admonished him. 'She cannot see you; she is blinded by sorcery. But question her as you will.'

'Sedet, tell me where you are, where I may find you!'

But the girl shook her head, sadly.

'Tell me, I command you!'

Sedet opened her mouth and began to speak. Her voice was faraway, faint, full of pain:

'I am cold, I am afraid, it is dark, I am lost . . . O Master, you have abandoned me and I am powerless . . .'

'No! You must tell me where you are being imprisoned!' he cried, and stepped out of the pentacle.

'Stop!' screamed Hedwige. But it was too late. With a terrible scream of pain, the apparition disappeared back into the body of the girl, who also began to scream, scream, scream. Her body was racked with convulsions, and she clawed the air with wildly-thrashing arms.

And then fell silent and very still.

'Dead,' sighed Hedwige, lifting up the girl's arm and letting it fall back on to her chest. 'You have destroyed the spell. We shall have to wait until the next new moon before we dare try again.'

Five days before the next new moon, Hedwige Lutjens was executed: suspected of being implicated in the von Stauffenberg bomb plot.

And so the Master's only link to his lost queen was gone, destroyed, useless. And without her, how was he ever going to ascend in triumph to his throne?

By the spring of 1945, the Master was on the point of leaving the Reichsführer to stew in his own juice. The Führer was growing cool towards him – stopping his ears to the truth, and making crazy decisions which inevitably ended in ignominious failure . . . which he then blamed on the Master.

Time to move on.

Of course, there were temptations to remain. Such as the orgies organised by the arch-libertine Goering, and the succulent girls who attended them, and offered themselves to him as though they had been sweetmeats on a silver platter.

On just such a night as that fateful evening in April when he had foolishly remained in Berlin instead of taking the opportunity to assume a new identity, forge a new path – perhaps surfacing next time as Eisenhower's trusted advisor, or Stalin's right-hand man. Instead, he had fallen victim to his own lusts, tempted to Hitler's bunker by the promise of delicate young flesh to taste and corrupt. And the prospect of looted art treasures, brought there to protect them and ripe for the picking.

And after all, why worry? Was he not immortal, invincible? Was he, the Master, not the very same

man who, as the great Rasputin, had defied death
and dismemberment and lived to fight again?

There were only four people present at that last
evening of delight: the Master, a magnificent body-
guard known universally as The Ram, a high-ranking
SS Officer called von Riesen . . . and the girl.

She was a morsel fit for any emperor's table; a ban-
quet of rosy pink flesh and golden hair: the perfect
Aryan *mädchen* who had come to the bunker from
her Bavarian village to offer herself to her beloved
Führer. But alas, the Reichsführer had taken a vow
of celibacy until the war was won, and so the poor
child looked to be going to waste . . .

Waste not, want not. She could serve the Father-
land just as ably by fucking the Führer's henchmen
as by fucking the Führer himself. She was pretty but
stupid. She soon saw things their way.

They took her into a storeroom, where they knew
they would not be disturbed. The walls were not
only strong, but thick: and, above the sound of
the approaching Russian guns, who would hear the
screams of a tender young girl?

The girl had clearly suffered: her clothes were
threadbare and ragged, and she obviously hadn't
eaten for several days, as she had wolfed down the
coarse black bread they had given her. But her eyes
were as bright as a bird's, and her mouth as rosy and
full of juice as a ripe plum, ready to be bitten and
enjoyed.

The drugged wine they had given her took rapid
effect, and her early reserve soon melted away. She
was laughing and joking with them. They put a
record on the gramophone, and she danced with
each of them in turn, responding with giggles and

sensual movements of her hips as they ground their hardening penises against her belly.

When the Master's turn came with the girl, he began to undo the buttons of her blouse. At first, she raised a feeble hand to prevent him, but he looked deep into her eyes and she let her hand fall back to rest on his shoulder. Slowly, he peeled the blouse from her shoulders and dropped it on the floor. Her breasts were pert and rosy-tipped under her silk slip. Licking his lips, he ripped the bodice down and bent to nibble savagely at her flesh, tormenting her nipples with such forcity that they began to bleed.

But she was enjoying the pain, dulled as it was by the spiked drink. She even began to unfasten her own skirt; but her fingers were clumsy, and he finished the job for her, tearing it downwards and leaving her naked, save for French knickers, suspender belt and stockings. The knickers yielded to the sharp point of his pocket-knife, and she stood shivering and giggling before them, nipples puckered with excitement and little brown pubic bush glistening with the first drops of her cunny-juices.

Von Riesen grabbed the girl by the wrist and wrenched her away from the Master, pulling her to her knees and forcing her arms behind her back. He manacled them together, and, unbuttoning his uniform trousers, he thrust his stiff cock into her mouth, almost choking her.

Whilst she was on her knees, helpless and sucking frantically at von Riesen's cock, the Ram began to pay great attention to her backside, thrusting his fingers deep inside and enjoying her moans of growing discomfort as he enlarged the narrow pathway with first one finger, then two, then his whole hand, up to the wrist.

Von Riesen came into the girl's mouth and pulled away, leaving her gasping for breath and with trails of semen running out of the corners of her pretty mouth. The Master, meanwhile, had taken up the whip he so loved to use and motioned to the Ram to move back so that he could take proper aim.

Oh, how she flinched and cried out under the lash, her pink and white skin reddening into stripes and weals as it cut into her tender back and backside. But von Riesen held on tight to her shoulders, toying with her breasts to amuse himself as the little charade played on.

When she had taken all that she could, von Riesen let her fall forwards and she lay face-down on the dirty floor, broken and humiliated, yet wriggling her hips in a lascivious manner that excited her torturers beyond belief. They flipped her on to her side, and the Master and the Ram lay down with her – one in front of her and one behind, so that they could both enjoy her simultaneously.

It was plain the girl was no virgin; but surely she had never had two big cocks in her at the same time – one filling her cunt and the other stretching her already-tortured arse to the very limits of endurance. And von Riesen, already excited again by this unusual and diverting spectacle, knelt down, raised up the girl's head in his hands, and forced her to suck him off yet again.

They were lost in their game. They paid no heed to the sound of artillery fire, which was still far away and surely no threat – the Russians would not be here for another day at least. Plenty of time to enjoy the girl . . .

They were so lost in their game that they did not notice the three shadowy figures that slipped unseen along the corridors of the Bunker; nor did they notice them standing silhouetted in the doorway of the storeroom, until a voice called out:

'Master! It is all over. We have come for you.'

With a roar of rage, the Master pulled out of the girl and leapt to his feet, turning his gaze upon the three sinister figures confronting him. Nothing to fear, surely, from three mortal men in raincoats. He looked deep into the first man's eyes and tried to burn out his brain with the sheer power of his thought. And, to his amazement, the thoughts simply rebounded upon himself.

A shield. A magical shield. These were no ordinary men. They were sorcerers . . . and sorcerers with powers he had never encountered since those days back in ancient Egypt.

Too late, the Master thought to flee; but the three sorcerers raised their hands and instantly he was paralysed, helpless, incapable of movement. Out of the corner of his eye, he saw von Riesen and the Ram, lying stone dead at his feet, their hearts stopped dead in their tracks. And the girl, also dead, still locked together with her tormentors.

The tallest man came forward and smiled at the Master. It was a cold smile of triumph:

'At last we have you. Such a shame to do this to you . . . your powers could have been such an asset to the Allied war effort . . . but even with the occult knowledge we have gathered through our experiments and through spying on you, your powers are too great for us to control, and you, my fine fellow, are much too evil ever to be trusted. Therefore we have sought for many years to destroy you . . .'

And that was the last he remembered before a cold hand touched his eyes and closed them in unconsciousness.

When he came to his senses again, it was with a searing pain that tore through him and then . . . nothing. He realised instantly what they had done. Unable to kill him or destroy his body, these amateur magicians had disabled him in the only way that their feeble sorcery could muster.

They had taken the block of crystal which had given him immortality, and – speaking the ancient incantation – had imprisoned him magically within it. They had taken away from him the power of sight, sound, smell, taste, movement. They had delivered him up from triumphant death-in-life to a living death.

As they left, Colonel Everett turned to his corporal and gave the all-important instruction:

'Ensure that these cellars are bricked up. *Securely* bricked up. We have to make sure that no-one ever comes down here again. Maybe we don't have the occult power to destroy him, but we have finally managed to disable him. At last the world is safe from this evil.'

And he turned and walked away up the cellar steps.

Trapped and blinded in the heart of the suffocating crystal prison, the Master's soul raged within his helpless, motionless body and would not be still:

'I shall return,' he vowed.

That night, Colonel Everett, his two magicians and his driver were mysteriously killed when their car crashed into a tree. It was never satisfactorily explained how their car could have run off the road on a clear, moonlit night.

Only the Master knew how.

13: The Joining

Andreas Hunt unlocked the door to his flat and tossed his hat inside, following it across the room and flopping down in his favourite armchair.

It had been a difficult day at work. Correction: it had been a difficult month. Ever since the Cheviot débâcle, the editor had regarded Hunt with suspicion – making sure he was the one sent out to cover all the crappy stories about cats up trees and crackpots who wanted to sail bathtubs across the Atlantic. No matter how hard he'd tried, he hadn't been able to make his experiences in Whitby sound anything other than the deranged ravings of a halfwit who'd been hitting the magic mushrooms. When he'd tried to interview Cheviot at the House, he'd encountered a predictable wall of polite uncooperativeness. Even Opposition MPs proved suspiciously cagey about discussing Cheviot's private life. It smelt mightily like a conspiracy.

But the editor wasn't interested in his 'fantasies', and retaliated by sending him to Barrow-in-Furness, to cover a story about a three-headed donkey. Hunt, in short, was not the flavour of the month.

Not that this had changed his mind about Sir Anthony Cheviot. It just meant that, from now on, his enquiries would have to be a little more unofficial.

Hunt poured himself a double whisky and kicked off his shoes. He switched on the television news: the balance of payments was looking even dodgier than usual, the Channel Tunnel had run into financial problems just for a change, and some poor teenage girl from Staithes had been found stone-dead with a human bite-mark on her neck. Funny thing was, the body had disappeared . . .

Now, why did that make the hair rise on the back of Hunt's imperturbable neck? Why? Because Staithes was a small fishing-village in North Yorkshire – in fact, in the constituency of a certain Sir Anthony Cheviot, MP . . .

The doorbell rang.

'Drat.' Hunt jabbed the 'off' button on his remote control and levered himself up out of the armchair. He supposed it must be that snooty French bitch from upstairs, come to register yet another complaint about the noises his plumbing made. He'd' have taught her a thing or two about plumbing, if she hadn't had starched knickers and a permanent smell under her nose. Whoever coined that old cliché about Frenchwomen all being raving nymphos must have been several bricks short of a load . . .

Hang on a minute, what was the matter with him? Hunt felt his prick rising to attention yet again, and was vaguely disturbed. These sudden sexual impulses were becoming more urgent, less infrequent. He hardly recognised himself any more.

The doorbell rang again, more insistently this time.

'OK, OK, I'm coming,' he grunted and padded

in stockinged-feet to the front door. Didn't bother squinting through the peephole, fumbled a little with the chain, drew back the bolt, and finally swung open the door.

'Hello again, Mister Ace Reporter.'

He looked into the girl's face and didn't know whether to laugh, cry or get his kit off.

'Do you still want me?'

Her words rolled off her pretty little tongue like honey off a cold silver teaspoon. Oh, how could she ask him a question like that, when for the last month he had been dreaming of feeling that tongue curling itself around his turgid prick?

Instead of answering her, he replied with a question of his own:

'Why did you run away from me?'

'I was afraid.'

'Afraid of me? But why?'

'No, not afraid of you. Not exactly. It's hard for me to explain to a . . . cynic like yourself. I was afraid that someone . . . something . . . might be using you to get at me. It was just a feeling, but a very powerful one. Did you not feel it, too: that first time we met at the fortune-telling booth?'

Hunt hesitated. Had he not just spent several miserable weeks under suspicion of terminal nuttiness, for propounding similar off-the-wall theories?

'I felt very strongly attracted to you, certainly,' he replied, cagily.

'But nothing else?'

He hesitated once again.

'Nothing else.'

He wasn't quite sure why he had lied, but he was

immediately glad that he had, as he saw the wave of relief pass across Mara's tired but oh-so-sexy face.

So maybe – just maybe – it really had all been a figment of her over-active imagination, a psychic hiccup? In that moment of relief, Mara decided to believe what she wanted to believe, and began to unbutton her coat.

'It's chilly out there – autumn in the air. I could use something to warm me up . . .'

'A whisky?' Hunt was all fingers and thumbs as he fumbled for the whisky bottle and knocked over his own empty glass.

Dear God, she was even sexier than he had remembered – and Lord knows, his every dream since that late August night had been filled with images of her. Images of the girl in all her miraculous nakedness, the glowing perfection of her tanned skin, her swelling breasts, her sinuous thighs that wrapped themselves around a man and took him prisoner for ever.

I surrender . . .

Mara smiled at his clumsiness.

'A drink wasn't quite what I had in mind,' she murmured huskily, taking hold of the end of his tie and pulling him closer to her. She could smell the whisky on his breath, the stale odour of sweat on his shirt. He smelt like a real man. And that turned her on.

Slowly and seductively, she slid down the knot of his tie and used the two ends like a horse's reins, steering his dumbstruck lips towards hers and crushing her mouth against his as though she wanted to suck the very soul out of him.

Her mouth opened slightly and her eager tongue

darted out, teasing apart his lips and sliding between them, to do battle with his own coy tongue within the warm cavern of his mouth. The taste of whisky filled her mouth as she withdrew and allowed his tongue to chase hers back inside her shameless mouth. And they jousted for a long time, savouring the taste of their mingled saliva, the warm gusts of their synchronised breathing.

'I want you,' he breathed into her mouth. And tried to push her backwards on to the threadbare settee that lay along one wall of the apartment.

'Not yet, not yet,' she murmured in reply. 'I want you to more than want me. I want you to need me: need me like oxygen. Watch me now: watch me but don't touch. Or you'll spoil the game.'

She pushed him gently away, and began to undress before him. Desperately, so desperately he wanted her as he watched her reveal those long-dreamed-of charms to his hungry eyes. Surely he could not want her any more than he wanted her at this moment?

But he was wrong.

The blouse had many tiny mother-of-pearl buttons which she lingered over, and which took an age to yield to her teasing fingers. One by one they slipped undone, revealing a little more of her exciting flesh to Hunt's yearning eyes. At last the final button was undone, and the two sides of the tight blouse sprang apart, revealing a diaphanous black lace bra. She peeled the blouse from her shoulders, but to Hunt's great chagrin made no move to remove the brassiere.

Now she moved her attentions to a lower sphere of activity: her long, fringed, peasant skirt. It, too, had buttons – a long row that extended right down the front from waist to hem. In agony now from his tortured prick, Hunt watched her begin at the hem and work slowly – agonisingly slowly – upwards. First a tanned calf, then a bronzed knee, and now a thigh . . . such perfect thighs, long and smooth and muscular. The thighs of a dancer or a beautiful athlete. She reached the waist of the skirt and unfastened the last button, allowing the skirt to slide down to the floor where it formed a colourful plinth for this breathtaking statuette.

She stood before him now, clad only in black lace bra and French knickers and Indian sandals. The sandals were easily kicked off, leaving only the tantalising barrier of bra and knickers. They were the perfect frame for her loveliness, setting off her bronzed skin to perfection. Her hips and buttocks swelled invitingly inside the lacy knickers, and her breasts bulged irresistibly upwards, defying gravity with their magnificent firmness and elasticity.

After what seemed an eternity, Mara walked towards Hunt and turned her back to him.

'Unfasten my bra – but don't touch my breasts,' she commanded him.

Swallowing hard, he obeyed with trembling hands. The catch took ages to give way beneath his clumsy fingers and, when at last it did, he was very nearly unable to control the overwhelming desire to grab overflowing handfuls of those soft, yet beautifully firm, breasts.

'Now the panties. Slide them down over my hips. Yes, that's right – like that.'

He slid down the filmy black fabric, and Mara stepped daintily out of the French knickers. Her

rounded backside brushed his hand as she bent down
to pick them up.

'No, don't touch me. Not yet. Don't spoil it.'

Almost sobbing with lust, he obeyed, though he
was not entirely sure why. She was quite small
compared to him; he could easily have imposed
his will on her, and he was confident enough to
believe that she wouldn't have had any complaints.
But something deep inside himself told him that she
was right, that it would be even better this way. He
had waited this long, so he could wait a bit longer.

She turned to face him, and he drew in breath
sharply as he got the full benefit of her exceptional
body. Long waves of glossy hair, so dark that it
was almost black, fell in a tumbling profusion over
smooth shoulders, swelling breasts with nipples that
stiffened even as he gazed upon them, transfixed
with lust. A taut belly and softly rounded hips flaring
out into kissable buttocks supported on those perfect
tawny thighs that made him gasp with pleasure to
see them. And in between those thighs, the luxuriant glossy curls that gathered like some mysterious
inflorescence, a floral celebration of the moist pink
mysteries within.

She came towards him again.

'No, don't touch me. Let me touch you now . . .'

Reaching out, she began to finish the task of
undressing him which she had begun with his tie.
First the shirt, then a deft flick of the wrist had his
belt undone. The zip yielded without a struggle, and
within seconds Hunt found himself stepping dream-
like out of his shoes, socks and trousers, leaving him
naked save for his underpants.

A wicked gentle small hand insinuated itself under

the waistband of his boxer shorts and began to
tease the flesh beneath, carefully skirting around
the burstingly erect penis which was thrashing around
frantically and helplessly on his belly. She knew how
to tease and arouse without satisfying; knew how to
provoke desire and not quench it until the moment
was exactly right. The tip of his prick was oozing
love-juice already, drooling for a taste of the flesh
it so desperately craved.

Then, to his immense disappointment, she took her
hand out of his underpants and moved it upwards,
stroking the dense hair on his chest, soothing his
flanks; sliding down again to stroke his legs and
thighs; now moving upwards again and – oh joy!
– wriggling butterfly fingers underneath the fabric
of the gusset and into the hot moist groin, there to
play with his most precious treasures.

His balls tensed with the immensity of the pleasure
Hunt experienced as Mara's knowing fingers tickled,
teased and then encircled them. He held his breath as
her gentle but insistent caress tormented him; letting
out a deep sigh of satisfaction as she began to squeeze
his balls, firmly but gently, so as to cause him only
pleasure.

Slowly – and with as much enjoyment as he himself
was experiencing – Mara took hold of the waistband
of Hunt's boxer shorts, and began to tug at it. They
slid down readily, enthusiastically even, as Hunt
wriggled his hips a little to hasten the process.

Now naked, his prick sprang out into the sudden
freedom and twitched convulsively, searching for its
target. Mara bent to kiss it and lick its head, but did
not take it into her mouth.

She stepped back from Hunt a little way, sat down

on the sofa and parted her thighs, so that he could see the pearly treasures within her fur-trimmed casket. They were already glistening with their own secret moisture and – as Mara pulled apart her cunt-lips to give him a better view – Hunt saw the erect bud of her clitoris, still swelling and pulsating with eager life.

Mara began to play with herself, revelling in the sensations of finger on clit, finger in cunt, finger on nipple . . . Hunt looked on, wild with desire yet not wishing to spoil the moment by leaping on her and taking her before she wanted him to. His only means of revenge was clear: he slipped his left hand under his balls and, with his right, began to masturbate himself, very slowly and very tantalisingly.

Mara was beginning to pant with pleasure, feeling herself dangerously near to orgasm. Hunt, too, was afraid that he would misjudge his manipulations and shoot his spunk all over the carpet before he had even had time to bury his prick in the delectable woman he saw before him, wanking herself off and daring him to intervene.

He need not have worried. For at that moment Mara opened her arms and said:

'Come to me. Take me. Unite with me.'

He needed no prompting. And he pushed her back on to the sofa, burying his prick inside her with one swift, smooth thrust that tore cries of pleasure from both of them.

'Fuck me . . . !' she breathed, thrusting forward her pelvis to take him deeper inside her. Her cunt was like an oiled machine, his prick the piston driving hard inside the cylinder: perfect precision, perfect harmony, perfect synchronicity.

Their fucking approached its crescendo and their

movements quickened as they climbed towards perfect simultaneous orgasm: an ocean-swell of spunk met an outrushing tide of warm cunt-juice, and they fell back exhausted and dizzy with the pleasure of it.

Perfect sex. No more. No hint of the supernatural, of any unseen presence. No cold hand upon the shoulder, no evil eyes burning into the soul, no practical joker using their bodies for its own sport.

Maybe that was the end of it. The end of their troubles, just as this was the beginning of their life together, their joining.

Mara tried desperately to believe it. But at the back of her mind she could still hear the mocking laughter and the chilling words:

'I will have you soon.'

They were days and nights of passion: the best days and nights of Andreas Hunt's entire life. Days of arriving late at work with dark circles under his eyes, after nights spent in lovemaking with Mara. Lovemaking that was sometimes tender, sometimes frenzied, even violent; but always intense. And just when he thought she had drained him of every last drop of spunk, she would wriggle that pretty little tongue around his bollocks, or force his tired head between the soft hillocks of her breasts; and he would be rigid and ready for the fray once again.

It was one Saturday morning, just over a week after she had arrived, that Mara awoke Hunt with a delectable kiss on his penis, then turned to him and made him an unexpected proposition:

'Are you willing to be joined to me?'

Hunt grinned, and made a grab for her pubic

hair, twisting the curly strands around his index finger.

'You know me: I'm always ready to be joined to you!'

To his extreme disappointment, Mara removed his hand and shook her head.

'No. I didn't mean that sort of joining.'

'You don't mean marriage, do you . . . ?'

Hunt had always been petrified of marriage. Sure, he liked the girl. Heck, no: he liked her a helluva lot. He wanted her to stick around for a long, long time. But marriage? He wasn't the conventional kind, and he was pretty sure she wasn't, either.

'Not marriage as you mean it, no. I mean a Wicca joining, the binding of our souls and bodies in a pagan rite. It is very natural, very . . . exciting. The ceremony would be performed before a group of pagan friends of mine, the members of my coven.' She smiled at him and began to caress his genitals, which were already rising nobly to the occasion.

'Well, I don't know,' said Hunt, doubtfully. Oh no, not more New Age weirdness, he groaned inwardly, and wondered if he was going to regret this intimate association with a real-life psychic. After all, he didn't even believe in the supernatural, did he? Why should he get himself mixed up with a bunch of nutters? And even if she did claim to be a white witch, did he really want to get himself involved in any sort of witchcraft?

He opened his mouth to say no, and was extremely surprised to hear himself say:

'OK . . . yes. Let's do it.'

The look of delight on Mara's face was almost sufficient reward in itself, for she immediately reached out and guided his hand once more to her pubic bush, inviting him to slide his fingers inside. She was already dripping wet and ready for him.

Maybe he wasn't going to regret it, after all.

Sky-clad and trembling with the cold, Hunt and Mara were brought forward into the clearing, to stand before the High Priestess, the embodiment of the great huntress Diana.

There were eleven other witches, six male and five female, which with Mara made up the coven of thirteen. They were of varying ages, shapes and sizes: some young and beautiful, others old and ugly. But all were naked, and all were obviously already in a state of some excitement. The men's penises were semi-erect and stiffening, and the women's nipples noticeably puckered, not simply because of the cold.

The High Priestess began the preparations for the Great Rite, casting the circle in which two worlds would meet: the world of men and the world of the gods and spirits. The sacred broom was used to sweep the area, whilst an invocation was chanted. Then the High Priestess took a dagger and used it to draw the circle, cleansing it with spring water and salt, and consecrating it to the mother-goddess. The attendant witches began to invoke the divine force, chanting:

> 'Bagahi laca bachahe
> Lamac cahi achabahe
> Karrelyos . . .'

'She is cleansing the circle so that it may be filled with our energies,' whispered Mara to Hunt, who was feeling distinctly uneasy. 'The ceremony will soon begin. See: she has placed the broomstick at the edge of the circle, to make a doorway through which we shall pass.'

The chant began again:

> 'Eko, eko Arazak
> Eko, eko Zamilak
> Eko, eko Cernunnos
> Eko, eko Aradia . . .'

Two witches – one male, one female – approached Mara and Hunt, and led them into the middle of the circle. They carried small earthenware pots containing some kind of aromatic ointment, which they proceeded to rub all over the bride and bridegroom's bodies – the female witch attending to Hunt, the male to Mara.

The very act of massage was in itself erotic, and Hunt felt his member uncoiling, rising, thrusting upwards; but it was more than just the feeling of a cool female hand rubbing ointment into his body – it was something in the ointment itself. As it was smoothed on to his skin, he felt a strange sensation – half-burning, half-numbing; a warmth that spread right through his skin, his flesh, deep down to the bones beneath.

Mara, too, was feeling the sensual warmth, as it spread to her nipples, her belly, her clitoris. The male witch was a skilful masseur, with a gentle but firm touch and bold, bold fingers. He had no qualms about massaging her most intimate places, and his fingers probed into the cleft of her backside, slid across her stiffening nipples, and down over her belly to her groin, rubbing the ointment right inside her vulva. It was the most exquisite sensation, like fire and ice mingled.

A bell was rung, and the High Priestess knelt before Penny, reciting the words of the fivefold kiss and touching each part of her body in turn:

'Blessed be thy feet that have brought thee in these ways.
Blessed be thy knees that shall kneel at the sacred altar.
Blessed be thy womb without which we would not be.
Blessed be thy breasts formed in beauty and strength.
Blessed be thy lips that shall utter the sacred names.'

She then knelt down before Hunt and repeated the ritual, paying particular attention to his wildly rearing prick.

She then took up a whip with silken thongs and scourged the two postulants lightly over their entire bodies.

'You must now speak the words of joining,' instructed the High Priestess, binding their right hands together with a silken cord.

Hunt turned to Mara and spoke the words he had been taught:

'Will you now pass through the veil and the gates of night and day? Will you be at one with me, who am both death and life? Will you kneel before me and worship me?'

Mara responded with a kiss, and replied:

'I am light and thou the darkness, I am darkness and thou the light, and there must be no separation between us. Will you love me beyond all things and be the instrument of my desire? Will you love the darkness that is within thee and open your arms to it? Will you flee not from shadows and the fears, but embrace them and so make yourself whole?'

'I will.'

Mara then knelt before him, and Hunt laid down the sword of mastery between her parted thighs: the symbol of their joining.

This was the signal for great rejoicing, and the witches drew nearer out of the shadows, bearing lighted candles and offerings of fruit and flowers. They rubbed more of the sweet-smelling ointment into their flesh, and Hunt's head began to swim as the hallucinations began.

The witches drew them to their feet, swaying slightly from the drugged ointment.

'Jump the broomstick!' cried the witches in chorus. And they helped the two postulants to step over the broom laid as a gate to the magic circle.

Hunt swayed on unsteady feet, now in the grip of a lust so powerful that it had changed his very identity. He was no longer simply Mr Andreas Hunt. He had become his own penis: nothing more of him existed. He lived for his penis, that proud, masterly staff which sprang godlike from his loins, full of the essence of life. It seemed to grow to immense proportions, throbbing with the insistent beat of his heart, quickening, rushing, impelling him towards the only goal it knew or desired or understood: Mara's delectable cunt.

Mara felt elated, hypersensitive; feeling every nerve-ending in her body tingling and singing with life. She needed sex: needed Hunt's big, insistent penis inside her belly, toiling away within her, rubbing against her throbbing clitoris and bringing her to glorious orgasm. She reached out and touched Hunt's penis, hungry for its smooth hardness within her, taking her to ecstasy and beyond. It twitched appreciatively in her hand, and Hunt knelt down, eager to have her right there and then.

The High Priestess walked forward and laid her hands upon their heads:

'It is now time for you to perform the Great Rite,' she intoned. 'Brothers and sisters, decree: shall they perform it in token, or in true?'

'In true, in true!' came the great cry. 'Let their loins be joined now, in our midst!'

Lying together on the dew-spangled grass, Hunt and Mara needed no further instructions. Their naked bodies were already entwined, glistening and fragrant with sweet ointments and the sweat of fast-growing lust.

'Fuck, fuck, fuck!' cried the witches, drawing nearer the two and running their lascivious hands over the two bodies. 'Enter her, enter her now!'

Responding well to such enthusiastic encouragement, Hunt searched out Mara's cunt and, with a great cry of pleasure, slipped into her. It felt exactly as if he were thrusting his entire body into hers, as though the whole world consisted only of prick and cunt and balls and clitty, of sticky spunk and slippery cunt-juice. His testicles felt huge, like great seed-pods, ripening, maturing, hardening, almost ready to burst. He reached out and felt for her clitoris: it, too, was a ripening fruit, a bud about to blossom. He could feel its hardness pulsating under his fingertip, and – feeling his own crisis drawing near – he pressed a little harder, to hasten Mara's climax.

He brought her off at just the moment that he felt the base of his prick grow still heavier with the coming outrush of spunk, jetting along his shaft like quicksilver, leaping out into the warm haven of Mara's cunt in long, luxurious waves of incredible pleasure.

They cried out their pleasure and lay panting together on the ground.

Hunt felt a hand upon his shoulder, and looked up into the face of the High Priestess.

'Now comes the celebration,' she told him. 'Now our brothers and sisters shall celebrate your joining in our traditional way.'

Hunt looked puzzled.

'She means that we may now all enjoy each other's bodies,' explained Mara. 'It is the way with our coven. Any man who desires me may have me, and any woman may claim your favours. The ointment will ensure that you are able to come as many times as you want to.'

Hunt was not sure he liked the idea of Mara being screwed by every man who desired her . . . but then again, he looked around at the sisters and had to admit there were one or two he wouldn't kick out of bed. That nice brunette with the pert little bum; and the blowsy redhead with the huge knockers.

Two women were tugging at his arm, one surely no more than eighteen years old, with perfect white skin and nice tits, and the other a middle-aged woman – not great-looking admittedly, past her best, but still well worth screwing, with her big soft body.

'Patience, girls – one at a time!' he joked. But that wasn't what they had in mind. The younger girl knelt down behind him and began to thrust her tongue into his arsehole, whilst the older woman – almost certainly her mother – knelt in front and set to work on his penis with her skilful lips and tongue. It was an irresistible combination of sensations, so mind-blowing that he scarcely noticed a fat, elderly man leading Mara off into the trees.

Mara lay down on the soft bracken and gave herself up to the old man's lust. Normally she would have been repulsed by this toothless old man, with his fat, pendulous belly and spindly legs. He was drooling with excitement as he began to paw at her perfect breasts and belly. There were so many folds of flesh about his waist that his prick was almost hidden from sight, only its dribbling tip poking out from underneath the fleshy curtain.

'Sweet flesh . . .' he wheezed, running his odious fat paws across her breasts, tweaking her nipples and relishing her slight grimaces of pain. 'And you're mine to enjoy. Let's see what you taste like, little princess . . .'

He ran sausage fingers up the inside of her thighs, pinching the delicate flesh and enjoying her evident discomfort. But she was clearly excited, too, by this fat old man with dirty fingernails who was poking and prodding at her most intimate places.

With some difficulty, because of his corpulence, the man knelt between her thighs and began to lap noisily at her cunt. In spite of her natural revulsion, Mara found herself responding instinctively to the contact of his greedy, rasping tongue. His saliva mingled with her abundant cunt-juices, and she almost came as his tongue darted into her wet tunnel like a lizard's darting after its prey.

Breathing heavily, he hauled himself off her cunt and crawled on top of her until he was right above her, looking down into her pretty face. She could smell his breathing: the sickly-sweet scent of decay, mingled with the heavy scent of her own cunt, and to her surprise the smell did not repel, but excited her, though he was all but suffocating her with the weight of his great flabby belly.

Without further preliminaries, his hand fumbled for his cock and stuffed it clumsily and rather roughly into her wet crack. She gave a sigh of perverse pleasure as he began to screw her. His breath came with difficulty, rasping out of his half-open mouth, the saliva dribbling disgustingly from the corners and down his unshaven chin.

'Fuck me . . .' she breathed, too far gone to care who or where or why, and only knowing that she must have an orgasm or go mad with frustration.

A final thrust did the trick, as he shot his load of spunk into her and ground against her clitoris, triggering off her own orgasm.

For a second or two, she lay with eyes closed, beneath him. When she opened them, it was with a low cry of terror. For she was looking up into the face, not of the disgusting old priest, but of the man who had called himself The Master. His eyes were burning into her soul, and there was an unspeakably cruel twist to the corners of his mouth as he smiled and said:

'Soon, very soon, I shall have you, little slut.'

And with those words, the image of the Master's face seemed to dissolve away, restoring the face of the priest who had screwed her and still lay on top of her, crushing her with his fat, malodorous body. And as she gazed up at him, his face changed yet again: this time twisting into an expression half-terror, half-pain.

Beads of sweat were standing out on his greasy forehead, and he clutched suddenly at his chest as he gave a rasping cry and fell, unconscious and unmoving, on top of her terrified body.

Her screams brought the others to the scene within seconds, but it was too late: The unwonted exertion must have brought on a heart attack.

So why could Mara still hear the mocking laughter echoing all around her in the darkness?

14: London

Things had settled down a little since that day, two weeks ago, when Mara had been so upset by the old man's heart attack. For several days she had been unable to sleep or eat and Hunt knew there was more to it than she was admitting to. But now she seemed to have put it all behind her, and he was greatly relieved to see her taking an interest in life again. She had even started work again, offering Tarot readings and palmistry to the bored housewives of suburbia.

Hunt, meanwhile, was feeling pretty good. The editor seemed to have relented somewhat and had recognised that his talents were wasted writing space-fillers that no-one would read. He had put Hunt on to a lead about a possible call-girl scandal in Whitehall, and he was delighted. This would provide him with the perfect platform from which to launch his second wave of discreet investigations into the fascinating Sir Anthony Cheviot.

He made repeated attempts to contact Anastasia Dubois, but there was no reply at her apartment and no-one at the club had any recollection of her. In fact, she seemed to have done a pretty effective disappearing act, just when he needed her to dish some more dirt on Cheviot. Without a glamorous

257

witness or a talkative victim, his front-page exclusive was just pie in the sky.

The phone call came around midday, just as he was about to knock off for a cheese sandwich and a liquid lunch in the local pub. The voice was female, breathy, seductive:

'Andreas Hunt?'

'Speaking.'

'Just listen. Don't say anything. I think I'm being watched. I was there, I saw it . . . the Knightsbridge murder . . . it was so horrible . . .'

'You mean . . . the call-girl who was bitten on the thigh and bled to death?'

'Yes, yes. Don't talk; we don't have much time. Listen: I was in the flat with her. We . . . you know . . . worked together, saw clients together. Some of them like to have two women together. Anyhow, he turned up, this guy, and I knew who he was straight away. It was that MP with the weird white streak in his hair, I don't know his name . . .'

'Meredith Parry-Evans?'

'Yeah, yeah, the Welsh guy. Anyhow, he seemed OK at first. Asked to be tied down and whipped, and then he wanted me to suck him off while Sonja sat on his face. It was OK, straightforward, I could feel him coming and I think he had Sonja excited, too. I could hear her breathing hard and I guessed she was about to come, and I was pleased for her . . . that doesn't happen much with clients, mostly it's just hard work.

'At any rate, he shoots off in my mouth and I give him a good long suck so as to make it last . . . and all of a sudden, he goes raving bonkers: starts thrashing about and shouting. Thrashes about so much, he breaks the leather straps we'd used to tie him down – he must have been incredibly strong, but he didn't look it.

'And before she has a chance to get out of his way, the bastard goes and sinks his frigging teeth into her groin. God, it was awful. He must have hit an artery. The mess – blood everywhere. And the way she screamed and screamed and then suddenly went quiet. It was all so quick, there was nothing I could do. I tried to stop the bleeding, but it was spurting all over the place. It only took a minute or two, and she went all pale and still. I knew she was dead.'

The girl's voice trembled, and she began to sob uncontrollably. Damn, thought Hunt. Won't get much sense out of her if she goes on like this. Got to calm her down. Get more details . . .

'Look, love, don't upset yourself,' he said, trying hard to sound sympathetic instead of impatient. This could be the big one . . . 'Come on now, take a deep breath and try and tell me what happened next.'

The sobbing went on for a while, and then the girl seemed to calm down a little and began again:

'I was so busy trying to do something for poor Sonja, I never thought to watch out for him – he looked like he was unconscious, laid out cold on the bed. I thought it'd be OK. Anyhow, next thing I know, he's coming towards me with a mad look in his eyes, and he's baring his teeth and . . . oh my God, there's blood dripping down his face and it's all over his chest; it's like something out of a horror movie . . .'

'So what did you do?'

'I hit him with the first thing I could lay my hands

on . . . it was a marble statuette I think . . . and that threw him off balance for a moment. And then I just ran and ran. All I had on was a waspie corset and high heels, and I had to take off the shoes so I could run. I wanted to get help, but at that time of night there was no-one around, it was four a.m. Eventually I got to my friend's flat and she let me in. I haven't spoken to anyone about it since.

'And there's something else you ought to know. I rang the hospital to find out if they'd let me see the body, and . . . it's disappeared. Gone. My God, what's happened to her . . . ?'

'Look, tell me your name and where you are. We need to get together and talk.' His pencil was poised over the shorthand pad, waiting with bated breath for the vital details. Come on, come on.

'My name is . . . oh no! No, please, please don't . . .'

'What's the matter – what's happening?'

'I . . . !' The girl's voice rose to a hysterical scream, which tailed off into a horrible hoarse groan, and then silence. Nothing but the dialling tone, insolently purring in Hunt's horrified ear.

Who was the girl? Where was she calling from? And how could he find out? She had sounded as if she was beyond help, but he had to try to trace her somehow. He had to think fast.

Feverishly, he scanned the previous week's papers, and found the story about the Knightsbridge murder. He didn't know why he hadn't paid more attention to it before, though there wasn't a great deal of detail. Apparently the victim was a high-class call-girl called Sonja Kerensky, who shared a flat with a friend called Teresa Monk, who also shared much of her work. Together, the girls specialised in 'threesomes' for wealthy clients. They didn't come cheap: it was rumoured the girls were pulling down £1,000 plus a night. Now Sonja was dead – in gruesome circumstances – and Teresa had vanished without trace. Intriguingly, the fact that Sonja had died from a vicious human bite was conspicuous by its absence. According to the newspaper article, she had been the victim of 'a violent attack, possibly by an intruder' – and that was all.

This stank of a cover-up by people who had an interest in not letting the public know how Sonja Kerensky had died. If the girl he had spoken to – and he had to assume it was Teresa Monk – was right about Sonja's death, a certain Mr Meredith Parry-Evans was in line to answer a whole lot of difficult questions. That is, if the truth ever came out.

And Andreas Hunt was out to make sure that it did.

On his way out, he rang Parry-Evans's private secretary at the House of Commons. He was 'out of the country on a trade mission, and won't be back for some time.' Very convenient.

Hunt scooped up the scrap of paper with Sonja Kerensky's address on it, and pushed his way through the swing doors, whistling with a savage glee. Andreas Hunt was on the case.

There was a pimply constable standing outside the entrance to the block of flats where Kerensky had lived, but that didn't pose much of a problem to Hunt, whose youth had been thoroughly mis-spent. He simply went round the back, and got in through the boiler room and up the back stairs to the fourth floor. Getting into the flat was a bit harder, but the month he'd spent in prison for refusing to pay a fine hadn't been wasted after all. You met some very useful people inside.

The door swung open with an eerie creak, reminding Hunt of the sound doors make in Hammer horror flicks when Igor invites the victim into Dr Frankenstein's laboratory. But Hunt was in no mood for macabre jokes as he stepped inside and closed the door behind him. He walked through the living room and towards the bedroom, scanning the scene: it was like a dress-rehearsal for Armageddon. Furniture overturned, the curtains torn down from the rail, papers knocked off a table and scattered like dead leaves on the forest floor.

He wrapped the handkerchief around his hand (you couldn't be too careful about leaving fingerprints) and turned the handle of the bedroom door.

Oh my God, screamed a voice inside Hunt's usually cynical brain.

There was blood everywhere: on the bed-sheets, the floor, in a big dried-up pool on the carpet, surrounded by a white chalk mark the boys from Forensic had drawn to remind them of the position of the body. It had even fountained up the wall at one point, and there were two bloody palm-prints smeared down the Laura Ashley wallpaper, as though the dying girl had tried to claw herself to her feet before finally collapsing on the floor. The windows were tight shut, and the air was full of the nauseating, metallic stench of blood.

He took several deep breaths – he didn't dare throw up, not here – and wondered where to start looking. What was he looking for anyway? He was no private investigator. But maybe . . . an address, a bit of paper with something meaningful written on it, a name . . . the address of Teresa Monk. He felt guilty about her: he was convinced she was dead, or worse – perhaps he should have contacted the police instead of taking matters into his own hands . . .

He rummaged in his jacket pocket and found the newpaper cutting. He smoothed it out and took another long, hard look at the photograph of Sonja Kerensky. 'Vice-girl found slain.' She'd certainly been a remarkable-looking woman: masses and masses of bright blonde curls hanging to the waist; huge, pale-coloured eyes with blonde lashes; creamy skin . . . The photograph was an old publicity shot from the days when Sonja had had a 'respectable' job as a photographic model. Even so, she was wearing nothing but a smile – still, it was a tasteful shot: she was lying face-down on a bearskin rug, just like one of those baby pictures only much, much sexier.

She was laughing into the camera and her knees were bent so that her feet kicked merrily in the air above her toothsome backside, dimpled and plump to just the right degree. Her nipples were hidden in the soft fur, but she was propping herself up on one elbow, so that her breasts hung down and Hunt could see that they were soft but firm, creamy-white and flawless. Her other hand was pushing her mane of golden curls seductively back from her long, slender neck.

An irresistible picture of her, rolling over on to her back, giggling and pulling him on top of her, leapt unbidden into Hunt's guilty mind. He felt extremely uncomfortable, having impure thoughts about this

263

poor woman who had just been horribly murdered, and yet . . . to look into that face was to feel sex surge through his helpless body; to gaze upon those breasts, those gently curving buttocks, was to feel the prick rearing inside his pants, nudging its head against the underside of his waistband, demanding release.

He was still looking at the photograph when a soft, sexy voice behind him spoke his name:

'Andreas Hunt . . .'

His heart was in his mouth as he turned on his heel to confront his discoverer, a plausible excuse already forming in his devious journalistic brain.

But he wasn't ready for this. No, not this.

Could Sonja Kerensky have had a twin sister? He knew in his heart that she hadn't. He'd read the cuttings. She was an orphan, no brothers and sisters, no family at all. Alone in the world. And now she was dead. Stone dead, with not a drop of blood left inside her poor drained corpse.

And that self-same girl was standing in front of him, smiling and beckoning him towards her.

'I . . . who . . . ?'

'I think you know who I am, Mr Hunt. My name is Sonja. Sonja Kerensky. I like you, Mr Hunt, and I think you like me too. Would you like to have sex with me? I won't charge you for it. I never make my men pay if they can satisfy me sexually. And you *can* satisfy me, can't you, Andreas?'

Her voice was like the distilled essence of pure sex, charming his too-willing prick as an Arab charms the deadly cobra with sweet, deceptive music. Hunt knew that this was ridiculous, horrible, macabre. He knew it had to be some sort of trick. Dead women don't just get up off their slabs in the morgue and come back to their apartments to seduce the first man who happens along. Dead women don't walk. And dead women don't smile at you and unzip your flies and pull out your prick and begin to suck it, to suck it like an angel . . .

He was speechless with mingled fear and excitement. Only moments before, he'd been paralysed with nausea at the thought of what had happened to this girl. He was still paralysed, but for a very different reason. He looked down at the girl as she knelt before him fellating him and wondered, wondered how this could be happening to him.

He stared at her, touched her hair, caressed the smoothness of her white neck – and it was all real solid flesh. A little cool, perhaps, and clammy – like the flesh of a small child fresh from bathing in the sea on a summer's afternoon. But real breathing flesh, none the less. The natural gold of her hair gleamed in the autumn sunlight filtering through the Venetian blinds, and he thought of the dulled eyes and matted hair of death, the blood; and the last foetid breath that belches from the corpse as it is lifted into the coffin.

And he thought to himself: how can this be death?

The girl was sucking away enthusiastically at his rigid tool, and he took her small white hands and placed them on his balls, showing her what he wanted her to do. She looked up at him and gave him a look of gratitude as she began to massage the two ripening fruits between his legs. The coolness of her hands and mouth seemed to soothe away the heat from his burning prick and balls; and yet he could feel his excitement growing, feel his reason ebbing away, his willpower draining out of him. He was now her prisoner, utterly – and he no longer cared. He wanted nothing more than to live within the pleasure-palace of her body.

He felt the pressure of her lips tightening about his prick, urging him on to orgasm; felt the incredibly sharp points of her teeth sliding over his hypersensitive glans; but he didn't care what she did to him: he just wanted it to go on and never ever stop.

The sound of footsteps in the living-room came too late for Hunt to pull out of the girl's mouth and make himself decent. And so, when the door opened a second later, his prick was still firmly lodged between her soft pink lips.

Hunt gazed into the eyes of three detective constables and wondered how the Hell he was going to explain why he was indulging in oral sex with a dead woman in the middle of her blood-spattered bedroom.

Except, of course, that all they could see was a mad journalist, standing on his own in the middle of the room, his erect prick thrusting obscenely out of the front of his trousers.

When Hunt got home from the police station, he thanked his lucky stars for friends in high places (that was one less favour he'd be able to call on in the future) and for the deplorable and very fortunate fact that all three detective constables had been drinking heavily and couldn't swear on oath to what they had seen. He only hoped the story didn't get back to the editor, who would be bound to start making pointed remarks again about

'nervous exhaustion' and 'overwork' – which was a
polite way of saying that he thought Hunt was about
to fall off his trolley.

Perhaps the editor was right. Perhaps he really
was inventing all these bizarre incidents in his own,
increasingly nutty, brain. Perhaps Sonja Kerensky
had just been an hallucination. Perhaps he ought
to forget about Cheviot and Parry-Evans and take
a holiday. A sun-kissed beach and Mara's nut-brown
nakedness within arm's reach . . . it sounded better
and better, the more he thought about it.

Mara was in the bath, looking irresistible as ever
and drinking Bollinger champagne out of a cracked
tooth-mug.

'What's the celebration?' he asked, sliding a hand
under the bubbles and toying with her right nipple.

'I've got the chance of a publishing deal!' she
giggled, unbuttoning his shirt and caressing his chest
with a soapy hand. 'A book on the power of crystals,
for a new occult publisher. Maybe even a video to
accompany it! Isn't it great?'

Hunt began to undo his belt.

'Yeah, great. But . . . why crystals?'

'They contain a very powerful psychic force, you
know. They can heal or harm, or tell the future . . .
I've become very interested in them over the last
few months. Anyhow this publishing company up in
Chester rang me today. Seems they've heard of my
reputation as a psychic, and wondered if I might be
interested in writing for them. I haven't signed up yet
but I'm so excited! Funny thing is, I've never heard of
the company. But who cares? Come on, have some
champagne and climb in!'

Hunt wondered why the hair was standing up on

the back of his neck; but he banished the feeling from his mind and kicked off his shoes, socks and underpants, leaping into the foaming water with such gusto that a tidal wave sloshed over the side and left a soapy pool on the bathroom floor.

Sitting at the opposite end of the bath from Mara, Hunt picked up the soap and began to rub it over her tits, lathering them until they almost disappeared under the bubbles, save for the pert pink nipples which protruded through the foam like the pink snouts of baby animals. She sighed with pleasure and retaliated by reaching under the water and playing with his cock. It responded in an instant to her familiar touch, growing and hardening between her gently teasing fingers.

Overcome by lust, Hunt lunged at Mara and fell on top of her, almost pushing her under the surface. Giggling like children, they struggled in the water until at last Hunt's superior strength won the day and his prick slid into Mara's slippery cunt like a warm knife into butter.

Maybe it wasn't such a bad day, after all.

After they had eaten, they drank a little more champagne and switched on the TV. More boring news about the EC, plans for a UN peacekeeping force in some Godforsaken banana republic, nothing worth listening to. Until the last item, which made Hunt prick up his ears and shush Mara into indignant silence.

'A bizarre incident occurred before this afternoon's Under-twenty-one international at Wembley,' began the announcer, 'when a naked woman ran on to the pitch and attacked Wayne Empson, the England

268

captain. She attempted to bite his neck before being apprehended by police. She appeared in court later this afternoon and has been remanded in custody pending psychiatric reports.'

The naked girl being led away turned her face momentarily towards the camera, and Hunt almost dropped his glass of champagne.

He was looking into the face of Anastasia Dubois.

The chapel at Longton Grange women's open prison was not usually a popular haunt for the inmates. Sunday morning service generally found ten or fifteen women in a chapel designed for two or three hundred: four or five of these would be prison officers, and most of the rest were only there because there was sod all else to do on a Sunday morning.

Under such trying circumstances, the job of prison chaplain was not an easy one. The Reverend Neil McCallister was an earnest, grey-haired man who regarded the prison chaplaincy as a vocation, if not a penance. Apart from anything else, it wasn't easy being the only man in a prison full of sex-starved women. If suffering was good for the soul, his place in Heaven was assured.

Preparing for Sunday morning service could easily have been a depressing experience, but Neil McCallister did his best to be enthusiastic about it. Maybe this Sunday the chapel would be packed to the doors. But he never really quite believed it. Which was why he was so surprised to turn round and see the chapel door swing open a good half-hour early, to reveal six prisoners, none of whom he recognised. Unescorted prisoners, at that. And that was strictly against prison regulations.

They were singularly attractive young women, no doubt about it. Rev McCallister had never married but he could still appreciate a pretty girl. Hard faces they had, though; and that was such a pity. Still, if they taken it upon themselves to come to him for spiritual guidance, all was not lost . . .

'Can I help you, my dear?' he enquired of the leader of the group, a tall brunette with muscular arms and a very nice bust, much of which was clearly visible as she had unbuttoned the top three buttons of her blouse.

She did not answer but just kept walking towards him, an odd smile on her face. McCallister began to feel slightly nervous. Maybe they were going to beat him up?

The woman was standing right in front of him now. She was half a head taller than him, and looked to be a good deal stronger. She raised her right arm, and beckoned to the other girls, who came forward and stood in a circle around the cowering vicar, who held on to his pile of hymn books for grim death.

'My dear, won't you tell me how I can help . . . ?'

He had no opportunity to say anything else, as they ripped off his cassock and stuffed the end of it into his mouth, to shut him up. They threw him to the ground and pinned him there, grinning maniacally but conducting their fiendish defilement in an eerie total silence. He writhed about as the tall girl stuck her hand up the leg of her knickers and he saw the knife-blade gleam in the candle-light.

But it was no good trying to wriggle free. They slashed at the fabric of his clothes and tore them from his trembling body.

O Lord no, not that, please, he prayed silently. But

it was too late. As they ripped off his trousers and underpants, his penis began to twitch and uncoil into rebellious life. The women were mocking him now, rocking with silent mirth as they saw this not-so-holy man so easily aroused, so easily led astray. And they began to undress.

As the tall girl stepped out of her knickers and forced him to sniff the damp, fragrant gusset, McCallister groaned and almost shot his load. He hadn't felt like this for years. He hadn't had sex for so long that he'd almost forgotten what it felt like, what the need felt like.

And as the naked women closed in around him, he looked beyond them and saw that there were more and more of them, flooding silently into the chapel.

As the first girl sat down on his prick, and the others began to lick him and nibble the flesh of his neck with their sharp white teeth, he had a strange thought which almost made him laugh: he hadn't had a congregation as big as this in years.

15: The Call

It had been a frustrating day. Hunt had got precisely nowhere with his enquiries about Anastasia Dubois: he'd drawn a complete blank with the police station, the magistrates' court, the lot. And the more he fetched up against a brick wall, the more convinced he became that he was dealing with a conspiracy of silence.

In desperation, he'd told the police everything he knew about Dubois and Cheviot, Teresa and Sonja and Parry-Evans. The Detective Inspector he'd spoken to had made encouraging noises, but Hunt wasn't fooled: he was damn well sure that the minute the door closed behind him, they'd torn up his statement and chucked it in the bin. 'We'll look into it,' they'd assured him. Well, he'd heard that one before and he wasn't holding his breath. He wouldn't be surprised if the bloody Police Commissioner was in on it, as well.

What made him even more suspicious was his own editor's attitude. Admittedly he had no hard evidence about either Cheviot or Parry-Evans, but he did have the tape-recording he'd made of Teresa Monk's telephone call. The editor was normally ready to take a chance, to tell Hunt 'Go for it,' publish and be damned. But, instead of the enthusiastic response he'd expected, Hunt was greeted by a stony wall of indifference which – if he wasn't very much mistaken – masked something else entirely. The rancid stench of fear.

Fear? Fear of what? And why? The libel laws had never held any terrors for the *Morning Chronicle* in the past.

Hunt stood by the bar in the Groucho Club and tried to look like a rising star of investigative journalism, instead of a frustrated hack rapidly subsiding into an alcoholic stupor. Bright young things and eminent literary figures rubbed shoulders all round him, but he didn't give a stuff. If it wasn't for the prospect of going home to Mara's soft tits and tight cunt, he'd have been totally fed up.

He beckoned to the barman:

'Another whisky, please. And make it a big one.'

The ice-cubes clinked invitingly in the amber fluid, but he just held the glass and gazed sightlessly into it for minutes on end. There must be some other way to get at the truth.

It was only the commotion in the lobby that brought him back to his senses and made him glance round. Through the double doors, he could just make out a tangle of three wriggling female figures, one of whom was obviously the club's rather sexy receptionist. There was a great deal of squealing and shouting. By now everyone in the club had turned to watch the riveting spectacle. Not one thought to go and lend a hand.

After a few moments, the receptionist went limp and slid to the ground, and the two other women broke free and burst in through the swing doors into the main bar. They were dark-haired twins, as alike as two peas in a pod, and pretty damn toothsome at that. Their crimson lips were full and glossy, and their slender bodies encased in body-hugging black Lycra mini-dresses which revealed far more than they covered up. Their breasts were small and round, like sweet apples ripe to be bitten into, and their tight little backsides were firm but mobile beneath the skintight fabric. Hunt could not suppress an appreciative shiver as they ran their hands sensuously over their bodies, as though actively seeking to arouse their audience.

No-one spoke or moved for a long time. All were transfixed by the sight of two identically sexy young women in black mini-dresses and fishnet stockings; identical sisters practising the ancient art of sex right before their tired eyes, suddenly grown brighter, more alert.

The girls began to dance slowly around the room, lingering at each table to stroke the men and rub their lithe bodies up against them. It was as though the men were hypnotised, unable to move or to speak. None made any move to touch the girls, though some were salivating – great drooling trails of spittle coming out of the corners of their mouths and running down their chins as they stood or sat there, open-mouthed and in an agony of desire.

Now the girls pulled down the tops of their dresses, revealing those rounded apple-breasts in all their rosy glory. Their nipples were hard as iron, the areolae puckered and glowing pink against the creamy-white flesh of their breasts. As they danced, so their breasts danced too, jauntily bobbing before them with all the lightness and gaiety of youth.

Hunt stared, unable either to believe or disbelieve

what he was seeing. He wanted to take out his camera and grab a few cheap shots of these two bizarre nymphos. He wanted to get out his shorthand pad and interview them – anything to prove his journalistic credentials. But instead all he did was goggle, just like all the other men. And women too: even the few women there were transfixed and clearly aroused, their pupils massively dilated and their breathing coming in fits and starts.

Hunt suddenly felt the connection between this incident and the other bizarre happenings he had encountered in recent weeks; and he sensed that, whatever else he did, he must resist the force which was being exerted upon him. The force was like a hand on his shoulder, guiding him in the direction it wanted him to go. He found that, by concentrating his thoughts, he could with difficulty detach that hand a little, or at least relax its iron grip.

Still fighting the compulsion to look at the girls, Hunt tore his gaze away and looked around the room. He realised that not everyone was equally affected: some were transfixed, helpless and clearly incapable of any voluntary gesture or word. But most people seemed, like him, to be only partially affected by what they were seeing. He wondered why.

The girls danced past, and lingered in front of a couple of middle-aged music critics at the table next to him. The girls beckoned to them and they immediately got to their feet, eyes bulging as grossly as the fronts of their trousers. Hunt, too, was aroused, but he could still think rationally, still distance himself a little from the weird experience he was undergoing. These men were enslaved, the empty puppets of these merciless temptresses. For the first time, Hunt noticed that the girls were wearing small crystal pendants, which dangled tantalisingly between their breasts and caught the light as they swung to and fro. They reminded him of Mara's crystal necklace, and the crystal-bladed dagger she had once shown him. She had never explained to him where she had got it from. And now she was writing a book about the bloody things. Hunt was growing increasingly suspicious of crystals.

All at once, the dancing stopped. Everything stopped. The silence was so thick, so oppressive that Hunt believed he might cut through the air with a sharp blade. The world was waiting, waiting.

The girls began to move slowly backwards towards the swing doors, arms outstretched in silent supplication. And, more slowly still, figures began to rise and walk towards them, followed them towards the door. A man here, a woman there, the two music critics, another man, and another . . .

The strange, silent procession, of ten or a dozen zombie-like figures, moved towards the waiting girls, who beckoned them on with smiles and welcoming arms. As they reached the doors, they swung open and an incredible, ferocious, unearthly whirlwind swept through the club, knocking over tables and chairs, breaking glasses. And ten of the Groucho Club's most eminent members simply walked out into the darkening Soho street: rats following the Pied Piper without a thought for the fate that might await them.

Hunt tried to follow, but it was like walking into the eye of a hurricane. It was all he could do to hold on to the side of the bar, eyes screwed tight with the effort of staying upright.

277

When at last the wind died down, they were long gone and the Groucho Club looked like a bomb had hit it. Dishevelled figures lay wide-eyed and pallid amid the wreckage, hardly daring to get to their feet. The ever-unflappable barman was the first to recover his composure, gathering up the fragments of a broken glass and mopping up the pool of gin and tonic on the polished wooden counter:

'Terrible weather we're having for the time of year, ain't it, Mr Hunt?'

Hunt took a long pull of his whisky and picked his way on unsteady feet towards the swing doors. Beyond, in the foyer, lay the unconscious figure of the receptionist, two tiny bite-marks marring the delicate whiteness of her neck.

Mara awoke in the night, suddenly aware that she was not alone with her lover. It wasn't the first time. And it wasn't just the aftermath of a bad dream, either: it was something much more concrete than that. She turned to Hunt and saw that he was still sleeping peacefully. There was no point in disturbing him.

She got softly out of bed, put on a dressing-gown to warm her fragile nakedness, and tiptoed to the window, parting the curtain slightly to look up at the sky. A big harvest moon, blood-red and low in the sky. Just looking at it made her stomach churn with fear. There was too much blood, too much blood everywhere: blood in her dreams, sudden strange visions of blood on her hands, and now Hunt was investigating these horribly bloody sex-crimes that seemed to defy the laws of reason. Of course –

and this was one thing that Hunt seemed incapable of understanding – in her world of the mind and the spirit, reason seldom had any significant part to play.

And a tiny, scared voice inside her told her that she had more than a little to do with it all. If only she could understand why. Maybe if she tried harder . . . used her skills, asked her spirit guides to point to some answers. Maybe she could get to the bottom of this bizarre and terrible persecution.

She went into the spare bedroom she used as a study and switched on the small table-lamp. It had a deep red shade and its reassuring rosy glow bathed the room in a comforting warmth. She drew her dressing-gown closer about her shoulders and sat down at the table she used for her Tarot readings. The ouija board was already set up, as she had held a seance the previous afternoon.

She rested the middle finger of her right hand on the upturned glass and asked her question in a hushed whisper:

'Is there anybody there?'

Nothing.

'Please answer me. Can you hear me?'

Nothing, and then the glass moved suddenly, jerkily; spelling out the letters:

'YES.'

'Why are you persecuting me?'

'FUCK.'

'I don't understand. What do you mean?'

'FUCK . . . FUCK YOU.'

Trembling, Mara let go of the glass and, to her horror, saw it continue to move without any contact from her – quickly, frenziedly, as though some demonic spirit were inside the upturned glass, desperate to express its unspeakable message:

'WHORE . . . WANT YOU . . .'

Mara got to her feet and backed away in horror: 'No!'

'YES . . . WHORE . . . HAVE YOU. HAVE YOU SOON. SOON.'

'Never . . .'

'VERY SOON NOW.'

She rushed out of the room and sat for a long time in the kitchen, drinking warm milk and trying not to think about the evil presence which was persecuting her. When she got back into bed, she was still shivering. The contact of her cold skin against his warm body awoke Hunt, and he pulled her to him, stroking and kneading her flesh back into comfortable warmth.

She began to forget her fears as the warmth permeated her limbs, her back, her breasts, her belly, her cunt.

'Want you, want you . . .' she murmured, running her hands over Hunt's warm body, kneading and massaging his flesh, revelling in the hardness of muscle and bone, and another hardness, burgeoning and thickening under her eager fingers.

Hunt threw back the covers and bared her slender body to the night air. She rolled over and lay face-down on the bed, exposing her delicious back and buttocks to his touch. Her skin felt as smooth as marble as he ran his hands over her back, running them down her spine until he reached the inviting crack between her satin buttocks and slid a finger inbetween. She wriggled with pleasure as he insinuated his finger further in and began to tickle the puckered amber rose of her arsehole.

'Yes, yes,' she moaned, as Hunt slid his finger further still and moistened it with the juices from her rapidly moistening cunt. When his finger was well-greased with love-juice, he slid it back up her crack and used the moisture to lubricate the doorway to her forbidden temple. He could feel her thrusting out her buttocks to meet his finger, trying to force him to penetrate her.

But he kept on teasing her, tormenting her, making her want him more and more. And he was enjoying the game, enjoying it more with every second. He felt huge, inspired, heroic, unstoppable. Perhaps he also felt the other presence, the evil presence, enter him – but he was too sexually aroused now to differentiate between his own identity and that of the evil soul which was manipulating him for its own amusement, its own devious ends.

His prick was ravenous for her: a mighty beast baying for its prey. And Mara was no less frantic for him, her cunt and arse pulsating in unison, opening and closing in a silent supplication.

At last he gave in to the overwhelming need for her and, sticking a finger deep inside Mara's arse, he placed the tip of his tool against her tight cunny-hole and gave a mighty thrust.

Mara cried out as the thick penis sank deep into her with that one mighty lance-thrust, running her through, impaling her, spearing her so she felt as though she would split in two.

'Fuck me, oh fuck me, tear me apart!' she cried, thrusting out her arse to take more and more of him, revelling in the double invasion of her innermost intimacy.

He rode her and frigged her with his finger, and she felt the warmth growing, spreading through her, localising around her clitty as the tip of Hunt's penis met his finger through the wall of her vagina. Hunt felt his own crisis approaching, and hastened his steed with ever-faster thrusts and the pressure of a finger directly on her love-button.

She came with cries of agonised enjoyment, weeping with the ecstasy of an orgasm with cunt and arse well-stuffed and stretched to bursting. And Hunt shot his load into her with a head-spinning orgasm that racked his body with wave after wave of perfect pleasure.

Afterwards, they lay locked together for some time, not moving, enjoying the sensation of semen trickling out of Hunt's penis and over Mara's trembling thighs and buttocks.

'I'll just switch the light on,' breathed Hunt at the end of a long silence. 'I'm going to get a drink.' And he climbed out of bed and groped his way to the light switch by the door.

Mara blinked in the sudden light, then looked up at Hunt and smiled at him. He smiled back and turned to leave the bedroom. As he turned, Mara caught sight of his reflection in the dressing-table mirror.

It was the reflection of the Master's evil face.

The next few days passed quietly, without incident, and Mara began to wonder if she had imagined that night – the ouija board, the evil eyes grinning out at her from the mirror. Yes, maybe she was beginning to imagine things. She even toyed with the idea of going to see the doctor and asking for something to calm her down.

On Saturday night, they went out for dinner with friends and came back late and rather drunk. Not that the drink in any way dampened down their ardour: in fact, Hunt felt randier than he had done for ages, and couldn't keep his hands off Mara in the taxi on the way back home.

They staggered, giggling, into the flat and the door clicked shut behind them. Fumbling for the light switch, Hunt knocked a book off the little shelf above the telephone table. It fell at Mara's feet, and she bent down unsteadily to pick it up.

It was a copy of *Halliwell's Film Guide*, and it lay open at a picture of Lon Chaney in full wolf-man make-up. Mara giggled and showed it to Hunt, who began to fool around, growling and pretending to bay at the moon.

'I used to be a werewolf . . .' began Mara, breathless with laughter.

'. . . But I'm all right now-oo!' Hunt grabbed hold of her and, picking her up in his arms, he slung her head-first over his shoulder and carted her off towards the bedroom, pummelling his back with hysterical fists.

Still in fits of laughter, Hunt threw Mara on to the bed and leapt on top of her, growling and snarling and tugging at her clothes with his teeth. He succeeded in biting off her two top buttons and began to probe around inside her blouse with his tongue.

'You're tickling!' exclaimed Mara, wriggling about with helpless mirth.

'Then I'll bite you instead!' And Hunt began to

nibble the sweet, soft flesh at the foothills of her breasts, tugging at the fabric of her blouse and wrenching it back off her shoulders to bare more of her utterly desirable body.

'It's a warm night,' whispered Mara, a sudden thought entering her head. 'Why don't we . . . on the balcony?'

'You have the sexiest ideas, you shameless hussy!'

And Hunt took her by the hand, unlocked the French windows and led her out on to the balcony.

Hunt had been lucky to get this flat. A wealthy friend had gone overseas for a couple of years and wanted a flat-sitter, so Hunt – who had previously been living in a grotty bedsit in King's Cross – had really fallen on his feet. The flat overlooked a quiet square, with an attractive park in the middle. The gardens were a little overgrown now, and the square had seen better days; but the trees whispered to each other in the light breeze, and the sulphurous light from the street-lamps suffused the whole scene with a soft and sensual glow.

They took a futon from the spare bedroom and laid it out on the balcony, added a few cushions and a blanket, and lay down together. The cool rush of air across her skin puckered Mara's nipples and brought a delicious thrill as it toyed with the tiny blonde hairs on her skin, making her breasts and thighs grow goose-pimpled and hypersensitive to Hunt's touch.

Hunt took one of the embroidered sofa-cushions and urged her to lift up her backside so that he could slip it underneath her buttocks. She wondered why – until she caught sight of the object in Hunt's hand. She hadn't noticed that he had brought more than cushions to ensure her pleasure.

He had been into the kitchen and brought back the object which most appealed to his sense of fun: it was long and thick and smooth.

'What are you doing with that candle?' demanded Mara, subsiding into giggles yet again – and knowing very well what he intended to do with it.

'Open wide!' commanded Hunt with a wicked smile; and he placed the end of the thick, smooth candle against the entrance to Mara's cunt. Then he gave it a good hard thrust. Fortunately, Mara's crack was so well-greased with love-juice that it opened willingly to the advances of this interesting dildo, and she thrilled to the thrusts of this substitute prick within her.

'Fuck me, fuck me!' she pleaded. And, ever her obedient servant, Hunt began to work the candle in and out of her cunt with long, slow, regular strokes.

As she writhed about under Hunt's exquisite tortures, Mara caught sight of something moving down below, in the park. At first, she thought is was just a stray dog, or a moving shadow made sinister by her lust-crazed brain. But a second, closer look revealed more shapes. And yet more.

Mara panted with desire under Hunt's conscientious frigging, thrusting her pelvis forward to enjoy the fullest possible sensation of being stuffed to the very hilt. She turned her head to look up into his face, and imagined that what she could feel inside her tight-stretched cunt was not a poor substitute but Hunt's own penis, grown surrealistically cool-fleshed and massive.

A sound from below caused her to look down through the railings again. Her heart missed a beat as she realised that she was listening to the sounds of a pack of baying dogs. As they moved forwards, into the light from the streetlamps, she realised something else. They weren't dogs.

They were wolves.

A pack of wolves – in London? But this was very nearly the twenty-first century and wolves had been extinct in Britain for hundreds of years! Surely they must be dogs? But even in her lust-crazed state she knew they were not dogs. They looked up at her with their yellow eyes, more sinister than ever in the orange-yellow light, and began to bay again, very quietly but very insistently. And she realised.

They were looking up at her. They wanted her.

The pack-leader was larger and more handsome than the rest, with a long, silky grey coat and penetrating eyes. Eyes she felt she had seen somewhere else before. He turned to the dominant female beside him and mounted her. Mara clearly saw his glistening penis enter the female, and heard her cry as he bit into the back of her neck to hold her fast.

And now all the other wolves were copulating, too: fighting and mounting each other and rutting and baying with the thrill of it all.

Mara felt the thrill, too. Fascinated by the sight of the pack-leader fucking his female, she imagined herself becoming that female, and the dildo inside her as the male's penis. She was nothing more than an animal, a wild animal chasing orgasm as it might chase its helpless prey.

She came with a great cry of excitement, and the wolves howled with her and were glad for her.

In a heavenly daze of ecstasy, Mara felt Hunt withdraw the candle and replace it with the warm, living flesh of his penis. It felt every bit as big, just as exciting. The flesh of her cunt still felt stretched and ready to burst.

And as she turned her head she saw the wolves still there in the gardens below, still looking up at her. The pack-leader was still fucking his mate, only now they seemed to be changing – at first subtly, then dramatically. They were assuming human form.

She came again and again: massive orgasms like surf crashing on a wild, deserted beach. And when she came to her senses and looked down into the gardens for a last time, she saw that the pack of wolves was still there, only now the beasts were surrounding two naked human figures: the figures of Mara Fleming and the Master.

And, as she suppressed a cry of terror, the Master raised his arm and beckoned to her, calling out to her in his quiet, but compelling voice:

'Come to me. The time is now.'

She swooned and could not be roused, and Hunt wondered what could have had such a profound effect upon her. For all he saw was a deserted garden, and all he heard was the barking of a small stray dog, looking for its master to come and take it home.

The following night, after they got back from a restaurant, they enjoyed the most exhilarating, passionate sex they had ever had. It seemed to have a mystical quality to it, to be governed by some huge cosmic principle which took away their power of rational thought and replaced it with a new guiding light: the drive to fuck and be fucked.

287

At last, exhausted but happy, they fell into bed and Hunt dozed off to sleep immediately. But Mara tossed and turned for an hour before at last she knew she would not be able to sleep, and got up to do some work.

She went into her study and sat down at the desk, to re-read the letter she had received from the publishing company that same morning. It was an odd sort of letter, but then again it was an occult publishing house and the publisher was clearly some sort of adept in the magical arts. And there was no denying the fact that it had contained a nice fat cheque. She shrugged her shoulders and thanked her lucky stars.

At that moment, there was a dull thud behind her. She swung round in her chair and saw that a book had fallen from the shelves: odd, that, seeing as the books were always pushed well back on to the shelves. It was almost as if it had thrown itself off . . .

She picked it up and saw that it was a book about the wartime Special Operations Executive and the training of its agents. It had fallen open at a photograph of a place called Winterbourne Hall, depicting a group of uniformed and plain-clothes army officers standing in a smiling line outside a big, rambling old house set in attractive grounds. She gave it a cursory look, closed the book and put it back on the shelf.

At that moment, she felt a sudden dizziness overwhelm her. She staggered back and held on to the desk to steady herself. Blinking and shaking her head, she opened her eyes and saw the image of Winterbourne Hall before her once again. But this time the picture had changed: there were no smiling officers in front of the house. It seemed to have been renovated, and the gardens were different too – more overgrown – and the house seemed to be surrounded by dense woodland.

Suddenly she realised that she was becoming a part of the picture, walking into it. It was impossible, but she could feel the gravel path beneath her feet. She was walking up the steps to the front door, ringing the bell. And the door was opening, someone was beckoning her inside. She looked into his face and saw that it was the Master, and he was smiling at her and beginning to undress her. And she felt the fear overwhelmed by the wanting, the wetness in her cunt banishing all doubts. He was caressing her breasts now, and whispering soundless words of arousal in her ear, stroking her neck, her back, her buttocks; sliding a finger into her cunt and back and forth across her throbbing clitoris.

'Come to me,' hissed the voice. 'You know you want to. You know you want my prick in your juicy cunt.'

'Fuck me,' Mara heard herself whimper, desperate for the feeling of hardness inside her belly.

'Then come to me. Come to me now. Come to me . . .'

The vision faded, and Mara found herself back in her own study, surprised to discover that she was now naked and her cunt dripping with wetness.

The doubts were gone, she knew not why. All she knew was that a sudden certainty had overtaken her and she now knew what she must do, where she must go. The call echoed loud and clear within her:

'Come to me now.'

She dressed quietly, swiftly, automatically; no

longer in command of herself or her own thoughts. And she opened the front door, walked down the stairs and out into the dark night air, the only sign of her sudden flight the front door swinging on its hinges with an ominous creaking like the articulation of dead bones.

16: The Acolyte

Little eddies of dust swirled around Mara's feet as she stood there in the middle of the deserted country lane in the gathering dusk. She felt something brush against her leg, and bent down to see that it was a newspaper, yellowed and torn. She picked it up, and saw with a start that the front page displayed a photograph of Winterbourne, much as it had looked in the book she had found at Hunt's flat. She glanced at the masthead, and a brief frisson of unease rippled through her dazed mind.

It was a copy of the *Daily Sketch*, dated April 1945.

She let the paper fall and began to walk on up the dusty track, hardly feeling the cold even though she was wearing only a thin jacket over her dress. The burning sense of purpose within her drove her on, though she hardly knew where she was going, or why. Somehow she knew that she would recognise when she had arrived, and that the purpose of the Master's call would become clear if only she obeyed. The fear was still in her heart, and the knowledge of the evil into which her powers were leading her: but all the will to resist had drained out of her, and a power beyond her own self led her onward.

Suddenly the road narrowed and came to an end

at the gate to a farmer's field. There was no signpost and no indication of which way she should go. But as she glanced round Mara caught sight of an overgrown track leading into the woods at right-angles to the road. This, she knew, was the way she must take.

She squeezed through the narrow gap, scratching herself badly on the brambles that grew in tangled profusion across the old track. They seemed alive, almost reluctant to let her go, wanting to touch and enjoy her body with their cruel fingers and keep her for themselves.

Pushing past, she found herself in a twilight gloom where the shafts of daylight penetrated only as intruders into a world where darkness was the natural medium. Although rain had not fallen for some time, the ground here remained slippery and there were patches of slimy black mud. Obviously this could not be the main way to the house she was seeking, for there were no footprints and it was clear that no-one had passed this way for a very long time. This must be some secret way, known only to a few. The way was so difficult that she even began to wonder if it was some sort of test.

Mara stumbled on in the half-light, feeling the prurient fingers of vegetation clutching at her, tearing her clothes, tangling her hair and trying to force their way into every fold of her fragile skin. In her trance-like state, Mara could do nothing to resist their rough embraces, and even began to become excited by the thorns raking across her flesh, the sharp branches tearing off her clothes and exposing her nakedness.

Gradually, as she pushed forward, her clothes were ripped in shreds from her body and her breasts and buttocks exposed. She stumbled and fell into a pool of mud; and when she managed to scramble to her feet and looked down at her mud-soaked hands and knees, she saw that the mud had formed curious patterns on her skin. Not amorphous patches of mud, but clearly defined characters, some of which she recognised as magical signs. Something very strange was happening to her.

She half-walked, half-crawled deeper and deeper into the woods, until at last she came to a fast-flowing stream at the bottom of a deep gorge with a fallen log lying across it. She saw immediately that the only way to cross was to pull herself across on the log. So she lay face-down upon it and began to edge herself over, inch by inch, terrified that she would fall to her doom.

The rough bark skinned her hands and knees and rubbed harshly against her now-naked flesh. But this roughness served only to excite her, stimulating her nipples and sending waves of sudden warmth flooding through her clitoris.

At last, she hauled herself off the log at the other side of the gorge, panting with exhaustion and almost sobbing with sexual frustration. Where to now? It was growing dark, and she had the odd sensation of being observed by many pairs of eyes.

At that moment, a dark shape glided out of the trees and into her field of vision. In what remained of the daylight, Mara saw that it was a huge, yellow-eyed wolf: the same pack-leader she had seen from the balcony, baying to her, urging her on. She recalled the image of the wolf transformed into human form, but the fear was slow in coming. She looked deep into the yellow-gold eyes and knew there was only one course left open to her: she must trust the wolf to guide her onward or perish in these dark and hostile woods.

The wolf led her on through the trees. The way was easier now, with a guide, and the path began to widen again, becoming a beaten track. At last they came to the place where the path crossed the main route to the house, and Mara stepped, weary and naked, on to the gravel driveway which led up to the front door of Winterbourne Hall.

She had long since lost her shoes and the gravel cut into her feet with agonising sharpness. But she stumbled on, oblivious to the pain and the danger, trusting only in the wolf as it led her on in the gathering gloom, towards the massive shape of the Hall, silhouetted like some malevolent demon against the darkening sky.

And moments later she stood before the great door of the Hall, filthy, torn and naked, raising her hand to ring the bell. When she turned round to look, the wolf had vanished. In its place, on the stone step beside her, lay the silver ring and the crystal-bladed dagger.

The door swung open and a dark, smiling figure beckoned her in.

'Welcome to Winterbourne, my dear girl. We've been expecting you.'

Mara was dazed and confused. She sensed that the aromatic ointment massaged into her flesh by Madame LeCoeur had been drugged, but knew instinctively that her confusion was more than the after-effect of an aphrodisiac massage. She felt as though a gateway had been forced open in her mind, letting in all manner of darkness and opening her up to be a channel for the will of far greater powers than those she herself possessed.

In her heart of hearts, she knew that the Master had brought her here because he had plans for her. And she knew that she should try to resist, but she could not.

She looked into the face of the man Delgado and understood that he, too, was being used by the Master for some evil purpose. But it was easy to read in his face that he was the willing tool of that evil, the eager servant of the Master's dark desires. And, seeing the shadow of that evil, the fear began to flood back into her.

The Master sensed that victory was near now, very near. At last he had succeeded in luring the girl to Winterbourne. Her spirit was broken now, and she would not resist him. She would easily be forced to lend her psychic powers to the cause of his salvation.

And he had Delgado to be the agent of his dark thoughts, to carry out his wishes until the moment of glorious liberation. Yes, Delgado had proved to be an admirable tool of evil: though it was undoubtedly a pity that his twisted body made him such an unworthy physical host for the Master's soul. For the perfect evil soul must be contained and nurtured within the perfect body. But, for these brief periods when he had the power to enter Delgado's body, the vessel would serve well enough.

Soon, very soon now, his own body would be free to serve him once again, as it had done for so many millenia.

He drank in the sexual energies emanating from England's finest whorehouse, and summoned all his powers to liberate his soul from its crystal prison for another brief spell. Tonight, through the agency of Delgado and the white witch, he would taste sweet flesh once again.

Mara had been bathed and perfumed, and robed in a long white shift with a silken cord at the waist. The crystal dagger hung from her waist in a pure white velvet scabbard and the ring sparkled on her finger. Strange how, when she had first discovered it, it had sat loosely on her slender finger; and yet now it fitted her perfectly – as though, like a living creature, it had adapted itself to its host.

Delgado was dressed in a similar robe, diaphanous as hers was; and Mara saw and was excited by the thick penis beneath, already hardening at the sight of Mara's exquisite body. Mara swayed with the intoxication of the moment: the drugs had dispelled the fear, arousing her to the point where she would have begged any man, woman or beast to fuck her till she screamed for mercy. Her pupils were widely dilated, betraying the trance-like state into which she was gradually slipping.

'Come,' ordered Delgado. 'It is time.' And he took Mara by the hand and led her out of the robing-room into a long wood-panelled corridor, lined with candles and torches hung in brackets on the walls. Mara blinked as the sudden light stung her eyes, and momentarily pulled back. But he forced her on, dragging her down the corridor, and she obeyed with uncharacteristic docility, following him as a trusting animal follows the farmer to its slaughter.

The corridor turned to the left, and then led down a steep flight of dark stairs. At the bottom was a door, which Delgado unlocked, and they passed through. It swung shut behind them with a dull thud. Inside the room was in darkness, save for the lantern which Delgado carried with him, and Mara shivered slightly with the sudden damp chill of the air, blinking in the gloom.

Delgado crossed the room and deftly pressed one of the panels. It immediately slid open and a current of ice-cold air rushed out.

'Inside,' commanded Delgado, and pushed Mara roughly before him. Once inside, he lit several oil lamps and Mara was able to see what manner of dungeon he had brought her to.

It was a dingy room with a musty smell. There were no windows and the walls were dripping with damp. But it was the most perfect example of a magician's workshop that Mara had ever seen. It was crammed with ancient leather-bound grimoires, fetishes, alchemical equipment, all manner of magical paraphernalia and vestments, jars containing magical ingredients . . . All lay in utter confusion: whoever the previous occupants had been, they had obviously left in some haste. The chamber had all the weird chaos of a magical jumble sale.

'This is a strongly magical room,' announced Delgado. 'As you with your exceptional powers will be able to deduce, it is located over the intersection of many ley-lines and other fields of power. It is also the secret room which was used by Allied magicians during the Second World War.'

'Why have you brought me to this place?' whispered Mara, realising for the first time that Delgado was speaking in the velvet tones of the Master. 'What is it that you want of me?'

'There is an object in this room which is endowed with a special power,' replied Delgado. 'You are to locate it and bring it to me.'

'But all the objects in this room are objects of power . . .' She looked around her in bewilderment. 'How . . . ?'

'If you are truly what I believe you to be, you will know it.'

Mara took a couple of steps forward into the room and closed her eyes to drink in the room's atmosphere. Delgado was right. The room embodied great power: neither good nor evil, but capable of being used for either end to great effect. But the messages she was receiving from the objects in the room were confused: there were so many conflicting signals. None stood out above the rest.

'What manner of object am I seeking? And to what purpose?'

She turned to Delgado for some signal, some word of reassurance or clue as to what she must do. But he was implacable:

'You will know it.'

Mara laid her hands upon several of the objects: a mouldering medieval grimoire, packed with rituals and incantations of enormous strength; an African fetish doll; instruments of torture and pleasure; a heap of magical vestments, embroidered with signs of the zodiac and images of the old gods.

But nothing spoke clearly to her. Only the confused jumble of signals she would expect from such old and powerful magical objects. None seemed to embody the extra-special qualities she had been commanded to seek out.

And then she felt it. The sudden heat from the blade of the dagger, hanging in its white velvet scabbard with its point gently stroking her pubis as she walked. The heat seared through her and she cried out, seizing the dagger and pulling it swiftly from the scabbard. Cautiously, she touched the glittering crystal blade. Nothing. It was as cool as a crystal should be. And she understood that the sudden surge of heat must be a sign.

She must use the dagger to help her find what she was looking for.

Holding the dagger before her, clasped in both hands and with point facing away from her body, she began to walk round the room, using the dagger as a divining-rod, feeling the vibrations which entered it at its point and flowed through it into the silver hilt.

At last: a force so strong she almost dropped the dagger. It trembled and shook in her hands and forced its point downwards towards the top of a rickety old table. But what exactly was it pointing at? Where was the signal coming from? She could see nothing but a small square of black cloth, covering . . . what?

She removed the cloth and saw that, underneath, there was an unremarkable wooden box carved with what looked like Egyptian hieroglyphics. She knew immediately that what she was looking for would be found inside that box. It radiated power: power that made the crystal blade of the dagger tremble so violently that it fell from her hands and on to the table beside the box. She too was shaking; for, even in the heavy, trance-like stupor which oppressed her and deadened her will and her sensitivity, she could tell that the force which emanated from the box was evil, dark, uncompromising.

'Open it,' hissed Delgado: the seductive voice of the serpent in Eden urging Eve to that first, irrevocable loss of innocence.

Bereft of the willpower to resist his command, Mara raised the lid and looked inside. Her eyes met a dazzling jumble of bright colours, gleaming precious metal and sparkling stones. The beauty of the necklace fascinated her, broke down her resistance, and she reached out and picked it up.

It was an Egyptian pectoral, exquisitely wrought and obviously very ancient, yet still perfect as she held it up to the lamplight and watched the changing colours dance hypnotically before her eyes. Precious stones and gold, wrought together into a heavy yet delicate profusion – a pattern of ibises and antelope, and at the very centre, placed exactly where it would hang between a woman's breasts, was a huge white crystal, carved into a multitude of glittering facets.

'Put it on,' ordered Delgado, mounting excitement in his voice. And, as she was slow to respond, he seized the necklace from her hands and hung it around her neck and shoulders himself, fastening it at the nape of her neck with a jewelled scarab clasp.

The moment the pectoral touched Mara's skin, an immense change surged through her. A terrible pain wracked her body, tore through her mind like a hurricane, and she cried out in an agony of fear as she witnessed, once again, the fate of the young Egyptian woman, screaming and screaming as they nailed down the lid of the coffin and spoke the incantation which would leave her hovering between life and death for all eternity.

But the scene changed. The pain ebbed away, and was replaced with a sudden calm, followed by a feeling of immense exhilaration. She felt the dark life-force of the undead priestess surging out of its place of captivity, flowing into her through the crystal, entering her through every pore of her skin, filling her up and banishing all traces of the woman who had been Mara Fleming.

Delgado felt the cold hand clutch at his heart, and knew that the Master had summoned the strength to overwhelm him once again. And he surrendered all consciousness of his own being as the Master took complete possession of his body.

Sedet glorified in the vitality of the young girl's body and gave a laugh of triumph: a laugh that echoed through the chill room as the raven's cry cuts through the air of the forgotten tomb.

'You have returned to me at last,' breathed the Master, cursing the imperfection of Delgado's body that caused him to be displayed so poorly to the eyes of his long-lost Queen.

'You abandoned me,' replied the Queen. 'Why did you abandon me, my one true Master?'

'I could not find out where you were . . . I could not contact you, though I used all my powers. The sorcery that veiled you from my eyes was too guileful, too strong. I have spent thousands of years searching for you and now you see me in this spent husk of a body – and even this poor body is not my own to possess. My body lies helpless and enchanted within this chamber. I can but steal brief moments of life before my strength is spent and I am driven back to my captivity. But soon I shall be free . . .'

'Take me!' cried the Queen, drawing close and laying soft hands upon the Master's shoulders. 'Take me now, for already I feel the power dragging me back to my death that is worse than death, my life that is less than life. Take me, fuck me, use my body as you used it that night in the Valley of the Tombs of Kings . . .'

The Master remembered that night, so long ago, when he had summoned Sedet to the dark valley with its many hidden tombs; and they had entered the tomb of the Pharaoh and had committed the vilest and most magnificent act of sacrilege: he had fucked his Queen on the very lid of the Pharaoh's sarcophagus, in their act of gleeful desecration defying the gateway of death through which all mortal men must pass.

He seized the girl roughly and pressed his lips to hers savagely, then grabbed handfuls of her flimsy garment and tore the fabric from her body, maddened by the hunger of millenia, the need to pull apart her cuntlips and have her, thrust his manhood deep into her soft belly and join his immortal, evil soul to hers for the first time in so many thousand years.

There was no gentleness in his touch, nor did she crave any: only the maddened greed of the famished, the urgency of the starving prick. He bit hungrily into her flesh, biting her nipples so greedily that she moaned with pain and yet urged him on:

'Harder, harder! Bite my tits until they bleed . . .'

But already he was moving down her body and biting into the soft flesh of her pubis, thrusting his tongue deep into her pubic bush and onward towards her already-throbbing clitoris. She tasted sharp, strong, intoxicating on his tongue. And she was clutching at him with her red-tipped talons, tearing at his hair and crying out her frenzy:

'Take me, take me! Give it to me, show me no mercy! Oh, use me, use my body . . .'

She began to rake sharp-nailed fingers across his back, tearing off his robe, pulling it down over his shoulders; and, impatient to have her, he unfastened the belt and threw the tattered garment to the floor. His manhood thrust impatiently out of the dark curls at the base of his belly, and his testicles felt unbearably heavy and bursting with their overload of hot, foaming spunk.

The Master caught sight of an upturned carved chair, lying in the dusty corner of the room. He set it upright and sat down on it. Immediately, Sedet flung herself to her knees between his parted thighs and began to lick the sensitive flesh of his groin, between the tops of his legs and his balls.

'Squeeze them, squeeze my balls,' he groaned; and she obeyed eagerly, clasping small brown hands around his bursting globes until his head began to spin and he feared he would shoot his load without possessing her.

He pulled her to her feet and made her turn round, so that her back was to him, backside thrust out slightly, and very invitingly, for his inspection and delectation. It was a wonderful backside: tanned and silky-smooth, rounded and downy like some huge juicy peach ripe for the eating.

Using a little of her copious cunt-juice, the Master began to lubricate the wrinkled brown arsehole which Sedet was so shamelessly presenting to him. She moaned with delight as he tickled her perineum, torturing her with half-forgotten sensations, gradually easing the tip of his finger inside her until at last he was able to thrust the whole finger into her arse. How she sang with pleasure as he moved his finger in and out, widening her forbidden pathway and pressing against the thin wall between arse and cunt.

He used his other hand to feel her cunt: it was ripe and juicy, overflowing with the nectar whose honey-sweet taste he so vividly recalled. He scooped up a little with his index finger and ran his tongue along it. Delgado's tongue, now pressed into his service, lending him the senses which had so long been lost to him.

Then he grabbed hold of Sedet's waist and forced her backwards and down, in one savage thrust impaling her doubly on prick and finger, filling cunt and arse to overflowing. His fat prick distended her cunt deliciously, and she danced on him like a music-box ballerina pirouetting on two spindles: one up her cunt and one stretching her arse.

Their souls met and mingled, and in their minds they were no longer in borrowed bodies, feeling borrowed sensations for a brief, stolen moment. They were once again in the dank darkness of the tomb, fucking shamelessly by the light of a single clay lamp, amid the dancing shadows. Fucking on the lid of mighty Pharaoh's tomb, the new gods for whom the puny gods of the underworld held no more terrors.

She rose and fell more quickly now, engulfing his penis and then levering herself up as far as she could go without losing its glistening tip; now falling suddenly, swallowing him up, until at last she cried out and the sudden delicious spasms of her cunt brought him, too, to a massive, crashing orgasm.

Sedet lay slumped forward, still impaled on his prick and panting heavily. As the last waves of pleasure ebbed away, a terrible cold began to steal over her and she cried out:

'No, no! I cannot go back, I cannot . . . !'

But it was too late. The Master could feel it, too. The union of their souls through incarnation in these two borrowed bodies had drained all their strength. And the power of sorcery which had held them fast for so long was once again clawing at them, dragging their souls back into captivity.

With a terrible cry of rage and despair, the Queen's soul fled its unwitting host, leaving Mara to slump forwards on to the floor, semen flooding out of her abused cunt. And Delgado found the power draining out of him again, leaving him once more a mortal and imperfect man, impatient to return to the dark immortality he had tasted.

Full of rancour, Delgado got wearily to his feet and looked down contemptuously at the prostrate form of the unconscious girl. He opened the door and called for two of his trusted henchmen:

'Give her to the guards,' he sneered. 'They'll have a few good ideas about what to do with her. Just make sure they don't kill her: we'll be needing her later on.'

As the Master's spirit returned, protesting but exhausted, to its place of imprisonment, he consoled himself with the knowledge that in Mara Fleming he had found the source of salvation, not only for himself, but perhaps also for his long-lost Queen.

17: The Quest

The heavy granite lid of the sarcophagus lay cold and unmoving. Dust sat thick upon its mirror-smooth surface. All around, the air hung foetid with the reek of death and decay. But within the unforgiving stone prison, his body frozen in the useless immortality of the crystal block like a fly suspended in amber, the Master's spirit raged and would not be still.

Although his body would not obey him, his spirit was gaining in strength by the hour. Already he had regained the power to see far beyond the confines of his prison and project his thoughts and wishes into the minds of mortals. Already he had drawn the white witch Mara to this house of ill fame; and, entering the body of Delgado, had been able through her to enjoy coition with his lost Queen. He lusted still as he recalled the sweetness of her living flesh and the delicious surge of sexual energy which had flooded from her youthful body into his restless spirit. Soon, very soon, he would feast upon her soul.

Nothing must stand in his way. The journalist, Hunt, was proving to be dangerously curious. He must be deluded, diverted from the trail that led to Winterbourne Hall. And if by chance or determination he should find his way here, then he must pay the ultimate price.

Above, in the mortal world, the sun had passed
behind a cloud and a sudden darkness presaged rain.
The Master could feel neither sun nor wind nor rain;
only the unstoppable dark force of his own desires,
and the exhilarating anticipation of the games which
he was about to play. He sincerely hoped that in Hunt
he had chosen a worthy prey, a victim who would
prove to be worth the trouble.

The Master's soul exulted, and the sky grew still
darker. He could almost feel a new life beginning
to surge through his frozen veins, the blood of
immortality envigorating his lifeless penis.

It was late in the morning when Hunt awoke,
dry-mouthed and with a throbbing headache. The
whisky bottle lay empty on the bed beside him, and
he realised with disgust that he must have drunk
the whole lot. He winced as he hauled himself to
his feet and staggered bleary-eyed to the bathroom,
emptying his bursting bladder with a sense of relief
marred only by the pain from his equally bursting
head. He looked in the mirror and did not like what
he saw. Unshaven, still wearing yesterday's shirt and
crumpled trousers, red-eyed and blotchy-faced, this
was not the image of the keen, clean-cut reporter
which Hunt had spent the last few years working
hard to achieve. He looked more like a stand-up
comedian's impression of a drunken old hack.

Memories flooded into his brain, sobering him
with the ice-cold truth the whisky had failed to
erase. Mara was gone. She had left no note; taken
no clothes with her: even her purse lay untouched
on the beside table. To all intents and purposes, she
had simply walked out into the night.

The police seemed less than interested: just the unpredictable sort of thing a woman like that would do, they had implied. White witch? Psychic? You couldn't expect these New Age crazies to behave like normal people, could you? But Hunt knew she wouldn't, *couldn't* have left him like that of her own accord. He had to find her.

He couldn't have imagined that he would miss her so much. As he stared listlessly into a cup of black coffee, he recalled that last night of lovemaking: passionate, frenzied, almost frightening in its intensity – as though she had known that this was the last time, the ultimate time, the once and forever and nevermore time.

The evening had begun ordinarily enough. A visit to the theatre; dinner in their favourite French restaurant – funny how Mara had lost her taste for her usual vegetarian dishes, and ordered only meat, craving the taste of warm flesh: red meat, so rare that the blood still oozed out of it and it had almost turned Hunt's stomach to see her tear into it with those pretty white teeth.

Afterwards, they went back to the flat and shared another litre of red wine. The room had started to spin and Hunt suspected that he was too tired, too drunk for sex. Perhaps he would just let himself drift off to sleep . . . But Mara had other plans for him. He remembered lying slumped on the settee, gazing up at her enchanted as she began to undress, slowly and provocatively. First she slipped off her elbow-length white gloves, tossing them teasingly across his face. Then she hitched up her skirt to reveal the tops of seamed black stockings, so fine that they were like a black mist kissing her shapely

limbs. Deftly, she unfastened them from the black
suspender belt and slid them down from her tanned
thighs to her slender ankles, stepping out of them
daintily and somehow reverentially, as though each
detail of the ritual was essential if her magic spell
was not to be broken.

'A charm to bind, a charm to bind,' she murmured
playfully, turning slow circles and taking the silver
combs from her dark, glossy hair so that it tumbled
down over her generous breasts.

Hers was a special rite; a special magic which never
failed to work its charms on Hunt. She was the sexiest
woman he had ever known: Monroe and Cleopatra
and Delilah with, that night, just a touch of Jezebel.
His prick began to rear its joyful head as he watched
her reach behind her and slide down the zip on her
tight black cocktail dress. It peeled away from her
golden back like the skin from a ripe, juicy fruit just
begging to be eaten. As she pulled the dress down
over her shoulders, her opulent breasts sprang free,
unfettered by any bra and as firm and soft as any
man could ever dream of in his wildest fantasies.

Now she stood naked before him, save for the
many-faceted crystal which she had recently taken
to wearing on a chain about her neck. It spun round
on its golden chain, hanging heavy in the deep cleft
between her breasts. Hunt groaned with pleasure as
she leant over him and let his face nestle between
her heavy globes, safe within the dark curtain of
her hair. Unable to reach her nipples, he took the
crystal momentarily into his mouth, accepting its
mystical coolness on his tongue like the Host of
some unholy rite, imbued with a sophisticated and
sensual and terrifying power.

It was as though Mara had suddenly been transformed at that instant: as though the communion
of flesh and crystal had allowed some other, wilder
spirit to enter her body as the spirit guide enters the
body of the medium during a seance. Her violet eyes
flashed fire. Hunt began to pant with desire and
tried to sit up, pull Mara towards him. But she pinned
his arms to the settee, staring into his eyes with a
greedy desire which would accept no challenges to its
mastery. He answered her gaze, but did not recognise
what he saw there. All was masked by a dark flame
of lust which terrified, consumed and excited him.

All at once she fell upon him as a wolverine falls
upon its prey – tearing off his clothes and laughing,
screaming with laughter like a madwoman. He lay
transfixed, between fear and ecstasy, as she worked
upon his thrusting penis with her skilful fingers.
The night air was full of the heady scent of her
sex, and clear, sweet fluid was trickling out of her
swollen cunt. He had never known her so aroused,
so . . . ferocious . . . in her desire. At last she
had taken his straining manhood into her cunt and
pumped away at him with all the savagery of a wild
beast in heat. And his ecstasy had mingled with the
pain of her long red fingernails, digging deep into
the flesh of his back.

Afterwards, she had seemed to return to her normal self again, and they had fallen asleep entwined
in each other's arms like sentimental young lovers.

And when he awoke, she was gone.

A quiet thud announced the arrival of the morning
post. Wearily, Hunt hoisted himself to his feet and
shuffled into the hallway. Nothing much. Just a
couple of bills, plus a handwritten white envelope.

He didn't recognise the writing. Tearing open the envelope, he read:

> 'FORGET HER, HUNT. FAR BETTER TO
> BE ALONE THAN DEAD. NEVER FOR-
> GET: YOU CANNOT ESCAPE THE ALL-
> SEEING EYE.'

It didn't make sense. Was this something to do with Mara's disappearance, or had one of his in-depth exposés finally driven someone to make threats against his life? All Hunt's professional instincts told him to put it out of his mind, throw the damn thing in the bin and forget about it. But – perhaps it was his imagination – he could feel a sudden coldness gathering around his heart.

He felt sick, dizzy, disorientated. At first he thought it was just the hangover, but that surely could not account for the blurred images forming across his field of vision. He blinked, trying to focus on the words; but a persistent fog clouded his eyes and he had to close them briefly, to combat the terrible feeling of falling, falling, into an icy darkness.

When he opened them again, the shapes were still there – but this time, they were vivid and sharp, frighteningly lifelike. Images floated around him. Images of naked men and women, the men with huge distended penises and the women with bulging breasts and dripping cunts. They were locked in an unholy orgy of coupling. Here, two men were using one woman simultaneously and, although the entire scene passed before his eyes silently, Hunt saw the woman's mouth open in a scream of exultation or pain – he could not tell which – as her cunt and arse were ravaged by her rampant suitors. One man was being held down by four dark-haired women who were laughing savagely as a fifth woman masturbated him violently whilst sinking her teeth into his thigh. His expression was one of mystical ecstasy, as though he had seen a vision of divinity. Everywhere men and women were copulating frenetically, as if this was their destiny and to fail it was to negate their very existence. None of them seemed aware of Hunt.

And then he saw another figure appear at the top of the staircase: the tall figure of a dark-haired woman in a long black cloak. A full hood concealed most of her face but, as she glided down the stairs towards him, she looked up at him, revealing features which were familiar, yet somehow strangely altered.

'Mara!' whispered Hunt. He tried to step forward, tried to touch her, but it was as though a glass wall separated him from his lover. She stood amidst the writhing bodies, part of the scene and yet set apart from it; and she stared straight into Hunt's eyes. He felt as if an electric shock had passed through him as she threw off her cloak and stood naked before him.

He gasped with desire and then horror as he saw her nakedness. For, where the crystal had hung between her breasts, he now saw the silver hilt of a dagger whose clear crystal blade vanished into her heart. Was his beloved Mara dead? Yet there was no blood, no agony, no look of death upon her face, and the most bizarre, cruel smile distorted her beautiful features so that he scarcely recognised her. Her long brown nipples were puckered and erect, and once again Hunt could smell her heady cunt. She was mocking him with her unearthly sexuality, and he longed for the touch of her slender fingers upon his manhood, which strained for release.

She was wearing a crystal coronet which sparkled like diamonds against her long dark hair. Its effect was as magical as the effect of Mara's luscious body was on Hunt. A sudden flash of light struck sparks from its thousand facets and the Dionysian revels came to an abrupt end. Each man and woman froze exactly where he or she was lying or standing, faces contorted as they were struck down in the midst of orgasm. And as they sank slowly to the ground, they turned their faces towards Hunt. Their dying eyes were full of an infinite ecstasy and an exquisite fear.

And, still smiling, Mara watched them die.

Lightning flashed across Hunt's brain, dazzling him for a moment. And when at last his eyes saw clearly, the visions had gone. He looked in vain for any sign of Mara's presence: it was as if she had never been there.

It must have been the drink. An attack of the DTs.

And then Hunt felt a sharp, burning sensation in his fingertips. Looking down, he saw that he was still clutching the threatening note, and inexplicably it was smouldering in his hand. As he looked at it, the note burst violently into flames. With a cry of pain he dropped it, and watched it reduced in seconds to a few charred fragments on the hall carpet.

Hunt spent what remained of the morning searching systematically through Mara's address-book and ringing up her friends. None of them admitted to knowing anything about her disappearance. In fact, none of them claimed to have seen her for at least a fortnight. Apparently she had been very preoccupied with the publishing project, but she had said nothing to anyone about any new fascination or sinister involvement.

Surely Hunt would have known if she was involved in anything dangerous? Surely she would have told him? He began to wonder if she had been seeing another man. Or maybe her friends were trying to put him off the scent? Many of them shared her involvement in the mysterious and the supernatural.

Hunt had never had much time for the occult until he met Mara, whose gentle insistence had forced the suspension of his disbelief. He was naturally suspicious of anything secret, anything vaguely forbidden. The mysterious note had only added to his suspicions. What if Mara was being held somewhere against her will by some group of New Age weirdos?

He made up his mind. He was going to see Eleanora. Eleanora was one of Mara's closest friends, and a fellow witch. Hunt had not been able to contact her by telephone and he reckoned she just might be hiding something. The only problem was, Eleanora lived in a remote cottage in some God-forsaken corner of rural Cumbria. No matter, he would drive through the night if need be.

Hunt was beginning to wish he had taken the M6 after all. It was one hell of a long way to Cumbria, especially when you went the pretty way. The trouble was, Hunt had a thing about motorways. Years ago, when he was a child, he had been involved in a terrible accident. The school minibus had been caught in the middle of a motorway pile-up, and his best friend had died before the ambulance got to them. You don't really ever get over something like that. Even though he was an experienced driver, Hunt still steered clear of motorways.

At least the B-roads were less crowded. He put a cassette in the tape deck and the insistent 4/4 beat of a rock anthem helped ease his troubled mind. It was getting dark and he realised that he hadn't eaten anything for almost twenty-four hours, so he stopped at a transport café for a burger.

The café was crowded with truckers, travelling salesmen and a party of schoolchildren on their way to an outward-bound course in the Lake District. Wandering round aimlessly with his tray of food, Hunt finally found a seat at a corner table, next to a very exotic, very desirable girl with the fullest red lips he had ever seen.

'Mind if I sit here?'

'Not at all. I'd be delighted.' The girl flashed him a smile which woke Hunt out of his depression and set something stirring in his loins.

She was delicious, and very vulnerable. Hunt found himself irresistibly attracted to her lithe body, those firm young buttocks and tanned thighs clad in flimsy shorts; that pert, eager bosom swelling stiff-nippled under her sleeveless T-shirt; those unbelievably full red lips and that great tumbling mass of dark hair. Feeling disgustingly disloyal to Mara, he realised that he longed to rip off her T-shirt and shorts, fling her down on the stained Formica table and ram his engorged prick into her like a stallion mounting a prize filly.

Hunt felt vaguely alarmed at the forcefulness of his response to the girl. He wasn't normally as oversexed as this. Since meeting Mara, his sexuality had scaled new heights; and ever since Mara had made violent love to him that night he had begun to feel as though some unseen force were constantly caressing him, maintaining him in a continual state of unbearable arousal. His unruly prick just refused to lie down and play dead. He took a couple of deep breaths, as though the oxygen might just help rid his body of such unclean thoughts.

The girl was toying with a sandwich and a cup of coffee but she didn't seem interested in it. Unless Hunt's instincts were letting him down, she had more of an appetite for him than for the food. Her T-shirt was cut very low at the neck and she kept leaning forward, to make sure he got a really good look at her deep, perfumed valley. He found himself thinking: 'I bet you're dynamite in bed, young lady. And you know I'd just love to stick my cock in between those gorgeous tits, you little prick-teaser.' And his cock twitched convulsively, wholly in sympathy with the thought.

'My name is Katya,' explained the girl, making endless circles in her coffee-cup with a plastic spoon. She was clearly foreign but her English was excellent, with just a hint of a sexy middle-European accent.

'Where do you come from? Are you on holiday over here?'

'I am a student in Romania. I come to England to . . . complete my education.' The luscious Katya was evidently a keen student, eager to perfect her technique, as Hunt felt a naked foot sliding up his leg, his thigh, caressing the aching hardness of his crotch. He was burning for her, and she knew it. And he saw that she was not indifferent to his charms, either: as he gazed at her, he saw her nipples stiffen visibly beneath the skin-tight T-shirt. God, he wanted her.

'I wonder, could I ask a very great favour?' She turned her enormous dark eyes on him, and it felt deliciously dangerous, as though some powerful cosmic force were threatening to rape his very soul.

He gave a little nervous cough: 'Ask away. But I warn you, I'm no good at robbing banks and I haven't slayed a dragon in months.'

She laughed. 'Nothing so exciting, I'm afraid. Tell me, are you travelling up to Cumbria tonight, Mr . . . ?'

'Call me Hunt. Yes, that's my plan.'

'I was wondering – would it be possible for you to give me a lift as far as Lancaster? I don't normally hitch-hike, but you know what it's like, Mr Hunt . . . we students have so little money.'

'Yes, well, I don't normally give lifts to hitch-hikers, either,' replied Hunt, trying not to betray the emotion he felt as her toes gently but expertly massaged his erect penis. 'But it's getting late, you're on your own and you look bloody freezing in that little T-shirt. OK – it's a deal.'

She smiled delightedly. 'I am so grateful. You are very kind, Mr Hunt.'

'We'd better get on the road, then. Finished your meal?'

'Yes, thanks. I wasn't very hungry.' Her food looked untouched.

Hunt groaned with desire as Katya got up from

her seat, revealing the full beauty of her well-muscled thighs, the poetry of her slender but powerful young body.

'By the way,' grinned Hunt, 'didn't your mother ever warn you about men like me?'

Katya nodded and gave a wry little smile. 'Of course – my mother was a very wise woman. But you see, I never was a *good* girl.'

Hunt swallowed heavily at this provocative remark, and sighed with inner agony as she opened the rear door of his car and bent down to push her rucksack on to the back seat. As she did so, her succulent arse thrust backwards and Hunt felt a sudden longing to wrench down her shorts and panties, unbutton his flies, take out his throbbing cock and wank himself to orgasm over her golden buttocks. He groaned as he got into the front seat beside Katya and turned on the ignition. He just couldn't get rid of the delicious mental image of his semen spurting out in great gobbets, splashing the amber flesh of Katya's backside.

They turned off the main road and set off along winding country lanes barely wide enough for one car to pass, let alone two. Katya babbled on in her excellent English about her home village in Romania, which was the sort of inoffensive chatter Hunt could cope with; but then she started talking about sexy underwear, which led her on to the subject of women's bodies.

'You like women's breasts, Mr Hunt?'

'Well, yes, of course . . . all men do, I suppose.' The discomfort in his trousers was now extreme.

'Then I am sure you will like these,' and without further ado, the dark-haired temptress stripped off her T-shirt, revealing the flimsiest of cotton bras which was quite inadequate to restrain her lively breasts. The fabric was so thin that Hunt could clearly see she had pierced nipples, and wore a tiny gold ring threaded through each. In the midst of his sexual confusion, Hunt noticed with vague surprise that she was also wearing a crystal on a chain round her neck. It hung, long and almost obscenely phallic, between her breasts – a potent symbol of the young woman's unfettered sexuality.

A car was approaching from the opposite direction and Hunt had to turn the wheel sharply to avoid a collision.

'For God's sake, Katya!' he gasped. 'This is neither the time nor the place . . . do you want to cause an accident or something?'

Katya's only reply was a little laugh which made her lovely breasts quiver and set Hunt's poor penis bucking and rearing within his underpants, especially when she peeled off her bra and flung it on to the back seat. His distress must have betrayed itself on his face for, the next thing he knew, slender tanned fingers were skilfully unbuttoning his flies and reaching inside for his pulsating member.

'No . . .'

But inside he was rejoicing, exulting, greedy for the glorious release which he had been longing for, and which he knew Katya would give him. Never before had he felt such an all-consuming need for sex: he could scarcely recognise himself. He groaned again, but this time with extreme pleasure, for the Romanian girl lowered herself over his penis and took it between her breasts, massaging it skilfully and sensually as she squeezed them together, and it was all he could do to keep the car moving along the dark, winding lane.

Katya could not have been older than seventeen, yet she had the skill of centuries in her fingers; all the mysteries of the ancients were contained in that knowing touch. Suddenly she was no longer a teenage strumpet amusing herself with an older man in the front seat of his car: she was a regal courtesan, a high-priestess of the arts of love.

Hunt's head was swimming. With one hand to guide the steering wheel, he used the other to caress Katya's firm breasts, revelling in the toughness of her erect pink nipples with their little golden rings. Her skin was strangely cool to the touch, more like a porcelain doll than a real live human being, thought Hunt, just as he poured forth his tribute on to her breasts – and moments before the Land Rover shot towards them round a blind bend.

Hunt's reflexes were good. Even in his post-orgasmic confusion he could have avoided the Land Rover if the girl Katya had not suddenly reached across and wrenched the steering wheel out of his grasp. If it hadn't seemed such a crazy thing to say, he would have sworn that she was actually forcing his car into the path of the Land Rover, willing the two vehicles to collide. And all the time she was smiling that secret smile.

The last thing he saw, before the cars collided and he lost consciousness, was an empty seat beside him. It was quite impossible, of course, but the mysterious Katya had vanished into thin air.

Hunt awoke in an unfamiliar bed, staring up at a clinical white ceiling. His head hurt, and when he reached up to touch it his fingers encountered a thick wad of lint and a crepe bandage. He tried to sit up but the room started to spin and he fell back, defeated. It wasn't until the nurse came along and propped him up on some more pillows that he fully realised where he was.

'You're in the Royal Infirmary, Mr Hunt,' explained the nurse, adjusting his backrest. 'And if I may say so, you're very lucky to be alive.'

'What happened . . . ?'

'You were driving along a country lane and you had a head-on collision with a Land Rover. It's a miracle nobody was seriously hurt.'

'What about the other driver? And what about me . . . ?'

'The other driver's fine – got away with a few minor cuts and bruises. And you've just had a bump on the head. You'll be fine in a day or two.'

Hunt's fuddled brain suddenly focused with razor-sharp clarity: 'What about Katya? How is she?'

'Katya?'

'You know, the girl in my car. Is she . . . ?'

'I don't understand, Mr Hunt. There was no girl in your car. I assure you, you were quite alone.'

'But . . . !'

'Don't worry. It's probably just a spot of concussion.'

The police came and interviewed him twice, evidently not at all happy with his story about the accident – especially the bit about Katya, the vanishing backpacker. Although they had been on the scene within a couple of minutes, and had interviewed dozens of people, no-one remotely answering Katya's description had been seen anywhere near the area.

The driver of the Land-Rover swore that Hunt had been alone in the car. The owner of the transport café remembered Hunt quite clearly, but was adamant that he had eaten alone. There had been no dark-haired girl, no Romanian hitch-hiker. And besides, how could a girl suddenly vanish from a moving car – by magic?

They tried pinning a drink-driving charge on him but he was lucky. The alcohol had worked its way out of his system and the police had to accept the official diagnosis of 'concussion'. That let Hunt off the hook, and yet it didn't make him feel any better. Was he mad? Had he been hallucinating? Was there some conspiracy against him? He was beginning to feel increasingly uneasy, incapable of trusting anyone.

Later that afternoon, they allowed him to telephone Eleanora. Although she clearly despised Hunt's professional scepticism, she grudgingly agreed to speak to him because of her close friendship with Mara. But as the details of his story unfolded, she became genuinely interested, concerned – almost agitated.

'Listen to me, Mr Hunt. You must not, I repeat, must *not* ignore these omens, these portents of evil. There are many, many things in this world of which you can have no comprehension. Only the sincere seeker after truth can hope to attain understanding. For a man like you, Mr Hunt, the quest for knowledge can be a mortally dangerous one. Give up your search. There are things which are better left untouched, unexplored.'

'I have no intention of ignoring these so-called "portents" – but surely you can't expect me to sit idly by whilst mysterious things happen to me and to people I care about? Look: Mara has disappeared, God knows where she's gone to – she could be in deep trouble. In fact, the more bad things happen to me, the more I'm convinced that she needs help and I'm the only one who can give it to her.'

'I see. So you are determined to proceed?'

'Of course I am. And any clues which you can give me – any information, no matter how insignificant it seems to you . . . well, surely you can see that it could mean the difference between life and death.'

'Indeed, Mr Hunt, but exactly whose life and death are we discussing? Mine, Mara's . . . yours?' For an instant, Hunt thought he caught just a hint of menace in that stern but sensible middle-aged voice. 'Listen to me, Mr Hunt. If you are determined to continue this foolhardy quest, I cannot stop you. But neither can I help you. I shall give you the little information I have, and then you must proceed alone.

'I can assure you that I do not, at this moment in time, know where Mara is. All I know is that she was very excited about an occult publishing house which was interested in signing her up. I think they were located in Chester. I personally had never heard of them, and warned her against becoming too involved. But apparently, she felt from the letters and telephone calls she had received that the publisher himself was a man of immense occult and spiritual significance. That is all I can tell you.'

'But . . . ?'

'No more. I fear for your soul, Mr Hunt; I fear greatly for your soul.'

Click.

She had hung up on him. And as Eleanora's

sombre words echoed in his mind, he realised that he was indeed utterly alone.

He discharged himself from hospital the following day. The car was a complete write-off: just a lump of twisted metal. How anyone could have survived such a crash was beyond him.

His head still ached, and he knew that he really ought to go back home and have a rest. Not to mention the fact that he hadn't been in to work for three days, and his editor was probably on the ceiling by now, wondering where the hell he was. He had a choice: do the responsible thing – go home, face the music and hope the police would find Mara before it was too late; or take off on impulse and try to track her down himself.

Sod it. He'd always hated people who behaved responsibly. Maybe that was why he was such a good journalist.

With his foot right on the floor, the hire-car got him to Chester by eight o'clock in the evening: this time, Hunt overcame his fear of motorways and sped down the M6 like a bat out of hell, lucky not to collect a speeding ticket to make his week complete.

All the glossy brochures described Chester as a pretty, touristy sort of place: a beautifully preserved ancient town complete with Victorian half-timbered buildings, Roman walls and a wonderful Gothic cathedral. But it wasn't living up to its chocolate-box reputation today. Hunt arrived in the middle of an unseasonal thunderstorm. It was a spectacular electrical storm – the sort you seldom see in Britain – with great jagged bolts of multicoloured lightning arcing across the dark looming sky and rain pelting down in great sheets, flooding the gutters and sending timid citizens running for cover. Early as it was, the old city seemed deserted: like Hamelin, five minutes after the Pied Piper had left.

Hunt pulled the collar of his coat up round his ears and stooped to lock the car door. At that moment a huge bolt of lightning caught the lightning-conductor on the cathedral tower nearby, then others began to strike the ground around him. Puddles sizzled like witches' cauldrons.

In the nearby cathedral close, lightning leapt to earth down the trunk of an ancient oak, splitting it in two and kindling foot-high flames which even the torrential rain struggled to extinguish. Hunt winced as the wild night closed in around him and the thunder rumbled deafeningly overhead. This was beginning to feel uncomfortably personal. Hunt wondered vaguely if God – or the Devil – was trying to tell him something. If so, he wasn't being very subtle about it.

He dismissed the thought with a smile and turned to run towards the door of a nearby restaurant. At that moment, an enormous bolt of lightning struck home just inches away from him, instantly blackening the overnight case which was standing next to him.

Suddenly more afraid than he had ever been in his life, Hunt pulled his coat around him and ran. He knew he must be imagining it, but he could have sworn he heard faraway mocking laughter as he scrambled for cover.

One good meal and two bottles of excellent wine later, Hunt felt distinctly better. There was nothing like a good claret for putting things into perspective. This whole catalogue of unpleasant coincidences now seemed nothing more than that. Tomorrow, he would do some local research on the publishing house. And maybe someone would have seen Mara. He was bound to turn something up.

A Hungarian gypsy band was accompanying a stunning dark-eyed girl who was singing folk-songs. She had a breathtaking body: firm and ripe as only gypsy girls can be and, in spite of his tiredness, Hunt felt an insistent stirring in his loins.

The girl was dancing seductively from table to table, singing her songs and laying a blood-red damask rose on each snow-white tablecloth. A nice touch, thought Hunt, wondering what it would be like to thrust his hand down inside her low-cut peasant blouse, to grab hold of those lovely bubbies and suck their teats until she cried for mercy, begged him to sink his prick into her sopping cunt.

She was at the next table now, dancing as she sang. Her spreading buttocks curved invitingly beneath her embroidered skirt, and Hunt could scarcely take his eyes off that wonderful arse. Almost as if she could feel the weight of his gaze upon her body, the girl turned round and looked Hunt straight in the eyes. The directness of her gaze unsettled him, making him dizzy with apprehension and desire. Those insolent dark eyes seemed to challenge him: 'Take me. Here. In front of everyone. Or not at all.' Their magnetism ate into Hunt's soul, sweeping away his inhibitions, his fears, his sense of who and where he was.

The girl lifted the hem of her skirt to reveal a generous naked thigh. She took a single, blood-red rose from her garter, and tugged down her crisp white cotton bloomers, baring a curly brown fleece. Parting her cunt-lips with the fingers of one hand, she wiped the flower-head lasciviously across her juicy quim and then handed the rose to Hunt. He inhaled its scent deeply – a rich mingling of rose-petals and the girl's own honey-dew.

Slowly, he began to unbutton his trousers and reached inside for his prick. He was unaware of anything but the terrible throbbing of his erect penis, the urgent rhythms of the gypsy music, and the gypsy girl with her dark eyes, her heavy breasts, her juicy backside . . .

Quick as a flash, she was on her knees before him, pushing the table back so that she could reach his penis comfortably. In one swift movement, she stripped down the front of her ruffled blouse, pulling out each brown-tipped breast in turn and running the head of Hunt's straining prick over the erect nipples. And then she gently took his purple-headed manhood into her mouth, never taking her eyes from his for a moment. It was as though, if she were to look away, the spell would be broken. He felt the tip of his cock slide smoothly against the back of her velvet throat, and he cried out with joy as she cradled his testicles in her cool, cool hands.

She sucked at him with a true delight, with all the naturalness of a country girl; and he surrendered to her utterly, rising on the dizzy tide of music and pleasure until at last he exploded in a cascade of falling stars and warm waterfalls.

He looked down at the girl. Thin trails of semen were running out of the corners of her parted lips. She stared deep into his eyes once again and this time she smiled a strange, wicked smile which Hunt knew only too well. His heart missed a beat. For her lips drew back to reveal two exceptionally long canine teeth, wickedly sharp and ready for the kill . . .

When he came round, the gypsy band were still playing and he was surrounded by solicitous waiters. There was no sign of the gypsy singer. He looked down and saw that he was unharmed and fully clothed.

'What happened?' he asked, weakly.

'You'd finished your meal and you were just drinking your coffee, sir,' explained one of the waiters. 'You were listening to the band. All of a sudden, you just collapsed. Fainted. How are you now, sir? Should I call an ambulance?'

'No, no. I'm fine,' insisted Hunt. 'Where is the girl singer?'

The waiter looked puzzled.

'We do not have a singer, sir. Only a gypsy band, as you can see.'

Hunt's head was spinning.

'Perhaps if I could just have a glass of water . . . ?'

As he was waiting for the water to arrive, Hunt suddenly became aware of a sharp pain in his right hand. Looking down, he realised that his fingers were tightly clasped over the stem of a blood-red rose. The thorns had bitten cruelly into his palm, and blood was oozing from between his clenched fingers.

In the centre of the flower-head he found a tiny rolled-up slip of paper. He unrolled it. On it was written a single word:

'WINTERBOURNE'

* * *

The wind rattled the windows and doors of Winter-bourne Hall and the rain lashed hard against the window-panes. Naked bodies writhed and sweated; the whores laughed and danced; and it seemed that there could never be an end to pleasure and desire.

The Master was well pleased with his work. His strength was growing; the day of his deliverance was near. Casting his spirit out into the stormy night, he looked down on a bewildered man in a restaurant, a blood-red rose crushed in the palm of his hand. Had the Master been capable of any movement, he would most certainly have smiled.

18: Sabbat

The following morning, still shaky and with his hand sore and bandaged, Hunt slipped out of the hotel after an unenthusiastic breakfast, and set out to look for the publishers Mara had been negotiating with when she vanished. Maybe they would be able to provide some clues to her sudden disappearance. It was about time somebody gave him some answers.

As he trudged the streets with his *A to Z*, Hunt's restless brain ran over the events of the previous evening. If it hadn't been for his bandaged hand and the weird note he'd found in the rose, he would have put the whole thing down to an attack of the shakes. He'd been drinking too much lately and he knew it. And then again, there was the road accident. He'd had a nasty bump on the head – maybe he was still suffering from concussion? Just maybe, even now, there was room for a logical explanation to all these illogical happenings . . .

Down the subway. Up again into Northgate Street. Where next? He consulted the map and saw that his best bet was to follow the city walls round to the Water Tower, and then take a left turn into a small alleyway. That in itself was odd. You wouldn't expect any respectable sort of publishing company to have its offices in a tiny backstreet, but these days nothing surprised him any more.

It was a pleasant enough walk round the walls, up above the town, looking down on the activities of the inhabitants in the autumn sunshine: delivery vans, housewives out shopping, businessmen walking to work . . . he even spotted one toothsome brunette getting dressed right in front of her bedroom window, pulling off her nightie and jiggling her breasts as she teased them into her bra – nice breasts she had, too. She might not have been an early riser, but Hunt certainly was. His penis sprang to immediate and insistent attention. Good God, he thought: there's no keeping the damn thing down these days. I'm turning into a sex maniac.

The thing felt so uncomfortable, poking through the front of his boxer shorts and rubbing up against the inside of his zip, that he checked no-one was about, ducked into a dark corner and had a quick wank. Thinking about that woman's big soft breasts as the come spurted against the sandstone wall made him think about Mara and her big firm ones. And the thought of Mara made him feel immensely guilty. He had work to do.

He put his cock away and set off in search of 3, Bishop's Yard, the address he'd found on a letter in Mara's desk. It wasn't easy to find in the rabbit warren of tiny backstreets. At last he came upon it, tucked away in the lee of the Cathedral, not so much a backstreet as the sort of dismal alleyway you might find *behind* a backstreet. It certainly didn't look the type of place where you'd find a publishing house. A couple of derelict warehouses, a car-repair workshop (closed of course), and an empty dustbin rolling around in the middle of the road were all the place offered at first sight. As he turned the corner into Bishop's Yard, a scrawny cat with extraordinary orange eyes leapt off the wall beside him and he almost jumped out of his skin. It was a spooky place, this. A place in hushed limbo, waiting for something to happen.

And then he noticed the front door: badly warped and cracked, with peeling and faded red paint. Number 3. This was it. But that was impossible: no brass plate, no painted sign outside. Nothing. Frankly, it looked completely deserted and run down. He rang the bell, but it was obviously not working; so he hammered on the door. The sound echoed through the building with an ominously empty sound.

He was just about to give up when an old woman with a halo of plastic curlers popped her head out of the door of the car repair shop:

'What you looking for, love?'

'Magus Press. This is the address I was given.'

'No use knocking there, dearie. Not unless you're trying to wake the dead.' She gave a horrible chuckle which pulled back her thin cracked lips to reveal toothless gums.

'What do you mean?'

'Why, the place has been derelict for nigh on thirty years, since old Mr Gittings was found there. Stone dead, he was. Heart attack they said, but he had a horrible look on his face. Sheer terror, I'd say. I always knew he'd come to a bad end.'

'And was this . . . Mr Gittings . . . he didn't happen to be a publisher, did he?'

The old woman laughed: the wheezing, sixty-a-day sound of a broken down accordion.

333

'Not likely. Undertaker, he was. Used this place as his workshop. There's some as say there's a few unfinished coffins still in there. Wouldn't care to look, myself. Might have left one or two of his clients behind.'

With a macabre chuckle, she popped back inside, and Hunt was left staring blankly at the door, a nasty feeling of having been thoroughly conned clutching coldly at his stomach.

If the Master had been capable of it, he would have split his sides laughing.

Hunt sat in his hotel room and racked his brains to think of some way of tracking Mara down. The publishing lead had drawn a pathetic blank; the police just weren't interested; and all he had left to go on was that mysterious piece of paper he'd been given in the restaurant. He took it out of his wallet and looked at it again:

'WINTERBOURNE'

It meant nothing to him. Well, not quite nothing. Somewhere in the back of his mind he thought he might have heard the name before, somewhere, somehow – but in what context, he couldn't for the life of him recall. It was like being a contestant in some macabre game-show: a game-show in which the stakes were life and death.

So who, or what, was Winterbourne? What did it mean? Could it be the name of a person? Or a place? Or something else entirely?

He was lost in thought and started abruptly when

the phone rang. He wasn't expecting a call from
anyone. Even the editor didn't know where he was.
Cautiously he picked it up.

'Yes?'

It was the switchboard:

'I've a call for you from a Miss Paolozzi. Will you
take it?'

He'd never heard of anyone called Paolozzi, and
he was getting a bit nervous about unexpected
telephone calls from mysterious women. But what
the Hell : . .

'OK. Put her on.'

The girl's voice was soft and husky, yet there was
a hidden strength in it. Hunt wondered idly if she was
pretty. His prick twitched appreciatively at her silky
smooth yet assertive tones, and he almost forgot his
determination to be suspicious.

'Hello, Mr Hunt. My name's Luisa Paolozzi, and
I'm a friend of Mara's.'

His ears pricked up, and his fingers tightened
around the receiver.

'Do you know where she is?'

'No, but I do know she's in trouble.'

'You've heard from her?'

She chuckled.

'Not in the way that you mean, Mr Hunt. You
see, I am a psychic, like Mara. I know that you are
a sceptic, but I hope that you will trust me when I
say that I have received a very clear message from
Mara across the astral plane.'

'Go on. I'm listening.' He sighed, convinced that
he was being led up yet another garden path.

'She appeared to me in a dream, and told me she
was being held against her will, I could not tell where

or by whom. But she was very distressed, and kept calling out for you by name. She told me to contact you, that you were the only one who cared enough to try to help her. And that is why I have called you, Mr Hunt.'

'Yes, well . . . I appreciate your concern, but I don't see how your dream is going to help me find Mara. At the moment, all I have is one word to go on: Winterbourne. And that means nothing to me. Absolutely zilch.'

'I think there may be a way. But you must co-operate with me, Mr Hunt. You must suspend your disbelief and do whatever I tell you to do. Can you accept that?'

His every instinct told him to tell Miss Paolozzi to go fuck herself, and slam the phone down. He was a respected investigative journalist. He couldn't trust some girl he'd never met who claimed to have had a vision. And yet . . . he knew that he must. There was no other way. And when all was said and done, surely it could do no harm.

'OK. Just tell me what to do.'

'I will meet you at your apartment at eight o'clock tomorrow night. There are many preparations that must be made. You must have ready as many of Mara's possessions as you can. Personal effects: clothing, jewellery, books, that sort of thing. That is all. I will see you tomorrow, Mr Hunt. Goodbye.'

Click. She had put the phone down on him. Already he was feeling uneasy. But what else could he do? He picked up his keys from the bedside table and went downstairs to Reception to settle the bill.

*　　*　　*

She was tall, dark, aristocratic; and more than
a touch sinister. Her spare frame reminded Hunt
of a thoroughbred racehorse – beautiful, lissom,
unpredictable . . . and just a little dangerous. She
looked into his eyes and seemed to scan his soul with
a single glance. She made him feel like a child in the
headmistress's office.

And she made him feel sexy, too. There was something exceptionally erotic about the way she moved:
something liquid, elegant, catlike. Her slender hips
swayed with an exquisite balance, and the strangely
pubescent swell of her tiny breasts invited the touch
of a bold, lascivious hand. It was all Hunt could do
to restrain himself.

Luisa had brought with her all manner of arcane
paraphernalia: pewter candlesticks in the form of
naked maidens, chafing-dishes full of incense and
sweet woods which she instructed Hunt to set burning
on a small side table, a magnificent long robe in red
silk, embroidered with gold, and a wicked-looking
scourge which Hunt eyed with mingled apprehension
and desire. He rather liked the idea of using it
on Luisa's taut young flesh. It would be just like
whipping a fine thoroughbred filly past the winning
post at Cheltenham. In spite of himself, he could not
suppress a wry little grin.

But Luisa was implacable: she had no time for
puerile games. Sternly, she ordered him to draw the
curtains and turn out the lights, leaving the room in
semi-darkness, illuminated only by the candles and
by two small oil-lamps.

'Have you prepared Mara's possessions, as I
instructed you?'

'Yes – I have them here.' Hunt produced a box

in which he had placed clothes, jewellery, a locket containing a little of Mara's raven hair, books, lots of little things that belonged to Mara.

Luisa searched through them diligently.

'These will suffice. Now, I wish you to undress.'

'What – completely?'

'Take off all your clothes. Now, please. We do not have much time.'

'I . . .'

'Oh, for goodness sake, Mr Hunt. This is no time to be shy. Look, I will help you undress if you won't do it yourself!'

And Luisa began to undo his shirt buttons with a resolute determination worthy of any prep-school matron. When she got to the trouser-belt and flies, turmoil erupted in his groin: his prick leapt to rigidity and he blushed deeply, unable to hide his excitement.

To his surprise, Luisa seemed pleased by this reaction:

'Good, good. This will prove of service later in our ceremony,' she said. 'The male essence possesses very strong magical powers.'

Soon he was completely naked before her, his prick ramrod-stiff with desire for her. She remained fully clothed, and he looked at her not just with a schoolboy's embarrassment but hopefully, expectantly, as she picked up the red silk robe. To his immense regret, she left the room and undressed in the bedroom, returning a few moments later wearing the silk robe, which hung loosely from the throat and chastely concealed those parts of her which Hunt most coveted a glimpse of.

'Now you must robe,' she announced.

'But there is only one robe,' pointed out Hunt. 'What am I to wear?'

338

To his dismay, Luisa pointed to the box containing Mara's possessions:

'You are to put on some of Mara's clothes,' she replied. And, just to ensure that he complied, she began to take out those items of clothing which she wished him to put on: a red satin bra and lacy panties and a crystal necklace.

'But why . . . ?' protested Hunt, as he strapped the bra, which was of course much too small around his torso.

'Because we are trying to invoke Mara's spirit on the astral plane, and by wearing her most intimate clothing you are emphasising the intimate link which exists between you. Trust me.'

Hunt felt like a complete fool, but he had no option. Trust her he must: at this point she was his only chance. And still he gazed at her and coveted that tall, slender body, so tantalisingly veiled by the silk robe, which swirled about her as she moved.

'Kneel before the altar,' she commanded, and he knelt obediently before the small table which they had set up with the candles and chafing-dishes. A swirl of scented smoke rose up from the smouldering sweet woods, making Hunt's head swim.

She began the incantation:

'Lords of the spirit world, we command you by our offerings to deliver unto us the spirit of Mara Fleming, that we may question her and know where she lies in peril.'

The rest of the incantation sounded like mumbo-jumbo to Hunt, a mere jumble of meaningless sounds that nevertheless possessed a certain strange musicality, a rhythm that was itself the meaning. He was beginning to feel very odd indeed: dizzy and other-worldly, somehow outside himself; yet exceedingly excited, aroused, lustful.

Luisa turned to him and beckoned him to his feet:

'It is now time for us to perform the Great Rite,' she announced. And, without further ado, she reached out her hand and pulled Hunt's engorged penis out of the front of the red lacy knickers. Then she bent forward, hoisting up her robe and supporting herself on the altar table. Her slender rump thrust out to him, inviting him inside.

'I . . . I want to fuck you,' gasped Hunt, uncomprehending. 'I want to stick it in your cunt.'

'You must bugger me,' hissed Luisa. 'It is the only way to empower the incantation. Take me quickly.'

Rather clumsily – for he had relatively little experience of such things – Hunt pressed the tip of his penis up against Luisa's hole and pushed. His first attempt at penetration ended in failure, for she was tight and dry. But a drop of saliva eased the way and, with a second thrust, he was inside. She felt wonderful, and he abandoned himself utterly to the rhythm which she set him, thrusting her buttocks out to receive him deep within her backside. But his confused brain could not understand why she removed his hands gently every time he tried to put them round in front of her and play with her clitty.

It did not take him long to come, and it seemed that Luisa had come too, for she gave a great cry of pleasure in harmony with his own.

As they lay locked together, slumped against the altar, something amazing happened. The room filled with a blinding white light, light that flashed like the many-hued glittering facets of a crystal. And, shielding their eyes and looking upwards, they saw in the centre of the light a tiny figure.

As they watched, the figure grew larger and more distinct until at last it became recognisable:

'Mara!' cried Hunt, trying to touch the apparition – but his hand encountered nothing more substantial than empty air.

Mara seemed to be gazing sightlessly before her, as though unsure that anyone could see her.

'Andreas,' she cried, but her cry sounded faint and very far away. 'Andreas, only you can save me now.'

'Tell me, tell me how!' he cried, sudden tears springing to his eyes. 'I will do anything, anything.'

'Look and you shall see the place of my imprisonment,' went on Mara. And she raised her hand and behind her appeared the outline of a large country house. It stood dark and sinister against the evening sky, a ravening beast waiting for its prey.

'Winterbourne . . .' whispered Mara. 'Winterbourne, where my body and spirit are enslaved . . .'

'Winterbourne!' exclaimed Hunt.

'Listen to me,' continued Mara. 'If you would save me, you must, tomorrow at noon, draw a picture of this house in your own blood. Draw it in the centre of our bedroom floor and stand in the place where you have drawn the door. Then wait . . . I can say no more . . .'

The image faded, and was replaced by a sight so terrible that Hunt cried out in horror: his beloved Mara, tied up on the floor of a windowless cell and forced to suck the cocks of fat old men with the faces of perverts.

'No!' screamed Hunt, pulling away from Luisa and trying to reach Mara.

But his efforts were in vain: the dazzling images disappeared, leaving the room once more in semi-darkness.

Luisa stood up and turned around, her silk robe still hitched up around her waist. Hastily she pulled it down, but not quickly enough to hide the horrible truth from Hunt, who recoiled in disgust and self-hatred.

For he found himself gazing, not upon a damp dark bush of pretty curls, but on the withered stalk of a satiated penis. This slender, boyish woman he had desired so much, who had ordered him to bugger her – small wonder she had been so reluctant to let him touch her cunt!

Hunt ran into the bathroom and was violently sick.

'Luisa' slept the night on the living-room floor, and left the following morning, unrepentant to the last.

'The incantation would not have worked if I had told you, for you would have refused to bugger me,' came the defiant explanation, delivered with a half-smile and a coquettish peck on the cheek. And then Luisa was gone and Hunt found himself automatically wiping away the traces of that final, tainted kiss.

He could scarcely believe that it would work – any of it. And yet Luisa, for all the deception, had delivered the goods. Somehow, impossibly, he had been able to speak to Mara and he knew deep inside him that the vision had been no deception, no illusion.

So he must carry out Mara's wishes, no matter how futile the exercise might prove to be.

The clock ticked round to eleven o'clock, eleven fifteen. He tried listening to the radio but the tinny jangle of techno-pop just irritated him. Eleven forty-five, and he knew he had to make a move soon. He had cleared a space on the bedroom floor and rolled back the carpet. He might be nutty enough to do this but there was no sense in ruining a perfectly good Axminster – especially since it didn't belong to him.

The big hand moved inexorably on, and he looked at the sharp blade of the carving knife and wanted to be sick all over again. He couldn't do it. He just couldn't. The slightest trickle of blood – especially his own – and he always passed out. But he had to do it. Mara's life depended on it, he knew it did.

Twelve o'clock. High noon. Now or never.

With a trembling hand, he raised the knife and – so quickly that he didn't have time to change his mind – used it to make a small incision in his forearm. At first, nothing: and then the blood came flowing out. Not much really, not enough to matter, but it mattered because it was *his* blood, besides which . . . it hurt. It stung like buggery. No, not buggery – he didn't want to think too much about buggery. Like Hell.

He squeezed the blood into an egg-cup and put a plaster on the wound. Now. He had no talent for drawing, but figured as long as the general shape of the house looked right . . . with a fingertip traced in blood, he began the outline, remembering to emphasise the steps up to the front door and the ornate portico.

It was done. The best he could do. Shaking and still nauseous, he stood up and stepped into the picture, making sure to stand right on the door he had drawn.

At first, nothing happened. He knew it. It was all hokum. Nothing was going to happen, it was all hopeless.

And then – the strangest feeling. Like dissolving, melting, floating away. The room was going all fuzzy, indistinct. He couldn't make out the hands on the clock any more . . . or the clock even. Everything was spinning, swirling, disappearing.

And then everything went black.

And Andreas Hunt vanished. Leaving nothing behind him save the crude picture of a large country house.

A house with an open door.

19: The Lure

Delgado awoke in the middle of the night with a thought that burned right through him, ate into his soul and refused to let him sleep or screw. The voice was inside his head again and its seductive whisperings would not let him rest.

There must be cellars under Winterbourne. Bricked-up cellars. He didn't know why he hadn't thought of it before. But now, suddenly, he knew that he had to find them, open them up right away, find out what was in there. It was very important. He didn't yet understand why, but he knew that it must be.

For the Master had told him so.

He slipped out of bed as quietly as possible so as not to wake the sleeping whore who grunted questioningly as he lifted her arm and took it from round his waist. Nathalie was a good screw – the best – but she had a feather duster for a brain. He didn't want her coming along, asking questions, getting in the way.

Got to do it now. Got to.

He got dressed hastily and crept out of the room. Luckily all the evening's guests had either gone home or retired to bed – their own or each other's – and the house was sleeping. Most of them were dead-drunk or drugged anyway. They wouldn't be any trouble.

Besides, soon it wouldn't matter any more. Very soon now, nobody would be able to cause trouble for Delgado and his Master any more.

He stepped over a couple who had fallen asleep after copulating at the top of the stairs, and hurried down the ornate carved staircase to the ground floor. He made a brief detour through the kitchens to the storeroom where he knew some builders' tools were kept, and selected a heavy long-handled pickaxe.

Then he set off down the long torchlit corridor, turned left down the dark flight of stairs, and through the secret panel into the hidden room where the soul of the Master's Queen had entered the succulent body of Mara Fleming.

It must be in here. Somewhere. The way through to the rest of the cellars. Delgado knew the house better than anyone and was certain there was nowhere else they could be. They had been cleverly bricked-up, certainly; made to look as if the cellars stopped here. But one of these walls was false: a much later addition.

Delgado tried knocking the walls with his fist. They all sounded the same. But just as he was giving up, a quiet voice spoke confidently inside his head:

'Behind the cupboard.'

It was a massive mahogany cupboard, full of magical regalia and mysterious jars and dishes; and it took all his strength to move it. Panting and groaning, he at last managed to edge it round so that it stood at right-angles to the wall.

'Take the pickaxe and strike the wall, three feet from the left-hand corner.'

Without thinking to question the command, Delgado took up the heavy pickaxe and swung it at the wall.

He was not a strong man, and the swing was an amateurish one – but to his amazement the pickaxe struck home and part of the surface of the wall fell away, revealing the almost-new brickwork underneath. Encouraged, he swung again and again at the wall, the sweat coursing down his brow and into his eyes.

Five or six more swings of the pickaxe and he managed to dislodge one of the bricks. Instantly, a current of chill air rushed into the room. Another brick, and another, and now the wall was crumbling away before him. He tore at the bricks with his bare hands, and they chafed and bled, but he did not care. He felt no pain. There was an inhuman strength within him tonight and he could not fail. Nothing could stop him.

After half an hour, Delgado had succeeded in making a hole large enough for a man to walk through. He picked up the oil lamp and held it up to illuminate the scene beyond.

Delgado found himself gazing down a flight of six or seven steps into another cellar, much bigger than the room he was standing in. It was completely empty, save for one single, dominating object: in the middle of the chamber stood a massive granite sarcophagus. Featureless, its smooth surface obscured by a thick layer of dust, it drew Delgado towards it as inexorably as a moth to a flame.

'You have done well,' spoke the dark voice within his head. 'Approach and listen carefully: for I have more work for you to do.'

Mara lay on the bed and tried desperately to project her thoughts into the mind of the transvestite witch she knew as Luisa. Luisa was the only person with whom she had consistently been able to hold telepathic conversations in the past and – ever since the brief but passionate affair which they had enjoyed a few summers ago – Mara trusted Luisa implicitly.

If anyone could get her message through to Hunt, Luisa could.

She strained against the leather straps holding her to the bed, but they were buckled tightly and cut into her skin whenever she tried to move. She sighed, and tears glistened at the corners of her eyes. Her bonds were far too strong for her to escape from them.

Why, why had she come here? What force had got inside her head and forced her to such madness, such degradation? And why had it chosen her?

The three guards had used her cruelly, handling her roughly and taking turns with her as though she were no more than a toy, provided for their sport. They were uncouth, thick-set, unintelligent men: mere animals for whom the gratification of their sexual impulses was a bodily function as basic as eating or pissing.

She had been forced to submit to every indignity as they explored each orifice with their fingers, tongues and pricks, mocking her growing discomfiture and satisfying themselves again and again with her sweet flesh. There seemed to be no end to their sexual appetites: they fucked and buggered and half-choked her with their big pricks until she was dazed and crying for mercy. And still they kept on abusing her.

After they had done with her, the man Delgado handed her over to a group of disgusting old men: rich elderly perverts whose money could buy them any gratification they desired. She shivered as she recalled how they had forced her to drink down their watery spunk and wank their world-weary pricks back into wakefulness.

It was late at night before they left her, strapping her tightly to the bed where at last she drifted off into a fitful slumber, bruised and aching from her ordeal.

She was awoken by the sound of the door handle slowly turning and, raising her eyes to focus in the gloom, she made out a shadowy figure framed in the doorway, a flickering candle in his hand.

Delgado. She trembled with the memory of what had passed between them in the secret room: the terrible change which had come over both of them as dark and hostile spirits used their bodies like dolls to satisfy their needs. She remembered, too, Delgado's cold satisfaction as he had handed her over to the guards and the reptilian old men.

He crossed the room to the bed and she looked up into his face, eerily illuminated by the candleglow which transformed him into a demon out of some medieval fresco of Hell. His expression was peculiarly blank, and he moved like an automaton as he unfastened the straps which held her to the bed.

He hauled her up into a sitting position, apparently indifferent to her bruised nakedness, and bound her wrists together behind her back with a piece of cord. She made no move to resist or to escape from him. She was too weary now, and too afraid.

'Come,' he ordered her and pulled her to her feet, pushing her out into the corridor and keeping tight hold of the cord binding her wrists. 'The Master has work for you to do.'

She stumbled as he pushed her, and almost fell

down the stairs; but he wasn't going to let her damage herself. She was too important, too useful. He guided her down to the ground floor, along the torchlit corridor which ran the length of the building, and down the darkened stairway to the secret door. It opened smoothly and silently, and they entered the secret room once again. Mara felt a pang of dread as she heard the panel click shut behind her, blocking off any faint hope of escape.

The oil lamps were still burning, and the room was filled with an unpleasant smoky-yellow light which lent the scene a dreamlike quality. Mara gasped as she caught sight of the wall which Delgado had hacked away, leaving a hole which gaped blackly like some ancillary entrance to the underworld. Beyond was only formless darkness. No light, nothing to lend hope. She shivered as Delgado pushed her towards the hole, clearly insisting that she should climb through.

'No . . .' she breathed. It was a plea for mercy, not a refusal. She was no longer in any position to refuse anything Delgado demanded of her. 'Please don't make me . . . not in there.'

But that was exactly what Delgado did. He used the candle flame to light a lantern, and held it aloft to light Mara's way as he pushed her through the hole, following close behind.

When Mara's eyes had become accustomed to the semi-darkness, she saw the outline of the massive stone sarcophagus, standing in the centre of the cellar. Delgado had lovingly cleared away the thick layer of dust from the polished lid, and it now gleamed with a malevolent intensity in the feeble yellowish light.

The moment she set eyes on it she could feel the power within, even without touching the stone. She could feel the evil seeping out of it, and knew instinctively what it contained.

To her surprise, she felt the cord about her wrists suddenly slacken and fall away, as Delgado sliced through the knot with a sharp knife.

'Lay your hands upon the surface,' he instructed Mara, pushing her forward towards the sarcophagus.

'I . . . I cannot. The power is too great – I fear it would destroy me.'

'Do it,' commanded a soundless voice within her own head. 'Or *I* shall destroy you. Do it now.'

Terrified, she approached the sarcophagus and laid her trembling hands upon the polished stone. Instantly, an enormous surge of power ran through her hands and into her body, searing like a massive electric shock; and she screamed with the sudden pain of it. But, try as she might, she could not take her hands from the lid. They felt as though they had been glued to the surface. She was a prisoner of its awesome power.

As she stood there, every muscle taut with agony and straining to free her from this evil force, an image flooded into her brain: an image planted, she had no doubt of it, by the Master. It was the image of what lay beneath the heavy coffin lid: the body of a man who was neither dead nor alive; a man imprisoned in a block of crystal; a man who was no longer a man, but an evil creature, intent on using her powers to liberate his own.

'No, no!' she sobbed. 'Free me, I beg of you. My powers are only for good. I cannot work for evil.'

She knew her pleas for mercy were in vain. For at that very same moment, the voice filled her head once again:

'Slide back the lid of the sarcophagus. I will give you the power.'

She gazed down at the heavy stone lid. It must weigh tons: how on earth could she hope to move it? And her hands were held fast against its mirror-smooth surface.

'Push it away from you,' came the voice again. 'I will give you the power. Do it, I command you. Or die . . .'

And the voice in Delgado's head told him:

'Take the girl now. Fuck her. As you fuck her, my power will enter her and she will move the stone. Do it now, I command you.'

The command seemed to electrify Delgado, up till now so impassive and machine-like. Unbuttoning his trousers, he took out his prick and began to wank it, caressing it into veiny-smooth hardness, breathing hard as he anticipated the warmth of Mara's secret cave. His prick was not slow in responding: the thought of flooding the girl with spunk soon had him hard and panting for her, his shaft throbbing and a bead of love-juice gathering already at the tip of his well-lubricated glans.

With a groan of satisfaction, he forced Mara's buttocks apart and sank into her delicious cunt, pumping away at her with furious lust. No woman's cunt had ever felt so good, so tight and wet around his eager tool. No fuck had ever made him feel so aroused, so immense, so powerful. With each stroke, he felt the Master's strength and dominion growing more complete, and his prick growing harder and more sensitive. And he rejoiced to be the servant of such awesome power.

With each thrust into her cunt, Mara felt her own passion rising in defiance of her fear and repulsion, her clitoris throbbing towards a massive climax; and she felt the Master's power flooding into her hands, her arms, her shoulders. Slowly, as she leaned forward to accept Delgado's tribute, the stone lid began to slide smoothly to one side.

And as Delgado inundated Mara with his spunk, and as she came with a great cry of bittersweet pleasure, their sexual energies united with the will of the Master and the lid gave way, sliding sideways across the coffin and falling to the cellar floor with a thundering crash.

Mara fell forward, Delgado still on top of her and the last drops of his semen trickling out of the tip of his penis and into her cunt. Her hands sought something to steady her, and came to rest upon another cool, hard, smooth surface. She opened her eyes and found herself looking down into the compelling, evil face of the Master, the handsome features distorted with agony and fear at the moment of his imprisonment, his sightless eyes gazing up into hers from the centre of a massive block of crystal, as clear and smooth as glass. And, glittering menacingly on the surface of the crystal, the magical dagger and the ring. So: they had followed Mara to Winterbourne, and now they had found their way inside the sarcophagus. Would she never be free?

For now, the Master's body was helpless, unmoving; but she knew instantly that the power within him was growing terrifyingly fast and that soon this evil presence would walk the earth again, if she could not find a way to resist him. And all her instincts told her that she could not. Her head swam, and she closed her eyes to dispel the vertigo.

The voice spoke again, sweetly evil, insinuating itself inside her head. She tried to fight it, but she could not.

'Place the ring upon the third finger of your left hand. Now take up the dagger in your right hand and place the point of the blade on the surface of the crystal, above my forehead.'

She obeyed, silent and submissive; defeated by the superior power of the Master's iron will. And the power flooded into her once again, and she became no more than a channel for his thoughts, his desires, his words.

As he fed the words of the incantation into her beautifully receptive brain (how well he had chosen!), the Master watched and waited and knew that he would soon be free.

'Asta, asta, Astaroth,' she began, in a voice that was no longer her own. 'Besra, besra, Behemoth. Azriel, Uriel, Shimoneth . . .'

It was working. He could feel the chains of sorcery beginning to dissolve.

'Mene, mene, Meroneth . . . Gazriel!'

The room was filled with a dazzling flash of white light, and the Master felt pain flooding through him, tearing him apart: pain such as he had never before felt. Such agony . . . a fire consuming him, raging through his soul and body and then . . .

Ebbing away, and leaving his flesh cold, unresponsive, imprisoned.

Mara lay unconscious, slumped across the crystal;

the unmoving body staring up at her with glassy, unseeing eyes.

The incantation had failed. And the Master knew why. His body had been irrevocably damaged by the long imprisonment. It was useless to him now; it could not be revived. Yet still he was shackled to it, for without a body to house it, how could his soul be liberated?

There was only one course of action left open to him now.

He must find a new body.

20: The Prey

The electric gates which guarded the hidden entrance
to Winterbourne Hall swung open on silent, well-
oiled hinges to allow the stretch limousine to pass
and glide on, beetle-black and sinister, past the lodge
and up the broad driveway to the main house.

The invited guests were gathering for one of Winterbourne's special evening entertainments. There was
a thrill of anticipation in the evening air, for Delgado
was one of the great showmen. He always gave his
guests their money's worth. They wouldn't be going
home disappointed.

Some of them wouldn't be going home at all.

Somewhere in the shrubbery, cold and shivering on
the damp earth, Andreas Hunt was coming to,
feeling groggy and disorientated and very much the
worse for wear.

The truth filtered into his mind and brought him to
his senses with a jolt. The impossible had happened.
He had stepped into a picture of a house and now,
hours later, he had woken up to find himself at that
very same house: and he couldn't remember a damn
thing about what had happened in those intervening
hours. Supernatural? He was long past asking those
sorts of questions.

He staggered to his feet and winced, brushing the leaf-mould from soggy trousers. His arm hurt. His head throbbed. His clothes were soaked through from lying on wet leaves. He peered out from between the foliage and watched the cars driving in slow procession up to the house. He couldn't risk walking up to the front entrance, but somehow he had to get into that house. He had no idea how he was going to do it, but he knew he had to make his mind up pretty damn quick if he was to stand a chance of rescuing Mara before it was too late.

Delgado walked out of the secret room and up the stairs. He didn't even bother to close the secret panel this time. There was no need. After tonight, there would be no further need to keep Winterbourne's dark secret from its pampered and privileged guests.

For they would have become a part of that secret.

He walked along the corridor and towards the main entrance lobby, immaculate in tuxedo and bow tie: still the consummate master of ceremonies. Already the guests were arriving, to be greeted by a tall and handsome black man in a white loin-cloth and very little else. Delgado scanned the guests with approval.

Soon they would all be here. Already he could see Cheviot, de Lacy, Parry-Evans, Blomfeld, the two princes . . . It was all going exactly as the Master had planned.

Delgado turned his attentions to the tall negro:

'Direct our guests to the ante-room, Ibrahim. It is almost time for the ceremonies to begin.'

And then he noticed the golden-haired beauty

358

walking through the door towards him: red lips, cool white skin, almost deathly pale in its trans-lucence . . .

'My dear Sonja! So glad you could make it . . .'

Hunt tried several windows before he managed to find one that yielded to his penknife and a little brute force. It took all his strength and resourcefulness to squeeze through, and he cursed his broad shoulders.

He jumped down into the room and saw that he was in the main kitchens of the Hall, thankfully deserted. A few bowls of evil-smelling red stuff stood on a table but he resisted the urge to examine them more closely. He crossed the room and opened the door. No-one was about. The corridor led to a narrow staircase which Hunt assumed must be the old servants' back stairs. He took them two at a time, anxious to find Mara before something terrible happened to her.

He reached the first floor and set off along a long, dimly lit corridor, lined with identical black-painted doors. Each had a hand-painted nameplate – Serpent of Nile, Revolution, Reichskammer, Lotus Gardens, Notre-Dame, The Winter Palace – and Hunt read several before plucking up the courage to turn a door-handle and look inside.

Hunt passed from room to room as though in a dreamworld. He'd never in his life been in a place like this, and he'd been in some pretty amaz-ing places. Each room mirrored the name on its door: decked out in loving detail to illustrate the chosen theme. Thus, Serpent of Nile represented Cleopatra's palace, complete with a basket full of very lively snakes; whilst Revolution recreated a

French Revolutionary court, complete with guillotine. All were deserted.

Except Orient Express.

When he turned the door-handle, a husky voice called to him:

'Is that you? I was expecting you hours ago, darling. Come in, I'm so hungry for you.'

Hunt was on the horns of a furious dilemma. If he went away, she'd probably come after him. If he went inside, she'd be bound to see that he wasn't the man she was expecting.

He compromised, and opened the door just a tiny crack. Mercifully, it was rather dark inside. The curtains had been pulled, and the only light came from a Tiffany lamp on the small table. The whole room was decorated to resemble the interior of a turn-of-the-century railway sleeping compartment, the height of decadent luxury.

The woman was sitting on the side of the bed, completely naked except for a pair of black silk stockings and a hat with a black veil which covered her face. She was slender, with nicely rounded breasts, a trim pair of buttocks and breathtakingly long legs, which she crossed and uncrossed with an erotic awareness which set Hunt's prick leaping about inside his underpants.

'You must be my guest,' she greeted him, sweetly. 'Señor Delgado told me to expect you. A very special guest, he said. Make yourself at home, won't you, my dear? Now, you know the little game we play in here, don't you? You're the guard on the train, and I'm the naughty lady who's travelling without a ticket. You have to think of the best way to punish me . . . Shall we begin?'

Hunt was completely nonplussed. He could hardly make his excuses and leave, not now. On the other hand, how could he justify wasting precious time playing silly games when Mara was in mortal danger?

'Would you like to punch my ticket, sir?' breathed the woman.

That clinched it. Hunt's prick refused to take no for an answer. He entered the charade with gusto.

'That's right, madam. All tickets, please.'

'Oh, dear – I'm afraid I've lost mine,' sighed the woman, pretending to search in her handbag. 'And I haven't any money. What am I to do? Are you going to throw me off the train?'

'That depends, madam,' replied Hunt, licking his lips, 'on how co-operative you're prepared to be.'

'Oh, I'll do anything, anything you tell me, sir,' breathed the woman, uncrossing her legs and stroking her dark pubic curls suggestively. 'I know I've been a naughty girl and I have to be punished.'

'In that case . . .' Hunt picked up the decorative parasol which lay, folded, on the table in front of the couchette. 'Turn round and bend over the bed.'

She obeyed, with evident enjoyment, thrusting out her backside and inviting him to thrash it. Which he felt obliged to do, since it pleased her; though he would really have preferred just to shove his dick into her and give her a damn good fucking. She squealed appreciatively as the parasol thwacked down hard on her backside, reddening it like a big juicy apple.

Next, he ran the tip of the parasol between her legs, enjoying the way she squirmed as the cold metal ferrule glanced fleetingly over her clitoris and slid through the delicious wetness of her cunt. As she was parting her legs wider and wider for him, he felt honour bound to give her what she was asking for, and shoved the parasol right up her cunt: the frilled fabric stuck out of her like the petals of some monstrous flower, but she loved it, and begged him for more, and more . . .

Finally, he could wait no longer; and, pinning her face-down on the couchette, he unzipped his flies and gave her the full benefit of his nice fat cock, right up her slippery cunt. Oh, how she howled with pleasure as he took her, sliding his hands underneath her to pinch her nipples as he rode her to orgasm.

It was only as he pulled out his still-dripping prick and climbed off her that she turned into a spitting fury, turning on him suddenly and lunging for his throat. In the struggle, her veil slipped from her face and he saw her for what she was:

'Anastasia . . .' he breathed – his mind now in total confusion. And, in fear for his life, he gave her a swift uppercut to the jaw. She fell back, unconscious, on to the bed. Frantic with fear, he tied her up with her own stockings and gagged her lightly with a pair of black silk knickers. He hoped that would give him time to do what he needed to do.

Swiftly zipping up his flies and locking the door behind him, Hunt stepped out into the corridor. It was still deserted, but there were some curious sounds coming to his ears from below. They sounded as if they were coming right from the bowels of the earth. From the cellars, perhaps?

Since Mara clearly wasn't in any of the upstairs rooms, Hunt decided he had better investigate.

* * *

Naked, giggling, high on Madame LeCoeur's aphrodisiac wine and the excitement of the moment, the guests followed Delgado down the stairs, through the secret panel and into the cellars, now impressively lit by burning torches hanging on the walls.

All around the room stood braziers full of burning sweet woods and incense to cloud the mind and inflame the senses. And in the centre, beside the open sarcophagus (its contents hidden from view by a black velvet cloth), a large pot of something warm and red and sticky was standing upon a bed of glowing charcoal. Beside it, an array of soft sable brushes.

Delgado cut an incongruous but elegant figure, fully clad in evening dress amid the host of revellers, naked save for their crystal necklaces. He clapped his hands and they fell silent, now sensing the power that flowed through him, attentive to his every word.

'Welcome, friends,' he said. 'Tonight is a night of great celebration at Winterbourne. Tonight we enter the spirit world: the world where darkness reigns, in which flesh and soul are one, and where all pleasures are permitted, nothing forbidden.'

Out of the corner of his eye, he spotted de Lacy and his stockbroker friend, Drew Pettifar, nudging each other and eyeing up the women. Time enough, he thought. Soon you'll have all the time in the world.

'First,' he continued, 'we must prepare ourselves for the sacred ceremonies of sexual conjugation which we are about to enjoy. Therefore, each of you must take a brush and dip it in this red . . . pigment; and then you must use it to paint upon each other's bodies whatever signs come into your minds.'

The guests came forward and dipped their brushes into the pot of sticky liquid. It had a strange and rather sickening smell, and Delgado was glad that he had ordered Ibrahim to add the incense, honey and sweet spices. The smell of blood was so difficult to disguise.

If some of the guests thought that this would be an occasion for horseplay, for joking around, for painting childish obscenities on each other's lewd bodies, they had not bargained on the all-pervading power of the Master.

Such sexual energy, such amazing power contained within these two dozen lustful bodies . . . The Master exulted within his prison and, using the strength of their own life-energies, cast forth his soul into their midst, clouding their minds with his dark desires. Their eyes became fixed, their faces distorted into grotesque parodies of their normal expressions, lewd masks that expressed only the principal desire within their minds at that moment: the desire and the soul-deep need to fuck.

Guided by the Master, untutored hands began to describe exquisite magical symbols on breasts and buttocks and bellies and balls: the pentacle and the horned ram; the goat; suns and moons and strange constellations beyond the edges of their imaginings. They began to laugh, no longer the innocent giggling of naughty children but the raw, demonic laughter of the lost, the eternally damned.

And Delgado threw back his head and laughed with them, the voice of the Master issuing forth from the depths of him like a wind sweeping through the wastes of Hell: cold, chill, exulting in the anticipation of powers soon to be enjoyed.

Delgado raised his arms above his shoulders, the staff and flail of mystic Isis held aloft and their gilded surfaces gleaming ghostly in the yellowish light. And those who heard the words of the Master could not but obey:

'Fuck, fuck my children!' he cried. 'Your Master bids you fuck, that in your bodies you may concentrate all the energies of the earth, the sea and sky, of air and of water, of celestial ether and sulphurous hellfire. "Do what thou wilt" shall be the whole of the law. Therefore fuck, my children: consecrate yourselves to the Master, and in fucking know that you are the chosen ones, who need never again fear death or decay . . .'

With animal cries of lust, the revellers fell savagely upon each other's hideously painted bodies and the orgy began.

Through Delgado's obedient eyes, the Master surveyed the scene and was well satisfied.

Gavin de Lacy was at the mercy of not one, but two, handsome young bodies – one female, the other male. The girl was straddling his face and pressing her cunt-lips up against his mouth, forcing him to drink in her copious juices, mingled with the nauseating paint he had daubed liberally upon her pink lotus-blossom. Meanwhile, the slender young man had pulled apart de Lacy's thighs and was kneeling between them, eagerly sucking his prick whilst tormenting his arsehole with a wand made of springy hazelwood, in preparation for the assault which his own stiff rod was already craving.

Harry Blomfeld was in paradise. After a lifetime of imposing his own bizarre tastes upon unwilling sexual partners, the tables were at last turning and he was getting a taste of his own medicine. And, to his immense surprise, he was loving every minute of it. Three strapping girls were whipping him with bundles of birch twigs, whilst a fourth was astride him, furiously riding him bareback and squeezing his balls so hard that the intense pain almost made him come straight away.

Cheviot had thrown Viviane forwards over the back of a chair, and she was supporting herself there on her arms whilst he – ever the moral hard-liner – rammed into her slippery cunt with his ferociously erect penis. And all the while a naked girl with pierced nipples bearing small gold rings was kneeling before Viviane, teasing her breasts with needle-sharp teeth, whilst a buxom Valkyrie flagellated Cheviot's eager back with a cat-o'-nine-tails.

'Katya, do it to me Katya . . . !' moaned Viviane, thrusting backwards to take in more of Cheviot's erection, and wishing Katya had a mouth big enough to accommodate not just her nipples, but a whole breast at a time.

Meanwhile, the two princes were forcing their near-bursting shafts together into the accommodating mouth of a smooth-skinned negress with pendulous breasts and heavy hips. She was sucking at them greedily, enjoying the sensation of having two pricks together in her mouth, and teasing their balls with skilful fingertips, running them lightly over the princes' pubic hair, sending delightful shivers through their groins. The princes, too, did not seem indifferent to her ministrations, or to the subtle sensations of two stiff pricks rubbing their sensitive heads against each other within her hot, moist cavern.

Salome and her twin were fucking lustfully on the cold stone floor, a massive double-ended dildo between them, playing the part of the man they had no need for. A pretty youth was savagely buggering a TV weatherman, who was being sucked off by an even more toothsome female talk-show host. Two actresses were demonstrating their versatility as they coupled with the aid of two massively endowed members of the Bolshoi Ballet, who impaled the women on their pricks and then hoisted them up off the ground. The girls then hooked their legs tightly around the men's waists and enjoyed a frenzied *pas-de-deux* which could never have seen its premiere at Sadlers Wells.

The Master looked around the room and was content. The energy was rushing into his soul, strengthening it for its final ordeal. Tonight he would be free. Tonight he must be free.

Delgado opened his flies and pulled out his own stiff prick, offering it to two lust-crazed girls who fought viciously for the right to suck him off. The blonde won the day and fixed her hungry mouth around his shaft. It felt utterly amazing, every movement of her lips and tongue giving him as powerful a sensation as ten orgasms; and he grabbed hold of the girl's hair and forced her to take him deeper, deeper into her throat.

Delgado spoke once again for the Master:

'Let the white witch enter the temple.'

Ibrahim appeared at the top of the steps leading to the secret room, naked and magnificently erect. He was leading a small, naked, trembling figure by the hand. A woman, slender but with softly-curving buttocks and swelling breasts. Her dark hair fell in glossy waves to her waist, and her large violet eyes shone with an unnatural brightness as she gazed blankly in front of her, apparently seeing nothing of the Dionysian revels in the cellar below. The ring sparkled on her left hand, and in her right she clutched the crystal-bladed dagger, her knuckles white with concentration or fear.

She was led down the steps and followed Ibrahim as obediently as a ewe-lamb follows her shepherd to the slaughter. The crystal pendant swung gently to and fro between her breasts as she walked, casting flashes of multi-coloured light across the gloom.

She paid no heed to the revellers as she passed through them, stepping over intertwined bodies, avoiding the sticky hands as they clutched greedily at her tanned limbs, seeming not to hear the moans of pain and pleasure and desire that rippled through the heaving mass of flesh, a grotesque tableau of sexual depravity and perversion whose participants had passed beyond the reach of human emotion and now lived solely in the world of sensations.

'Approach the altar,' the Master's voice commanded her; and as Ibrahim led her towards the sarcophagus, Delgado pulled his prick out of the blonde girl's mouth, crossed to the coffin and took away the black velvet covering, once more revealing the ghastly sight beneath: the sightless eyes gazing upwards from the helpless body which still chained the Master's unwilling spirit.

'Lay your left hand upon the crystal, above my penis,' instructed the Master. 'And with your right hand, touch the crystal above my heart with the point of the dagger.'

The voice cut into Mara's brain, slicing through

her willpower and imposing its own will upon her reluctant mind. She knew that the Master was using her superior psychic powers to control her: the very abilities which had given her strength were now being manipulated for the Master's evil purposes, as easily as a child manipulates a handful of modelling clay.

She reached out with her own mind, tried desperately to resist him with all the strength of her spirit; but it was like trying to batter down a steel wall with bare fists, and she slumped forward on to the crystal, exhausted and once more subjugated to the Master's will.

'Now fuck her,' hissed the voice in Delgado's head; and, obedient to the last, he pulled apart Mara's buttocks and slid into her, slipping a hand beneath her so that he could manipulate her clitoris. In spite of herself, Mara began to pant with desire, the pleasure beginning as a small area of warmth but spreading like a forest fire through her body, taking her over, making her the Master's willing tool.

Her left hand moved to touch the area of the crystal above the Master's penis, and she placed the point of the dagger above the Master's forehead. Immediately, she felt as though she had been plugged into a massive network of power, a ring-main of sexual electricity. And she realised the part that she was playing, the part played by the revellers, who were still fucking and groaning about her feet on the bare stone floor.

She was the missing link. The last link in the chain that would bring the Master back into his kingdom. Nothing could stop him now.

'The incantation. Speak the incantation,' commanded the Master's voice through Delgado, still pumping away at Mara's cunt, and rubbing her clitoris with increasing intensity.

'Asta, asta, Astaroth . . .,' she began, half-sobbing, half-sighing with pleasure, with the absence of will, with the desire only to be the vessel for this so-evil, so-irresistible force. 'Besra, besra, Behemoth . . .'

As the last words of the incantation were spoken, Mara felt a sudden presence behind her, and looked up to see a figure standing silhouetted at the top of the cellar steps. A figure which, somewhere deep inside her memory, she recognised. But the pain and pleasure of recognition were swamped by the sudden orgasm which raged through her and threw her forward on to the smooth face of the crystal.

'Mara!' The voice was heavy with anguish.

Andreas Hunt.

Hunt hesitated for a moment at the top of the steps, aghast at what he saw beneath him. The writhing, naked bodies of men and women, covered with sticky redness, fucking and buggering and sucking pricks and beating each other and racing towards orgasm. But he had no time to stand and look. No time to lose.

Hunt rushed down the steps and towards Mara. Got to save her, take her away from this hell-hole.

The writhing bodies made no attempt to prevent him from passing through. Delgado pulled out from Mara's cunt and stood aside, not apparently surprised by the sudden intrusion. Hunt reached the girl without hindrance, touched her naked shoulder, put his arm around her and raised her head so that she could see his face.

'Mara . . . come with me, quickly . . .'

She gazed at him questioningly, not quite recognising, not quite understanding . . . And then she drew away from him, taking his hands from her head and pulling herself slowly to her feet. She looked from him to her hands, and began to stroke the crystal blade of the dagger.

Then she raised the dagger and pressed its point to her chest, at that point between her ribs, just above her heart . . .

Hunt remembered the vision he had had of Mara, surrounded by naked fornicating couples, a crystal dagger sticking out of her chest. And with a cry of anguish he raised his hand to stop her.

'Do it,' hissed the Master's voice inside Mara's head. 'Do it now.'

And, before Hunt could stop her, Mara seized the silver hilt of the dagger in both hands and, quick as a flash, reversed it, plunging the crystal blade deep into Andreas Hunt's chest.

As the blade sank into his heart and the strength ebbed away from him, Andreas looked up at Mara and saw a tear winding a slow, glistening trail down her cheek.

'Mara . . .' he gasped, but already the darkness was closing over him. Strange, he hadn't expected death to be like this at all. He had expected it to be peaceful, like going to sleep. But this felt as though some dark presence was pushing his soul out of his body, forcing itself into him, annihilating his identity . . .

The world grew suddenly very dark.

And, as he sank silently to the ground, the writhing figures around him became more savage still, lunging for each other's throats, thirsty for the blood, the blood, the scarlet life-force spurting from a bitten throat . . .

And in a little while, all was still.

Mara gazed down at Hunt's unmoving body, the dagger still protruding from his chest, and as the Master's presence withdrew from her mind, she realised with horror what she had done.

She looked down at her hands. They were covered in blood. The blood of her lover, Andreas Hunt. He was dead and she had killed him. Delgado lay slumped nearby, eyes closed, hand clutched to his unfeeling heart. And all about her lay unmoving, bloody corpses, still locked in passion's final embrace, the death-rictus on their faces.

With a cry of agony and despair, Mara turned and ran from the cellar. No-one tried to stop her, and she did not stop running until she was far away from Winterbourne Hall.

The Master got slowly and rather unsteadily to his feet, easing the dagger out from between his ribs and casting it to one side. He would not be needing it any more.

He liked this new body. It was perfect: young, strong, handsome, virile. Already he could feel the blood pumping into his new prick, stiffening it, making it ready for its first sweet taste of cunt. Andreas Hunt's misfortune was his gain.

He turned to Delgado, touching him upon the forehead. At once, his eyes opened and he scrambled to his knees before the one true Master. And all around, bodies were stirring, the dead quickening, rising silently to their feet as though their souls had never slept; gazing at the Master in mute adoration.

The Master turned his new face towards Delgado, and gave the order:

'Seal the sarcophagus. And then have the cellar bricked up. Securely.'

Then he turned to his new followers, smiled, and beckoned to them to follow:

'Come, my children. There is much work for us to do.'

21: Epilogue

No glimmer of light penetrated the deep cellars of Winterbourne Hall. The sarcophagus lay dark and massive in the airless gloom. It looked for all the world as though it had lain untouched for centuries.

But within the sarcophagus, trapped within the Master's deserted body which still lay at the heart of the great crystal, something stirred.

Locked in its crystal prison, the lost soul of Andreas Hunt screamed for release. But no-one heard. There was no-one to hear.

The sarcophagus lay silent and unmoving. And the dust began to settle slowly on the polished lid.